NO PLACE
FOR A
DAME

Also by Connie Brockway

NO PLACE FOR A
DAME

CONNIE BROCKWAY

Montlake
Romance

Published by Montlake Romance, Seattle, WA

www.apub.com

ISBN-13: 978-1-477-80858-0
ISBN-10: 1-477-80858-2

Cover illustration by Dana Ashton France

Library of Congress Control Number: 2013906195

*For Maureen Enger, thanks for being so special
(and tolerant!)*

Chapter One

November, 1819

It had been a mistake bringing Sophia to Killylea Castle, Giles Dalton, the Marquess of Strand, acknowledged as he sat staring broodingly into the Great Hall's hearth fire and waited for his guests to join him for dinner.

Upon their arrival late last night, his bride-to-be had wasted not five minutes before launching into complaints about the castle's inadequate lighting and frigid temperature. They were not unwarranted criticisms; Killylea did seem unusually cold and gloomy, made even more so by the winter storm blasting the ancient fortress's sea-facing walls.

During his childhood here, he'd loved nothing better than a violent storm. He would stand on the parapets, the wind whipping his bare head, arms raised to the heavens, pretending he was a wizard conjuring the elements. Sophia did not share this predilection. But then, she shared nothing else with him either, not conversation or interests, ambitions or goals. Nothing except, a few times, her beautiful young body. Unfortunately, even that lovely vessel had ceased to hold his interest. Especially here.

How odd. But true.

When Sophia had invited him to her room last night, he'd found the notion disconcerting, even distasteful. It had been weeks since she'd sought the only sort of companionship they'd ever enjoyed with one another, not since she'd lost the child she'd allegedly carried. *Allegedly.*

Giles did not think her duplicity was at the root of his reluctance to renew that most intimate of relationships. He'd known all along that she might be lying. Even if she wasn't, she'd readily admitted that the child she'd claimed to carry might not be his.

No, it wasn't anger or disappointment that kept him from accepting her invitation. He was an old friend to duplicity and deceit. Such acts held no fresh surprises, nor their perpetuators the power to offend, let alone wound him.

It was something else that made him resist. This was his home. His real home. A wave of fierce pride swept through him. For two hundred years Daltons had lived here, fought from here, loved and lived and died here. He resisted dishonoring its ancient walls by using it as a place of . . . sport.

Though, he glanced around impatiently, such sport would risk a woman's health in such a cold, dank place. What in bloody hell *had* happened to the lights? Though it was only five o'clock—dinner was always served according to country customs at Killylea—the sun had already quit the sky and the room was steeped in gloom, with only a few of the dozens of sconces and tapers that decorated the walls and tables lit.

For that matter, where were all the servants? Rather than the usual, seemingly endless line of servants that generally met his infrequent homecomings, only his steward, Travers, and a single maid and footman had met their arrival. The same maid had set his fire this morning and the same footman had attended him at breakfast, while Sophia and her father, Malcolm North, acting as chaperone in only the loosest sense of the word, had breakfasted en suite.

He knew for a fact that he employed forty-six at Killylea. Thus far he'd seen only three.

And then, of course, there was Avery Quinn, but she was hardly a servant. She was . . . well, what matter? It had been several years since his visit to the castle and hers had coincided. Indeed, he might never see Avery Quinn again, because he could not envision Sophia living here as

Killylea's chatelaine. And during those rare times Sophia was in residence, he imagined Avery would disappear. He could not imagine two women with less in common. His small female scholar liked Killylea's solitude while Sophia was far better suited to the bright artifice and sophistication of London

As, he reminded himself, was he.

"Strand? Is that you? I can't see. 'Tis too dark," a female voice announced from the doorway. "Do not think I shall stand for such cheeseparing measures when I am marchioness. We shall have lights to rival Carleton House!"

Strand looked up from the fire, relieved to be distracted from the uneasy passage his thoughts had been taking. His bride-to-be had arrived.

Sophia North frowned pettishly as she peered about. The Great Hall looked just as dim, grim, and uninviting as the rest of this godforsaken castle. Only the muffled moan of the wind flinging itself against the thick stone walls broke the eerie silence. At the far end of the room a wingback chair stood facing a huge bed of embers in a hearth so high a man could walk into it upright. The only other furnishing was the monstrous banquet table.

"One might as well dine in a charnel house," Sophia muttered.

"Best get used to it, Sophia," her father said from beside her. "Strand's ancestral home, don'tcha know."

Ancestral home, bah. Who would willingly live in such a place? She knew little about Giles Dalton's immediate family. No one did. His father had not taken his place in Society, seemingly content to stay in this godforsaken castle with his books and letters. Strand's mother, the marquess's second wife, had relocated to Italy with Giles's sister long ago, before Giles had become heir to the marquisdom. The first marchioness had died in childbirth.

Sophia didn't recall much about Giles's older brother, the first heir, other than that the boy hadn't lived long, either. She had never thought to ask why; she wasn't interested.

"Strand can stay here for all I care. *I* shall be in the London town-house, until I can find better." She'd no more live here than she would in Seven Dials. "Where is Strand? Why isn't he here?"

Before her father could reply, a deep masculine voice spoke. "How happy the groom must be whose bride counts the hours she doesn't spend in his company."

Sophia wheeled around, looking for Strand, the owner of that deep, velvety voice.

A dark shadow moved in the chair before the fire and a log fell suddenly, the burst of light limning the famously classic profile, curling over a strong, long-fingered hand, and tracing a muscular leg stretched out before him. It caught the glint of a silvered eye and burnished the dark glow in the shock of tumbled guinea-gold hair.

Giles Dalton, Marquess of Strand.

He was as handsome a man as Sophia had ever seen, even now, about to enter his thirtieth year. And if the deep shadows beneath his eyes and the lines bracketing his sculpted Roman nose in any way diminished what was said to have once been Apollonian looks, well, she'd not known him then and thus had nothing to compare this version of Strand to that earlier one. And this version of Strand in no manner disappointed.

He hesitated just an instant and then with fluid grace, rose to his feet. The barbaric surroundings should have dwarfed him, made him look small, should have rendered him insignificant. It couldn't. He owned this room as he surely owned any London salon.

The exquisite cut of his cobalt blue coat, his flawlessly arranged cravat, the buff-colored trousers that molded to his long legs, were only trappings. Even without them he would draw the eye and fix the attention. He was not merely beautiful, he was riveting.

He sauntered forward and bowed. "Sophia, my dear, I doubt these poor walls have ever seen your like. And Malcolm, I trust everything is to your liking?"

"Must allow it ain't, Strand," her father said, striving to emulate Strand's air of masterly nonchalance and failing utterly.

"No?" Strand's brows rose. He took her father's elbow and led him towards the table. "Good heavens, sir, please have a seat and tell me all about it so I can make reparations at once. But first, let us fortify ourselves for the night ahead and all the subsequent nights ahead."

Sophia smiled, unable to keep the triumph from her expression. Let him mock all he wanted. It was too late for him to change his mind. He'd sent the announcement of their engagement to the papers, the ring had been bought, the chapel reserved. He would never be able to show his face in Society again if he threw her over. And Strand lived for his position as Society's premiere dandy, whip, and nonpareil. Or so he'd always said.

No, she had nothing to fear. Everything she wanted, money, pleasure, and celebrity, would soon be hers. They might as well already be.

Strand saw to it that first she and then her father were seated before returning to his chair and motioning for Travers, whom she assumed to be the butler, to fill their glasses. He drained away half of his, then rolled the crystal stem between his long fingers, regarding them from across the great table, like prisoners in a docket set before a judge.

He gestured for the sole footman in attendance to bring in the first course. When she became marchioness they would have a staff to rival any of the great homes in England. Even here. Even though she would not be in residence. She intended to spend and spend lavishly and live even better and Strand could well afford it.

"Now then," Strand said, "tell me, Malcolm, how has Killylea failed in your expectations? For there is nothing as demoralizing as being led to expect a thing only to have something else foisted upon you." Strand's voice was as smooth as oiled silk and dark as a moonless sky.

Sophia froze, her glass halfway to her lips. Her father's heavily veined cheeks turned bright. He'd been part of her plan to leg shackle Strand from the start. Unfortunately, while as ambitious as she was, he had not a tenth of her nerve. "Well, for one thing, it's cold."

"Cold? Good heavens, we can't have that." Strand raised his eyes to the butler, standing motionless at the end of the table. "Have the wood burning in Mr. North's room doubled at all times, Travers."

"Yes, sir."

"Anything else?"

"Well," Malcolm pursed his lips, "it's gloomy."

"Gloomy. What might we do about that, Travers?"

"I am at a loss, sir."

"As am I. Hmm . . ." He snapped his fingers. "I know. Exchange the drapery in Mr. North's bedchamber for something more festive. Yellow, I should think. Yellow is such a gladdening color, don't you agree?"

Sophia snickered at Strand's mockery. A mistake. Strand's mercury-bright gaze slewed towards her.

"And you, my dear, have you any complaints?"

"Not a one." *None that I'm likely to give voice. At least, not until after the wedding.*

"Ah, then you like Killylea. Such a relief."

"I did not say that. I said I had no complaints."

"So you did." Strand sank back in his chair. "What an accommodating wife you shall make."

"I shouldn't rely on that." Malcolm signaled the butler to refill his glass. "Sophia has always been too spirited, too headstrong. She'll need a strong hand."

Sophia shot her father a poisonous glare.

"Spirited." The word fell dryly from Strand's lips. "You are a far fonder parent than Society credits you, North."

"I don't understand."

"I refer to the generosity of your depiction. I myself would have used a different adjective to describe my future bride."

Malcolm started. "What adjec—"

"Do *not* ask, Father," Sophia cut him off sharply. "Don't you understand what he's trying to do? Strand is relying on you asking how he would describe me so that you will be forced to call off the wedding once you hear his reply."

Strand's gray eyes widened with feigned surprise. "Good heavens, Sophia. How diabolical you think me. And I must protest, because believe me, my dear," his tone abruptly hardened, "should I wish to be rid of you, I need hardly resort to baiting your father."

As quickly as it had appeared, his antipathy vanished. "Do not fret, Sophia. I have every intention of wedding you."

"Wed?"

At the sound of the whispered word, Sophia turned. What she saw made her gasp.

A small female figure stood swaying in the doorway, clutching a single taper that bobbed and dipped in her hand, spilling wax on her fingers and the floor. A dingy, oversized bed gown covered her from neck to feet in layers of dirty, gauzy material. Long, matted yellow hair fell about her shoulders and over her face, obscuring her features. She hunched a little, head stuck out like a dog sniffing poisoned meat.

Sophia's skin rippled into goose flesh at the sight of her, remembering the freaks and loonies that had rushed her when she and her friends had toured Bedlam. They'd looked like this thing: Revolting. *Wrong.* "Who is that? *Who is she?*"

"I am sorry, sir," Travers said to Strand. "I couldn't do anything to stop her and I didn't see it was right to do so, either."

"*Who is that creature?*"

The butler looked at her mournfully. "That, miss, is his lordship's sister."

Chapter Two

Julia Dalton? *This* was Julia Dalton? Giles's mother was supposed to have spirited her away to Italy and never returned. But here was proof, horrible proof, that the marchioness had left this cretinous creature behind. God knew how long she'd been here.

Now Sophia understood why the Daltons had seemingly eschewed Society. They were *tainted*.

"*My* wedding?" the girl whispered in a singsong voice, sidling towards Sophia with an outstretched hand. With a cry, Sophia recoiled. Her chair's legs scraped loudly on the flagstone floor. The girl's hand dropped.

"I'd like to be wedded. Or," the girl's voice thickened with animal cunning, "bedded. Nice and wedded; good and bedded," she sang and began spinning around in slow circles, her arms held out straight at her sides, the long gossamer sleeves drifting out like tattered moths' wings. "Good. And. *Bedded*."

Frantically, Sophia looked at Strand. He was staring at the creature, his expression tense. "Travers. What is this?"

"I am sorry, sir." The man had visibly paled. "I could not stop her. Nor did I want to. I didn't think it was right, what you were going to do."

"Damn you for an interfering scoundrel, Travers." Strand rose to his feet, his eyes narrowing on the girl. *"That's enough."*

At his sharp command, the girl collapsed on the floor like a marionette whose strings had been cut. *"Nooo!* Don't make me go back!"

"Dear God," Sophia whispered.

At once, the girl's head snapped around towards Sophia. Quick as a rat, she scuttled towards her on hands and knees. With a squeal, Sophia bolted from her chair. It fell over with a crash, causing the girl to flinch back and flee into the shadows along the wall.

"What sort of foul trick is this, Strand?" Sophia cried. "Did you think to spring your insane sister on me *after* the wedding?"

Strand's eyes narrowed and he regarded her closely for a long minute before answering. "Actually, Sophia, my dear, I wasn't going to 'spring' her on you at all."

"Then when were you going to tell me that this . . . this *freak* was your sister?"

Not a hint of embarrassment showed in Strand's expression. "I wasn't."

The enormity of his confession, the treachery he'd been plotting to perpetrate upon her, staggered her. "You . . . you *swine!* You unutterable villain! What if I bore something like . . . like that?" She pointed towards the shadowy figure that hunkered in the gloom, giggling. Horrified, Sophia scrambled behind her father, clutching his arm and setting his bulk between her and Strand's hideous sister. "Have her taken away!" she shrieked at the butler.

"I shouldn't like to try, Miss North. It is only bound to provoke a nasty scene," Travers said mournfully.

"Ah!"

Malcolm swung around and grabbed her upper arms, squeezing hard. *"Stop it*, Sophia! Strand is healthy and sound. Your babes will be perfect."

"But what if they aren't?" she cried, sick with growing fury.

How *dare* Strand have a sister like this? How dare he? He'd ruined *everything*. Yet he just stood there, his eyes hard and cold, judging *her*. She could *feel* his contempt.

"Then you give them to the wet nurse," Malcolm ground out, "and from there to a nurse, and then"—he glanced at Strand—"send them here. Eh, Strand?"

An ugly smile twisted Strand's beautiful mouth. "Certainly. Plenty of rooms for rejects at Killylea. We'll just have to keep you bellyful until you pop out a promising looking specimen and then perhaps a couple more as a contingency. I know my pater would have liked to have had a few more spares laying about. Unfortunately, my mother fled before he could implement the plan. You wouldn't do that though, would you, Sophia?"

"You . . . *monster*. *This* is why you've never wed. You knew that once a lady had seen *that*"—she pointed at the creature—"she would never accept you. God, how you must have laughed when you thought you'd got me with child!"

"I assure you, I did not so much as crack a smile."

"And what of that half brother?" She turned to her father. "No one ever saw him, did they? Was he as repellant as she is?"

Something dangerous sprang to life in Strand's gaze, like a red-hot epee slicing through snow. "I have no doubt you would have found my brother quite loathsome."

"You see? I am right! He thought to trap me into being his brood mare. But I won't. I will not bear your idiot children! Do you hear me? I *will not marry you*, Strand!"

"Please. You break my heart." His mockery was knife sharp.

"*You bastard!*" Tears of fury and frustration streamed down her cheeks. Her voice quivered with hatred.

"Shut up, you stupid bint!" Her father raised his hand to deliver a stinging slap. "You'll—"

Strand's suave voice cut like a whip across the room. "I shouldn't if I were you, Malcolm, old man." Her father's hand dropped to his side.

"The lady has made her position clear. Even should you by force of . . . shall we say personality? . . . compel her, I can't think the marriage would be comfortable. And I do so value my comfort.

"Besides, a fellow likes to be welcomed into the conjugal bed, don'tcha know? Not greeted with shrieks of horror. Bound to upset the servants and, let us be frank, have a dolorous effect on one's, er, constitution."

"No. No. She's just unnerved," her father insisted desperately. "She'll come round once she's had a chance to think things over. Took her by surprise, is all."

Strand turned his gaze to her. "Tell me, Sophia, and consider carefully, my dear, before you answer because I will not ask a second time: Do you think there's any chance at all of you 'comin' round' as your father so quaintly put it? Because I will still have you, if you do."

God, how she wanted to say yes! She wanted the jewels, the houses, the title, the fawning of her friends, the envy of her enemies, the power, the privilege, the license, and everything that came with being the marchioness of Strand. But . . . She stared at the creature.

The girl had crawled out of the shadows on all fours and was now stretched out flat on her belly, her face half covered with the matted hair, her mouth ajar, a little line of drool oozing from the corner. Sophia's stomach seized into knots and her gorge rose thick in her throat. No. She choked back a sob of rage. She *couldn't*. She glared impotently at Strand. "I hate you!"

"Ah, well, there you have it," Strand said, sinking down in his chair and giving Malcolm an apologetic smile. "I hope this doesn't cast a pall on the rest of your stay. I'm sure we can all rub along together pleasantly enough. And now that you know about . . . her"—he glanced down at the girl, his silvery blue eyes glittering strangely—"well, I won't have to keep such a tight vigil, will I? She's harmless. Mostly. Still and all, I'd keep the doors latched at night. You never know where she might show up."

Dear God. "No. No! I insist we leave here at once. Tonight!"

"Tonight? But the darkness, the cold," Strand objected in a monotone. "Surely you'd be more comfortable—"

"I won't be *comfortable* until I am far away from here. And her. I *insist* we leave at once."

"Well, Travers? Can this be done, say, within the hour?"

"I am certain we can accommodate the young lady's wishes."

Strand looked at Malcolm. "Sir, I fully realize that no restitution can possibly compensate for such an outrageous machination. Nonetheless, my man of business will be in touch."

At the hint that money might be forthcoming, the dusky purple receded from her father's face. "One should hope," he huffed. "Really, Strand, 'twas a foul bit of business you meant to deal us."

"I agree. The situation is deplorable."

"Luckily, I am a man of honor. You can be sure no one will hear of . . . of any of this"—he glanced down at the girl lying on the floor tracing the cracks around a flagstone—"from my lips *or* Sophia's. Which ought to make you *doubly* grateful, since I don't doubt eventually you'll offer for some other poor, unsuspecting girl."

"Not only a man of honor, but of subtlety," Strand said. "I cannot think how I will ever be able to express my gratitude. Luckily, between you and my man of business, I am confident you will find a way.

"Now, Travers, if you will escort Mr. and Miss North back to their rooms and then inform the stable master to have the carriage readied?" He raised an elegant brow in Sophia's direction. "That is, unless you've changed your mind about dining? Cod, I believe."

He was sophisticated and brilliant, beautiful and wicked, and she hated him in that moment more than she had ever hated anything in her life. Hated him with the virulence of a woman who'd held a future of munificence and prestige within the palm of her hand and knew she would never see its like again.

"Damn you, Strand!"

"Likely already been taken care of, my dear."

With a muffled cry, she edged past the girl and fled, Malcolm and Travers following close behind.

Strand remained seated, his gaze moving to the disheveled figure at his feet. As the sound of footsteps receded, the girl raised her dirty face and listened intently a few more seconds before springing lightly to her feet. She glanced at the mantle clock perched above the hearth.

"Drat," Avery Quinn said. "Twelve minutes. I bet Travers a quid she'd bolt in under five."

Chapter Three

"Kindly remove that monstrosity from your head," Strand said.

Avery pulled the antique wig off, sending her own auburn locks spilling down her back.

Strand did not *sound* angry, but it had been four years since she had seen him and she'd never presumed to know his thoughts. The times he'd visited Killylea, first from Eton and later from Oxford, he'd seemed more like some young god descending from Olympus then a son returning home for a visit.

She'd heard about Giles Dalton long before she'd ever seen him. The servants' hall had been filled with tales about the strapping, handsome heir to Killylea. He was golden and gifted, amiable and charismatic, privileged in every aspect by countenance, station, and wealth. The term "to the manor born" might have been coined for him.

Even at ten years of age she had decided that no one could possibly live up to such fanfare.

Except he had.

She'd been eleven and hanging over the tower parapet the first time she'd seen Giles, having been alerted to his impending arrival by the flurry of activity below stairs. He'd left behind the carriage conveying his things from Eton, choosing to arrive on horseback ahead of his custodians.

The morning sun had burnished his golden head as he rode up the lane, lithe and graceful, his face alive with the pleasure of homecoming, his gaze traveling with pride over Killylea's ancient facade. He must have felt her gaze for he'd looked up and spotted her. She'd frozen, red-faced at having been caught spying, and scowled down at him because she hated feeling awkward. Then he'd compounded the injury by winking at her. *Winking.*

It had been Avery's first experience with masculine charm and it proved a disconcerting one. She could not explain it—it was ineluctable, mysterious, and confusing—and even at such a tender age she had distrusted anything she could not explain. It also irritated her. He wore the unassailable certainty of his own consequence with as little self-consciousness as another man wears shoes and used his magnetism as easily as another breathed, and she'd despised herself for falling prey to it after just one wink just like everyone else, because she was *not* like everyone else.

She never had been.

She never could be.

By eleven years of age, she had not only reconciled herself to that knowledge, but in some small way had even begun to take pride in it. And to have it so blatantly demonstrated that she was made of the same base stuff as everyone else . . . well, it hadn't seemed fair to be so rudely made aware that, in this instance at least, she was not so very special. She was, in fact, just one of a crowd of acolytes surrounding Giles Dalton's altar.

Not that there were all that many opportunities thereafter to feel the unwilling fascination Giles held for her. She and the future marquess spent little time together. Why would the future marquess of Strand and his father's accidental protégé, the gamekeeper's daughter, spend time together? Oh, there'd been a few meals made uncomfortable by the obvious strain between Giles and his father and the sullen demeanor she seemed incapable of shedding whenever she was around him, but other than that, she tried to avoid him.

No. That was not true. She tried to avoid him *seeing* her. She found plenty of opportunity to overhear him in conversation, to study him from a discreet distance, to . . . well, spy on him. She'd been a girl; he'd been a godlike adolescent. Of course, she'd been fascinated.

When Giles *had* spoken to her, he had always been unfailingly polite or lightly teasing, the same way he treated any of the servants. But the manner in which the housekeeper, Mrs. Bedling, pinked up at his blandishments and Avery's own father puffed his chest out at Giles's compliments only made Avery all the more keenly aware that he stooped to conquer. So, of course, when he did speak to her, she'd gone out of her way to be a little beast in order to make him see *her*, not just another in the ranks of servants on which he'd polished his address.

She'd been, truth be told, awful, and Giles Dalton, Marquess of Strand, had no reason to feel magnanimous towards her. Which is why now she must rely on the hope that, like his father, Strand always paid his debts.

"You are going to have to face me eventually," he said.

She took a quick, steadying breath and turned, struck anew by how much the years had changed him. Gone was the bright, devil-may-care young godling and in his stead was a man whose golden beauty seemed fire wrought rather than light given.

It was not simply the lines bracketing his mouth or the bruised flesh beneath his eyes. An assessing gleam had subverted what had once been a candid, open gaze and tension had taken up residence in the set of his jaw and shoulders. He looked brooding and wicked, a touch of cruelty in the curl of his lip and the angle of brows. What had happened to him . . . ?

She banished her curiosity. Whatever had happened to him, she would never know. Nor did she need to. Once he'd helped her achieve her goal, there would never be another reason for him to speak to her again.

If he helped her.

"Face you? You make it sound as if I were reluctant to do so." She hoped she sounded braver than she felt. She lifted the hem of the grubby night rail, dipped it into the water glass sitting on the table, and began wiping the grime from her cheeks.

"My mistake." He sounded amused. "Where did you get that rag you're wearing? And please do not tell me it ever belonged to any relative of mine, dead or alive. I refuse to believe any of my forebears would have ever fallen so low."

This was new, too, this over-arch tone, the languid sardonicism.

"Mrs. Bedling made it up out of an old bed netting." The thought reminded her to clear the other servants of any complicity. "She had no idea what I meant to do with it. And none of the other servants had anything to do with this evening's, er, entertainment, either."

"*What* other servants?" he asked dryly. "The place seems deserted. And why is it so dark? Has the staff been pilfering candles?"

"No. Of course not. Mr. Travers let everyone have the week off because, well, we just thought that the scene played better with less light. And, mind you, Mr. Travers wasn't a willing coconspirator."

"Blackmailed him, did you?" He showed not the slightest outrage at the suggestion.

"No! No. I begged."

At that, his brows shot up. "Avery Quinn? *Beg?* The girl I remember would have walked across burning coals before asking for help, let alone begging for it."

"The woman that girl became knows better."

He gave her a quick, unreadable glance. "Does she? Pity." His gaze had softened but then he shifted on his chair, as if physically divesting himself of whatever emotion had prompted the words. "Did you ever worry that you were overplaying your role with all the dirt and such?"

"No." She'd finished wiping her face and moved on to her hands. "Not really. The plan was either going to work or not, though I concede it occurred to me that any discerning individual would be bound to wonder why the sister of a marquess, demented or not, should be allowed to wander about unwashed and unkempt."

"Lucky for you that the Norths are not known for their discernment."

"Exactly!" She pounced on his words. "How could you actually offer to marry such a—" She paused to scratch behind her ear. Her eyes flew wide. "Good heavens. I believe there were *fleas* in that wig. Which makes you *doubly* indebted to me for saving you from having to marry that vile girl."

"*Saving* me?" For the first time that evening, he looked taken off guard. "Is that what this was about?"

"Yes."

An odd expression crossed his face. "How touching. But did you ever consider I might not *want* saving?"

It was her turn to be taken aback. In point of fact, she hadn't. But she wasn't about to admit it. She would lose whatever higher moral ground she had. "She was using you. Manipulating you."

"I daresay, but those sins are hardly unique to Sophia. Certainly others have fared similarly. Some by my own hand, as it happens. Including her." His gray eyes had darkened. "As they say, turnabout is fair play."

"No," she insisted. "You could never marry her. Not once you knew what she was like. Not once you knew her feelings about 'freaks and aberrations.' God help any child of hers that did not meet her standard of perfection. Like Louis."

Giles's older brother had spent his brief life at Killylea cocooned from the world and, more specifically, the cruelties of people like Sophia. He had been born short in stature, a dwarf, and had also suffered from a weakness of the heart. Though he had died a full year before Avery and her father had arrived, he had been still mourned as the loss of a good and gentle soul.

Soon after her stepson Louis's death, Giles's mother, the second marchioness, had gone to Italy, taking Giles's sister, Julia, with her. Giles, already at Eton, had asked to stay in England. If he had ever felt abandoned by his mother, he had never evinced it. He loved Killylea. His pride in his heritage and his home were obvious. But that had changed soon after Giles's eighteenth birthday when he had gone to London and discovered how gratifying it was to be fawned over and celebrated. Or so it seemed. Why else would someone appear so changed?

She had been surprised that he had become such a raffish dandy. Despite what she said in public, in her heart she had always thought better of him. Yet each year, his notoriety grew.

But while she might have been wrong about Giles's character, she was not wrong about his love for Louis. Of that, she had no doubt.

"You're right," he said now. "I wouldn't have offered for Miss North had I known about her phobia. And I didn't know. The question is"— he regarded her thoughtfully—"how did you? Or perhaps you're telling me your masquerade was simply fortuitous? What if Sophia had revealed herself to be soft-hearted and thrown her arms about you and called you 'sister'?"

She gave him a sardonic smile. "Killylea may be remote, but the mail comes regularly. I subscribe to a number of London papers and journals, both the scientific ones and . . . otherwise."

"You mean you read the *rags*?" He looked politely astonished.

"Religiously," she confirmed a trifle defensively. "They are filled with the most illuminating information. For instance, that opera dancer you involved yourself with last summer? She was not up to your usual standards."

He raised an eyebrow. "My dear, you have no idea the sort of standards by which I measure my female companions."

She felt herself flush but refused to be distracted. "Had *you* perused the rags," she said, "you would have read a dozen stories about 'Miss N's' aversion to 'freaks and monstrosities.' Last spring she fainted at the appearance of an armless juggler hired to entertain at Lord Crabbe's fete. And any number of newspapers reported how the beautiful 'Miss N' caused a near riot at Bedlam this past spring."

He tipped his head. "In what manner?"

"She and her party were viewing the inmates when some poor wretch followed an ill-conceived impulse to touch her, seeing how pretty she was. Your happily former fiancée reacted by howling so loudly and for so long that she roused the entire population of the ward to a frenzy. It took three days to settle them down.

"So you see, you *are* indebted to me. Admit it," she said, willing him to meet her eye. "Admit you owe me whatever I request of you."

He leaned back in his chair and regarded her with open amusement. "Good God, my girl, do you think me mad? Why ever would I give you such power of me?"

"Because you're a gentleman. If you proposed to that vile girl just because she *might* have been pregnant with your child and then remained engaged to her even *after* discovering that she wasn't, I expect you'll act no less honorably towards me for getting shut of her and her repulsive parent."

Such intimate knowledge of his affairs caused his smile to fade. "The servants' network, I presume?" he asked after a minute.

"How else? You lords and ladies have no idea how accessible your lives are to those of us you barely note."

"Oh, I've noted you," he murmured. "And I am sure you are correct. But that's beside the point, that being, I don't recall asking for your aid."

"You didn't," she conceded. "But if someone were drowning and I could save him merely by pushing a log out, I would do so without his having to holler for help."

"Confounded as I am by such selflessness, I must nonetheless protest: I never *holler*."

"I wasn't speaking of you," she said, "I refer to your father. I could hear him thrashing about in his grave the moment that little harridan entered the castle. You may not honor your family name anymore, but he did. So, out of both my respect and obligation to him, I acted."

At the mention of his father, Giles's face grew shuttered.

"Ah. I should have realized. Your éminence grise."

She flushed as his hand hovered over the platter of sweetmeats the footman had brought in. Giles had never understood the relationship between his father and her. Nor had she, not entirely. There had been respect between them, but never warmth. Never anything like friendship. The old marquess was not a man given to warm personal relationships except, reportedly, in the single instance of his devotion to his firstborn son, Louis.

"He was my benefactor. I am indebted to him for what he did for me."

"And what was that?" he asked a little tersely, confusing her. Then, seeing her expression, his own smoothed. "Despite what you think, I am aware of my familial obligations and those include producing heirs. Miss North comes from a genteel and unremarkable family. Believe it or not, in my own poor way I was attempting to ensure the family line." He reached for a candied fig.

"I shouldn't eat that if I were you."

"Why not—" His hand fell abruptly away. "You didn't actually *poison* the food?"

She shifted uneasily. Perhaps she'd overextended herself. "*Taint* is more appropriate. And only the figs. She looked like a fig eater to me. Is she?"

"Is there anything you won't stop at? You should have been with Wellington. He could have used such a ruthless advisor. The war might have ended earlier."

How would he know what Wellington could have used? The marquess, concerned over the fate of his only heir, had refused to buy Giles a commission in his chosen regiment. Avery had sometimes wondered whether it was only coincidence that shortly thereafter, Giles had embarked on a career of gambling, drinking, and excess. He had spent the war in London pursuing opera dancers. The marquess had been disgusted.

Only near the very end of the marquess's life had father and son achieved an uneasy reconciliation. At least, Giles had come home for the months before his father's death.

"*Taint,*" she repeated. "Not poison. It would have only given her a bellyache. And if I consider something important enough, I would do whatever I deemed necessary. And making sure you didn't marry that sod-awful little trout fell into that category."

He *tch*'d lightly. "What a vile tongue you have, Avery."

"I'm a gamekeeper's daughter. What else would you expect?" She hiked up her skirts and hopped up to sit on the edge of the table, her legs swinging indecorously. "The pickles are safe."

His gaze fell casually upon her bare limbs and lingered long enough to send little frissons racing beneath her skin. Slowly, his gaze lifted to her face. He smiled and she remembered too late how easily he'd always countered her defiant demonstrations of low-class behavior, sending her fleeing with just a look, a word. But she was not a girl anymore. She would no longer take to her heels when he played at roué.

"From someone with your education?" he asked. "With the advantages you've known? I'd expect a great deal more."

She resented that. Not because it wasn't true but because she knew Giles didn't believe it. Long ago she'd overheard him tell his father that the education he was giving her would make her an outcast at every level of society. Afterward, Avery had walked in terror of the marquess terminating her education. She needn't have. Being the marquess, he'd had no choice but to continue. He'd given his word and a Dalton always honored his debts.

In the course of a highway robbery committed during the first week her father had worked for the Marquess of Strand, Dermot Quinn had dove in front of a highwayman's bullet aimed at his new employer. He'd been nearly killed. Upon his recovery the old marquess had asked him to name whatever he wanted for his reward. Quinn had made a seemingly simple request: that the marquess see to the education of his motherless, ten-year-old daughter, Avery, "until she stops askin' all them bleedin' questions."

Forthwith, the marquess had hired a tutor for the girl, thinking, no doubt, that within a few months she would tire of the classroom and go back to . . . wherever it was she'd been before the robbery.

But she never had stopped asking questions; the questions just grew harder.

And the marquess, whose sense of honor was as unassailable as his sense of duty, and who'd adhered strongly to the belief that a deal struck was a deal met, continued to find teachers, instructors, and tutors to keep pace with her curiosity.

But an education and an intellect that far surpassed most of the ton's prominent members, male and female, did not make her a lady any more than slumming in Spitalfields made Giles a day laborer. Giles had made that clear. It was a fact she had never allowed herself to forget.

"But I prefers the cant of me own," she said now in her father's broad provincial accent before segueing into the haughty tones of a lady, "to the arch drawl affected by yours."

"You are a consummate mimic, Avery. You ought to consider a career on the stage. You'd do so well there."

In spite of herself, she felt heat flood into her face. Though a virgin, she was no innocent. The plainspoken Cornwall folk and the marquess's more sophisticated, but no less earthy staff had seen that she received an education every bit as enlightening as the one she'd received from the marquess's hired teachers.

She knew there were few ladies on stage who were ladies anywhere else. Most actresses were also mistresses, their finest performances given for an audience of one on a satin-covered stage. Giles was reported to have been the recipient of many such performances.

She looked away, but not quickly enough.

"I did not mean to imply that you would ever—"

"Ever what? Become a paramour?" She lifted her chin. "I suppose not. I should make a most uncomfortable mistress, since in all likelihood I would be a great deal more intelligent than my so-called protector and categorically unwilling to mask that fact in order to preserve his self-importance."

He inclined his head. "Allow me to apologize for my unfortunate comment."

His composure only made her more flustered and words tumbled out before she could stop them. "I daresay you would be happy to have me taken off your hands. As would I."

"You are overreacting."

"Am I? Shouldn't you like to come to Killylea without worrying about encountering me?"

"I never worry."

She steeled herself against the unexpected stab of pain his words caused. *Of course he wouldn't worry; why should he spare any thought to her at all?*

"And this is your home," Giles added.

"No. It is *your* home and it is high time I arranged for my future elsewhere."

"Don't be ridiculous." He sounded curt and she felt again the same unworthy pang of pleasure she'd had in provoking of him when she'd been a twelve-year-old girl. The realization rattled her. Would she ever grow up where he was concerned?

"Who will take care of your father if you leave? Where would you go?"

His words caught her by surprise. "But . . . my father no longer works for you. He married Madame Turcotte. They retired to her native town in Normandy six months past. He wrote you . . ." She trailed off, her eyes narrowing. "That old dog. He *didn't* write to you, did he?"

"*He married my cook?*"

Her indignation fell prey to the humor in the situation. "I'm so sorry." She was trying not to smile. Her dad always had done whatever he deemed necessary to win the desired results. She supposed she was like him in that. "He swore he would, even though he was worried you'd try to dissuade Madame Turcotte from accepting his offer."

"Damned right, I would have."

His tone was so honestly aggrieved she could not keep from chuckling. "Perhaps that explains his reluctance to inform you. Poor man knew his charms would not stand up to the lure of a doubled salary. So, now you see that I no longer have any excuse to live here." There. That was better. Reasonable. Calculated. Thoughtful, not like some panicked girl throwing out threats in the hope that someone would tell her not to be silly.

"That's ridiculous. You don't need an excuse. My father—"

"Your *father* has been dead these four years," she interrupted calmly. "And you have more than fulfilled any obligations he may have undertaken. Besides, I have plans."

"Oh? Off to foment a rebellion in some unsuspecting principality or other?"

"Very amusing."

She had spent fourteen years living on the marquises of Strands' charity and might have done so indefinitely had she not read the announcement of Giles's upcoming marriage. She'd blinked at the page like a blind woman suddenly developing sight as it had slowly dawned on her that Giles would be bringing his wife to Killylea. That he would raise his children here. *Her* children.

She had never considered Strand marrying before, or if she had, had relegated it to some vague future, a possibility that one must acknowledge but not necessarily anticipate. Like the plague.

But in that instance she'd realized that of course Giles would marry—and soon, if for no other reason than to secure the line. She could not stay here when he did. The new marchioness was bound to take exception to finding an unmarried woman in an unidentifiable position living in her new home.

Or worse, she might not.

And then what would Avery be? An uncomfortable phantom haunting the netherworld between upstairs and down? A topic of post-dinner conversation? A means to congratulate the new marchioness on her forbearance or exalt Giles's father on his odd sense of fair play?

No. She could not stay. She must find employment somewhere. Not as a governess. She could not imagine herself being dependent on the sufferance of recalcitrant children. But she'd heard mention of new types of schools opening in London and abroad, schools catering to older female pupils who desired to learn academic subjects. Perhaps one of these would hire her. Or she might apply to one of her former instructors to fashion the new lenses she'd designed. It wasn't the same as being a milliner—hats apparently being the one item ladies were allowed to manufacture without social censure—but then she wasn't a lady.

No. She did not doubt her ability to make a living for herself, but she recognized that once she left Killylea there was little likelihood she would ever again have the freedom or opportunities to learn, to explore, to *discover* that had been hers.

No matter now. What would be must be.

But first there was something she needed to do.

"Avery?" Strand's voice pulled her from her thoughts.

"There is something I want very badly," she said. "I would like you to help me obtain it. But not because of some long-paid debt your father incurred but because *you* owe me." For some reason this was important. "Do you agree?"

He reached out, refilled his wine glass and regarded her for a long moment before taking a sip. "What matter?" he finally murmured. "Why not?" He tipped the wine glass in her direction in a toast. "I am obliged to you. Ask what you will."

She closed her eyes, her head swimming with the abrupt release of tension. She hadn't realized until now how very much this meant to her. It would be the only thing she might ever have to show for her years of study, tangible proof that she'd achieved something through all her hard work. That her education had mattered. That she *was* someone. She was special.

She exhaled unsteadily and opened her eyes to find him studying her curiously.

"What do you want, then?"

She hopped off the table, picking up the discarded wig and tucking it under her arm. "I'd rather show you."

He set his glass down and rose to his feet. "Lead on."

Chapter Four

A very led the way down the castle's long central corridor to the base of Killylea's east tower, where the old marquess had converted what had once been a guards' room into her study. Since her arrival back from Ghent several months ago, she'd once again taken possession of the room, and now star maps and books, prisms and lenses, navigation instruments and polishing stones covered the tables lining the walls.

She heard Giles murmur, "What are you up to now?"

She motioned him to follow her up the steep spiraling staircase that led to the tower's upper room, a tiny sentry's apartment. The brazier she had lit earlier that afternoon still held enough live coals to heat the small space and it was warm inside. A large telescope set on a wheel-driven platform stood against the wall, leaving little room for anything else.

She opened the door to the ramparts outside and at once an icy blast of wind hit them, whipping her hair around her face and plastering the lawn gown tight against her body. She barely noted the cold, too excited by the prospect of sharing her discovery.

With a muttered oath, Giles shed his coat and draped it over her shoulders.

She gave him a quick, distracted smile before tipping her face to the cloud-clotted sky and searching the heavens.

"What are you looking for?"

She didn't answer, her concentration being wholly overhead . . . There! She spun about, elbowing her way past him and back into the sentry's room, returning a moment later rolling the telescope ahead of her.

She pushed it into position next to the crenelated wall and peered into the eyepiece. Carefully, she began turning the rings orienting the various lenses. And then all at once, the night sky opened up around her, unfolding before her eyes and she was falling through the firmament, swimming in an ocean of brilliant pinpoints, white and pinkish, palest blue and tinted green, and, darting amongst them like silvery minnows, dozens upon dozens of shooting stars.

It took her breath away now just as completely as it had the first time she'd looked through a telescope.

"Look," she said. "Quickly, before the clouds cover it."

Giles bent to the eyepiece. She watched him intently, alert to his every movement, willing him to experience something of her awe. When he didn't speak she reached out impatiently to adjust the scope but he brushed her hand away and leaned closer.

She heard the quick intake of his breath. He looked up.

"What am I seeing?"

She gave him the same reverence-touched answer her own teacher had given her when she'd asked the same question all those years ago. "The playground of God."

His glance was quick and sardonic.

She cleared her throat, embarrassed to have been caught rhapsodizing. "Or you might also call it a meteor shower."

He turned back to the lens. "Impressive."

"Yes, but that's not what I wanted you to see." She restrained herself from edging him out of the way and retaking possession of the telescope. He was warm. She could feel the heat radiating out from his tall, broad-shouldered body and checked the impulse to move closer. "Pretend the center of the field is the middle of a clock. Now look where the minute hand would be if it were *not quite* ten minutes past the hour. Follow that imaginary line in about a third of the distance to the center.

"Do you see? A barely visible ball of light just a shade larger than those around it? It will look fuzzier than the others, too, and you might just make out a little plume of pinkish light behind it."

He frowned, peering closer before stilling. He did not lift his head, but she could see in profile his lips move in a smile.

"Yes. I see. What is it?"

"My comet," she said.

Chapter Five

Giles straightened, inspecting her as if she were indeed an inmate of Bedlam.

"It's my comet and I am going to keep it," Avery repeated. "And you are going to help me."

"I see. Shall I take the barouche or will it fit in the phaeton?"

"You know that's not what I mean."

He raised an elegant brow. "Do I?"

With a muttered imprecation, she pushed him out of the way and dipped her head to look once more through her telescope. "I discovered her," she whispered. "She's mine."

"You *discovered* it? You are certain?"

She glanced up to find him studying her closely. Though Giles might know little about the science of stargazing, he clearly understood that amongst astronomers such a claim would carry considerable weight.

Avery straightened. "Yes. I found her three years ago in Austria when I was studying with Herr Vandervort. It won't reappear again until 1821."

She wrapped her arms around herself, as much to bolster her confidence as to keep the driving wind from finding her bare flesh. He reached up and tucked his coat collar closer about her. "You're cold. We should continue this conversation inside—Good God, your feet are bare! Are you purposely seeking death or was what I witnessed downstairs not an imitation of madness but the real thing?"

"No. I just—"

He scooped her up into his arms before she could finish. Startled, she gasped and clutched him around the neck. "Let me go!"

He looked down at her, something heated and elemental glittering in his eyes. She had to be imagining it. Giles had no more interest in her than he did in Mrs. Bedling. He was holding her only because he'd been trained since birth to be all but incapable of witnessing a woman's discomfort without acting. And the intensity in his mercury-bright gaze? He was a rake; that's how a rake looked at a woman. Any woman.

"Soon enough." He strode back into the sentry's room, kicking the door shut behind him.

"Put me down."

"Of course." His gaze held hers as he released her and she slid down his length. She felt every hard inch of that journey and when her toes finally found the ground for a second she feared her legs wouldn't hold her. But they did.

She backed away. She couldn't go far. The room was too small, providing barely enough room to turn without brushing against him. The only light came from the glowing brazier at their feet and the starlight glimmering intermittently through the square window cut high in the wall. It molded his face in shadows, sparked his eyes with silver.

He leaned back against the wall and crossed his arms, looking down at her. "What do you mean you plan to 'keep' your comet?"

Gratefully, she returned her attention to the matter at hand. The moment had come for her to reveal her plan. After that it would be up to him. He would either help or refuse her. She *had* to convince him this was the only way.

"I intend to present my discovery to the Royal Astrological Society. In six weeks they convene for their winter meeting, at which time I estimate my comet's visibility will be well past its zenith but still visible."

He nodded. "I see. And you need me to escort you to the meeting? Perhaps to set you up in accommodations for the duration of your stay?"

"No."

"Of course not. That would be too easy." He sighed. "What then?"

"I mean to become a member of the society and submit my research on the comet to their board. Such a discovery should all but guarantee my being presented with the society's Hipparchus medal *and* its attendant monetary award." She smiled. "And then I will be able to continue my research."

"I'm sure that will be most gratifying. But I don't see how this involves me. Unless . . . do you think I can somehow influence the membership?" His lips twisted into an acerbic smile. "Well, of course. That's the way of things. You'll have to provide me with a list of names—"

"No!" she burst out, appalled. "No! That's not what I want! I would never ask you to try to influence people into voting for me. It isn't ethical."

"Ethical," she heard him murmur in an odd voice. She could not see his expression any more. The clouds had covered up the slice of star-strewn skies and it was dark. "My mistake. But how was I to . . ." He laughed softly. "But now I am even more at a loss as to my role in all this. How exactly am I to aid you?"

She took a deep breath. "The Hipparchus medal is an annual prize bestowed on the man making the most significant contribution to astronomical study in the preceding year."

"Man." He repeated the pertinent word.

"Yes. Only gentlemen are invited to join the society."

He hesitated. "So you wish me to stand in for you?"

The idea horrified her even more than his proposed use of influence. "Good heavens, no. You wouldn't last five minutes of interrogation by men of their expertise."

She saw his teeth glint in the darkness. "Come now. I have every confidence I should last six."

"No."

"Then I do not see any way for you to achieve your goal. Unless you mean to change gender . . ." He trailed off. "You mean to try to pass yourself off as a man, don't you?"

"Yes." She nodded. "Yes."

"And you want me to support you in this outlandish charade? Even though if we are discovered it could mean banishment from Society?"

She lifted her chin. "I am not *in* Society."

He pushed off the wall and the glow from the embers in the brazier caught his profile from beneath, illuminating him like a portrait of the fallen angel he so resembled. "I am."

Heat piled into her face. Of course, she'd considered that when she'd formulated her plan. She understood that what she was asking could damage his reputation, but after having read about his exploits in the penny press for years, she was also fairly certain that any harm would be negligible and that he was the sort of golden being whose misdeeds the gods forgive and mere mortals celebrate. Still, that didn't make her request any less presumptuous. It was unforgivably audacious to ask and she knew it.

But oh! How very, *very* much she wanted this.

What could she say to make him agree? What promises could she make? What did she have to barter with? Nothing. She could only give him the truth.

"I want this. More than anything," she said, moving closer and tilting her head back to search his shadowed face, *willing* him to understand. "My discovery will stand on its own merit. If some other person has a greater claim to that award than me I shall be the first to congratulate him.

"But I *deserve* it. I do not want the money for carriages or dresses or frivolities. I want it so that I can continue to work. *My* work. And yes, I know you could easily finance me and would probably do so if only to force me to sign a document promising never to darken your door again." She gave him a twisted smile. "But it's more than the prize money. It's what it means. It's . . . recognition."

She was so intent in making her plea that she didn't realize her hand had risen to lay against his heart in unconscious supplication. His dark gaze fell on it and lifted slowly to hers. Her fingers curled into a fist against his hard chest. She could feel his heart beat, deep and steady.

"I know it must appear I am motivated by nothing but excess pride, but can you possibly understand what it would mean for someone like me to be recognized for what I have accomplished? To have my name attached forever to that comet's discovery?"

"Someone like you?" he echoed in a strange voice.

"Yes, someone who is . . . no one." She hunted his face for some sign of empathy, some clue as to what he was thinking. He frowned down at her, his dark brows knotting and for a long moment was silent. She could feel his gaze on her, the tension beneath her hand, the rise and fall of his chest. Finally, he spoke.

"And just how do you intend we should go about deceiving the entire Royal Astrological Society and, for all practical purposes, every member of polite Society who will then be in town? Which, I am loathe to point out, will be primarily members of Parliament, who are not generally the most gullible of men."

He was going to help her! She felt the smile bloom on her face and in her elation patted him approvingly on his chest before she realized what she was doing and snatched her hand back. He bit back a half smile. "I have a plan."

"Why am I not surprised?"

His sarcastic tone didn't dim her exuberance one bit. "I will pose as your protégé!"

"My protégé?" he echoed incredulously. "No one who has the slightest acquaintance with me will believe that."

"Why not?"

"My dear girl, I am hardly the sort of man to have *protégés*."

"True, the tradition has gone out of fashion, but in the past many of Society's most exalted gentlemen kept entire stables of protégés: artists, writers, composers, poets. It was," she added archly, "one of the few things such gentlemen were any good for and is a practice that ought to be returned to favor."

"You really must try to not to be so liberal with your compliments."

She grinned. "I have it all worked out. You were traveling in the Netherlands in order to recover from the disappointing dissolution of your engagement." Giles snorted. "There you discovered a fascination with the heavens and in wishing to educate yourself further were introduced to me, a student from England studying in Ghent. I consented to tutor you. You were so impressed that you decided forthwith to foster my brilliance." She beamed at him. It was a perfect plan.

"That is one of the most idiotic plans I have ever heard."

"No, it's not," she said, stunned he should think it so. "It's brilliant."

"No. It's not brilliant. First of all, no one is going to believe that I would need to travel in order to recover from the disappointment of losing Sophia's hand. Second, neither will they credit that I have developed a sudden fascination with stars. And finally, no one will believe I would play pupil to a pup such as you are likely be mistaken for, *if* you manage to convince anyone you are a lad in the first place, *which* I greatly doubt. Greatly." His gaze flickered over a figure she knew to be more curvaceous than most women's.

"If anyone does think you are a male and I try to pass you off as my protégé, they are much more likely to assume I am embarked on an exploration of new ways to err against the flesh."

She wasn't entirely certain what he meant by this but it sounded a little depraved and so she blushed. Upon witnessing this, he made a rough sound of exasperation. "There. You see? You are the merest babe. You don't even know to what I refer, and nor should you, but if you were to live in my house, as a male, you would soon learn all manners of things you shouldn't know. I do not need that particular sin on my head, having a full contingent already."

"No," she protested. "No. I won't interfere in your life. I promise. You won't even know I am there. I shall keep entirely out of your way."

"My dear. A great mimic you may be, but let us be frank, if not with each other at least with ourselves. You have as much ability to remain unobtrusive as an elephant has to fly. I recall you thundering about Killylea, arguing with your tutors, fleeing from the staff when you broke something during one or the other of your experiments, and generally terrorizing the household."

She hadn't thought he'd noticed.

"Besides, the entire scheme depends on me taking you about and introducing you to the right people, does it not? How are we to do that if you're sitting quietly unobtrusive in my sitting room." He spoke this last with heavy sarcasm.

"*Please.*" She felt her comet slipping from her grasp. Desperation brought tears to her eyes. Valiantly, she sought not to shed them. "Please. I *can* be unobtrusive. I have lived alone for years. Do you think I was welcomed as a member of the family in the homes of the men under whom I studied?"

She saw his mouth tense with unwilling sympathy. So, he had not grown entirely callous over the years he'd ruled Society's fashionable set. She pressed her suit. "I am used to my own company. I will stay to my room when we are not actively pursuing our goal. I swear it."

He did not reply but looked away, the set of his jaw tight.

She reached up, clasping his shirt front in entreaty. "A couple of luncheons, an afternoon or so, just a few hours here and there and the rest of the time you will not have to bother with me at all.

"I *know* it will work! If you tell people what they will be seeing, then show them something, almost always they will see what you've led them to expect. Just like your one-time bride did. It's human nature.

"It's like one of those silhouette portraits where the same profiles are facing one another. If I tell you it's two people looking at one another, that's what you see, but if I tell you it's actually a single vase in the center then that is what you perceive. *Please.*"

"Bloody hell," he muttered.

She could not lose this. Not now. Not when she was so close.

Tears spilled over her lower eyelids. *Angry* tears now. Throwing all pretenses of gentility aside, she bunched his shirt tighter and yanked his head down, forcing him to meet her eye. "Is this really so much to ask for releasing you from the life sentence you would have entered into with that wretched girl and her horrific father?" she demanded fiercely.

She waited for him, breathing hard, certain he would either respond in kind with anger, or denounce her and her plan entirely—

"All right."

"What?"

"I said, 'All right.' "

She let out the breath she'd been holding with a whoosh.

"Apparently, I have no choice but to acquiesce. Though I warn you, this mad scheme of yours is certainly doomed to failure and will expose you to great condemnation. Have you thought of that? Of the consequences?" he asked. "How such an eventuality might affect your future?"

She had. If she were exposed as a hoaxer, no one would hire her as their assistant. She would not be welcomed back to study at any observatories or with any of her former mentors. But then, long ago Giles had said she would never be welcomed in any of those places anyway. So, yes, this was a risk she was willing to take.

"I have," she said. "But . . ." She hesitated, her conscience railing against her practicality. "But what of you? What of the censure you would face?"

His beautiful mouth curved in a smile that for once held no mockery. "I daresay I shall survive. If nothing else, the tale of our attempted deception shall provide entertainment for an untold number of my peers. So, there you are. I believe I have agreed to help you, you wretched little extortionist."

"Thank you. Oh! Thank you!" She suspected her smile was more of a foolish grin. She struggled to restrain it but she was so . . . so *gratified*. She cleared her throat. Grinned wider. Cleared it again. "We should make plans. Time is of the essence and there are so many variables to consider and—"

"Yes," he interrupted. "And we shall make plans. *Tomorrow*. Today, I have had enough planning." He held up his hand when she started to protest. "Tomorrow."

"As you wish." With a happy sigh, she raked back her hair, reached out for the wig she'd set on the casement, and plopped the hideous thing back atop her head.

"What are you doing?" he asked as she shoved her dark red hair beneath it.

"I am going to scratch on Miss North's door. Perhaps snuffle. Definitely giggle. Manically." She grinned again. "We can't have her reconsidering now, can we?"

Chapter Six

Giles watched Avery disappear, the filthy gown swishing around her bare feet. He closed the damper on the brazier then headed down the spiral staircase, wondering if Avery really was moaning at Sophia's door.

Of course she was.

Bollocks.

In the course of one short evening, she had managed to make disarray of the ordered if unprepossessing plans he'd made for his future. He had arrived home with every intention of making Sophia deliriously happy. And if her happiness was not contingent on sharing his bed, body, or company but would come primarily from acquiring his name and fortune, and even though at one point he might have hoped for more from his wife, he was older now and expected nothing else. Nor did he deserve it. He had wasted any opportunities he'd had for something better.

He'd intended to spend a few days here acquainting Sophia with the staff and his home, present her with a few choice bits of jewelry from the family coffers to tide her over until after the wedding, then send her off to wherever it was North lived during the winter. He'd then intended to return forthwith to London with the single goal of finding out what had happened to Jack Seward, his friend and fellow agent for the crown, who'd disappeared along with his wife some weeks ago.

But now, somehow, he'd promised himself to take part in a havey-cavey charade that hadn't the slightest hope of success. And while he couldn't in all good conscience regret the loss of Sophia's hand in marriage, he did begrudge the time taken away from his investigation. He must somehow contrive to do both for as long as necessary. Which likely wouldn't be long.

No one would mistake Avery Quinn for a young man, not with her figure. Tonight when the wind had plastered the lawn gown tight against her small body, exposing her lushly curved shape as clearly as if she'd been naked, his body had tightened in quick and heated response. Which was strange since Sophia's determined and skillful touch had not roused him in the least for several months.

Now, his mind's eye could not dismiss the image of Avery, her breasts full and round, her waist small, and her hips sweetly curved. No, he couldn't imagine a shirt and trousers would ever adequately conceal that womanly form. And all the binding in the world wasn't going to force that diminutive but well-endowed figure into a masculine silhouette.

As for her face? Admittedly, she had strong features: a crisp jawline, deep-set eyes, and a wide mouth. But the arch of her brow, the length of the swanlike neck, the succulent ripeness of her lips . . .

A man would have to be blind.

He reached the bottom of the stairs and headed for the library, hoping that Avery's "scene setting" had been relegated to only those rooms Sophia was likely to visit and that a nice, warm fire would be burning in the hearth. He was gratified to discover this was so and entered the warm and welcoming room with a sense of homecoming. Here, he'd spent countless hours pouring over the well-stocked shelves. As had Avery Quinn. Sometimes he'd find evidence of her recent habitation: a scribbled note, a half-empty cup of tea, a book left on a table. It had always made him feel as though he shared the room with a particularly companionable little ghost.

He moved to the window and looked out. The unassailable fact was that he did owe Avery. Until this evening, he'd no idea Sophia had a hysteria about people less perfect in form than herself. And he should have. It would have been embarrassing had it not been pathetic. Because he hadn't known for the very simple fact that he hadn't extended himself to discover anything about her. He'd assumed Sophia was nothing more or less than what she appeared to be: ambitious, sly, vain, and sensual. And while he may have decided that he'd found in Sophia exactly what he deserved, she was not what his children deserved. Particularly not since dwarfism ran in his family.

He hadn't investigated Sophia adequately and for that oversight his presumed progeny might have paid a terrible price. Oh, he had asked plenty of questions about her father. He knew all about North's finances, both what he owed and what he was owed. He knew the man's weaknesses, which were legion, and his strengths, which were few. After all, finding out about people was what *he'd* done for all the years that England had been at war with France.

While he'd never held any commission, long ago he'd been recruited into a different service, one where wits and wiles replaced rifle and sword, a world where information was traded for darkest secrets, a world of subterfuge and duplicity.

He'd been very good at it, too. Not just at information gathering, but at engineering events, setting people in the right place at the right time and then manipulating their reactions with just the right trigger to affect the most specific of outcomes. Oh, yes. He'd been very good at it. Better in some ways than even the best of such agents, Jack Seward.

At the thought of Jack, Giles gave the bellpull a tug then poured himself a glass of port. Thoughtfully, he lowered himself into an armchair.

He'd been surprised when Seward had sought him out a few months back and asked for his aid in finding a petty thief that had stolen an important government document. At the end of the war Giles had resigned from the Home Office's Secret Committee thinking the government would have little need for spies during peacetime. Still, infrequently, his talents had been called upon by Sir Robert Knowlton, who, along with Sir Jameson, oversaw the Secret Committee. Even more infrequently, he'd actually agreed to undertake whatever request they made. In fact, he'd considered refusing Jack until his friend had made it clear it would be a personal favor.

It was to be a onetime arrangement. He would facilitate Jack's entry into Society and little more. But things had gone terribly wrong. Jack had made discoveries he had never been intended to know and now Jack was suddenly gone along with his beautiful wife, Anne. Giles was almost certain Jameson was responsible.

Just before his disappearance Jack had broken rank with Sir Jameson, relating sensitive information to Jameson's rival, Sir Knowlton. Jameson did not tolerate betrayal. Soon after, the Sewards had vanished.

Some part of Giles, tired and worn by the dark echoes of his past, wanted to leave it be, afraid he would discover they'd been killed. But there was still some portion of him that would not tolerate the thought of his friends being murdered. If Jameson had killed them, Giles needed to know and bring him to justice.

How quaint. After all he had seen and done, apparently he still had faith that justice could be served. He tipped his head back and drained the contents of his glass.

"Sir?" Travers had entered the room.

"Still playing the butler, you dog?" Jacob Travers had been his father's estate manager from before Giles was born. After the old marquess's death, he had continued on as Giles's general factotum. "That was an amusing tableau you helped orchestrate this evening. Why ever did you agree to it?"

"She saved you from a terrible situation from which you were incapable of extricating yourself."

"I assure you had I wished I would have—"

"No, sir," Travers interrupted staunchly, "you would not. You were honor bound to marry that young woman and so you would have. You are, like your father, a man of integrity."

Giles did not reply, feeling the burden of Travers's faith as keenly as a dead weight.

"Miss Avery wants this, m'lord. She's worked hard for it." Travers broke his silence in a low voice. "She deserves it."

Giles leaned back in his chair, drumming his fingers on the armrest. Travers had always been fond of Avery, though why remained something of a mystery. As a girl Avery had been a prickly little hedgehog. Brilliant, certainly, but she'd put him in mind of the fledgling crow Travers had found after a storm and kept. Josephine, he'd named her.

Travers had taught her all manner of tricks and yet he never could get Josephine to take a treat from his hand without drawing blood.

So it was with Avery, spouting Cicero and drawing metaphorical blood wherever she went.

"Whatever happened to that crow of yours, Travers?"

"Josephine?" Travers asked in surprise. "Why, she flew away, sir."

"You must have had her a dozen years. What happened?"

"One day I took her out of her cage and she simply flew out the window. That was the last I saw of her." He sounded more bemused than aggrieved.

"Perhaps she grew tired of her cage," Giles said, thinking of how shocked he'd been when Avery had said she intended to leave Killylea. He couldn't envision Killylea without Avery and even though in the last years they'd rarely been here at the same time, he always imagined her here, studying in the library, tromping through the orchards, stretched out on her back on the topmost crenellations and staring into the sky. Why, there'd been a time . . . but that was long ago when he'd been hardly more than a boy.

The pertinent point was that Giles had inherited Avery as part of his bequest. Despite what he owed Avery for her timely intervention with Sophia, he felt the obligation his father had incurred far more deeply. *Something* must be done with her and this, apparently, was what she wanted.

He poured himself another glass of port, fully aware of Travers's expectant gaze, so different from Avery's challenging glare.

She'd looked unearthly attractive standing on the ramparts this evening, her eyes so dark they seemed to have drunk the midnight hue from the heavens and her deep auburn locks coiling and dancing out behind her in the wind.

"How in the name of all that's holy does she ever hope to fool anyone?" he muttered. "She is too . . . her form . . ."

"She has enlisted Mrs. Bedling's aid in manufacturing a wardrobe suitable for a young country gentleman. She has a plan to deal with her, ah, her silhouette."

Giles gave a short laugh. "Avery has a plan. Ah, well then, we're all fine as five pence." He heaved himself to his feet. "You might as well start packing."

"Sir?"

"As soon as the Norths have left, we'll ride at breakneck speed to the coast, cross to the Netherlands, and ramble about for a week or so before hieing ourselves back to London in all due haste that we might meet up with Mr. Quinn, whom I shall then inform all and sundry that I met while in the midst of said rambling. During which time I also happened to develop a sudden passion for stargazing. Oh, yes. No one will think anything smoky in that. Not at all."

His sarcasm was lost on Travers. "But . . . *we*, sir?"

Giles was not above enjoying Travers's discomfort. Between them, he and Avery had all but assured his own. He clapped the older man on the shoulder. "Yes. If this rattle-pated plan has a chance of succeeding, Avery will need an ally in the house. Someone amongst the servants who knows who she is and can protect her identity from the others." He smiled. "You, my friend, have just been demoted."

"Sir?"

"You're Avery's new valet."

Chapter Seven

Miss Avery was gone. She'd disappeared, having been last seen entering a private sleeping room in a coaching inn forty miles north of London. She never emerged to rejoin the stage coach on the last leg of its journey. But as the room had been paid for in advance and was left neat as a pin and with no hint of anything untoward having occurred within it except, perhaps, for a plethora of shorn mahogany-colored locks found in the waste bin, the innkeeper decided not to pursue the matter. Why, girls eloped all the time and in truth, Miss Avery had hardly been a girl, being clearly on the wrong side of twenty.

However, the stagecoach gained a new passenger to replace her. A small, fat, and flushed young man found shivering on the bench outside the inn early the next morning joined them. He gave his name as Mr. Quinn as he handed his single piece of luggage, an over-stuffed valise, up to the driver and climbed aboard.

For all his youth—and he *was* young, having skin as smooth and soft looking as a puppy's belly—the matronly lady seated across from him gauged Mr. Quinn to be a rustic scholar. The scholar part she based on several observations: the pair of glasses perched on his nose, hands that had certainly never seen manual labor, and the set of books bound with a leather strap he carried. Rustic she judged from his hat, a low-crowned and wide-brimmed felt one fashioned in the country style that shadowed his features, and from his coat which, though made of good, sturdy material, was ill cut and swiftly made. The matron had sewed enough clothing herself to be a fair judge.

Possibly he was a tutor on his way to his first employer, she thought. For his sake she hoped not. Boys could be so cruel. Especially to someone . . . different. Like this young man. For though his arms and legs were spindly, his torso had a pronounced spherical contour that began beneath his chin and ended at the tops of his legs, the effect being as if a melon had sprouted limbs.

A pity, she thought, for he might have been a handsome enough lad otherwise. He had even features and dark eyes from what she could see behind the glasses—though an unfortunate single heavy brow marched straight over the bridge of his nose—and a clean, clipped jawline. Curious creature. He'd spent the entire trip mute as a mummer and for the past half hour had covered his mouth and nose with a handkerchief, his eyes watering.

She sympathized. She remembered her first visit to London and her own reaction to its potent reek. "You never been to London afore, have you, Mr. Quinn?" she said.

"No, ma'am." He had a soft, raspy voice as if his throat had been injured at some point in time. Perhaps in his childhood. If he'd been invalided as a boy, he would not have the opportunity to pursue those activities that turned baby fat to muscle. It would also account for his lack of manners. He hadn't even offered her his seat when she'd climbed inside and had even neglected to doff his hat. Mothers always tended to overindulge a sickly child.

"I been," she disclosed with the serene satisfaction of the well traveled. "Many a time and always for the same reason, that being tending my brother's nippers whilst his wife produces another. You get used to the stench and the air being so thick. Be folks expecting you?"

He nodded. She didn't think him surly, but rather painfully shy and all her maternal instincts came flying to the fore at the thought of this babe lost in the Sodom and Gomorrah that was London. The stagecoach rocked to a halt.

"You have a job waiting for you then, Mr. Quinn?"

He shook his head. "No. That is, not exactly."

So, he'd come hoping for a particular job but not yet having secured it. She studied him pityingly. She doubted he'd get it unless he was the only applicant. He hadn't much to recommend him.

One of the postboys clambered down from his perch and yanked open the door, revealing the Gloucester Coffee House's well-tended courtyard.

"Well, good luck to you, lad," she said as she accepted the postboy's hand and climbed down out of the carriage.

"You'll need it," she muttered and then her brother and at least a half dozen of her young nieces and nephews swarmed around her, shouting and laughing, and she forgot all about the unfortunately shaped Mr. Quinn.

How in the name of heaven did people live here?

Avery, last to climb down out of the carriage, shivered violently and stood in the courtyard, transfixed. Even though it was just past two o'clock in the afternoon, it was already dark. Well, not dark precisely, but dim, muted, the air coalescing into a thin, freezing mist, the pools of water standing in the courtyard rimed with ice. She pulled her coat closer around her throat and tipped her head back to stare in horrified fascination at the patch of sky revealed overhead. It was dingy and low, the indistinct disc of the sun sunk into it like a tarnished coin at the bottom of a dish of milky tea. It would be impossible to see the stars through that opaque mantle.

She had been to other cities in the course of her education, generally small university towns, but never to London. In her imagination it had loomed as a repository of all that was great in England: art, music, mathematics, science. But this was noisome and cold and *loud*! Horses neighed, dogs barked, hooves clattered, and axles squealed. Heavily laden carts rumbled over the cobbled pavement, an underscore to carters bawling, coachmen shouting, and vendors hollering.

And it stank! She pushed the handkerchief to her mouth again and looked about. Surely all of this great city could not be so foul?

"Here, boy!"

She turned in the direction of the shout and the stagecoach driver tossed her valise to her with so much velocity that she staggered backward as she caught it. He smirked. "London's gonna eat you alive, youngster, lest you grow some muscle 'neath all that fat."

She flushed, clasping the valise to her chest. She realized her disguise made her a target for censorious eyes, but there had been no practical alternative. After several hours of experimentation, she and Mrs. Bedling had agreed that the amount of constriction necessary to bind her bosom flat would have rendered her unconscious. So instead, they'd concocted a way to hide it amidst layers of padding sewed into one of Mrs. Bedling's corsets.

Had she been vain she would have been embarrassed by her appearance. She was not vain. Having people think she was a fat young man suited her purpose. If they were looking at her waistline they would not be looking at her face.

She and Strand had parted ways nearly three weeks earlier. Strand had given her a purse full of coin and explicit instructions: In twenty days' time, Miss Avery was to take the stagecoach to Whitchurch, procure a private room at the last coaching inn, and there transform herself into Mr. Quinn. Before daybreak the next morning she was to leave the room by way of the window and wait outside the inn until the coachman arrived to rouse the other passengers. Once in London she was to hire a hackney carriage to take her to Strand's house. She would be expected.

"You planning to stand there interferin' with traffic all day, son?" the innkeeper shouted at her from the tavern's open door. She looked around uncertainly and spied a hansom carriage parked just outside the courtyard. Hefting the valise to her shoulder, she trudged through the icy muck to its side. The driver leaned over from his seat, looking her up and down. "You kin pay?"

"Yes." She nodded, squinting up at him through the thickening drizzle.

He eyed her doubtfully. "Let's see the color of yer coin."

She reached into her pocket and withdrew the tightly laced purse, untying it with cold fingers. She pulled a pair of shillings out and held them up for his inspection. He gave a grunt, bent at the waist from atop his perch, and yanked open the door.

"Where to?" he asked as she shoved the valise inside.

She gave him the address on Half Moon Street, drawing a low appreciative whistle as she climbed in and shut the door. "Is it far?" she called up once settled inside.

"Far?" She heard him laugh. "Nay. T'aint far. But in London, lad, it's never how far a thing is away, it's how long it takes to get there!" And with a flick of his whip, he sent the carriage lurching forth.

An hour later, Avery understood what he meant. They seemed to spend more time standing, backing up, and skirting around things than moving forward. Traffic choked every avenue and street. A van lying on its side obstructed traffic for blocks, its spilled contents swarming with a hoard of raggedy children darting beneath the cudgel-wielding arm of the driver trying futilely to defend his goods. Men unloading a brick wagon clogged another intersection and everywhere a river of pedestrian traffic flowed thick as sludge.

Just when she thought she might never reach her destination and that she would end her days in this carriage, the traffic abruptly loosened. The congestion petered away in mere blocks. She stared out the window as the carriage entered a short block lined with tall, white edifices built cheek-to-jowl across from a small park blanketed with a recent snow, a hedge of holly brilliant against the white.

Each house looked much like its neighbors. White Greek columns flanked the entrances and each one boasted identical sets of tall French doors along their first floors. These, in turn, opened to identical balconies enclosed by shining black wrought-iron rails. More rows of windows gleamed in orderly procession from the upper stories.

The carriage halted midway down the street and the driver jumped down and opened the door. She hesitated only a second before leaping down.

" 'At'll be a shilling three," the driver said as he pulled her luggage free and dumped it at her feet.

She dug the coins from her purse and handed them to him. He tipped a finger to his hat and climbed back to his perch, setting off at a smart pace. Wearily, Avery trudged up the stairs, her valise bumping her thighs on one side and her books bumping the other. At the top, she set the valise down and rapped on the door.

She waited, cold and weary, but with an undeniable sense of achievement. She'd done it. She'd passed her first day as a male without being found out. The older lady in the coach had given her a few tense moments, but in the end people had done exactly as she'd expected them to do: They'd accepted what they saw without questioning it.

Now, all she wanted was a bath and out of this contraption. Later she could meet with Strand and find out what arrangements he had made to introduce her to various members of the Royal Astrological Society. Perhaps they could dine together in her room with Travers—who'd arrived earlier in the week—to attend them. Then she could dispense with the male garb for the evening. Though masculine clothing *should* have allowed for greater and easier movement, the cotton batting protruding like a prow from her front curtailed any benefits the attire might have offered. It would take some getting used to.

The door swung open. A footman in livery stood before her. He was tall, at least a head taller than she, and very blond and startlingly handsome—almost as handsome as Strand. He looked down at her, his expression carefully neutral.

"Mr. Quinn?"

Where was Travers? Travers was supposed to meet her. Or at least that's what she had assumed . . . She nodded, resigning herself to prolonging her charade for a bit longer.

"You're expected, sir. I am Burke," the footman said, taking her packages from her and stepping aside.

She looked around the entrance. The walls were painted a pale, celestial blue surmounted by a white ceiling, the plaster moldings carved into an intricate Greek key motif. A single round pedestal table stood in the center of the entry, graced by a silver bowl brimming with yellow hothouse roses and blue larkspur.

"If you'll follow me, sir."

She nodded and Burke led the way down a long hall, stopping at the first door and opening it, then stepping inside. She frowned. She would rather go to her rooms and clean off the travel muck before seeing Strand but she supposed she had little choice.

"Mr. Avery Quinn, m'lord," Burke announced.

"Strand," she said a little irritably, starting past the footman, "if it is all the same to you might we delay this interview until after I've changed clothing and . . ."

Her voice trailed off as a room full of strangers turned towards her.

Chapter Eight

At the sound of her voice, Giles turned, saying, "Ah, this must be"—his eyes widened at the sight of her—"my boy genius."

Whatever surprise Avery's appearance might have occasioned, it took less than a heartbeat for him to recover. "I was just telling my guests all about you and here you arrive, like Hamlet's father, and no less pale." His gaze swept over her. "Though a good deal more corpulent. We shall have to withhold the sweets, m'lad, lest you need a new suit of clothes before week's end. Here, let us at least shed the coat. You're dripping."

He came towards her, his back to the assembled company. "And take off your hat," he said in a voice pitched for her ears alone. "You're supposed to be a young gentleman and there are ladies present."

She flushed and snatched the hat from her head, tousling the short auburn curls beneath. How dare he chastise her when he was the one who'd played foul?

He stared at her cropped curls, his hand moving fractionally as though to touch them before falling to his side.

She attempted a smile, speaking in an equally low voice through clenched teeth. "If you hope that by thrusting me all unawares into the middle of a party I will reveal myself and you will be done with our bargain, you are doomed to disappointment. I am made of sterner stuff than that."

"I should hope so," he replied. "Or we are, indeed, doomed." He looked her up and down. "The glasses are a nice touch."

He turned to the footman. "Burke, take Mr. Quinn's things to the garden-facing bedchamber and have the maid dry his coat."

"Good heavens, Strand, are you never going to introduce us?" A stout middle-aged woman resplendent in a purple velvet turban slapped her fan on the table beside her.

"I hope I'm not interrupting, Lord Strand," Avery announced in the low raspy whisper they'd agreed she'd adopt. If queried, she could claim it was the result of a childhood infection that had affected her voice.

"Not at all." He took her by the elbow and propelled her over to the couch where the lady roosted like a fat pullet alongside a tall girl with overly frizzed yellow hair and a shy smile. At Strand's approach, the girl shrank back against the cushions.

"Lady Demsforth and Lady Lucille Demsforth, may I present Mr. Avery Quinn?" Strand said. "Make pretty, Avery."

Avery pushed the spectacles up higher on her nose, uncertain what "making pretty" entailed, while the ladies regarded her in offended puzzlement.

With a light *tch* of his tongue, Strand bent confidingly towards Lady Demsforth. "Brilliant," he said apologetically, "but, as is so often the case with these brainy sorts, lackin' in the social arts, eh?"

With a quick start of understanding, Avery jerked forward at the waist, feeling the blood rising in her cheeks. "A pleasure to meet you, ma'am. Miss."

Lady Demsforth took one look at the pedestrian cut of Avery's coat, sniffed, and nodded dismissively. Lady Lucille, however, gave her a sympathetic smile. "How do you, Mr. Quinn?"

Before she could reply, Giles secured her elbow and led her towards a pair of gentlemen standing at the far end of the room, one quite large and young and the other a haughty-looking fellow closer to Strand's age.

"Vedder," Giles said to the older man, "my protégé, Avery Quinn. Avery, Lord Vedder."

Lord Vedder, Avery felt confident, was what the popular press deemed "an exquisite." He was good enough looking, with heavy-lidded eyes and a haughty expression, and with somewhat pinched nostrils. Though if his nose had not been so elevated, this minor detraction would not have been nearly so notable.

His indigo blue coat fit him as seamlessly as a second skin, a spray of pink sapphires securing the snowy folds of his cravat beneath his chin. Pink threads also embroidered his gold-colored silk waistcoat and encrusted the ebony head of the cane he swung lightly from his fingertips.

He smiled and something in his hooded eyes told her that he intended to have a spot of sport at her expense. It did not alarm her. In fact, it felt oddly comforting. She had seen that look countless times in the eyes of young men who thought themselves her intellectual superior and wanted to draw attention to their primacy in front of an audience.

They invariably failed.

"I confess," the exquisite said, "I find the notion of Strand suddenly showing up towing a protégé in his wake most curious. How do you account for it, young sir?"

She'd anticipated a question like this. "Lord Strand recently experienced an epiphany."

"Yes," Lord Vedder drawled, "but I wasn't talking about his revelations concerning Miss North."

His words obviously intended to shock and succeeded. She glanced at Giles. Though his expression remained perfectly neutral, he could not be amused by the inference that he had discovered something about Sophia that caused *him* to break off the engagement. No gentleman broke off an engagement, for *any* reason. To do so was unspeakably dishonorable. And a gentleman was nothing without his honor. Or so Avery had been told.

"Whatever do you mean, Vedder?" Giles asked.

Vedder's brows rose. "Why, only that you made the unhappy discovery that Miss North did not wish to marry you," he said innocently. He turned back to her. "What epiphany were *you* referring to, Master Quinn?"

She pushed her spectacles back up her nose, buying time. She felt out of her depth and did not like the sensation. "I meant that Lord Strand realized that by acting as a patron to the intellectual community he might benefit society rather than"—she looked pointedly at Vedder's walking stick—"adorn it."

Lord Vedder's head snapped back. Avery carefully refrained from glancing at Giles. She suspected he'd like her *bon mot* no better than Vedder's.

"Oh, my!" Lord Vedder murmured. "It has teeth. What a fierce little cub you've found yourself, Strand."

Giles gave an exaggerated sigh. "You can appreciate how hard it's been for the wretched boy to find himself a sponsor," he murmured. "I believe I am one of the only people in Europe he hasn't managed to offend."

"How do you do it?" Vedder asked.

She fumed inwardly. She hated being spoken of as if she weren't present.

Giles's smile was beatific. "I take the higher ground. For all his faults—and you are seeing but a scant portion of them—the lad *is* a genius."

She could stand it no longer. "The lad is *here.*"

"So, you are," Giles said in the kindly manner of an uncle speaking to a spoilt child.

"What a collector of oddities you've become, Strand. First you sponsor the redoubtable Colonel Seward and now this boy."

Giles did not reply. Though not a muscle moved in his face and his smile remained unaltered, an alertness had entered his gaze that been missing before.

"Where is your erstwhile friend, Strand? I haven't seen him or his delectable wife in a cat's age." The salacious quality flavoring the query made Avery shift uncomfortably.

Giles tipped his head. "Why do you ask? I had the distinct impression you and Seward found little to recommend in one another."

Vedder shrugged. "Just curious." He turned to Avery. "And now you've plucked another unknown from thin air. Tell me, boy, what is it you are genius at?"

"I am an astronomer, sir."

"I see. Perhaps you can tell me my fortune?"

"Astronomer, sir. Not astrologer. One is science, the other is poppycock."

Giles sighed again. "He has opinions."

"So I see."

"I only tolerate them because this very year he discovered—" He broke off as if recalling himself, pressed a finger to his lips, and smiled from behind it. "But I speak ahead of myself. Leave us say, Avery's mental prowess is even more pronounced than his social deficiencies. But I am remiss. I have yet to introduce him to Lord Neville. Neville, may I present Avery Quinn. Avery, Lord Neville Demsforth."

"How d'you do?" The young man who had been standing nearby attempting miserably to pretend he hadn't overheard every razor-edged word inclined his head, the tips of his ears burning brightly.

He was a very large young man who held his shoulders slightly bunched forward as though uncomfortable with his size. Avery supposed him to be fresh out of his teens and that a last minute spurt of growth had made him self-conscious and awkward. He had a nice, open sort of face, his nose snubbed and freckled, his jaw a trifle heavy, and his carefully combed flaxen hair already receding from a high forehead.

"Come, Vedder, let us leave these two young bucks to trade confidence of the sort we did at that age," Giles said, and led Vedder towards the settee occupied by Lady Demsforth and her daughter.

For a moment, Avery and the young man stood silently regarding one another. Lord Neville seemed to be waiting for something. She couldn't imagine what.

"You are an academic then, Mr. Quinn?" he finally asked.

"I am a scientist."

"I see. And what do you study?"

"The stars."

"My uncle likes stars." He looked at her expectantly but she could not think what to reply to this.

She did not simply *like* stars. They were her life. But she very much doubted Lord Neville wanted to hear about Fraunhofer lines. Her gaze drifted uneasily around the drawing room looking for inspiration, noting the marble mantle, the white painted woodwork, the light green damask-covered furnishings. Should she perhaps comment on how chilly the room felt? Did men say things like that to one another?

Lord Neville cleared his throat. "You must be very smart to have attracted Lord Strand's notice at so young an age."

"I am." She reseated the spectacles on the bridge of her nose.

Once more they fell silent, she with mounting frustration, he with an increasingly sympathetic expression.

Why was he looking at her like that? As though he felt sorry for her. Why should he feel sorry for her? She had discovered a comet. What had he ever done? She glared at Giles. He'd put her in this fix. He caught her eye and gave the smallest jerk of his chin in Neville's direction. Fine.

"You must be great friends with Lord Strand," she said.

"What? No." The lad looked taken aback. *Now* what had she said? "I mean, not *great* friends. Why do you say that?"

"Well, here he is back in town but a few days and after being thrown over by his fiancée and here you are. I should think only a friend of long standing and intimacy would present themselves thus."

She watched in fascination as Neville's ears once more grew crimson. She bet an anatomist would enjoy dissecting his arterial system. . . .

Neville cleared his throat, glanced at her, cleared his throat again and stared, stricken mute. Suddenly, she felt impatient with the inanity of it all and frustrated and rueful that she'd unintentionally discomforted this nice boy.

"I'm sorry," she said. "I've done it again, haven't I? Strand is right. I oughtn't be allowed out in polite company."

He searched her face and whatever he found there seemed to reassure him, for he blew out a gusty sigh and his whole large, well-dressed, ungainly body relaxed. He grinned ruefully. "No, no, you are quite correct." He glanced around before looking back down into her face. "But as the old marquess and my father were at school together, and my father once made some mention of how nice it would be should one of his children wed one of the marquess's and the old marquess didn't bother to disagree, my mother feels a bargain has all but been struck—and let me tell you she was not happy when Lucy was displaced by Miss North—and that it gives us permission to arrive here so precipitously upon Strand's return to London and stay far too long."

Avery regarded him quizzically.

"What I mean to say, Mr. Quinn, is that we *are* being unconscionably forward. But my mother wanted to steal a march on the other Society ladies with marriageable daughters."

Avery furrowed her brow.

"Now that Strand's once more in the market for a bride."

Avery stared at him in dawning horror. "You mean we might expect more ladies to arrive with their offspring in tow?" she asked. This was not how things were supposed to evolve. Not at all.

"I expect so, yes."

Avery looked at the proposed bridal candidate with increased interest but after a few seconds decided there was nothing there to engage Strand's notice. Just a pretty girl in a pretty, frothy dress, sitting prettily.

"And you say these ladies will parade their daughters in front of Lord Strand like cattle at a county fair waiting for him to choose from amongst them?"

Neville burst out laughing. His mother glared at him from across the room. He quickly stifled his amusement. "Ahem. In a manner of speaking, I suppose so."

"But that's barbaric."

"You really have been living the life of an ascetic, haven't you?" Neville asked wonderingly. "Whatever were your parents thinking to let you come to Strand so unprepared?"

Avery was astounded and not only because, frankly, Neville Demsforth did not look any more prepared to deal with Society than he seemed to feel she was, but because no one had ever spoken to her like this before, as though she was slightly below average in some area or other. It was a unique sensation. "I . . . ah . . . they're dead," she said, offering a silent apology to her very much alive father.

Neville studied her for a moment more before seeming to come to a decision. "You need a guide, my friend. Someone to enlighten you."

"Thank you, but Lord Strand—"

"Is a generation removed from you and has enough ton bronze on him to stand in for a statue. Besides, he is . . . well, I can't think you two have much in common."

She glanced at Giles. He embodied élan, his easy, clever manner merely an extension of his self-confidence, his unassailable superiority. Though only thirty feet separated them, she had never been more aware of distance. Not only physical distance, but the distance between their experiences and lives.

And futures.

Neville was right: Giles belonged to a world she would never fully understand, one that even in her disguise she could participate in only on the fringes. But while she was here it would be interesting to learn something of it. Like a tourist at some foreign port of call.

"I offer my services as a far more likely alternative," Neville said, smiling solicitously. It did not offend her since there didn't seem to be anything critical in his assessment, only honest concern.

She couldn't recall the last time someone had exhibited any sort of protective impulse towards her. She'd run free under her father's benign indifference, and the old marquess had shipped her off without a second thought to whatever illustrious scholar would have her. She knew how to take care of herself.

"And how exactly would you do that?" she asked.

"We could take a ride in my new curricle 'round St. James Park or even in the city proper. Streets aren't nearly so crowded now that the Season's over."

"I'm sorry," she said, mindful of her promise to Strand that she would remain hermitized in her rooms. "I came to London to study stars, not the ton."

"You will be studying stars. London has her own set of luminaries, Mr. Quinn, ones that can rival in brilliance any stars you have hitherto known. Though with the Season over they are much more elusive. Makes it all a better game, eh? It will be fun, I promise you."

Games? *Fun?* He was twinkling at her in such a good-humored sort of way that she didn't want to disappoint him. It had been a long time since anyone had suggested she do something simply for pleasure.

"We shall see."

"I'll come by Friday afternoon."

She had no intention of going, but neither did she want to get involved in some silly pull-and-push conversation and this had all the earmarks of becoming one. Neville looked so eager. So determined. He looked, she realized, more in need of a friend than she.

But she'd always been very independent and quite satisfied with her own company. Yes. Quite satisfied.

She would send written word tomorrow or the next day politely declining his offer and that would be that.

"Say you will."

"Perhaps."

Neville gave a knowing nod. "Good. Now, let us go rescue my poor sister from Strand's attention. She looks likely to disappear under the cushions at any moment."

Chapter Nine

G oodness. How ever did it grow so late?"
After stretching the bonds of even the most liberal rules of etiquette by more than an hour, Lady Demsforth finally noted the time and only then, Strand was certain, because her son was holding his pocket watch open five inches beneath her nose. Vedder had left a half hour earlier.

"If we have stayed a bit too long, Lord Strand, it is entirely your own fault for being such a congenial host," she cooed. "Naughty man. But then, time does have a way of disappearing when the company is so pleasing. Don't you agree, Lord Strand?" She tipped her head blatantly in the direction of her poor daughter. Lucille turned pink.

"Indeed, yes, Lady Demsforth," Giles replied, feeling sorry for the girl. She so clearly felt her mother's vulgarity.

Normally, Giles managed to dodge Lady Demsforth and her ardent and ill-fated pursuit of his coronet, but when Burke had brought her card, he'd remembered that her brother was president of the very society Avery wished to join and so had received her and her progeny.

But why *had* Vedder accompanied them? Though he and Vedder both belonged to White's Gentlemen's Club and moved in the same circles, they could hardly be called friends. Indeed, Vedder had never called on him before. It was a unique event and Giles distrusted unique events. What did Vedder hope to gain?

"You must promise me, *promise*, that you will call on us this week. We shall be home every day," Lady Demsforth said, interrupting his speculation.

Neville's cheeks grew ruddy with mortification.

"I shall try, ma'am, but I do have obligations to my protégé."

Lady Demsforth cast a quick glance at where Avery sat teetering on the edge of a chair like a giant egg about to topple over.

"Yes. Well. Bring him along." She reached out and rapped his hand sharply with her fan, smiling coquettishly. "Promise."

"I shall endeavor," he said, fearful he would otherwise end up spending the next hour fending off her demands. Happily, her son took matters into his own hands—literally—by clasping hold of her upper arm and hauling her bodily to her feet while still somehow managing to make it look as if he were simply a dutiful son attending his mother. Clearly, Neville had unforeseen potential.

"There, Mother. Off we go," Neville said with forced cheer. "Lucy?"

With what Giles would have considered unflattering alacrity had it not been so amusing, Lucille jumped to her feet and, with a quick bobbed curtsey, dashed out of the room, leaving her brother to drag their parent along in her wake. Giles grinned after them, turning to see if Avery shared his amusement—

She did not.

She'd stood up, hands on her hips, the furry brow lowered in a thundercloud of displeasure. The tip of her mud-encrusted shoe tapped ominously.

He strangled back the smile that threatened, deciding it would be impolitic, but really, what in the Almighty's name had she done to achieve such a shape? She looked like a giant apple. Every feminine contour had been obliterated by whatever means she'd used to achieve that figure. And she'd apparently glued something between her brows to make them meet over the bridge of her nose.

He approved the spectacles. They reflected back much of a room's light, hiding the extraordinary midnight color of her eyes and her long, spiky lashes. It would be better, however, if she didn't need to keep pushing them up on her nose. It drew attention to hands both too elegant and too slender to be masculine.

And though it had been necessary, he regretted the loss of her hair. It had been irrepressibly feminine, falling about her shoulders in a riot of undisciplined auburn coils, like shining corkscrew ribbons on a present. The thatch of remaining curls looked boyish enough, though still untamable.

"You set me up to fail!" The words exploded from her. "You wanted me to be discovered. But I wasn't. I won't be."

Her accusation produced an unexpected twinge of hurt. How odd. What did he care that she'd misconstrued the situation and misjudged him? She just as easily could have been right. It was just the sort of thing he might have done.

Except he hadn't.

He lifted his hands from his side in a placating gesture. "You are mistaken. Hard though it is to imagine, I wasn't entertaining the Demsforths for the pleasure of their company but rather to recommend you to them."

"Why?" she snapped. "Were you thinking of offering me as your substitute suitor? I doubt Lady Lucille's mama will approve."

He arched a brow to keep from smiling. "What a piquant notion! I'm sure Lady Lucille would find you vastly preferable to me."

"Don't be ridiculous," she muttered. "She would have to be an idiot. You're . . . *you*."

He chuckled. He couldn't help it. Not at her notion of him, but that she had felt compelled to voice it. She was the most ingenuous, candid creature he knew. His smile widened as he realized the absurdity of such a notion, for here they were in the midst of perpetrating a whopping deception on the decent members of the Royal Astrological Society. If she was the most honest person he knew, he really must get to know a better class of people.

Except he didn't want to.

She cocked her head, eyeing him darkly, and he realized she was awaiting his response.

For a second or two, he toyed with the idea of demurring but, confound it, it was rather fun playing into her concept of him. When was the last time he had thought of something as *fun*?

"I am, aren't I?" he agreed pleasantly.

She gave a short snort of disgust.

"However, I was not alluding to my exceptional recommendations as a suitor, but to your scheme. You see, Avery, Lady Demsforth's brother is Samuel Isbill." He watched with gratification as her eyes grew round behind her glasses.

"*Sir* Samuel Isbill?" she whispered reverently.

"Yes. The president of your Star Club thingie, I believe."

"Neville said his uncle liked stars but I never imagined he meant . . ." she murmured. "Good heavens."

"Neville?"

"Yes. He's invited me to go driving with him later this week."

"He did, did he?" Giles didn't know much about the lad. A large, innocuous-seeming boy newly up from Cambridge. Second son of the very wealthy Earl of Demsforth.

"Yes." Avery pulled a face. "He thinks I stand in need of a . . . less sophisticated, shall we say, companion than you."

The impertinence of the pup. Yet, one could not fault his discernment. "Well, high points for the lad's acumen. And by all means, should you meet him again, be pleasant. He might prove useful."

She frowned at this. "Do you judge everyone's value by their usefulness?"

He forgot how little she knew of him. "In terms of your goal, yes."

He watched her mull this over, discontent pleating her brow. She was not meant for intrigues. "What of Lord Vedder?" she finally asked. "Why was he here? Don't tell me he's a member of the Royal Astrological Society?"

"No. The only society Vedder is interested in is the ton and the only interests he pursues are his own. For some reason, he attached himself to the Demsforths today."

"I don't like him and I am glad you don't like him."

"Did I say that?" he asked mildly.

"You didn't have to." Apparently he was back in her good graces.

"As for driving with Lord Neville, I will ask you to remember your promise to me not to leave the house. It offers too many opportunities for discovery."

"Must I really remain inside for weeks?" she asked in a small, dismayed voice.

"Of course not. I expect I shall have to show you off a few times and there's a lending library and a coffee house the next square over that you can visit. But take Travers with you. I doubt you'll excite much curiosity at either place. But riding out with young Demsforth? No."

"As you will," she said. "I shall send word saying I am committed to my studies." She sighed and he wondered if she had been looking forward to riding with young Neville. "What do we do next?"

He tugged the bellpull. "*You* are shown to your rooms where you shall unpack. I shall have Travers bring dinner to your room in, shall we say, three hours? If you don't mind, I'll join you so that we can discuss strategy without interruption." And in the meantime he would do what he could to flush up some information about Jack. He'd been in town four days with nothing to show for all his ferreting about.

"Of course," she said eagerly, then paused. "Where *is* Travers?"

"Lurking in the servants quarters, doubtless, waiting for someone to scream, 'That's a woman!' "

"I cannot believe he has such little faith." She sniffed derisively.

"I can't claim to have had any more confidence," he said. "And I did allow you to walk into the lion's den, so to speak, not only because it provided an opportunity to introduce you to Lady Demsforth but also because I knew that you were most likely to fail during your first moments under scrutiny and if you did I could try to pass the whole charade off as part of a silly wager."

"Good heavens." She looked more disquieted than angered. "Are you always so Machiavellian?"

Machiavellian? Well, he supposed he was. Treacherous, double-dealing, devious, designing, they'd all once applied. Perhaps they still did. Because, when war translated you into someone, some *thing* else, could you ever return to a semblance of the man you once were? He wasn't sure he wanted to know the answer.

The door open and Burke entered. "M'lord?"

"Burke," Giles said, "please show Mr. Quinn to his rooms then return to me."

"Yes, sir." The young Adonis turned to Avery. "If you'll follow me, sir?"

But Avery was still studying Giles with an odd, contemplative air, as if she'd seen something unexpected in the night sky and was reassessing an earlier hypothesis. He strongly suspected he'd been downgraded from comet to flotsam. He did not much like it.

"Run along, Avery. And in answer to your question, yes, I am," he said. And wished he lied.

"Relax, Burke," Giles said to the strapping young footman standing at attention. "This isn't the Inquisition."

"Yes, sir. Sorry, sir."

Burke had been one of Jack Seward's men. Four years earlier, Jack had found the illiterate cockney lad running a rigged game of dice on the docks. Burke had attracted Jack's attention not because he wanted to save the lad from a potentially dangerous occupation, but because the boy had been so good at it. Jack had taken the boy, taught him to read, write, and speak, and how to be a footman. Then he'd inserted him where he would prove most useful.

Upon his return to London, Giles had sought out Burke to see if he knew anything about Jack's fate. He hadn't, but he'd been as keen to discover what had happened to Jack as Giles was. He was a very loyal young man. And so Giles had offered him a position, both as a footman and in his old capacity.

"Before you tell me what you've learned regarding Colonel Seward, I have a task for you."

"Yes, sir."

"Mr. Quinn is unused to a household such as this. He is a very private young man. Make sure the staff does not enter his room without first knocking. And I should not be surprised if he locks the door on you."

Strand had vacillated over whether or not to include Burke in his confidence and had finally decided against it. He did not doubt Burke's discretion, but he did not know him well enough to trust his acting ability.

If Burke knew Avery was a woman he might inadvertently react to her in such a way as to invite comment amongst the staff. It was hard enough for Giles himself to remember she was supposed to be a man. From there it was a short step to discovery and, as had been so recently illustrated to him at Killylea, the servants' network was a potent source of information. No, the fewer who knew, the better.

"He's very different from your usual friends," Burke said carefully. It was as close as he was likely to allow himself to asking a question.

"Yes," Giles agree. "Well, we must allow ourselves a few eccentricities."

"As you say, sir."

"Now, what have you learned?"

The young man's face mirrored his distress. "Nothing useful. Can't rightly make up to Sir Jameson's staff as he doesn't have much of one. Just his housekeeper, and if she knows where her arse is without looking, I'd be surprised—pardon, sir—and a deaf scullery maid and his valet. No cook. No other maids. No footmen. And he don't keep a carriage."

"What of the valet?"

"Finical, egg-peeling bloke. Don't have no, er, *any* vices nor habits nor pleasures. I think he considers polishing his gentleman's boots a high lark." Burke's face twisted in disgust. "I've managed to encounter him a few times, but seeing how housebound he is, to chance upon me any time soon is bound to wake his suspicions. Besides, he didn't want to trade words with me."

"So, he's loyal to Jameson?"

Burke shrugged. "Loyal or afraid. Hard to say. I'm sorry, sir."

Giles waved away the apology. "It was a long shot at best. Jameson is hardly likely to have brought Jack or Anne to his house, either alive or dead. We shall just have to search elsewhere."

"But where, sir? I've kept my ear tuned to the servants' chatter and haven't heard mention of Colonel Seward or his lady."

"Then we shall have to broaden our scope beyond the ton. If something nefarious was done, I'll have to go where nefarious acts are for sale."

Burke nodded then glanced sharply at Giles. "You, sir?"

"Yes, Burke. You needn't look so alarmed. I assure you, I am quite capable of making inquiries without getting killed." The footman's incredulity might have offended another man, but not Strand. It rather amused him. Burke had not known him when he'd worked for Knowlton.

"Beggin' pardon, sir, but are you sure?" Burke asked.

"Oh, yes." He smiled, though he doubted it reached his eyes. "Quite sure."

Chapter Ten

Giles had shaken off introspection by the time he knocked on Avery's door. Travers answered.

"Ah-ha! Now that the crisis has passed you appear, you bounder," Giles said amicably. Travers managed to look offended without moving a single muscle in his face.

"Don't tease him." Avery waved her fork commandingly at him from her seat at a small table set before a crackling hearth fire. Various dishes of cold meats, cheese, bread, and vegetables cluttered its top. "He had gone down to the inn specifically to find me so I wouldn't have to meet your guests unforewarned. Unfortunately, he thought I was to disembark at three o'clock, not two."

"So he says."

"Milord, I must protest," Travers said. "I would never purposefully compromise Miss Quinn's mission."

"Oh, it's a mission now, eh?" Giles pulled out the chair across from Avery. She'd returned her attention to the cold joint and boiled potatoes on her plate. He snapped open the spare napkin and settled it across his lap, regarding her obliquely.

She looked very different from the egg-shaped youth who'd entered the drawing room. She'd scrubbed her face and though her dark brows still angled in rather fierce winged arcs above her dark eyes, they no longer bristled, meeting in the middle like furry caterpillars butting heads. She'd also shed Mrs. Bedling's attempt at making a gentleman's coat and was swathed in what he recognized as one of his own silk damask dressing robes. The rich blue hue acted as a foil to her auburn hair but the sleeves were far too long, forcing her to roll them up over slender forearms. He made a mental note that she was never to roll up her sleeves. Her arms were as smooth and graceful as a sylph's.

"Am I mistaken or does the banyan you're wearing look familiar?"

"I begged Mr. Travers to find me something to wear."

"You must call him Travers now. He's supposed to be your valet and you, a gentleman. And I hope Mrs. Bedling was able to manufacture more than just the clothing you arrived in."

"I meant that I asked Travers to find me something *comfortable* to wear," she explained. "I have with me the complete wardrobe of a young country gentleman, but I neglected to bring anything to wear when I am not on stage, so to speak. I did not think it advisable to risk the maids finding a dress amongst my clothing."

He felt his lips twitch appreciatively. "Indeed. Well considered."

"Thank you," she said, her attention returning to her food.

"How did you achieve the brows?"

"Hm?" She pierced another bit of boiled potato with her fork and carried it halfway to her mouth. "Oh. Binder's glue and a sable's tail I liberated from an old tippet I found at Killylea. I anticipate I shall be able to harvest around another two dozen appearances from it before I am forced to find another carcass."

He shuddered. "Must you say 'carcass'?"

She popped the potato into her mouth and eyed him mischievously. "Corpse?"

Travers cleared his throat. She darted a guilty glance at him.

"May I serve your lordship?" he asked.

"Would you even know how? I didn't think so. No, thank you, Travers. I seem to have lost my appetite." He replaced the napkin on the table.

"Liar," she muttered.

He ignored this, studying her. Seen in the daylight—such as it was; London was enjoying another of her infamous black days—all suggestions of immature girlishness disappeared. She was a woman in full bloom. The banyan skimmed over her breasts closely, leaving him to wonder what, if anything, she wore beneath. It was an uncomfortable conjecture.

"I hope the spectacles don't strain your eyes," he said. "I understand the reason you've adopted them, of course. Your eyes are simply too"— he smiled—"too beautiful to belong to a boy."

She started, a rosy blush spreading up from her throat into her face. Her gaze flickered up to search his, then fell self-consciously to her plate.

He frowned. Didn't she know she had beautiful eyes?

"Bosh."

Apparently not.

He considered pursuing the matter but decided it would only cause her further discomfort. "And your new silhouette? A stroke of genius. You look exactly like I always imagined Humpty-Dumpty to have appeared."

"Humpty-Dumpty?"

"A character in a book of juvenile rhymes my mother gave me when I was a lad."

The slight defensive tension in her shoulders relaxed. "Thank you. I think. I own I do consider the disguise rather ingenious."

How poignant that she so readily took this sort of praise as her due while doubting compliments other ladies would take for granted. What a waste.

"How did you do it?" he asked. "It looks quite authentic."

"Basically it is several pillows sewn over Mrs. Bedling's corset."

"I applaud your ingenuity. I was rather afraid you were going to try to pass yourself off as a pretty, lithe young lad à la Caroline Lamb." He leaned forward confidingly. "She never really fooled anyone, you know."

She sucked in a tiny breath, deliciously scandalized. "I read about that! She was mad for love of Byron."

Giles sat back. "She was mad for love of attention. Always has been."

"You don't think they loved one another?" She seemed indignant.

"I think both of them loved the celebrity their affair generated far more than one another."

"I am sure you are being cynical."

"I am sure you are correct," he replied equitably.

She frowned. "Is there no romance in you?"

"Not a whit," he said. "And neither should there be in a scientist. I am surprised you are not grilling me about when we can breach the front door of the Royal Astrological Society rather than rhapsodizing over what is in fact nothing more than a sordid little affair." He was as surprised to hear the words coming out of his mouth as she looked. When had he become a prig?

She lowered her gaze, a little flustered. "Yes, of course, that is the most important consideration and I am a scientist first and foremost. But that doesn't mean I am without sentiment." She had put her elbow on the table—a deplorable habit he would have to convince her to eschew—and set her chin in her hand, regarding him as though he were one of her science experiments. "Hasn't your heart ever urged you to pursue where your reason resisted?"

"Once or twice." He shifted in his seat, ambushed by a long ago memory of a girl running through spring grass, a tumble of lithe limbs, breathless laughter . . .

She smiled and he had the lowering suspicion that she realized his discomfort and it amused her. "Oh . . . ?" The word was drawn out invitingly.

If he were the sort given to snickering—which he wasn't—he would have snickered then because really, did she honestly think he was going to sit here trading girlish confidences with her?

"Yes. Twice. Both times at Tattersall's," he said. "And a damned good thing much-reviled reason held sway, because to date neither filly has ever won a race."

She sat back with a snort of disgust.

They had much work to do before he introduced her into Society. Even given her genius, no one would believe he would *ever* tolerate a protégé who snorted.

"That's not what I meant," she said.

"Really?"

A light blush tinted her cheek. She dabbed her mouth with a napkin and set it beside her empty plate. "Fine. I understand. I am overstepping. But pray recall that I was never schooled in deportment. Now, what do you propose is the next step in our plan?"

"I shall invite Sir Isbill to dine with us during which time you shall dazzle him with your astronomical expertise."

"Excellent." She rubbed her hands together. "At your club?"

"Hardly," Strand said. "No woman has stepped foot in White's in forty-one years. There are some holy of holies that I refuse to trample just so you might achieve astrological immortality."

"Ach." It was not *precisely* a snort, this time, though it carried just as clear a message. "So what if a woman's feet tread across a few yards of marble and her hands touch a fork and she wipes her mouth with a linen napkin? Bury the fork, burn the napkin, and salt the tiles."

He pressed his lips together to keep from laughing. She was so utterly unimpressed with his consequence. Not to mention his club's sovereignty. It had been years since anyone had surprised him like she did. But then she always had.

"Besides . . ." She stood up, spurring him to rise hastily to his own feet. She might not think of herself as a lady, but she was, and, despite some proof to the contrary, he was still a gentleman. She blinked at him owlishly and a scowl started as if she thought he was mocking her.

"Now what insult were you about to levy?" he quickly prompted.

"What makes you think it was going to be an insult?"

"Let's call it a hunch. You had said, 'besides.' Besides what?"

She grinned. "*Besides*, you're the only one who would know. The rest of your precious club members would be blissfully ignorant, a state in which, I am loathe to say, it appears the majority of the peerage spend most of their time. Why are you smiling like that?"

"It's gratifying to have one's predictions fulfilled," he said. "And I don't believe you are loath to say that at all."

"You may be right," she readily admitted. "But the fact remains that given how perceptive the average aristocrat is, I'd bet there have been women loitering undetected about the halls of your clubs for decades."

He burst out laughing. He couldn't help it. The picture she painted was too delicious. After a second of looking alarmed by her own audacity, she joined him, her laughter rich and beguiling. Alas, that was not the only thing about her that beguiled.

As she'd risen, his silk dressing robe had fallen open at her throat, exposing a pale, satiny looking expanse of skin and the shadowed vale of her breasts. Her dark blue eyes glittered like sapphires and her lips, curv-

ing in a smile, looked as red and lush as if she'd been eating bramble-
berries. And it was then, quite without volition, that he realized
something he had almost forgotten, as he had forgotten so much of who
he'd been.

Four years ago, he'd thought her the most desirable woman he'd ever
known.

And that was as far as he would allow that particular thought to
travel, because his father had already done quite enough to complicate
Avery Quinn's life and he wasn't going to do more. He would instead
continue doing his damnedest to see that something of value came out
of the old marquess's interference and machinations.

And if that allowed him to enjoy her unique and interesting company,
that was all he would enjoy.

By God.

Chapter Eleven

Sir Jameson had seated Lord Vedder in the only other chair in the room besides his own and inquired whether he would like something to drink. Upon receiving Vedder's assent, he poured him a glass of port.

Tucked away in an inconvenient corner of Parliament, Jameson's office was quite unlike that of his counterpart, Sir Robert Knowlton, whose large airy rooms on the top floor overflowed with artifacts and maps; deep, cushioned chairs that invited lengthy stays; and a host of libations to please any palate.

In stark contrast, besides the two chairs, Jameson's office held nothing but a desk, a wall of shelves, and a small sideboard where a few bottles of indifferent liquor waited for those infrequent visitors who expected such things.

Jameson desired nothing of the trappings of wealth and aside from a predilection for exquisitely tailored—if uniformly dark—clothing, he lived the life of an ascetic. His appearance could not have better illustrated his nature. His head was aristocratically molded and sharp boned, a cadaverous Caesar, the skin cleaving to the underlying structure so tightly the flesh appeared painted on, and any smile he offered endangered splitting his mouth at the corners. Likewise, his body carried not an ounce of excess flesh and, though elderly, he held himself with rigid exactitude.

He considered himself in all ways superior to all men with such conviction that he felt not the slightest need to verify it. Certainly no one observing his cordial ministration of Lord Vedder would ever suspect he was anything other than a rather finicky, though polite, gentleman from a previous generation. Though he no longer felt the necessity of cultivating Vedder's cooperation—he held far too many of Vedder's secrets—he understood to a science the benefit of providing a carrot alongside the whip.

A few months earlier Vedder had been pushed into actions to which his puerile—and need it be said, facile?—sense of honor had objected: He had been instrumental in an attempted assassination of Jack Seward. But he'd made a muck of it and Jack had survived.

Now Vedder must try again. And try he would.

Because whatever Vedder told himself at night—probably that whatever he did, he did for the good of the nation—the simple truth was that Vedder lived beyond his means. When he'd first been recruited, Jameson had provided Vedder with the wherewithal to accommodate his lifestyle. But as his desperation had grown—because the appetites of such men were always unquenchable—so, too, had his involvement in less savory undertakings until finally . . . well, Vedder was completely Jameson's creature.

Sir Jameson had achieved his current position of power through a combination of ruthlessness and guile, statesmanship and fear, and a remarkable ability to subjugate emotion to cold impeccable reason. Indeed, he took great pride in his clinical dispassion.

Which is why it was so important to put this issue of Jack Seward, his adoptive son, his heir, and now his most dangerous enemy, to rest. Because when he thought of Jack, of how the most effective and lethal of all his agents had betrayed him, it filled him with pure, unadulterated rage. Such extreme emotion inevitably led to disaster.

Eventually his rage would cause him to make a mistake, make him vulnerable. And that was something he would not allow. The Prime Minister had voiced "grave concerns" over Jameson's handling of his last assignment. He needed to be able to concentrate his full attention on overseeing his portion of the Secret Committee, lest Knowlton be given sole directorship. He could not afford the distraction of hatred, of this . . . this *need* for revenge.

Which is why his hands shook with anticipation, with the *hope*, that Vedder had some information, some clue as to where Jack had gone to ground. He handed the glass of port to Vedder.

Vedder took the proffered glass. "Scant as it is, you don't have pretend at civility. I could just as well have told you in the hallway everything I learned."

"Pretend at civility?" Jameson echoed. "Good heavens, Lord Vedder. We are nothing without protocol." He meant it, too. He firmly believed in keeping to a proscribed standard of behavior. At least, whenever possible. He smiled, though he knew his smiles did little to set people at ease. "One would think you didn't enjoy my company."

Vedder looked away, red spots appearing high on his cheeks.

"So then." Jameson returned to his chair behind the desk. "What did you learn?"

"Nothing," Vedder said gracelessly. "I asked the footman who showed me in if Seward had been there recently but the fellow had only just been engaged. When I asked Strand what had become of his friend, he asked why I wanted to know."

"Did you press him?"

"There was no opportunity. I arrived at the same time as Lady Demsforth and her progeny. She's angling for her daughter to become the next marchioness. The damn woman wouldn't leave!

"I had begun to think she intended to take up residence in Strand's drawing room until he agreed to wed her chick." He snickered. "Though it wouldn't have mattered if she had left, all of Strand's attention was taken up by his new protégé."

Jameson tipped his head inquiringly. "Protégé?"

"Yes. Some boy genius he picked up on the continent after throwing over his fiancée." His lip curled at Jameson's raised brow. "No one believes Sophia North would have ended the engagement of her own volition. Anyways, apparently the young man impressed Strand enough that he decided to bring him back to London. He's some sort of stargazer chappie."

Jameson's eyes narrowed. Strand was not a patron of the sciences. He was entirely a creature of the ton: facile, ready with a quip, as easily bored as he was distracted. True, Knowlton had considered him useful but his activities always seemed to Jameson fairly inconsequential. Besides, immediately after the war he'd gone back to his pursuit of pleasure. That is until this past summer when Jack had applied to Strand to smooth his way into Society while he'd hunted for a thief that had been plaguing the prince regent's wealthy friends. Such an entry would have been impossible without Strand's cachet.

There had been more to it than that, of course. The thief had inadvertently stolen an extremely sensitive letter that would have granted whomever held it unprecedented power. Jameson had intended to be that person. But then Jack had betrayed him, the letter had been returned to its owner, and afterward several of Jameson's more sensitive operations had been reviewed. He had very nearly been stripped of his position. He might still be yet.

For the first time in his life, Jameson felt vulnerable. And he would continue to be vulnerable as long as Jack Seward remained alive. But where the hell had he gone?

Knowlton would not have helped him disappear. Not only was Knowlton far too shrewd to make an open enemy of Jameson, but he doubted Knowlton had the wherewithal to accomplish such a thing. Jameson knew all of Knowlton's agents and operations. It would be impossible for him to pull off Jack's disappearance without leaving some trace of his involvement behind. Which left Giles Dalton, Lord Strand, the closest thing to a friend Seward had, as rich as Croesus and, as such, the likeliest person to have aided him in vanishing.

Unfortunately, one did not simply kidnap a marquess and force him to talk.

Well, Jameson conceded, one *could*, but the repercussions might prove problematic. Better to go about his investigation obliquely. To find Strand's weak point and then exploit it. All men had weak points. It seemed even he was not exempt.

"Tell me about this protégé."

As there was no table alongside the chair, Vedder finished his port and set the glass at his feet. "Chawbacons little fellow, quite a quiz. Shaped like a squab, all breast and belly with spindly little legs and arms. Eyebrows like a Russian bear. Wears spectacles. Manners of a colonial."

Jameson steepled his fingers together.

"Strand's inexplicably taken with him. Always seemed to have an ear tuned to the boy's voice and kept a close eye on him throughout the afternoon. If the lad were a few years younger—and a great deal better looking—I would suspect him of being Strand's by-blow."

Jameson puzzled on it. There was something here. He was certain of it. Whether it led him to Jack remained to be seen. He noted Vedder watching him uneasily.

"Well. There you are, Lord Vedder." Jameson got to his feet, indicating the interview was at an end. Vedder bolted from his chair, eager to be released.

"You said you knew nothing and yet you have reported several interesting things. Find out more about this protégé of Strand's. You say he picked him up on the continent? Where? Get close to the boy. Gain his confidence. Find out where he met Strand and if, when he did, Strand was in the company of anyone else."

"You want me to take up with that little country bumpkin? Without arousing comment? How?"

"I'm sure you'll think of a way, Lord Vedder," Jameson said mildly. "In fact, if I were you, I wouldn't rest until I did."

Chapter Twelve

A very awoke long before the sun breached London's rooftops. She snuggled deeper into the thick featherbed, drawing the blanket up under her chin, her breath forming little vapor clouds in the air. The weather had been brutally cold since her arrival three days ago, and when the fire in the hearth had died down, glacial air had crept down the chimney and seeped through the walls.

She knew it would have helped if she'd closed the draperies but she disliked the claustrophobic feeling imposed by the heavy gold brocade drapes. She kept them open so that she could see the sky as she had at Killylea.

Not that there was any night sky to speak of. A freezing sleet had followed dusk into the city, glazing the windows with ice and nearly obliterating her view of the heavens or anything else, for that matter. The only things visible were the streetlights in the park across the street, indistinct globes of light suspended in the gloom. The days had been little better, a dingy woolen firmament hanging low over London's towers and turrets.

Dolefully, she looked around. Like the rest of the house, the bedroom was beautiful and cool, elegantly appointed with gilt furniture clad in gold satin and damask, the walls tinted icy blue. She had never slept in a room like it before. When she'd boarded with the astronomers with whom the old marquess had arranged for her to study, she'd lived apart from their families, often in what was meant to have been the governess's room. No one ever allowed her to mistake herself for a guest.

Her stomach growled. The ton, Travers had informed her, never rose before nine o'clock, but she was famished now. Bracing herself, Avery clutched the blanket around her shoulders and gasped as her feet searched the cold floor for her slippers. Shivering, she trudged to the ornately carved marble hearth and stirred the embers. She tossed in a few chunks of coal and squinted at the mantle clock. It had stopped. Her stomach growled again. It had to be close to breakfast time.

She wrestled herself into the padded corset, donned one of the three shirts she'd unpacked, pulled on a pair of trousers, and shrugged into her coat. The cravat, as usual, proved her undoing. After a quarter hour of trying unsuccessfully to get the wretched thing to look like Giles's, she gave up and called it good enough. She then went in search of sustenance.

The breakfast room, too, was bitingly cold, a fire only recently having been laid. The dining table sat empty and the curtains were still drawn. It reminded her of a theater stage minutes before the audience arrived. The whole house felt like that, as though no one truly lived here. It was too perfect, containing none of the detritus of an individual's history, those little misjudgments in taste that lent personality and originality to a home. It was nothing like Killylea. It had nothing of Strand to it.

As she hesitated over what to do, a maid bustled in carrying a whisk and dustbin. Upon seeing Avery, she gave a start. "Oh! Sorry, sir. I'll fetch Burke at once!" Before Avery could reply, she'd bolted back out the door.

A few seconds later Burke appeared, hastily smoothing a nonexistent rumple from his spotless livery. She eyed his cravat appreciatively.

"Sir." Hastily, he pulled a chair out from the table for her. "I'm sorry for the delay, Mr. Quinn. We'll have things right as rain in a moment."

"There's no hurry. I can wait."

"That's very kind of you, Mr. Quinn. There won't be but a few minutes delay."

As if on cue, the maid returned with a single table setting and delivered it to Burke. Hard on her heels came a ruddy faced, middle-aged woman with an old-fashioned lace cap sitting squarely atop a coiled loop of dun brown hair, clucking like an alarmed pullet.

"Beggin' pardon, sir. We haven't been introduced yet due to what oversight I am sure I do not know, nor do I judge. But I am the house-keeper, Mrs. Silcock. Allow me to tender my apologies that the room has not yet been readied." She speared sharp glances at both the maid and Burke.

"Thank you, Mrs. Silcock, but it really isn't necessary," Avery said, growing more self-conscious by the minute.

At Killylea, she'd always had her first meal sitting at Mrs. Turcotte's kitchen table. When she'd been boarded in the homes of her tutors, most of her meals had been delivered to her room. No one ever made a to-do over when she ate. Or even if. It all seemed rather silly. "I have no wish to turn the household on its ears."

The housekeeper's mien froze. She drew herself up, her expression oozing affront. "*Mr. Quinn*," she said with carefully mustered dignity, "it will be a sorry day indeed, when the Marquess of Strand's household is 'set on its ears' by the simple prospect of serving breakfast at a guest's preferred time."

Avery should have known better. Even at Killylea a servant's pride was inexorably aligned with his master's.

Avery hurried to soothe Mrs. Silcock's ruffled feathers. "I didn't mean to imply a deficiency, only that it wasn't necessary to extend your staff and yourself—"

"We are *not* extended, Mr. Quinn," she cut in coldly. "You will find your breakfast waiting for you whenever you choose to dine, be it at one in the afternoon or three in the morning." And with that, she spun around, skirts rustling, and stalked with exaggerated dignity from the room.

An hour later, her stomach fair to bursting after dutifully consuming the enormous breakfast ordered up by The Silcock, as Avery had silently dubbed her, Avery fled back to her room. There she had sat, half afraid to leave lest the housekeeper be lurking outside her door with a bowl of treacle pudding. With a sigh, she wound the mantle clock and then proceeded to spend the rest of the morning trying not to watch it. Time dragged by at a snail's pace.

Each day she'd been here had been a duplicate of the preceding one. Until this morning she'd waited dutifully until the clock struck nine before descending the staircase. Each morning the beautiful footman, Burke, politely informed her that Giles had left for the day. Each afternoon, she retreated to her room where she could shed the increasingly hated padded corset, don Strand's silk robe, and tuck herself into a chair near her fire where she stared at nothing. Even Strand's library provided little interest, being primarily stocked with military histories, agriculture tracts, and political discourses.

She hated politics, she knew nothing about agriculture, and military histories unnerved her. All that analysis about the best way to kill as many people as possible.

There was little for her to do. Her papers outlining the discovery of her comet and the calculations by which she'd anticipated its appearance had already been polished. She didn't have the necessary equipment to pursue other lines of investigation, and she hadn't brought the books or star maps she would have needed to research her latest cosmological theories.

So she sat. And wrote a letter to Mrs. Bedling. And another to her father. Then tore them up as she could hardly post them herself and she dared not give them to any of Strand's servants. She wasn't supposed to know anyone in Killylea and that was just the sort of information servants would be likely to speculate about with one another.

By the time the mantle clock struck two, she had decided she could not take a moment more in this gilded prison. Strand had mentioned a bookstore. Well, she was going to find it.

She went in search of Travers, only to discover he'd been commandeered into polishing the silver by the inimitable Mrs. Silcock who, Travers explained, had taken one look at Mr. Avery Quinn's toilette and decided that whatever talents Travers possessed did not include valeting and posing as one was a case of malingering in the highest order. As

Mrs. Silcock did not tolerate such nonsense in her household, she'd found good honest work to occupy him.

Oddly, Travers didn't seem all that unhappy. In fact, he looked quite comfortable sitting at the butler's table wiping down the saltcellar. Avery considered asking him to put off the task and accompany her but she was uncertain just how much power a young man as she was supposed to be enjoyed in a household. Enough to trump Mrs. Silcock's decree? It seemed unlikely.

And if Travers declined, she'd have told him her plans to leave the house and then he would explicitly forbid her from doing so. And she couldn't disobey a direct order. Not a *direct* one . . .

So, instead, she headed to the front hall where Boote, the second footman, leapt to attention. Half expecting him to bar the door, she tentatively asked for her coat. He fetched it at once. Without asking a single question. Without raising a brow.

Grinning like a cat let into the dovecote, Avery shrugged into it, clapped her hat on her head, and stepped outside. Closing her eyes, she tipped her face back and inhaled deeply. She smiled. True, it stank of coal smoke and sewage and the sky was still dim and the air was still cold, but at least she was out of the house.

Stepping smartly, she descended to the sidewalk and followed it to the corner. Ahead of her stretched a far more crowded thoroughfare than Strand's relatively empty street. Elegant barouches and landaus moved up and down the broad boulevard, maneuvering around the dray carts stopped at the curb. Despite the cold, a number of people hurried along on either side of the street, their heads tucked down and their collars pulled high. A man selling roasted nuts from a cart sat huddled at the corner, shoveling chestnuts into twists of paper for a few pennies. A clutch of youngsters surrounded him more, she suspected, to be near the warmth from his brazier than to make a purchase.

Avery spied the bookstore Strand had mentioned behind the vendor. She entered and was at once approached by a pleasant young clerk who asked if he might assist her. She was about to ask him to direct her to those shelves dedicated to scientific subjects but something stopped her.

She had always had a secret penchant for melodrama, romance, and commedia del'arte. But the old marquess had condemned such books as "low-brow pap, unworthy of a person of intellect." Later, in the homes of her tutors, being sensitive to how her tastes in literary entertainments might reflect on her intelligence, she'd never allowed herself to enjoy them.

But now there was no reason she shouldn't read whatever she wanted. There was no marquess to disappoint and no scholars to disapprove. It was a mildly thrilling idea.

And so, for the next two hours, she happily pottered about the bookstore, leafing through the various books the eager young clerk gladly provided. She would be lying had she not admitted that part of her pleasure derived simply from being in the company of others. For while the store was not precisely busy, a steady stream of people came and went, sometimes alone, but often in company with others. Avery eavesdropped shamelessly, listening avidly as they argued the merits of one author over another, taking note of particular titles that sounded intriguing, and silently adding her own voice to the discussions.

She finally made her selection, paid for it, and waited while the clerk wrapped the book in brown paper. She tucked it under her arm, intending to head back to Strand's townhouse, when her eye was caught by the coffee shop placard. Coffee houses were mostly male enclaves. She'd been a male for four full days now and not experienced any of the advantages. And it was still early in the day. . . .

With a dawning sense of adventure, she ducked into the coffee shop and looked around. It was just a smallish, rather unadorned room holding a dozen tables of varying sizes, all empty save for two: a pair of young men sitting in deeply earnest silence occupied one while the only other customer, a plump, balding man in early old age, pored over a newspaper at the other. At the back was a counter on which stood a large samovar.

She doffed her hat and headed towards a table well back from the diamond-paned front window. As soon as she sat down, the proprietor hurried over. "What'll it be then, young sir?"

"Coffee."

He nodded, leaving her to return to her study of the room's other occupants. She made a little game of it. The younger men were bank clerks, she decided, and they hated their employer and were here building up their courage to quit their jobs. She turned her attention to the older gentleman.

He wore half mittens and licked his fingertips before turning the page of his paper. He had a comfortable look, the complacent air of a regular customer. An accountant, she settled on, newly retired or so near retirement that no one would bother to chastise him for being too long at his supper and he knew it. He caught Avery's eye and nodded.

Startled to be caught staring, she returned his nod with an apologetic smile. Apparently the older gent decided to take this as some sort of invitation, for after a second's hesitation, he lumbered to his feet—he weighed a bit more than she'd realized—and waddled over to where she sat.

"New up from the country, I see," he said without preamble.

She blinked up at him through her spectacles. "Excuse me, sir?"

He smiled, a merry twinkle to his eye. "Your shoes, sir. Your shoes. They're brogues made in the country. Tell me I am wrong. Tell me. I dare you."

She looked down at her shoes. Whatever he saw was not so obvious to her. But one glance at his avid expression and she could not take offense.

"I do not know how you divined that my shoes are country made, but you are correct. They are and I am newly arrived in the city."

He beamed with delight.

"It's marvelous," she said, enjoying being able to give the gentleman such obvious pleasure. "What gives them away?"

He waved his hand at the empty chair across from her. "May I join you?"

She ought to demur. She ought to leave. But the dodger was so patently harmless and just as patently eager for companionship and heavens knew she was, too. What harm would there be in spending ten minutes taking coffee with him?

"Certainly."

He pulled out the empty chair and dropped into it, stretching his legs out in front of him. "What makes them country is the buckles, lad. No young gentleman wears buckles these days. Why, *I* don't even wear them anymore and if *I* don't wear buckles, you can be well assured that *no* one wears buckles. Tell me I'm wrong!"

His bonhomie was contagious. She shook her head. "Not I!"

"Good lad," he approved. "What I *don't* know is what part of the country is so misguided as to still put buckles on their brogues. Enlighten me."

"Cornwall." The answer popped out of her mouth before she knew it. At once, she realized her mistake. She wasn't supposed to let on she had ever been anywhere near Killylea.

"Excuse me? I didn't rightly hear that. Your voice is not much more than a whisper and my ears ain't what they used to be."

She sighed with relief. "Sorry," she said a little more loudly. "Cumbria."

"Well, that is a mite far off in the country. Somethin' happen to yer voice, son?"

She felt herself blush. She disliked lying outright to the old gentleman. "Happened when I was a boy. I got sick and my throat just seized up on me like. Been like this ever since."

The man nodded again and Avery shifted uncomfortably. She would pay her bill and leave. This had been a bad idea after all. She was about to motion the tavern owner over when the older gentleman leaned back in his chair.

"Let me tell you about when I first come to London, young sir. Like you I was from the country, but from the coast and it was there that I become a sailor and sailed off to war with the colonies in the Americas. . . ."

The next half hour flew as the he regaled her with tales of fighting the colonists at sea. When she finally glanced out the window, she was shocked to see that the light had faded from the sky and it was coming on dark. Travers was bound to notice her absence soon if he hadn't already.

She bolted to her feet. "I'm sorry, sir. I . . . the time." Hastily, she collected her package and scattered some coins on the table. "I hadn't realized. I'm sorry but I must go. I apologize for being so abrupt—"

"Now then, don't you worry about it. I tend to ramble when I get started. So my daughter says. Off you go!"

"Thank you!" She shoved her hat on her head, grabbed her greatcoat from where it hung, and hurried out the door.

It only took a few minutes to navigate the short distance back to Strand's townhouse. She headed round to the mews entrance, generally reserved for delivery and tradespeople, and slipped inside. There was no one around. This close to supper time they would be busy preparing the meal. With one last quick glance around she scooted up the servants' stairs to her bedchamber. She hadn't even doffed her coat when she heard a knock.

"Yes?"

"It's me. Travers," came a low reply.

"A minute!" she called out, jerking off of her coat and flinging it behind the bed before letting him in.

He crossed the room without glancing at her and dropped heavily into a chair. "That woman is indefatigable."

"Something tells me your romance with the silver shining has waned."

"The silver shining was not the problem. The iron dog blacking, chandelier polishing, hauling water for the laundress, turning of mattresses . . . *those* were the problems. And I can see in the shrew's eye she means to have her pound of flesh tomorrow, too."

"What are you going to do about it?"

"I don't know yet. But *something* will be done." He puffed out his cheeks and then looked up at her. "Where have you been all day?"

She hated to lie to him. Luckily, she didn't have to.

"Hiding from her?" He answered his own question. "I shouldn't wonder. She's taken a great dislike to you. Thinks you are 'a trumped-up little toad.' Still, it must be stultifying having to be up here all day. I complain about having to do a spot of work but at least I have people to talk to." He regarded her sympathetically.

She smiled weakly. "I managed to keep occupied."

Giles drummed his fingers on the top of his desk, carefully scanning the list of names on this particular ship's manifest. The records he'd requested for the dates in question had been delivered at noon. Since then he'd sequestered himself in his library searching for . . . damn it! That was the problem. He wasn't certain what he was looking for. If Jack and

Anne had left the country, they'd have done so under assumed names—obtaining the necessary paperwork would have been a small matter for someone with Jack's connections. Making things even harder, they wouldn't necessarily have shared the same last name. Or perhaps even the same mode of transportation.

And that assumed that they'd left the country alive and well. Because that is what Giles wanted to believe. But that also meant they'd left without betraying a hint of their intentions or a whisper of forewarning and that, Giles knew, was a bloody, bloody hard thing to do.

He'd spent the last four days knocking on various doors and calling in favors—the ships' manifests were the results of one such conversation. His frustration was palpable.

Now, compounding his bad temper, Travers had just delivered what Giles' old nurse would have called "an earful" regarding his dereliction of duty towards Avery Quinn. Apparently, he'd neglected, ignored, and disregarded the poor girl who, bless her valiant, long-suffering soul, had not complained once—though, knowing Avery, Giles was not at all sure he believed that. But that was neither here nor there.

The fact was, Travers was right. Giles *had* ignored Avery. Because she was too distracting, too appealing, and the things that prowled the back corridors of his imagination whenever they were together were wrong. Far more wrong than leaving her alone for a few days. *Not* leaving her alone, now *that* would be wrong. And he didn't want to leave her alone. She . . . *damn it.*

He set down his pen, staring sightlessly at his blotter.

Avery Quinn was becoming something of a problem.

It wasn't just that sexual desire awoke when he was in her vicinity, she plagued other parts of his mind, too. He spent too much time thinking about her, arguing with her in his imagination, wondering what her reaction would be to such and such an eventuality, plotting for her installment in the Royal Astrological Society. He didn't understand it.

Twice in his adult life, Giles had thought himself in love: once with a beautiful, vivacious girl and once with a lovely widow. Both times, he'd entered the contests for their hands too late and they'd chosen better men. The last lady had become Jack Seward's wife, Anne. And that had been not two months ago.

And yet, even before Anne's disappearance, he'd begun to realize that the ache of loss he'd felt had been for what he'd wanted there to be, not for what had been. He might not be capable of the sort of connection he'd witnessed between Jack and Anne. He might be akin to a connoisseur of the arts, able to recognize the beauty of what others created without having the least talent for creating it himself.

He had been blessed with nearly every endowment a man could hope for: good looks, a healthy body, an agile mind, and spectacular wealth. He called few men friends but those he did he trusted with his life, He was surrounded by admirers and sycophants, and he was wise enough to know the difference. The only thing he needed was an heir.

Perhaps he ought to have married Sophia.

Then he might not be thinking about Avery, who was unrefined, unsophisticated, and unmannered. She was opinionated, brilliant, uncertain, and gauche. She knew nothing about feminine wiles and yet she used them ruthlessly to her advantage, a conundrum if he'd ever encountered one. She'd no conversation, though she'd make a damned good lecturer; she had no idea how to dress, yet still managed to make his blood stir; she knew nothing of music or art. . . .

And she loved the stars. When she'd tipped her face to Killylea's heavens, it had been filled with a reverence and beauty that had taken his breath away. Not only was she smart and beautiful but she was wise, a woman who knew the value of a thing—

Someone knocked on the door.

Thank God.

Chapter Thirteen

A very pushed open the door to Giles's library and stopped, twisting her hands together. Burke had relayed the message that Lord Strand would like a word at her earliest convenience. Not one to postpone bad news, she had come at once but now she hesitated, apparently not as brave as she liked to think herself.

Strand sat behind a beautifully crafted mahogany desk, its fluted legs curving out to end in clawed feet. Untidy stacks of papers cluttered its surface, the larger ones weighted down by ornate paperweights. A pen lay in an enameled trough alongside a crystal inkwell. He'd glanced up when she entered and quickly returned his attention to studying the top sheets of two stacks of paper set before him, his gaze moving between them, comparing whatever he read. He looked entirely preoccupied.

"Don't stand there lurking in the hall like some uncommitted specter," he muttered without lifting his head. "Come in. We have things to discuss."

She'd been dreading this. Someone had reported seeing her sneaking into the house through the mews and now he meant to put an end to their bargain. She walked in, stiff-backed, stopping in front of his desk like a schoolboy called before the headmaster.

"Well?" she said.

He looked up. "*Well?* What with all the instruction you received from any number of scholars—many of whom were gentlemen—didn't one take it into his mind to teach you the rudiments of polite behavior? 'Well' is no proper way to begin a conversation." He fell back in his chair, his brows rising challengingly.

Even when she was a girl, Giles had been able to rouse her where none of the other children could: neither the cook's nasty boy, nor the stable lads, or the under maids, some no older than she, all of whom resented her exemption from their long hours of exhausting work. Mistress Mongrel, Blue Bottle Bluestocking, Fair-haired Folly—none of their names or taunts had been able to provoke her. She'd been too well aware of the truth of them and the unfair advantage she'd been given.

But Strand was a different matter. A tipped eyebrow, a faint smile, and the hairs on the back of her neck rose. She didn't even try to ignore it. Which is why she lifted her chin now and stared haughtily down her nose at him. "A conversation? Is that what we're going to have?"

He looked puzzled. "What else?"

"What else, indeed?"

"For the love of all that's sacred, take off those spectacles. I can't see you properly."

She snatched off the offending glasses and glowered at him. He tipped his chair back, balancing on the back two legs, folded his hands over his flat stomach, and regarded her quizzically. His cravat was twisted a little askew and his hair looked rumpled. Clearly, he'd run his hands through it many times.

Had he done so while deliberating over her? Trying to decide the best way to go about ridding himself of her?

The idea brought with it a certain satisfaction, followed by horror that she could find satisfaction in so small a thing. One rumpled one's hair while fretting over the disposal of a favorite dog's pups. Without warning, the hot promise of tears pressed against the backs of her eyes.

"Here, sit down," he said, studying her intently. "You look strange. Are you feeling all right?"

"I'm fine."

He got up and came to her side, caught hold of her wrist, and groped for her pulse.

"I'm fine," she repeated, pulling her hand away.

He took her chin between his thumb and forefinger, lifting her face and turning it towards the light. He really was, she thought apropos of nothing, so very handsome.

He smelled faintly of cedar and spearmint and this close she could see the starburst of lines radiating from the corners of his eyes, the cut-glass glitter of his irises framed by gunmetal gray auroras, the hard line of his jaw smudged with a nascent beard, and the deep lines scored on either side of his nose. Lines of dissipation? Or weariness? Could they be erased with a caress . . . ?

She jerked back.

Where had that thought come from?

He released her chin and she released her breath. Thank God, he didn't seem to notice.

"Your heart is racing and your eyes are dilated."

Treacherous pulse. Feckless eyes. "I forgot to eat lunch. It may have made me faint."

"*You?* Forgot to eat?" His patent incredulity rekindled her indignation. She nearly thanked him.

"Am I to presume *that* is how one is supposed to commence 'a polite conversation'?" she asked. "Such helpful instruction. I shall endeavor to remember it next time I am in polite company."

His lips twitched in an unfairly attractive manner. "I see that whatever ailed you was only temporary and that you are back to your customary contentious self."

"I am not contentious."

"You are. Decidedly contentious." He went back round to his chair behind the desk.

"Only with you."

This took him by some surprise. "Is that true?"

"Mostly."

He gave her a crooked smile. "And why is that do you suppose?"

"You provoke me."

"I most certainly do not," he said.

"Intentionally, I suspect."

"Good God. You don't really believe that? I will allow that, perhaps, at times, I do provoke you," he said. "But *never* intentionally. Such behavior is beneath a gentleman and, for all my sins, I am still a gentleman."

"Except when you are with me."

An odd light banked deep within his gray eyes. Then he tore his gaze away and quaffed back the glass of port that had been near his hand. "Madame, *especially* when I am with you."

"Have it your way," she said, afraid she knew which way this was heading. "You're the consummate gentleman and I am a contentious, troublesome burden and now you can tell me that having made one minor misstep you no longer feel under any obligation to aid me in my endeavor and can, with clear conscience, rid yourself of me."

Very carefully, he set down the empty glass. "What are you talking about?"

She scowled. "Isn't that what you meant when you said we needed to talk?"

"No." He tipped his head, his eyes narrowing. "What misstep did you make?"

The bleak future yawning ahead of her receded like the tide racing from the shore. "No?"

"No," he repeated. "Again: What did you do, Avery?"

She looked him dead in the eye. She wasn't about to make it easy for him to get rid of her. "I forgot to wear my spectacles to lunch yesterday."

For a long moment, they battled each other in a contest of stares. He clearly didn't believe her. Her eyes dared him to make the accusation. In the end, he was too much of a gentleman to do so.

"I would never use so flimsy an excuse to rid myself of you, as you so colorfully phrase it. When we say our final farewell, I shall have the distinct satisfaction of knowing I carried out my part of our agreement honorably." His gaze became hooded. "I trust you will be able to say the same?"

"Why, of course," she said feigning hurt that he could think anything less.

"Then we're of a like mind."

"Like two peas in a pod." Now that she knew she wasn't about to be sent packing, she allowed herself to saunter over to the chair positioned across the desk from him and take a seat. "What did you want to talk about?"

Giles shifted his shoulders uncomfortably. "Travers informs me that I have been unfeeling, insensitive, and boorish in regards to you."

Her eyes flew wide. "Travers said that?"

"Yes. Amongst other things."

"Why would he say such a thing?" she asked, completely baffled.

He opened his mouth, apparently decided better of what he'd been about to say, pressed his lips tightly together, and spoke. "Because it is true."

She stared for a second, trying to . . . Ah! She had it. She smiled. "I see. You must have said something especially nasty about me in front of your servants. What did you say? Something about me being a horrible glutton? Whatever it was, I assure you, I fully understand that you would have done so only to lend credibility to my masquerade and that I take no offense." He was regarding her strangely, like she was speaking a foreign language.

"Frankly, while Mr. Travers is a very good man, he really doesn't seem to, well, understand what a gambit such as ours entails, does he? Obviously you can't act towards me as if I were a woman." She paused, frowning. "I mean, I *am* a woman. Obviously." She gave a nervous chuckle. "Well, maybe not so obviously right at this moment.

"As I said, in my current disguise you can't react to me like a man would a woman, can you? I mean not that you *would* even in normal circumstances, but you *could*."

Dear heaven, why was she babbling like this?

"I mean—"

"That's not what Travers meant."

She regarded him gratefully. Thank heaven he'd interrupted her. Lord knew what she might have blurted out next.

"He meant that I have marooned you in my household with no company, no conversation, and nothing to do."

"I see."

His brow creased. He looked troubled. "Has it been simply awful for you? Travers seems to think it has."

"Oh. Oh, not really. No," she equivocated. She was distinctly uncomfortable because clearly this was one of *those* conversations. *Polite* conversations, she assumed one would call it. She'd observed enough of them to be of the opinion that they revolved mostly around people asking questions to which one was not expected to reply honestly but instead in whatever manner would make the questioner feel good about himself. It seemed an exhaustingly circuitous means of communication.

To keep Giles from probing further, and because she just wasn't all that confident in her ability to dissemble further should he do so, she got up and strolled over to the bookshelves.

"Why have you leapt from the chair and streaked over to my bookshelves?" he asked. "Are you suddenly inspired to look up a word?"

She turned her head and smiled sunnily, refusing to be baited. "No. I am just interested in what masterpieces you may have acquired. Oh. Look. *The Wayfarer of Lachamoor.*" She widened her eyes innocently. "Is this not a *romance*, Lord Strand?"

"It was a gift."

"From a lady, no doubt. Poor thing."

"Pray why is this hypothetical lady 'poor'?"

"I can only imagine she gave you such a book either because she assumed you were given to romance or because she was hoping you might become so. In both cases, by your own testimony, she was bound to be disappointed. Ergo my sympathy."

"Actually, the book belonged to Louis."

She turned fully around, interested. "Then I'm surprised to see it here."

He frowned. "Why is that?"

"There's nothing else in this house from Killylea. It's as if this house and Killyea belong to different people."

His gaze grew shuttered. She had gone too far. Been intrusive. For a moment, she thought he would freeze her with silence but then, he surprised her yet again. "Maybe they do."

He exhaled slowly, his expression relaxing, and gave her a rueful smile. "You never met Louis, did you? It's too bad. I think he would have enjoyed your company."

"I'm flattered. But do you think would *I* have enjoyed *his*?"

The question seemed to startle Giles. He didn't look offended, simply as if such a thing would never have occurred to him. "I don't know," he finally said. "I expect so. He was kindhearted and thoughtful and," he added with a glint of humor, "had a decidedly romantic nature."

"Why do you say that?"

"Well," Giles smiled. "There is the book. It wasn't the only such title he owned. It was simply his favorite. And before you ask if the story is any good, the answer is an emphatic 'no.' It's a dreadful conceit in every sense. You know the sort of thing, filled with perennially endangered damsels and perfunctory villains, noble sacrifices and hopeless, though worthy, crusades. He thought I ought to use it as a template for my life."

The pleasant memory had caught hold in his imagination. She could see it in the loosening of his shoulders and the softening of his gunmetal gray gaze. But all she could think of was his last sentence. Why would Louis presume to arrange Giles's life for him?

"I would go to his room directly after lessons," Giles continued softly. "As soon as I arrived, he would make me recite everything I'd learned that day. He took his role of big brother very seriously"—a slight smile— "but then, afterwards we would turn his bed into whole new worlds of make-believe.

"That book"—he nodded at it in her hand—"was often our script, the source of countless adventures. A pillow became the insurmountable Lachamoor Mountains, a blue scarf, the raging river Jesset. We would play for hours on end. I'm afraid I was not always mindful of his fatigue."

She conjured up an image of Giles, not as the adolescent paragon she'd met, but years earlier, a sensitive boy worshipful of an extremely sickly older brother, aware that each time Giles saw him, it might be the last. She glanced away. Giles would not thank her for her pity.

"You must miss him."

He gave her an odd, twisted smiled. "Thank you for using the present tense."

She looked at him askance.

"His death happened so long ago. Most people would have said, 'You must *have* missed him very much,' as though as time goes along one stops missing the person who has died."

A little warmth crept into her cheeks. "It is not my experience," she said.

Her mother had died when she was five and though she could not recall with certainty her face or voice, she only needed to let her thoughts drift to remember how it felt to be held by her, the feeling of safety and contentment and love. She sometimes missed her with a yearning that was visceral. Her father, though fond and bluff, had been more of an uncle than parent, a protector but not a guide. She shook off the melancholy moment. "And how have you done?" she asked.

"Excuse me?"

"As the would-be Wayfarer of Lachamoor?"

He grinned. Sitting there with his hair rumpled and his cravat slightly askew, she realized how young he still was and saw an echo of the sensitive lad who'd waged bloodless warfare on his brother's counterpane.

"Poorly, I'm afraid. I am too lazy to commit myself to any crusade, hopeless or not. Villains terrify me. Noble sacrifices invariably entail self deprivation of some sort and as for perennially endangered damsels . . . ? As loath as I am to point this out, generally I am the one doing the endangering."

She couldn't help it. She burst out laughing.

Chapter Fourteen

L ouis used to say that I must live to have adventures for us both."
Giles wasn't certain just how he had become entrenched in this conversation, spilling out a history he had kept to himself for fifteen years. But he did not regret it. He tipped his chair back, clasping his hands behind his head and speaking with the sort of thoughtless candor one used with an old and trusted friend.

Avery had moved the chair alongside the hearth and was holding a poker. Every now and then she'd give the fire a good hard jab, sending a fountain of sparks sailing into the air to disappear up the flue. She watched the miniature fireworks display with quiet glee. She found pleasure in a great many things he took for granted.

When he'd sent for her, it had been with no other goal than to assuage Travers's concerns—and his own guilt—with a twenty minute or so conversation. He would ask her about her stars. She would ramble on a bit. He would contrive to look interested. She would ramble on a bit more. Then she would leave. Of course, since it was Avery Quinn, she was bound to find something to rail about and, truth be told, that was the part of the conversation he'd most anticipated. It was fun locking horns with Avery Quinn.

But instead, he found himself talking about things and people he hadn't spoken of in years. Like Louis. How strange this conversation had become. Here he sat revealing his history to a beautiful young woman hiding beneath the guise of a fat and unhealthy-looking lad, a woman who seemed as impressed by his title and consequence as she was with head lice, who aggravated him at least once during every encounter, charmed him a half dozen times during the same period, and who increasingly roused even more increasingly inappropriate desires.

And, for the life of him, he couldn't imagine having this conversation with anyone else.

"And just how were you to have these adventures for both of you?" she asked now.

Behind the lenses, her blue eyes gleamed as brightly inquisitive as a robin spying a worm. She exhibited not a whit of pity or sorrow or judgment, simply curiosity. It was oddly liberating. Perhaps that was why it was so easy to speak with her. Avery didn't recognize sacred ground and that meant no topic was burdened by hallowedness.

His hands dropped from behind his head and he straightened a piece of paper on his desk. "I was to be his avatar. To rescue maidens, slay dragons, right wrongs." He gave her a crooked smile. "I was to do all the things he would not live to do. Even before it became obvious he would not reach adulthood, he used say I must have adventures enough for us both. He made me promise to be his champion."

She sighed, shaking her head slightly. "I see. Well, he was just a lad himself. You mustn't think harshly of him."

Her words caught him off guard. He'd expected her to show at least *some* sympathy for a boy who hadn't lived long enough to see even his secondhand dreams come to fruition. "Of course, I don't. Why would I think harshly of Louis?"

She eyed him as though uncertain whether he was being serious. "For asking you to live out his dreams rather than pursue your own. For assuming the life he would have led, had he been able, was somehow more valid than one you would have chosen for yourself."

He stiffened. "That's not how it was. Louis meant to exhort me to being a better man, to give me an incentive to become that man. Because *he* was the better man."

She contemplated this and he found himself growing irritated. She shouldn't be pondering his pronouncements about a brother he'd known and she hadn't. He hoped she had the good sense not to forward an opinion.

"I don't think so."

He should have known better.

He regarded her coolly, refusing to ask her to elaborate. He had lived for years with the knowledge that were Louis alive today, he would have been disappointed in him.

She thrust the poker into the heart of the fire and stirred it into a conflagration. She looked over at him. "I mean *literally* he wasn't the better man because he wasn't a man, at all. He was only what? Fifteen? Sixteen? He was a boy who had spent the majority of his life in a bed."

He inhaled sharply, but she wasn't looking at him, she was frowning, peering sightlessly into the hearth as she worked something out. "If he had been a man, he would never have asked you such a thing. He would never have presumed. *You* never would have asked such a thing."

He scowled. "I am impressed you feel confident enough to make these assertions about a young man you never even met," he said coldly, but he could not deny that her words made him reflect.

He realized he hadn't *thought* about Louis or himself or their relationship since his brother's death. Everything concerning Louis—Giles's feelings for his older brother, his perception of him and their relationship, his assumptions about Louis's character and identity—existed in stasis, formed by the memories of the thirteen-year-old boy Giles had been, none of it reexamined with the objectivity, experience, and understanding of the man he'd become.

And here Avery was questioning all of it. While apparently trying to set his house afire.

"I think . . ." she started to say, then stopped to stir the damn embers again.

"Pray tell what you think," he drawled unwillingly. "I am on tenterhooks."

She gave him a distracted smile, not a bit offended by his cool tone. "Louis wasn't some selfless shriven saint sending forth his champion.

He was a boy taking a spot of comfort in imagining all the grand adventures his handsome younger brother was going to have. He was a little jealous perhaps, so he asked you to do them for him, too. I don't think he ever meant it to be a sacred pact or a holy inspiration. I think Louis was a just boy who didn't want to be forgotten."

Her words caught unexpectedly at his heart.

"You don't know what sort of man Louis would have become," she said. "Are you the person today you thought you'd be at sixteen?"

She had him there. Was she right about Louis? Had he done his brother a disservice by thinking of him as a paragon? Had he unwittingly drained the personality—the *humanity*—from his memory of Louis? "God, no."

She grinned. "Exactly. Had Louis lived and come to London, he might have decided heroism was too much work. Apparently you did." The barb was not lost on him, but it was well timed, a bracing little reminder that he'd not find easy comfort or undeserved sympathy from Avery Quinn. He respected that.

"Louis might have settled for something less lofty but more fun." Her blue eyes grew round in inspiration. "Maybe he would have become a *dandy*."

How had she done that? What alchemy had she employed to turn atrophied grief into gentle humor? Despite the aura of sanctity he'd built around Louis's memory, Giles found himself chuckling at the thought of his diminutive brother tricked out like a Bartholomew babe. Louis might have liked such a thing, at that. He'd always had a penchant for the dramatic.

"Or," she continued, "he might have followed a course similar to mine and become a scientist."

Giles shook his head. "Never. He couldn't add a double column of numbers."

"A gambler?"

"Now *that* I could easily see. He loved games of chance. Especially card games."

"Was he any good at them?"

"A disaster."

She laughed and he joined her, and when their laughter had run its course, he settled back, more at ease than he could remember being in a long time. "Louis believed he had the most formidably impassive face in the kingdom but whenever he drew a decent card his left eyebrow twitched like it had St. Vitus's dance and he would gulp. Audibly. He would have made a run at the tables and been broke inside a week."

They smiled at one another, in perfect accord. Her lips softened into a natural curve. The fire fanned a rich color to her profile and licked her tousled auburn locks with a plummy sheen. He itched to test the texture of those silky curls.

"I would have loved to have watched him have a run, though," she finally said.

"Liar," he accused softly. Her gaze flew to meet his.

"You would have loved to have a run at the tables yourself. I could see it when I mentioned Louis's betraying signals. Your hand moved towards your brows and you are trying not to swallow."

"That's not fair!" she burst out. "You can't just watch people like that and then tell them what they're thinking."

She did not, however, deny it. "Why not?"

"It's not nice." She sniffed. "Besides, I am sure I would be able to cozen you if I'd a mind to do so."

He feared his face betrayed how utterly ridiculous he considered this claim because her mouth formed an "o" of outrage. "I could so!"

"Hmm."

"You don't think I can. In spite of the fact that I have managed to fool your entire staff into thinking I am a man."

"Oddly, my staff is not expecting to be 'fooled'—which is one of the prerequisites to a successful confidence game. In a card game, the players expect each other to bluff. It is you who would be at a distinct disadvantage."

Her magnificent eyes narrowed to sapphire slits, glittering between the dark banks of her lashes. "What hubris. Let's see if you can back up your words with action."

He wasn't sure he was hearing her right. "Are you *challenging* me, Miss Quinn?"

"I am indeed, Lord Strand."

"And what will we be playing for? Because without something of value to back the play, there's no point in bluffing."

She considered this a moment. "We shall divide the walnuts in the bowl on your desk equally. Whoever has the most nuts at the end of the game gets to name his prize."

He smiled at her. He'd played similar games with other ladies before, but he would hazard a guess Avery had no idea the sorts of forfeits those games had entailed. "Aren't you taking an awful lot for granted?"

She shrugged. "I doubt it. You're a gentleman. I, however, am not. I'm not even a lady. If I were you, I should be the one feeling some trepidation. You have no idea what I'm capable of demanding. But I can assure you, you won't like it."

"You intrigue me. It might be worth losing just to find out what you have in mind," he said. "But then winning will provide its own rewards."

"You accept then?"

"I accept."

The game went on past the dinner hour and far into the night. The servants, mindful of their master's order to leave them strictly alone, did not once offer to tend the hearth, close the drapes, or in any way disturb the pair.

A housemaid was replenishing the water in the vase of flowers outside the library door when a tousle-haired Giles stuck his head out, spotted her, and snapped: "Sandwiches and port. At once." When she returned as ordered, she managed a fleeting glimpse of what was happening behind those otherwise closed doors and reported later at the servants' dinner table to an avidly interested group.

"I knocked on the door and Lord Strand himself answers. He steps aside and says where I'm to set the tray and I goes about doin' so. Straight off, I see Mr. Quinn in that great chair that generally sits by the fire, only it's been pulled up before Lord Strand's desk.

"Mr. Quinn's kicked off his shoes and I can see his stocking feet is curled up beneath his great belly and he's perched in that chair like . . . like . . ." Her eyes lit with sudden inspiration, "that statue of Bud-hah I seen in Prinny's dining room at Carleton House."

"When did you ever see Prinny's dining room at Carleton House?" a scullery maid asked scornfully.

The housemaid lifted her nose. "Last winter when I paid a ha-penny to take a look-see after one of them grand dinners he has, that's when. But it ain't right, if you ask me, for a young whelp like Mr. Quinn to sit like that in the presence of his betters."

"What were they doing?" Burke asked, to keep the story moving along.

"Well, now, Mr. Burke," the housemaid dimpled at the handsome young footman, "Mr. Quinn is peering ever so hard at a fistful of playing cards and chewing his bottom lip and there's a pile of walnuts rolling about by his elbow and on the other side of the desk is another pile only somew'at larger."

"They were gambling," intoned Mrs. Silcock, just to make sure everyone understood. "Using walnuts as currency."

Everyone had understood the implications except the second footman, Boote, who nodded his enlightenment. "I see."

"Well, Lord Strand comes back round the desk and sits down and just stares at Mr. Quinn. But he's smilin' and I don't mind telling you I wouldn't like it if his lordship smiled at me like that, his eyes all sharp and shining, like a cat's in moonlight. Would scare the daylights out of me, it would!"

"Now, girl, don't you be comparing his lordship to some filthy cat unless you want to go to bed with no supper," Mrs. Silcock scolded then added, "go on."

"I didn't mean nothing disrespectful," the housemaid sulked. "Only meant to say his lordship looked in fine fettle. Like he's having a fly old time, indeed, and it's all at Mr. Quinn's expense.

"And his smile makes Mr. Quinn right nervous, too. You can see that. And I expect it's *been* making him nervous for some time, for ain't Mr. Quinn's cravat been pulled clear off and his collar come undone from 'round his neck? And a right scrawny neck it is, all apiece with his scrawny legs and arms."

Mrs. Silcock looked disapproving at this criticism of a guest but as it was now an accepted part of the house mythology that she disliked Mr. Quinn, it came as no surprise when she didn't voice a complaint.

The housemaid continued. "Then, all of a sudden, Mr. Quinn slaps his cards face down on the desk and says, 'Stick!' "

"Ah!" intoned Burke knowingly. "They were playing *vingt-et-un*."

"Well, ain't you a one, Mr. Burke," the housemaid tittered. "And do you play this 'Vinty Own,' yerself?"

To which Burke's only reply was a broad wink.

"What happened next?" Boote asked.

The maid shrugged. "Don't know. I left."

"Why?" asked the scullery.

"Because I'd done what I been told and there weren't no reason to stay. So I left."

At which point everyone moaned except Mrs. Silcock, who refrained only at the last moment and only because, just in time, she remembered her dignity.

Chapter Fifteen

How many nuts did you say you had over there, Strand?"

"None."

"Why, begad, you don't, do you?" Avery's eyelids batted up and down in a parody of stunned surprise. "Which means . . . I win!"

Pleasure spilled out of her like light from a lantern. Her head fell back and the low, musical laughter rippled through the room. "I win! I win! I win!"

"And gloat."

Her eyes grew round as if the idea delighted her even more. "*And* I gloat!" She sobered. Not much, but enough to peep at him sidelong. "You don't mind, do you?"

How could he? "Not at all. Gloat on. I expect I have it coming. Beside, you look as pleased as if you'd spotted a pony on the lawn come Christmas morning."

She puzzled over that one. "I'm not sure what you mean."

Of course not. She had never been the daughter of the house. It would never have occurred to her to ask for a pony for Christmas and suddenly he found himself wondering if she had ever asked for anything for

Christmas and if so, what it had been and if she had gotten it? He wished he had given her something. He hoped his father had.

"I know. It's part of your charm."

She went quite still. "You think I have charm?"

"Yes."

He didn't know how he'd expected her to react to that. A blush, a humble look to the side, a little modest smile of pleasure, perhaps? He did *not* expect her to leap to her feet with a little shout of triumph. But that's what she did.

She bounded out of the chair, the hideous stuffed corset wobbling around her, and wheeled around, her arms outstretched and her head thrown back. Comical, ridiculous, absurd. Yet his breath caught in his throat and he found himself wishing she hadn't cut her hair and that it was streaming behind her, as it had the night atop Killylea when the icy wind had pulled it into long, auburn pennants. "I do, don't I? I have charm *and* I am a better gambler than you."

"Now, I never said—"

She stopped spinning, laughing his words down. "*And* now you shall have to pay the forfeit!"

"Which is?" he prompted with a touch of alarm. She'd been sincere in warning him. This woman *was* capable of anything. She might demand a world tour, take his house, his Shakespeare folio . . . his heart. He scowled at the random thought.

The fake brow had started to come undone. It angled above her natural brow, making her look ridiculously quizzical. "I don't know. I haven't decided yet."

"You can't do that," he protested. "You have to decide now so I can pay my debt and be done with it."

"Of course I can and no, I don't." She hopped over to where he still sat, putting her palms flat on the desk and bracing herself as she leaned over it towards him. She gave him an entirely mischievous, triumphant grin. "You'll just have to wait."

She tapped him lightly on the chest, her teeth flashing white in the firelight, her skin rosy and satiny where it lay exposed by her open collar.

It was late. Going on two o'clock in the morning and he hadn't had much sleep in the preceding nights. He'd drunk most of a bottle of port. He hadn't been with a woman in weeks.

But all the reasons in the world didn't change the fact that he wanted her more than anything he'd ever wanted in his life.

Or could belie the fact that he always had.

He'd been twenty-one, returned home for a short visit from London, when he'd realized Avery Quinn was something extraordinary.

Marooned on England's shores by his father's refusal to let him buy a commission in an active regiment, he'd set about becoming in fact what his father always considered him: an ornament, a dandy and a fop, a drunk and a gambler. But then he'd been recruited by the Secret Committee and by twenty-one had already done things of which he would scarce have believed himself capable. So when he had ridden up to Killylea that day he'd been pathetically eager to be home. At Killylea, the sea wind would scour the stench from one's clothes and heart, one could sleep without dreams and speak to people without wondering what one might be required to do to them on the morrow.

He'd reined in his horse at the bottom of the drive to simply drink in his fill of the sight. On his left was the orchard, on his right the wide lawn, and before him, cresting the prominence that looked out over the sea, rose Killylea, splendid in her great, gray substance, her durability, a castle built not to impress but to shelter.

He was about to remount when he heard wild laughter and a dog barking furiously, and as he watched, a girl dashed from out of the orchard. Hard on her heels bounded an enormous brindle mastiff. The girl was waving what looked like a piece of thick rope over her head and as he watched in growing concern, the dog leapt and seized it, knocking her over. She fell with an *uff!* grabbing the dog around the neck and carrying him with her to the ground.

They tumbled together in a flurry of paws and bare feet, silky brindle flanks and long, shapely legs amidst a swirl of skirts and petticoats. Not a girl, then, but a woman, at least from what he could see of her lithe limbs and pert derriere. Her auburn curls cascaded around her shoulders, obscuring her face from his view. She was laughing again, a rich, unfettered sound of pure enjoyment.

It drew him like a fire on a cold night, warming and loosening the cold knot that he carried within his chest. He found himself smiling as the wrestling match continued. The dog growled fiercely and the girl laughed louder, leaping to her feet and heaving back on the rope. The dog hauled back as well, pulling even harder. She fell forward flat onto her stomach as the rope was wrenched from her hands and, with a toss of his head, the dog dashed away with his prize.

She flung back her hair, lifting herself up on her forearms and screeching after him, "You come back here, you miserable great cheat!"

He knew that screech.

"Avery?"

Her head swiveled round. Beautiful eyes, deeper than the blue in a peacock's feather but just as rich, turned towards him and, as he watched, the smile slowly faded from her lips, but, even worse, from her eyes. Her expression grew shuttered and a flush stained her cheeks. She bolted to her feet, dusting the grass and leaves from her skirts, her dress a trifle too tight for the ripe figure blooming beneath. The prickly little girl who'd so enjoyed proving her superiority over him had become a woman.

Of all those who lived and worked at Killylea, Avery Quinn had been the only person whom his much-vaunted charm had failed to impress. She always seemed to go out of her way to pick a fight, or point out an error in his facts or reasoning. He'd found it amusing. So much so that whenever he visited he purposely erred in making some assertion just to give her the pleasure of correcting him.

He'd always felt a little uneasy about her, thinking she must lead a strange and lonely existence, educated like a daughter of the house—no, make that a son of the house—but with none of their expectations. What did his father think would become of her when all was said and done?

But apparently she was not the overly serious, unhappy creature he'd believed. Her laughter had come easily and her glee had been uninhibited and expansive. Perhaps she had finally looked in the mirror and seen what he'd always suspected: that the promise contained in the strong, angular child's face would be fulfilled in the handsome, arresting visage of a woman. A woman who looked anything but scholarly, with a gypsy mane of tangled curls and eyes that seemed lit from within by some internal fire. She was regarding him watchfully, as if she expected to be reprimanded. Or mocked.

On any other day, he would have obliged. It was part and parcel of his new persona. But not that day. Perhaps it was precisely because he had so recently played the role of condescending exquisite that he resisted now. Perhaps it was because she'd been so happy just moments before and his arrival had taken that from her, or because he wanted someone to think better of him and it had been a long time since he'd given any one cause to, but for whatever reason he did not say a word. He only remounted his horse and continued on his way.

He could not put her out of his mind, however, and decided that before he left Killylea he would win a laugh from her, somehow flush the beguiling joy from wherever she hid it. As she was ubiquitous within Killylea's halls, he could pursue every opportunity.

She was not receptive. Not at first. She seemed to view every comment he made as a test, every subject as an opportunity to prove she'd made good use of the education the marquess had provided. His father encouraged her to exhibit her vast amount of knowledge, seemed even to take pride in her achievements.

But, eventually, as Giles refused to play the "quiz Avery" game and it became apparent that he would not judge her based on her academic achievements, her stiffness faded and she relaxed her vigilance.

Finally, one day while they were taking lunch with the marquess, Giles said something that made her laugh. To this day he could not recall what it was. He only knew that it hadn't been anything witty or sophisticated but it had been enough to free the same delighted, joy-filled laughter he'd heard on his arrival. It had made him catch his breath. And in the next instant, he had to catch it again as she peeped at him from beneath the thick sweep of her lashes and an unexpected dimple appeared in her cheek.

An image of her lying beneath him, her face flushed with the after-glow of lovemaking, her eyes glittering with that same soft joy, waylaid his imagination and left him dry mouthed and yearning.

His father's gaze had swung from Giles to Avery and as soon as lunch was done, he'd requested Giles to join him in the library. Once there, he had rounded on him.

"What do you think you are doing?" It would have been better if his father had been angry, but he was not. He had been aghast, shocked. "Avery's father entrusted her welfare to me as well as her education. I thought you understood that."

"I don't know what you are talking about."

"I saw the way you looked at her. I may not be one of your sophisticated ton friends, Giles, but I can see clearly enough when a man has designs on a woman."

He wanted to protest but he could not, because no matter how innocent his motives might have been to begin with, in the end desire had proved paramount. He did want her.

"You've been trying to seduce that girl for days and now you're on the cusp of achieving it and I will not stand for it. Do you hear me? You are not going to make Avery Quinn your mistress. She is better than that. She has a greater vocation in this world than pleasuring you!"

His words were as effective as a blow and just as painful. Anger boiled in to replace the guilt the accusation had awoken. "Oh? And what vocation is that?" Giles drawled. "At which college is she going to teach? Which scholar is going to accept her as their associate? What press is going to publish her? Where will she continue her research?"

The marquess's face had turned bright red.

"What do you think *you* are doing?" Giles had countered. "Giving this girl a false sense of her own worth. Encouraging her to make assumptions about a future that will never materialize. *She's your gamekeeper's daughter*, by all that's holy. And now she has no place in *any* society, either that to which she was born or that which her father serves."

His father stared at him, the bright color slowly receding from his cheeks. He furrowed his brow, peering at Giles as though seeing something unexpected. "I confess, I find it surprising you've given the girl any real thought."

Giles turned away. "Of course you are."

"But that doesn't change the fact that she is under my protection." He put his hand on Giles's shoulder. It been years since his father had touched him and Giles could not keep from turning back towards him. His father's eyes bore into his. "I would consider it the most morally reprehensible of offenses if you were to offer her any other sort of protection. I would not like to think you capable of such a thing."

"Not even the protection of my name?" He didn't know what made him say it. Perhaps he'd just wanted to shock his father.

Instead of flinching, her father simply shook his head rather sadly, for all the world as if he'd actually pondered such a thing himself. "Your name would be no protection at all. You would simply make outcasts of you both.

"I know how well you love Society. If you wed her, soon enough you would abandon her for your mistresses and then she would be unutterably lonely." He gave a half smile. "And bored."

So much for his father's good opinion. But he had made his point.

Not that Giles was considering marrying the girl. She was sixteen. She knew nothing of the world or men. She was prickly as a hedgehog and about as unsophisticated. He was a sophisticated man with sophisticated tastes. And very sophisticated sins.

He rarely saw Avery after that visit. Each time he ventured home she seemed to be gone, installed in the home of some newly hired professor or expert far away. It was probably for the best.

But for all these years he had kept close to his heart and cherished the knowledge that he had once made Avery Quinn laugh. . . .

Chapter Sixteen

Three days later Avery had still not decided what to ask of Strand in payment for his debt. Not that she could have collected even if she had, for she hadn't seen him since the night they'd played cards. Once again, he vanished early, ate out somewhere, and returned only after she'd retired for the evening.

She might have been tempted to sneak out again herself if it hadn't been for the book she'd purchased. It kept her riveted. Like a miser with a bit of cheese, she'd parsed her reading out in two-hour allotments, tucking herself away in Strand's library every afternoon where she eagerly cracked open the pages of the anonymously written *Frankenstein; or, The Modern Prometheus*.

Which is where she was when Travers found her.

"Here you are!" he said, hustling in to the library. He carried her coat over his arm and in his hand held her hat and a pair of gloves. "Lord Neville is in the front saloon waiting for you! He says that it's been arranged that you would go driving with him."

She bolted upright. She'd forgotten all about Neville Demsforth, including her plan to write him a note declining his offered carriage ride. "Oh, dear. I forgot."

"Clearly. As well, apparently, as your promise to Lord Strand to stay out of the public eye."

Heat piled into Avery's cheeks.

Travers clucked his tongue, looking over his shoulder to make sure they were not overheard. "Nothing can be done about it now. Lord Neville is expecting you. You are hardly dressed for an excursion in the young lord's company, but that can't be helped either. You can't keep him waiting. He has far more consequence than you *or* the character you pretend to be."

Guiltily, Avery stood up. "Please, can't you tell him something?"

"What?"

"I don't know. I'm indisposed? Unavailable? Ill?"

"No. I cannot. A gentleman would have sent word if he were discommoded and, even if you are not a gentleman—a fact, I daresay, which will soon become clear to Lord Neville if it hasn't already done so— Lord Strand is, and *he* would never allow his protégé to be so cavalier with another's time."

"But you said yourself that I oughtn't go," Avery countered worriedly. It was one thing to gull a young man for an hour in a room filled with other distractions; it was another to do so while closeted with him in a carriage. Not to mention the whole "carriage" aspect of the outing. She didn't trust the high-wheeled contraptions young "whips" insisted on driving. "He's bound to find me out. I shall make any number of mistakes, I know it."

"It's too late to think of that now."

"What will we talk about? I have nothing to say to him."

Upon hearing the panic in her voice, Travers relented. "You say no more than necessary. You keep your face averted as much as possible while still remaining polite. Remember, you are a young man. Do not titter."

The idea of her giggling like some idiotic girl acted as bracingly as a face full of cold water. She sniffed. "I have *never* tittered."

Her outrage did not impress him. "Do not start now. And do not attempt to emulate the manner of a young buck. Promote yourself instead as being that which you are: a scholar. At least no one can doubt the veracity of *that* representation. Anything else is bound to raise speculation if not downright skepticism."

He fussed about her person while he gave his advice, brushing off a few bits of toast left over from the morning's meal and tugging at her feather-augmented corset, the billowy parts having shifted to her side while she sat curled in the chair.

He motioned for her to turn around and held open the coat he'd brought. She obliged, sticking her arms through the sleeves. He came round to her front and buttoned her up. Then he draped a scarf around her neck, handed her the gloves, and plopped her hat atop her head. Finally, he picked up the glasses she'd left on the table and seated them on the bridge of her nose. He stood back, eying her with what she could only think was extreme misgiving.

"I have reconsidered." He shook his head. "Do not talk at all. Your best hope of success lays in drawing as little attention to your face as possible. Say you have a sore throat and leave it at that. And do not, for any reason whatsoever, remove your glasses."

Avery stared unhappily up at Lord Neville's carriage. It shone black as a cormorant's wing, a pair of light gray horses, perfectly matched in height and conformation, shifting restlessly in their traces. High, high above her, perched on slender black springs, awaited a seat upholstered in rich, claret-red leather.

With all the excitement of a boy with a new toy, Neville hurried to the driver's side of the vehicle and clambered up. He settled himself, took up the reins, and looked down at her expectantly. Abruptly, she realized he was waiting for her to climb aboard unassisted. Of course he would. She was supposed to be a healthy—or at least relatively healthy—young man from the country.

But she didn't know how. She had never ridden in such a vehicle before. It looked dangerous. She'd only ridden in rented hacks or, on rare occasion, with the marquess in his barouche, a low-slung, cumbersome vehicle. Carriages like this one invariably seemed to be traveling too fast, the horses barely under the control of their red-faced and often terrified-looking owners as pedestrians, livestock, and fowl fled from beneath thundering hooves and screeching wheels.

"Come along, Quinn. Me cattle's getting restless."

The "cattle," weren't just restless, they were fraught. Their ears lay flat back against their heads as they blew vapor clouds out of dilated nostrils and stomped impatiently.

Dubiously taking hold of the rail, she raised a foot high up on the metal step forged to the side of the carriage. The alien and altogether indecent sensation of having her legs spread so wide apart caused her to blink. Neville looked down at her. "Is something wrong?"

"No!" she croaked, scrambling up the side and into the seat next to Lord Neville.

He regarded her approvingly. "I confess I wondered whether we ought to have Strand's footman fetch a block of steps but you are certainly light-footed for someone so . . ." He broke off, the color rising in his cheeks.

She took pity on him. "I know what I look like and you are correct. I am more agile than one would suppose," she said, hoping conversation would distract her from the height of the carriage and its team of feral horses. One rolled its eye towards her in malicious promise. She could see the white of it.

He turned to her gratefully. "And *I* suppose I shouldn't expose you to the elements like this, but she was only just delivered to me and I could not stand to let her sit idle."

Avery looked about for the "she" to whom Neville referred and caught his eye.

"The curricle," he explained, with a return of the pitying expression he'd worn in Giles's drawing room.

"I see." Apparently young men were wont to ascribe inanimate objects a female gender. How peculiar. But then, given what she knew of female aristocracy, perhaps not so peculiar. Certainly this curricle had more personality than most of the grand ladies she'd encountered. Not that she'd met that many. When she'd been living with her various tutors, she had not spent any time in the company of the mistresses of the establishments and she had been kept entirely from associating with any daughters of the house lest, she supposed, something as indecorous as genius be contagious.

And now here she sat next to a young, eligible, bona fide peer. How many of those young ladies from whom she'd been so carefully segregated would have traded all their family's silver for such an opportunity? A trade she'd have been glad to have made if it meant getting off this ridiculous, precarious-looking contraption.

Perhaps she could just close her eyes for the duration for the drive.

"Are you ready?"

Before she could answer, the team bolted forward and Avery clutched the rails, slamming her eyes shut, and praying that she lived long enough to tell Giles she was sorry she'd broken her promise.

Very sorry.

Chapter Seventeen

"Blister me! Would you just look at that cow-handed clunch!" The exclamation broke the hush that generally permeated White's Gentlemen's Club during the afternoons. Most of its members were either at their own homes or sunk into comfortable chairs scattered throughout the front room, snoring away the last remnants of the previous night's folly before seeking out the next.

"I have a guinea says he upends his rig by the time he reaches the end of the street," said another man.

At the casually tossed-out bet, several of the club's more ardent gamblers hastened to their feet. No one bothered to secure White's infamous book on their way to the window; there wouldn't be time to enter any bets into it.

Giles set aside the note containing Sir Isbill's acceptance of the invitation he'd sent him and glanced without much interest out the window. He'd spent a long night unsuccessfully hunting for some clue as to Jack Seward's whereabouts. The suicidal antics of would-be bloods held little—

With an oath, he surged to his feet, drawing the attention of those nearest him. He barely noted them, his gaze fixed on the certain disaster unfolding on the street below.

A black curricle barreled down the avenue, its steaming, lather-flecked team stampeding in their traces. Their young driver stood straight up on the floorboards, frantic-eyed and hauling ineffectually on the reins. The vehicle careened and teetered as it came, each rut in the road threatening to tip it over, each icy cobble the potential for disaster.

"Best call out now, Strand," one of the club members advised. "Does the driver make it to the end of the street or not?"

"He damn well better make it," Giles said grimly. "Because that's my protégé clinging to the side."

"Oh! *That was glorious!*" Avery cried out when Neville finally managed to haul the team to a halt. "Can we do it again? Let's do it again!"

"No," Neville barked with unnecessary force before he folded like an accordion and landed heavily on the seat. His hands were shaking and sweat beaded his brow.

Startled, Avery studied him and was amazed to realize that rather than being flushed with excitement, he was ashen faced with terror. For the first time, it dawned on her that their race down the avenue hadn't been planned. Hard on the heels of this realization came another: not only hadn't it been intentional but the horses had been completely out of Neville's control. Only dumb good luck had saved them from disaster.

The knowledge should have frightened her. It *should* have made her go weak in the knees like apparently it had Neville. It should have made her head spin and her stomach clench. But it didn't. Oh, it made her pulse race faster, all right, but out of pure exhilaration.

Who would have guessed speed and danger were such a heady combination? Or that she would find oscillating wildly atop a high moving perch so electrifying! And all the more so for being unanticipated.

"I say, Lord Neville, terribly kind of you to take young Quinn driving and all, but do you think it was necessary to scare him half to death while doing so?"

At the sound of that dry, soft, and unmistakable drawl, Avery's head snapped around. She looked down into the enigmatic, cool gray gaze of Lord Strand. He stood in the street below her, his golden head bared to the elements, a few flecks of snow melting on the wide expanse of his jacket's shoulders, and spatters of mud debasing the mirrored shine of his boots. Though it was cold and dank and he wore no coat, he looked no less at ease than if it had been high summer.

"I trust you aren't going to toss up your accounts?" he asked her. The sobriety of his searching gaze belied his insouciant attitude and caused an unexpected feeling of warmth to blossom in her chest.

"No, I—"

"*He's* not the one likely to retch," Neville broke in. He found a handkerchief in his greatcoat's pocket and mopped his forehead. "You misunderstand the situation entirely."

"Do I?" Strand tipped his head. Though his words were no louder than a murmur, the color came rushing back into Neville's face.

"Yes, sir," Neville said miserably. "I mean, no. 'Struth, the damned horses *had* bolted but young Quinn here wasn't shouting out of fear, he was screeching at the bloody beasts to go faster!"

His pronouncement caught Strand off guard. His brows dipped and an unmistakable flicker of surprise crossed his face. He looked at her. "Have you lost your mind?" he murmured.

She followed the direction of his gaze, noting a half dozen finely dressed men standing outside the door of a white stone building with a large bow window, watching them. Too late—far, far too late—she remembered her promise to be inconspicuous.

She wet her lips. "Possibly."

"Damned if Providence don't always shine on you, Strand. You are truly her favored son." A man Avery recognized as Lord Vedder sauntered over. "Take your winnings."

Strand turned and smiled, holding out his hand. Vedder dropped a gold coin into it.

"Tell me," Vedder said. "What made you think the bloody carriage would stay upright? By all the laws of nature it should have tipped over halfway down the street."

Avery started. That Strand had wagered on her physical well-being both shocked and distressed her at some elemental level. She looked at him, afraid her hurt was clear in her eyes, but he only affected exquisite indifference.

"'Tis as you said, Vedder. Providence would never inconvenience Her favored son with having to arrange a funeral. And just think how the obligatory mourning period would wreak havoc with my social calendar." He shuddered. "No. She could not be so unkind."

He glanced up at Avery. "I commend you, Mr. Quinn, on having the good sense not to make the transition from celebrated pet to annoying corpse."

The men behind him broke into appreciative laughter. Avery's head snapped back as if she'd been slapped.

"Lud," another man exclaimed, "I believe you've hurt the whelp's feelings. Look at his expression. He's wounded, by Jove. He thought he held a greater portion of your affection, Strand."

Heat flamed in Avery's cheeks. How dare the fellow presume to interpret her expression! She'd thought no such thing! She'd simply been shocked that Strand could be so caustic. In the library discussing Louis and later playing cards he'd been so . . . so unlike this.

"Fustian," Strand said, without a glance at her. "The boy thinks no such thing. I only met him a few weeks ago. Picked him up as a project to chase away winter's ennui.

"It was either take up with Quinn here or go to Italy to visit me mum and frankly, my Italian is atrocious. Why, last time I was there I gave orders that the landlord send 'un piccolo agnellino' to my room for supper. Imagine my embarrassment when a signorina in a state of interesting dishabille showed up instead."

"Embarrassment or delight?" someone asked.

"Oh, embarrassment. I already had company, you see." The men guffawed appreciatively. Including Neville, Avery noted venomously, who was trying too hard to sound hearty.

"Here, Strand. You're making the young man uncomfortable," a handsome young man with military bearing said. "He isn't used to your debauchery."

"I suppose not, Mandley. And God forbid he ever is."

"What's this? Sentiment, Strand?" Vedder asked with a light sneer.

The corner of Strand's mouth lifted. "Not a bit of it. I just don't want those stargazing chappies after my head. They would be most unhappy if an intellect of Mr. Quinn's caliber threw over his studies for my sort of pursuits. I may be a wastrel, me dear fellow, but I abhor waste."

More laughter greeted this.

"If we stay out here much longer we shall soon make the transition from uncelebrated life to celebrated death," another gentleman said. "At least me wife will celebrate it. Let's adjourn inside. Bring your baby genius along, Strand. You come, too, Demsforth. We'll have a groom take your carriage 'round to the mews."

Neville nodded eagerly and leaned towards her. "That's White's Gentlemen's Club," he whispered. "One of the most exclusive clubs in all of London."

"We don't have to go," she whispered back.

"Yes, we do!" Neville's eyes were wide with shock. "It will add greatly—*greatly*—to our consequence."

She couldn't help but smile. Neville's longing to be accepted by the elite members of the ton was almost painful in its conspicuousness. "*Our* consequence? What consequence do I have that I need to add to it? Oh, don't look like that. Of course, I shall go in with you if you deem it important."

"I do."

"If you are quite finished with your little tête-à-tête, perhaps you would care to join me inside?"

On hearing the cool note in Strand's voice, Avery looked down. He still stood in the street below them, looking both bored and annoyed.

Flushing deeply, Neville scrambled down from his perch and withdrew to the far side of the street, leaving Avery to face Strand's inimical silence alone.

She turned and took hold of the side rail, sticking one leg down to hunt around for a toehold. Her leg dangled ineffectually for a few seconds. Drat and drat! She squatted lower, angling her head to see where the despicable foot bar had been hidden—

She heard a low curse as suddenly large hands clasped either side of her waist, plucked her bodily from the side of the carriage, and deposited her on the street. She turned, intensely aware of Strand's hands skimming over her waist. Even through layers of padding she imagined she could feel their heat and strength.

Strand's hands dropped to his sides. "You were beginning to look ridiculous."

"I should expect I did. I've only ever seen such a vehicle as this a few times in my life. I certainly have never ridden in one."

She gazed up at him. He hadn't stepped back and this close she could feel the slightest aura of heat rising from his lean, broad-shouldered body. She had the sudden, insane desire to take a step forward and press herself against him, to absorb some of his warmth. Except any physical warmth she managed to steal would be offset by an emotional arctic blast.

He looked aloof and disdainful. And he had every reason to be. She'd not only failed to stay inside his house, but she'd appeared in public in such a way to draw intense scrutiny. She swallowed, prepared to take the dressing down she richly deserved.

"Damn it, Avery." Though he spoke quietly, his words rumbled up between them like a growl. "A few weeks and this would be over. Was it so much to ask?"

"I'm sorry. I shouldn't have accepted. I didn't mean to. I forgot to send word and he arrived and then . . . I was lonely." The words came out in a rush.

A shadow passed over Strand's gray eyes and his expression went from cold anger to dismay. For a second, he didn't say anything but when he did, the frost had disappeared from his voice. He shook his head. "Well, at least you seem as if you enjoyed yourself."

Her response was immediate, stemming as much from relief that he was not angry as from her enthusiasm for the carriage ride. "Oh, yes! It was so . . . Oh, I felt so alive, Giles! Invulnerable and fearless and free and . . . and . . ." She trailed off, at a loss as to how to put words to her feelings. He was regarding her with an odd expression.

"What?" she asked.

"I don't believe you've ever called me Giles before."

"I beg your pardon. I forgot myself." He didn't seem angry anymore. In fact, all traces of coolness had disappeared from his expression, yet she could not read what supplanted it. Her heart seemed suddenly too large for her chest, thudding like a panicked prisoner against its walls.

"Strand. The boy will be cold." She turned her head and realized a trio of men were still standing just outside the club's door—the man Strand had called Mandley, another middle-aged fellow with graying ginger hair and a sneering mouth, and Lord Vedder. Mandley's gaze was too sharp and intelligent by half.

"Dear me, Mandley," Giles said, turning around, his sophisticated indolence slipping back into place as easily as an old pair of gloves. "Marriage has made you quite the old woman."

Without a glance in her direction, he motioned for her to follow. "Come along. Lessons are about to begin."

Chapter Eighteen

H e ought to put an end to this lunacy now. It was bound to come undone at any moment.

He had no doubt that Captain Mandley, the only fellow here he counted as close to resembling a friend, would have tumbled to her gender had he stayed but as soon as they quit the streets, Mandley excused himself, a more and more frequent occurrence of late as his new bride apparently proved better company than his old cohorts. Giles couldn't blame him: He'd seen Mandley's wife.

But it was nothing short of astounding that not one of these other so-called men had yet denounced Avery as a fraud. Her femininity announced itself as clearly as a trumpet blast.

Giles studied her from across the room where several of his fellow club members were busily regaling her and Demsforth with sensational tales of mad, breakneck carriage races. Everything about Avery betrayed her gender: the satiny sheen of her skin, the carnation-pink color in her cheek, the unconscious way she tucked her lower lip beneath her front teeth when she was nervous, how she pressed her knees together tightly and skewed sideways when she sat down, the way she tipped her head as she listened, *everything*. The sweet swell of her derriere, the narrow, elegant wrists, the tender length of neck . . .

And yet, not one man had cast her a single questioning look.

Giles sloshed some brandy into a glass and quaffed it back neat, his mood growing darker with each moment. She should have been somewhere else. She should be living some other life. She should have been improving some worthy man by bullying him into planting more acres, buying more cattle, or printing more books. She should be dragooning their clutch of bright-eyed children into finishing their lessons. Or she should be lying soft and yielding under that same, worthy man's straining body, her head thrown back in ecstasy, her hands fisted in the sheets, her legs—

He poured himself another glass, forcing back the unbidden red-hot flash of desire. Avery Quinn, he thought, should be wedded, bedded, and happily somewhere far away from here.

But she wasn't and could never be and the fault for that lay at his family's feet. He was honor bound to help her in her quest because his father had turned her into a woman without position or situation. She was far too well educated to ever fit into the social stratum into which she'd been born and too low born to ever fit into the class that in every respect, aside for the circumstances of her birth, she exceeded. A husband, children, a home, those things which she might have had before his father had embroiled himself in her life, had been replaced with dry books and cold, distant stars.

How could he refuse to help her attain the one thing her education had *not* precluded her from obtaining?

Demsforth's nervous laugh broke Giles's reverie. He set his glass down half-unfinished, his gaze slewing towards Avery's companion.

If he couldn't end this masquerade, at least he should be allowed the satisfaction of killing Lord Neville Demsforth. That great blond *boy*, he thought with unnatural venom, had risked Avery's life. He had lost control of a team he should never even have owned, let alone driven, and in doing so had stopped Giles's heart in his chest.

He'd stood in the window above the street, watching helplessly as the over-balanced carriage lurched out of the path of an oncoming hansom and nearly keeled over. And there hadn't been a thing he could do to prevent it, not a single *damned* thing. Except nod numbly when Vedder had suggested a bet.

Apparently, he did not handle helplessness well, because his response to the feeling was downright feral. Ergo his desire to throttle young Demsforth. Giles was not given to violent responses. It disconcerted him to find himself in the throes of one—though again, there didn't seem to be a bloody thing he could do about it. His reputation amongst the ton was built on his sangfroid and amused indifference. He'd learned his heart was an untrustworthy advisor and, if he did not always successfully ignore it, at least he'd learned enough detachment that he could find his occasional, ungovernable lapses into sentimental yearning amusing.

He was certain if he considered it in the proper light, or with the proper amount of gin, he would find it excessively droll that when Avery had said, "I was lonely," he'd felt as though he'd been kicked in the chest.

However, he'd never find anything amusing about Neville putting Avery in danger. Nor was it amusing to witness some of White's more dissolute members segueing from telling mildly rakish tales of highway bravado to more illicit stories. Which was all too obviously what was happening now.

The men stood winking and elbowing each other's ribs like lascivious schoolboys, pointing at the pages of a ledger laying open on a table before them: White's infamous betting book. It was a decades-long litany of wagers, all the way from an innocent bet over the color of the resident mouser's first kitten to far more salacious wagers.

Damn it.

God willing, no one had pointed out any involving his name. But then, even as he watched, Avery's eyes grew round behind the obscuring spectacles and a rich rosy hue deepened the color of her face as, hovering over her shoulder like some dull-witted Norse demigod, Neville's mouth dropped open.

Bloody hell, Giles thought impatiently and irritably and, worst of all, regretfully, what had they seen? The wager that he'd have a certain opera dancer in his bed by nightfall on the same day he met her? Or—

With a muttered oath, he slammed down his glass and stalked over to the group examining the betting book.

"I can't imagine there is anything worth your perusal in there, Mr. Quinn. I should think it beyond, if not beneath, the scope of your studies." He glanced down, his eye catching on a particular entry. Relief flowed through him.

He looked around at the men surrounding them. They were regarding him in bemusement. "Now there's a wager I was amazed anyone took." He tapped his finger against a scribbled line of text:

5 quid M. of S. arrives drunk to Almack's 1st salon of 1817

"Why is that?" someone asked.

"Because of course I arrived drunk. 'Tis the only conceivable way to tolerate the place."

He flipped the book shut with an unmistakable air of finality and divided his gaze amongst his fellow club members who, one after the other, had fallen into an uncomfortable silence. Then he straightened the cuff of his sleeve and asked casually, "I trust no one wishes to sabotage my attempt at redemption by despoiling my pet genius here?" He was acting out of character and he knew it and he didn't give a bloody damn.

One of the younger men chuffed derisively. "Why should you care about redeeming yourself, Strand? We like you quite well enough unredeemed."

"Terribly gratifying," Giles said, "and for myself, I don't. But my mother does. Come now. You all look as if the concept of my having a mother were as alien as Douphton here having a mistress." He nodded at the ginger-haired man.

The men laughed. Though Douphton drank like a fish and had gambled away several fortunes, he still fancied himself morally superior to, well, just about everyone. From what Giles could gather, it was a viewpoint based solely on his much-vaunted celibacy.

"I assure you," he continued, "I have a mother. A bluestocking, no less. Worse, a bluestocking with spies—though she insists on calling them friends—who over the years have been assiduously following my career and reporting to her in Italy.

"No, no. Pray do not look so contemptuous of the poor fools. We must be charitable. One must assume that relating my exploits to her are as close to having their own as they are likely to come."

Appreciative snickers met this sally. Avery's was not amongst them. He did not look at her. *Damn the girl, anyway.* She'd promised him she would stay discreetly tucked away in his house. She was never supposed to be here, with these men. She was never supposed to see him like this.

Now he had to come up with some viable excuse for his concern over her continued innocence. Dammit all.

"Alas, my mother's coterie of toadeaters have been busier than usual of late," he continued with sigh. "She has written, making clear her disappointment. She threatens to return to London to exert her saintly influence over me unless I reform. I admit, having lost the bride with which I'd hoped to placate her, I was at a loss." Snorts of amusement and nods of approval greeted this callous admission. "But then I met Quinn here and saw the perfect opportunity to establish myself as a benefactor of the sciences."

Vedder openly jeered. Giles turned on him, playing the role of facetious dilettante to the hilt.

" 'Struth, Vedder, I did consider doing something geniusy myself, but it seemed an awful lot of trouble to go through when I could just as easily sit back and accept the accolades for ferretin' out genius. And, of course," he added confidingly, "pay for the boy's odd spots of cheese and books and ink."

He touched his finger to his lips as though a momentous thought had just occurred to him. "Begad, if I don't think I may have a knack for this sort of thing! Mayhap I'll find meself a painter fellow next year."

He waited for them to laugh but they simply stood like befuddled sheep, unsure whether he was having them on or not.

A chuckle drew his attention. He swung around to identify the canny cove who'd tumbled to his mockery and found himself face to face with his little pear-shaped protégé. Her chuckle turned into a full-throated laugh. But then she realized she was the only one laughing. From behind her spectacles, she stared at his fellow club members. "You don't actually *credit* all that fustian?"

Their uncertain glances turned faintly hostile. These were men who prided themselves on being awake to all suits. To have their gullibility pointed out to them by a chubby, oddly shaped country mouse of a scholar would be intolerable. Worse, at least two of these men had strong ties to Avery's astronomical society. That's why he'd come here today: to set the groundwork for her introduction. Now, unless he acted quickly, her laughter would undo any social coin he might have earned.

"What fustian is that, Mr. Quinn?" he asked, moving closer to her. He let his eyes go cold and his voice colder still. "Is it fustian to suggest that if I am your intellectual equal?"

She searched his face, her amusement fading into confusion. "Well, I . . ."

"Or perhaps you consider my patronage fustian?"

Behind him he could hear someone exhort him, "That's the way! Take the little blighter to task, Strand."

Damn the man's impudence.

Avery opened her mouth to reply. Closed it. Glanced in confusion at Neville, who quickly looked away. Smart lad. Now was not the time to come to the aid of a new acquaintance. Not if one wanted entrée into the most exclusive club in London.

"No," she finally managed in a much-subdued voice.

"Or is it fustian to think I am canny enough to recognize the spark of genius in others? Or do you think your genius must shine especially brilliantly, seeing how it was able to attract the attention of a fainéant such as myself?"

Her chin wobbled, her eyes stricken. "No! I swear. I would never think such a thing!"

He reached out and casually flicked her beneath the chin, then spun on his heels, grinning. "Well, you should have; you would have been right."

His companions burst into laughter, clapping him on the back and naming him a wag and a regular out-and-outer and a right cock of the game and then called for him to stand them all drinks in the next room. One would think he had traded barbs with some premier farceur rather than made mock of a defenseless boy.

But he went with them.

By all appearances, they'd forgotten Avery. Giles hadn't. He couldn't. He glanced back over his shoulder. She stood staring at him, looking small and stricken and vulnerable.

He crushed the desire to go back, to explain that this was who he was required to be, that this is what people expected of him, and that he had used their low expectations to achieve certain ends he would never have been able to as another man. A better man. The question of Jack and Anne's disappearance still needed answering and he intended to do that. And this, he'd learned, was the best guise in which to ask questions.

So, instead of following his impulse, he waved his hand at Lord Neville who, God love him, had not abandoned Avery to follow after them. "Best take Mr. Quinn home, Neville. The lessons for the day are over."

Chapter Nineteen

A very watched Giles disappear into some back antechamber. She felt bruised and lost and quite, quite out of her depth. There hadn't been the faintest echo of the youth she'd known or even the Giles she'd thought she'd come to know in the man who'd so callously dismissed her.

"Stings a bit, doesn't it?"

She looked around. Lord Vedder was standing next to the table, casually leafing through the betting book.

"Being the target of Strand's rapier tongue, that is," he said.

She turned her head and snatched off her glasses, polishing them assiduously as she blinked away the tears blurring her vision.

"I'm sorry."

The unexpected sympathy in Vedder's voice threatened her composure anew. She took her time putting her glasses back on before turning round. "Thank you, but you have nothing for which to apologize."

"I suppose I am apologizing for my species."

She tipped her head inquiringly.

"The London Dandy. An oft-vicious, purposeless breed known for its incessant barking and insatiable appetite."

His attempt to ameliorate the situation surprised her. He must have read the confusion in her face for he closed the book. "I'm afraid we got off on the wrong foot the other day. I was intent on barking, you see."

She smiled faintly at his cajolery. He was a very handsome man, she realized. When he was not sneering.

"There. That's better," he said, smiling approvingly. "Let's start afresh, shall we? I promise to behave. I know how it is to feel out of place."

"You, sir?" Neville asked. She'd almost forgotten him.

Vedder looked at Neville, none of the sympathy he had shown Avery in that brief glance. It roused a tingle of wariness in Avery. But his answer was friendly enough. "Oh, yes. I came to London from the country myself and received any number of lessons similar to the one young Mr. Quinn here has just learned." He turned back to Avery. "Strand didn't mean any harm by it."

"It certainly felt like he did," she said impulsively, still raw from the encounter.

"Well, you don't really know him very well, do you?" Vedder asked, coming round the table. He held out his hand, gesturing to the nearby chairs. "If you'd care to have a seat, I shall reveal all."

She hesitated, unwilling to turn down an opportunity to understand the vast discrepancy between the Lord of Killylea and the Prince of Fops. On the other hand, Giles had clearly wanted her to leave.

Neville had no such misgiving. He plopped himself down as Vedder took a seat. They regarded her askance until she followed suit.

"Something to drink?" Vedder asked. "No? Where were we? Oh, yes. You're unfamiliarity with your mentor. Tell me, how long have you known Strand?"

It was just a casual question. "A month."

Vedder clapped his hand on his knee. "There you are. I saw that you did not know him well. His conduct disturbed you. 'Tis clear you've involved yourself with a stranger."

Avery frowned. "I wouldn't call him a stranger."

"No? But you said a month. Perhaps I misunderstood. Was there some earlier association?"

"No." She shifted uneasily in her chair.

"I shouldn't tease you. I forget how it is to be young, when within the space of a conversation a chance acquaintance can become a treasured friend and one makes choices based on whim and impulse."

Avery blinked at him. Whim and impulse were anathema to a scientist. "I assure you, sir, I don't do *anything* based on whim or impulse. It would taint the scientific method."

"You don't?" Vedder looked faintly taken aback. "Ever?"

"No."

"I do," Neville interjected eagerly then flushed. "At least, I'd like to."

"Not I," Avery said. "I am a scientist."

Vedder studied her with what Avery very much suspected was pity. She scowled. "No," he said, "I don't suspect you do. No matter. You did entrust yourself to Strand and you must allow if that was not capricious, at least it was precipitous."

"I trust my instincts. A good scientist must also trust his inner voice."

"Of course," Vedder agreed.

"I would like to trust my inner voice," Neville murmured, drawing their attention. "But it too often suggests impossible things. Things mo— others would never allow."

What, Avery wondered, would this nice young boy consider impossible? Flouting his horrible mother's orders?

"You shouldn't ignore it," she said decisively.

"I agree," Vedder said. "Nothing is impossible."

"You don't understand. My mother . . ." he trailed off miserably.

"But I do," said Lord Vedder. "This is London, Lord Neville. Anything is possible. Anything can be done. Anything *is* done. And nothing is disallowed. Trust me. If you don't allow yourself freedom here, you will be a slave everywhere."

Avery wasn't sure she'd go quite *that* far.

With a little groan, Neville slumped backward in his chair and fell silent, his brow furrowed and his chin resting on his chest as he stared sightlessly at his boot tips.

"Where did you meet Strand?" Vedder asked her.

The abrupt question caught her off-guard. "Strand? I . . . in . . . in the Netherlands."

"Where in the Netherlands?" He brushed a bit of lint off his leg.

"Ghent."

"Ah, Ghent." He nodded comfortably. "I have relatives there. They live near the cathedral."

"You mean the basilica."

"Of course."

She was beginning to feel anything but comfortable. The conversation had taken on the flavor of an interrogation. Rather than learning anything about Strand, she was revealing things about herself. She swiveled around and fixed Neville with an imploring stare. "Lord Neville, did you not say you were bespoke to your mother this evening? It's close on six o'clock."

"What was he doing in Ghent?" Vedder asked. Neville was still lost in unhappy contemplation of his boots.

"I am sure I do not know," she answered stiffly. "Nor would I have asked."

He ignored her icy tone. "Was he with friends?"

"Friends? No." A bead of sweat had started trickling down the back of her neck. "I mean, I don't think so. We didn't travel back to England in the company of anyone else."

"Oh? Hm. Odd. I thought I'd heard him say he had joined up with friends on the continent."

He had? Wouldn't Strand have told her if he had made up a story about their supposed meeting? But what if he hadn't had time to tell her? She had to be careful.

She shrugged. "Oh? Perhaps he did so before we met. I cannot be certain, I didn't really pay much heed to what he was doing, or with whom, before we met."

"And how did you meet?'

"At a planetarium. Neville!" She pushed to her feet, startling the large young man out of his stupor. "Your mother will be anxious."

"Mother?" Neville blinked and looked at the standing clock by the doorway. He jumped to his feet. "Oh, lord! We best be straight off! Thank you for your good advice, Lord Vedder. And thank you for your hospitality."

He secured Avery's upper arm in one ham-sized hand and hauled her bodily out the door. Or would have, had not Avery broken free and got there ahead of him.

"Something odd there."

Vedder swung around to find old Douphton standing in the doorway opposite the one by which Mr. Quinn and Lord Neville had just left. He was scowling. But then Douphton was always scowling about something or other or what someone had done or might do or shouldn't do. The man was a bore and a pedant. But in this case Vedder agreed with him. There was something odd about this Mr. Quinn. He just couldn't quite put his finger on what it was.

"You mean his appearance? Podgy little blighter. I suspect some sort of family taint accounts for the shape and beardlessness. Good enough features, though." Which made the portly little physique all the sadder. He wondered if Quinn were a castrato. Shouldn't be surprised to find out that he was. Likely an accident of some sort.

"You think so?" Douphton sniffed. "I daresay Strand shares your same opinion."

Vedder, who had learned a few things in the years since he'd somehow become Jameson's cur, knew a man who wanted to say something when he heard one. Douphton was dying to add something to his comment.

The older man contrived to look casual as he came into the room, but he moved too quickly and his attitude was eager. "I saw him helping the boy out of that gig in the streets. He caught him round the waist to do so."

Vedder shrugged. "So?"

"It made me uncomfortable. *Damned* uncomfortable. Looked like he was . . . well, more interested than was natural."

Vedder regarded Douphton with pity. The man was pathetic. Seeing sin and depravation in every act. And while Vedder certainly allowed sin and depravation to be in no short supply, the idea that Strand might be a molly was absurd. Not only had there never been a hint of any such thing attached to his name before but there were any number of ladies who would happily testify to his sexual preferences.

Besides, if the gloriously handsome Lord Strand were going to experiment with boys, he would certainly pick an equally glorious-looking one, not some bushy-browed little dumpling.

Douphton was watching him intently, waiting for him to speak. Vedder hesitated. He didn't want Douphton to think for an instant that he gave any credence to the idea. There was no end of ears in a place like this and even if Douphton didn't have a care for his hide, Vedder did. One did not make that sort of suggestion without courting severe consequences. Strand was not only a dab hand with a pistol but a brilliant swordsman.

Douphton would get himself killed if he didn't watch his mouth. But he was the sort of lunatic who felt he had a sacred duty to reveal whatever sins he'd unearthed. His eyes practically glowed with religious fervor. Tiresome man. Still, Vedder already had enough worrying the little kernel of a conscience that had managed to survive all these years. Besides which Douphton sometimes lent him money at the gaming table.

"Shouldn't let it make me too uncomfortable if I were you, Douphton, lest you find yourself discomforted into sporting a bullet hole in your head, if you take my meaning."

Douphton glowered at him. With an inner sigh, Vedder decided to give him one last warning. "I'm sure it was nothing to speak of. Nothing at all."

And without looking to see how this was received, Vedder gave a quick tip of his head and went in search of his greatcoat.

He had a report to make.

Chapter Twenty

B oy says he met Strand in Ghent." This time Vedder did not make the mistake of taking a chair but remained standing. The sooner he'd finished his report, the sooner he could leave Jameson's domain, always an uncomfortable province.

"Do you doubt it?" Jameson asked without looking up from a map spread across the otherwise empty table.

"Not really. I told him I had relatives in Ghent. Had he been lying he would have equivocated. He didn't. He knows Ghent. Whether that's where he actually met Strand, I don't know." He shrugged. "But I would wager there's something he knows that he's not saying. Makes him uncomfortable, too."

"He might be one of Strand's little rabbits," Jameson mused, using the term that he'd coined for the boys who carried gossip and bits of overheard conversation.

They scurried about all strata of society, unnoticed and unremarked, their ears aquiver as they swept streets, emptied slops, sold nosegays, and bore the torches that lit dark streets. Later they would find people like Strand to whom they could sell all sorts of interesting information about the people who used their services without realizing that even gutter-snipes had ears and eyes and mouths.

Vedder shook his head. "Too old, and besides, I think he's what he says he is: a scientist. At White's, old Ned Coles asked him some sort of astro-nomical question and the boy spouted off the answer quick as a penny is lost in a faro game. No. I think he's here for just the reason Strand claimed he was, to broker an invite to this star club. But there's more to it than that."

"So you keep repeating." Jameson's tone hadn't modulated a bit, but Vedder could feel his impatience. "Pray make every attempt at elucida-tion. *Why* do you think this?"

Vedder wet his lips. If he were wrong, things could get worse for him, and they were bad enough as they were. He was on the rocks again, the creditors lining up outside his door, damn their impertinence.

"I swear there is more history between Strand and this Avery Quinn than can be accounted for in a few weeks' time, a familiarity that is not altogether comfortable. Perhaps a bit, well, strained."

He had Jameson's full attention now. "Strained. What do you imag-ine is at the root of this strain?"

"I don't know. Douphton thinks Strand has predatory designs on the young man." He laughed to show how ridiculous he considered this sug-gestion.

Jameson did not laugh. His eyes narrowed to slits, all but hidden be-neath the heavy overhang of his lids. His fingers drummed lightly atop the map. "You don't think so."

"Patently absurd." Vedder did not want Strand coming after his head should such rumors find their way to him. One never knew what informa-tion Jameson might leak, nor when and certainly never why. "Never heard so much as a whisper in that direction. Not even the shadow of a whisper."

"And you would know."

"I appreciate a catholic variety of acquaintances," Vedder allowed. "I believe I would have heard had there been any suggestion of such, yes."

"But you can't be certain."

Of course, Jameson would like Strand to be a madge cull. Then he could bring him to heel with hardly any effort at all and finally find a worthy replacement for Jack Seward.

"No," Vedder agreed. "I can't be sure. But even if Strand were so dis-posed, the boy's formed like a misshapen dumpling and with the same complexion: pasty and soft. Strand's mistresses have always been prime pieces. Can't imagine that developing a predilection for young men would affect one's eyesight."

"That's because you think every sexual encounter fulfills the same need. Different desires require different partners."

Vedder shivered, not because Jameson had said anything he did not already know—he understood the varied compulsions to which men were subject—but because of the gloating in Jameson's pronouncement. Jameson was relishing the idea of all the useful men out there whose weaknesses were just waiting to be exploited.

"I don't think so," he repeated.

Mild disappointment flickered across Jameson's face before he raised his hand, flicking his fingertips invitingly. "Then, by all means, tell me your theory."

"I think the boy saw or heard something in Ghent and is canny enough—Lord knows, he seems smart as a whip—to realize that Strand doesn't want him talking to anyone about it. I suspect he's offered Strand quid pro quo: Strand uses his influence to get him into that astronomical society and Quinn stays dutifully mute under Strand's watchful gaze."

"You think this dumpling of a boy is *blackmailing* the Marquess of Strand?" Incredulity filled Jameson's voice.

"No. Of course not. Strand would squash him like the bulbous little fly he resembles. No, I think it's subtler than that. An agreement made and met. But it's clearly caused friction. Strand was furious when the boy showed up with Demsforth's halfwit cub this afternoon. My theory accounts for both his ire and the boy's sudden appearance. At least, it is a better tale than the one Strand used to explain his sudden interest in acquiring a protégé."

"And what was that?"

"Something about his mother wanting him to have a higher purpose. In other men I might accept it, but I've known Strand a long time. He's never mentioned his mother before. I'd actually thought she was dead."

Jameson leaned over the table, his deep-set eyes as fathomless as awl holes in his elegant old head. "Do you think this boy knows where Jack Seward is?"

The slightest tremble had entered Jameson's voice, a violin string still quivering after the bow had been drawn. There was also a fervor in his face Vedder had never seen before. Frankly, it frightened him.

He recalled the king cobra his uncle had brought home from India. It had looked dangerous enough just lying in the sun in its cage. But then his father had put a rat into the enclosure. The snake had come to sudden, stunning alertness, rising up and spreading cape-like flanges wide on either side of its head. From dangerous to lethal. Vedder felt a sense of recognition; Jameson had become lethal.

"No," Vedder said. "If his knowledge had been that specific, Strand would have had him silenced."

Even now, even after all the things he'd done, it still surprised Vedder that he knew men who "silenced" people simply because of what they had seen or heard. It surprised him even more that he had become one of them. But he wasn't going to think about that now. "I suspect rather that he *might* know something that would lead to them."

Jameson thought a moment then shook his head, his frustration and disappointment manifest. Vedder watched him warily. This was not the same man who'd enlisted Vedder's "occasional help" some years back. Jameson had never before allowed anyone a glimpse into his emotions.

"So, you believe that Strand brought the boy to London, arranged for his nomination into the Royal Astrological Society, and is keeping him under his thumb so that he will not unintentionally let slip a piece of information he may or may not be aware he possesses?"

"Yes."

Vedder sank back in his chair, his lips thinning with derision. "And how long do you think he intends to keep the boy around? A year? Two? Perhaps he'll adopt him."

His words startled Vedder. Sir Jameson never mocked. He considered it coarse and unmannerly.

"Sir, if I may pose a theory?" he asked carefully, recalling that when the cobra had finally struck its prey, the rat had been scrambling futilely, trying to climb sheer glass in its terror to get away. Vedder had always thought the cobra had struck not out of hunger but out of simple irritation. Jameson might destroy him for no other reason than that he was irritated.

"By all means."

"It is my belief that whatever the boy knows is time sensitive. I heard Strand say to him, 'a few weeks and this will done.' I hypothesize that wherever Seward is, he will not be there in a few weeks' time and it will not matter then what the boy says or does."

For long moments Jameson said nothing, his gaze fixed on the map of England on his desk. Little pins with various colored flags dotted the coastline, a cluster over Brighton.

"He's somewhere," Jameson whispered. "And Strand will tell me where. By God, he will."

Vedder did not ask him what he meant. He did not want to know.

Chapter Twenty-One

By the time the dinner hour had arrived, Avery had worked herself into what Mrs. Bedling would have recognized as "a fine fettle." The magnitude of Giles's shabby behavior that afternoon had grown with each passing hour, until she had gone from feeling hurt to furious. When Travers announced that Lord Strand would be dining in and requested the pleasure of her company, she sniffed and quite seriously considered declining the invitation.

But that would mean she would forfeit the opportunity to put a large and noisome bug in his ear and that, she decided, was a pleasure she could not quite deny herself.

So, it was with considerable anticipation of the battle to come that she pushed open the dining room door and announced in her coldest voice, "Lord Strand. *So* kind of you to condescend to dine with me. However do you control such charitable impul—" The rest of her words faded into silence.

Because rather than Giles's polished golden perfection, she found herself facing a large, barrel-chested man with thinning, thatch-colored hair and enormous side whiskers, standing on the far side of the dining table. He was dressed immaculately and tastefully, a testament to his tailor's skill, as not a single crease marred the cut of cloth across his meaty shoulders or thick middle. He had the affable, blocky features of a yeoman except for his nose, which was unexpectedly small and neat. At the sight of her, his brows climbed towards his receding hairline.

"Is *that* your boy genius, Lord Strand?" he asked, looking past her.

Avery swung around to find Giles standing beside the door. He gave her a lazy smile before returning his attention to the stranger. "Yes, Sir Samuel. This is Avery Quinn."

She started and stared. *This* was Sir Samuel Isbill, the president of the Royal Astrological Society, inventor of the Isbill refractory lens? *Oh, my.*

Burke, who'd been hovering behind Sir Isbill, angled the dining chair behind him a bit closer, making it easier for him to sit down. Wincing, Sir Isbill lowered himself into it then returned his speculative gaze to Avery, still standing transfixed in the doorway. "Gout," he explained. "I am a martyr to it. What's your excuse?"

"My excuse, sir?"

"For your deplorable lack of manners? My excuse is the gout. What's yours?"

"I . . . I . . ." Helplessly, Avery looked at Giles.

"I did mention he lacked polish, did I not?" Giles asked.

"You did," Sir Isbill allowed. "I suppose it makes no matter. We must make allowances for genius." Then he smiled. It transformed his face and she suddenly saw Neville in him. "Suspect there's more than a few out there who think I'm a bit of a clunch myself. What strange bedfellows the stars make, eh, Lord Strand? Great bear of a man like me and this little duck-shaped fellow."

He spoke so matter-of-factly she could not take offense.

"Please, Mr. Quinn, come in. You do speak. I heard you. Now it only remains to be seen whether what you say is worth hearing. Is it?"

"Yes, sir. I mean, I think so, sir. I hope so."

"Good. Lord Strand here tells me you have discovered amazing things. Come and tell me all about them."

And with a sense of unreality, Avery did as she was told.

"Do you realize that Sir Samuel Isbill just agreed to read my treatise on predictive anomalies influenced by the orbital patterns of Jupiter and Saturn on the Quinn comet?" Her hands were shaking. "The *Quinn* comet! And *he took it with him*. He said he would give it his every consideration. Do you know what this means?"

"I am confident you will tell me."

"If he likes it, he will nominate my name to become a member of the society at its meeting at the end of the month. If I become a member, I will be eligible for this year's Hipparchus Award."

"I am agog."

He was teasing her; she didn't care. *Sir Isbill had taken her monograph.*

The illustrious scientist had refused to "talk stars" during the lengthy course of dinner, devoting himself fully to enjoying each dish as it appeared. Avery, overwhelmed with the importance of the meeting, knowing she had to be on her very best behavior, and sadly aware that her best might not be near good enough, had retreated to silence over the three-hour span, drawing curious looks from Giles, who, thank heaven, took it upon himself to provide the congenial company Avery so categorically could not.

But as soon as the last Eccles cake and jelly tart had been cleared away and they had retired to Strand's library for port, Sir Isbill had turned to Avery and said, "Now, then. What is this Strand tells me about a comet?"

And with that invitation, Avery found her tongue. She feared she might have found it a little too much because, thinking back now, it seemed that she had done nothing but chatter for the last half hour.

"Did I talk too much?" she now asked Giles worriedly.

They were still in the library, Giles stoppering up the crystal decanter while she stood rooted in place, staring at the doorway through which Sir Samuel had departed.

"Did I make sense?"

He smiled at that. "My dear, I am hardly in a position to judge."

"Did he *look* like I was making sense? I'm afraid I was talking too fast and sometimes when I talk too fast, my reasoning might not appear very cohesive. Did he look like I was making sense?" she repeated.

"Do you mean was he openly snickering? No."

"Oh, no! Was he *surreptitiously* snickering?" she asked, horrified.

Giles laughed and took her hand reassuringly in his. It seemed the most natural thing in the world for her to clutch it, a talisman against fear. It wrapped more securely around hers, warm and strong.

"Take a breath, Avery. No. He wasn't snickering at all. You acquitted yourself well. Did you not see me, nodding and preening, as proud as if I had discovered your comet myself?"

His reassurance meant everything to her. In truth, he *had* been nodding and smiling and following the conversation as if truly interested. She had little doubt that this was not the case and that it had all been for effect and for her benefit. Overcome with gratitude and relief, she pulled her hand free of his and flung her arms around him, hanging around his neck like an awkward pendant, her tiptoes scraping the floor. "He didn't snicker!" she burbled happily. "You're *sure* he didn't snicker? Oh, thank you, Strand. Thank you!"

In answer, his arm wrapped around her, pulling her tight as he straightened, lifting her off the ground. She twisted her head to smile up at him and say—

Whatever words she'd been about to utter died. His gray eyes found hers, soft as ashes, banked and heated. There was nothing cold or arctic in his gaze tonight.

Even through the padded corset separating them, she was intensely aware of the muscular planes of his chest, of his long, powerful thighs and the strong arm binding her to him like a steel band. She wished she wasn't wearing the wretched corset so she might be even more intimate with the body next to her own. Her heart fluttered like a trapped bird in her chest. Her arms simply would not release their hold.

She wet her lips with the tip of her tongue, hoping some words would come. His free hand drifted up her back to cup her head. She had all the time in the world to turn away, every opportunity to break their intermingled gazes. She didn't. He lowered his head, slowly, purposefully.

His lips touched hers. She sighed, nearly swooning with the tenderness of it, the promise. Or was that him? And then his mouth was covering hers, deeply, completely.

As a kiss went, it was fairly shattering. The world spun away and all sensation narrowed to the point where his lips covered hers, warm and vital and urgent. His fingers speared through her short curls as he bent her over the arm bracing her, following her down.

No cautionary story she'd ever heard—and Mrs. Bedling had made certain she'd heard plenty—had prepared her for such a kiss. Because even though her intellect stood back, aghast and fully cognizant that what was happening shouldn't be happening, her blood sang in her veins, an intoxicating primal song that drowned out all the warning from her higher faculties.

She wrapped her arms more tightly around his neck, not to keep herself from falling but to urge him closer. He tasted of port, his lips firm and warm, stirring a fire that ought not to have been lit. She kissed him back, deeply, fiercely, giving a little gasp of ravished discovery when his tongue touched hers and stayed.

But at that utterance, at the very moment of trembling surrender, as abruptly as it had begun, he ended the kiss. With a rough sound, he pulled his mouth from hers and straightened. Gently, he set her on her feet. She swayed and he caught her elbow, steadying her, his gaze intent but shuttered.

She didn't know what to think. How to react. She fought the impulse to demand to know why he'd stopped, fought an equally strong impulse to flee in mortification, and ended staring at him, trying to decipher what she saw in his face. Like an *Ombres chinoises*, the shadow puppet plays she'd seen in France, indistinguishable emotions flickered across his countenance too quickly to interpret or even define.

Then he smiled at her, a little crookedly, and touched a finger to her chin.

"My pardon, *mon chat*. 'Twas force of habit, I'm afraid. Put a female—even one disguised as a male—in my arms and I cannot help myself."

She blinked at him.

"Come now, Avery." He sounded calm, perfectly natural—except his chest was moving a little too deeply, as though he were forcibly regulating his breath. "Don't look so tragic. It was only a kiss."

"Yes," she said, terrified her voice would quake. "Yes. Of course. How provincial you must find me."

And before he could answer, she turned and fled.

Chapter Twenty-Two

Giles cursed silently as he watched Avery disappear down the dim hallway outside the library. His hand curled into a fist by his side and he closed his eyes tightly, tipping his face up towards the ceiling and breathing heavily. He wanted very much to hit something. Hard. And if it hit back, all the better.

Her scent had been his undoing. She'd thrown her arms around him in a moment of unfettered exuberance—only a blackguard would have mistaken it for anything else—and he'd been about to give her an avuncular pat on the shoulder when he'd inhaled. She'd smelled of wool and faintly of soap, but above all she'd smelled like Avery, a fragrance subtly sweet and deeply earthy, as vibrant and feminine and thought-clouding as an opiate. Her scent had been the inciting spark, but he would be lying if he didn't admit that other factors had contributed to that kiss, too. He hadn't been able to keep his eyes off her all evening.

When Sir Isbill had asked her to describe the process by which she predicted the appearance of the comet, her pupils had dilated, her indigo irises shining and the color rising with a flush of excitement to her face. All he could do was watch in astonished wonder, asking himself how Isbill failed to *see* her, recognize the lovely, sylphlike woman sitting across from him beneath the ridiculous lumpy padding and bushy brow?

How could Isbill think skin that translucent, that satiny, could belong to a man? The shape of her ear, the slender throat, the subtle dishing at her temples, the blue-green tracery of veins on the inside of her wrists—all of these things declared her. Was Isbill blind?

Or was *he* mad?

Undoubtedly mad. It wasn't just how she looked that had his heart thundering and his hands clenched at his sides. It was so much more. Her spirit, her laughter, her irreverence . . . everything. Giles opened his eyes as he banished her image, the memory of her mouth yielding beneath his, her arms tightening around his neck, her heart beating wildly—

Damn it to bloody hell! What if one of the servants had come in and seen them? It was only a stroke of luck they hadn't.

As if in answer to a premonition, a pair of maids appeared in the doorway to clear the tables. The sight of him standing alone in the middle of the room clearly startled them. They bobbed twin curtseys, muttered, "Pardon, m'lord," and made to leave.

"Come in. I'm done." He brushed past them and headed for his chambers with a grimly renewed sense of purpose.

That kiss could very well have destroyed Avery's hope of realizing her dreams. Not only that, but it would have jeopardized his own quest to find out what had happened to Jack and Anne Seward.

He'd done as much as he could do on Avery's behalf. The next move was up to Sir Isbill. At least for a short time, he was free to pursue his own investigation. Besides, he needed to clear his head. For the time being, this *was* Avery's home. And as such, she should be safe from the sort of attentions he had offered. It was his duty to provide her a safe haven and he failed miserably, *because she smelled good*. Good God. Where was his self-restraint? His discipline? His sense of honor?

Had another man taken such liberties with her, he'd have called him out. The very least he could do was make sure he did not repeat the offense. He should take to heart the very words he'd said to her: It was just a kiss. Avery was not some seventeen-year-old chit. She was twenty-four, damnably attractive, and had lived in more places than he. Somewhere in her past, surely some young man had stolen a kiss. . . .

Perversely, the idea did nothing to improve his mood. In fact, it fouled it further. He swore again, taking the stairs two at a time, refusing to allow himself to glance at her door.

Once in his rooms, he traded his tailored clothing for the worn, ill-fitting, but warm clothing of a tradesman. He donned a heavy greatcoat, tucking a loaded pistol into an inner pocket. Where he was headed a wise man armed himself for any eventuality and he was, at least in most instances, a very wise man.

Then, he headed down stairs and out into the night.

To hunt.

The noise grew to deafening proportions as the tiers of benches lining the small, converted mews filled with people. Costermongers and soldiers, tinkers, rag pickers, butchers, and servants crowded the room. Intermingled amongst them was a spattering of apprehensive-looking young blades come down to the docks for a night's entertainment. A couple of lorry men began hauling out rats' cages and stacking them in the pit, its sides boarded four feet high. A few of the canine "contestants," quivering like violin strings on their masters' laps, began whining nervously.

Giles stood near the doorway, waiting for the man he'd arranged to meet. He hoped to be done with his business by the time the ratters were loosed. Dog fighting and animal baiting had always seemed to him a despicable and cowardly amusement. If one found bloodletting necessary to be entertained, then one ought to have the balls to offer up one's own blood in its pursuit.

A boy, his feet bound in rags against the icy ground and an inadequate coat hugging his narrow frame, appeared next to him and handed him a note. "Mr. Bees said to give you this and that you'd pay me a shilling when you got it," the boy muttered.

"Did he?" Giles pressed a pair of shillings into the boy's palm, being careful to do so out of sight of interested eyes. If anyone knew the boy had been given money, he wouldn't get far before someone tried to take it. Rather than leave at once, the boy lingered, provoking Giles's curiosity.

"What is it, lad?"

The boy's small face puckered, resentful and angry. "You rich?" he finally blurted out. "Mr. Bees says you'd gimme a shilling 'cause you're a toff. You don't look like no toff to me."

Giles supposed he ought to be gratified. "I make do. How does it concern you?"

The boy's gaze darted across the room to where a brutish-looking man with a carbuncle for a nose stood above a small, cowering, dirty-tan terrier bitch. "That there is me dog. Were me dog. You ought ter buy her off that bloke. Ye won't be sorry. She's a fair devil on rats when she's got her 'ealth."

Giles regarded the boy soberly. "I don't fight dogs. I don't bet on ratting either." He turned but the boy grabbed his sleeve.

"That's fine then. Fine." The words tumbled out of the boy in a desperate rush. "You take her to your house and you'll never see another rat again. She got good manners. Don't piss in her cage. Don't bite. Much."

Giles smiled ruefully and reached into his pocket for another shilling, thinking it would put an end to the conversation. He handed it to the lad, but he shook his head, angrily refusing it. An urchin who wouldn't take a coin? Something was off.

He lowered his voice. "Why are you so eager to get rid of the dog?"

For a moment the boy stared at him, hard-learned caution and mistrust warring with a greater need. "She's a good dog!" he finally blurted out in a low, fierce voice. "But she's old. Four or five years. And she ain't won a penny in months. She's warshed up and he's gonna sell her to the dog fighters tonight fer a bait dog. She'll fetch him a good price counta she'll fight back."

"He," presumably, was the apish man with the bulbous nose. Giles stared down at the young, dirty face, sickened.

"Listen, mister. Yer rich enough to gimme a couple shillings to fetch a note, you kin pays a couple quid fer her. She's a good dog. *Please.*"

"Please" wasn't a word that came easily to the wiry, hard-faced boy. Nor were the tears pooling in his lower lids. Sentiment was a liability in these slums and hard streets. Yet somehow he'd managed to find something to love here. Something he cared enough for to risk exposing his vulnerability.

"Listen, lad. I'll give you a crown to buy your dog then—"

"No! He'll only take her away agin."

He looked about. The dog's owner was shouting at one of his mates. The spotted dog had crawled beneath the bench. "Isn't there some place you can go with her?"

"Where?" the boy asked, his face contorted in impotent fury and misery. "He's me *dad.*"

Of course. Disgust and pity filled Giles. He had no need for an old, half-feral ratter. But then he had no need for a prickly astronomical genius with a smile that made his breath catch and lips like velvet, either.

"Fetch her."

What the hell was happening to him?

Chapter Twenty-Three

Giles quit the building just as the first dog was dropped into the rat-filled pit amidst a roar of approval from the spectators. The white-and-tan terrier he'd become the unwilling owner of alternately slunk along and fought the rope the lad had tied around her neck. He had no idea what he was going to do with her but right now she was coming with him.

As he headed deeper into the city, away from the docks, a squat, hairy man detached himself from the shadows and followed Giles into a twisting lane. Little light penetrated its narrow confines, the cobbles buckling under his feet. At his side, the terrier bitch emitted a low, throaty growl. Giles stepped back, pulling her with him behind the skeletal remnants of a long abandoned, wheelless cart, and waited. A moment later, the hulking shadow passed him. Giles stepped out behind him.

"Why are you following me?"

The man jumped and spun, peering into the gloom. Giles recognized him as the boy's father and former owner of the dog at his feet. She'd drawn her lips back in a silent snarl.

"Bloody 'ell. You gimme a start lurking back there."

"Again, why are you following me?"

He was as stupid as he was brutish. His gaze darted around until he spied the dog at Strand's feet. "Come to get me dog, that's all. Will said as how you'd pay a crown fer 'er, but I didn't see no crown. Next thing I knows, Will's grabbed me dog and I see you leavin wid 'er."

Giles almost laughed. Having seen the color of Giles's gold, the bastard had set out to rob him and, gauging by the glint of the wicked-looking skiver he'd palmed and tucked in his sleeve, perhaps worse.

"I saw the boy give you the money," Giles said.

Indecision warred across the man's coarse features. He could withdraw, by far the most sensible action, or try his luck.

The fool decided to try his luck.

With a roar, the hand clasping the knife punched out of the end of his coat sleeve. He launched himself at Giles, his arm raised to strike down with the skiver. Giles could have easily sidestepped the attack but the terrier bitch suddenly pulled free of his hand and leapt between them, tripping Giles. He fell sideways, the hot stab of the knife slicing though his upper arm, hitting the icy ground with bone jarring force, fully expecting to be stabbed again. Instead, he heard a yowl of pain and rage.

In one liquid movement, Strand was back on his feet, facing his adversary. The terrier bitch had sunk her teeth into the man's calf and clung like wet on water, shaking her head like she was killing a rat. The man swore viciously, twisting to plunge his knife into the dog.

Giles caught his wrist inches before he sank his blade into the bitch, locking his fingers backward and yanking until he heard the bones snap. The man screamed, the blade clattering to the street. Strand kicked the skiver away, sending it skittering into the darkness as the man fell to his knees and wrenched the dog from him, flinging it against the alley wall. She hit the wall and crumpled silently to its base.

The man grinned up at Strand. "Well. Now it looks like we're both out a dog."

With a muttered oath, Strand grabbed the man by his coat collar and yanked him to his feet. Too late, he realized his mistake and twisted. The man kneed him savagely, just missing his groin. Pain lanced through him as he doubled over and the man's unbroken fist slammed down on the back of his head. Light-spackled darkness exploded across his vision.

The man leaned over, wrapping his beefy arm around Giles's throat, intent on choking the life from him. Giles hooked his foot behind the man's leg and jerked backward, sending them both toppling to the street. The man landed on his back, refusing to release his chokehold even when Giles landed heavily atop him.

Giles's throat ached, his lungs burning for air. But now he had a slight advantage. He lifted himself, then slammed back, knocking the man's head against the stone cobbles. Again and again he did so, his heels scrabbling for purchase against the icy pavement as the man choked him with tenacity born of desperation.

Giles fought against losing consciousness, his thoughts clouding, the blood roaring in his ears. Just in time, the arm around his throat loosened. He rolled sideways, free of the deadly embrace, and rose to his hands and knees, gasping for breath. The other man moaned. Lurching to his feet, Giles snatched up the skiver and staggered over to where the man lay.

"Whatcha gonna do now?" the man mumbled, spitting a tooth out of his bloody maw. "Kill me? Over a useless old bitch?"

Giles wanted to. He wanted, he realized, very much to do just that. But if he did, what would become of the boy and whatever other siblings he had? Undoubtedly they'd be a great sight better off without him. In fact, the world in general would be better off without him, starting with the dogs he abused, to the children, and the women he likely did as well. And anyone and anything else smaller, less vicious, or weaker than him.

A faint shiver ran through Giles as he realized that he was standing in a dark alley, calmly debating whether to kill a man who no longer posed a physical threat to him. Worse, there was nothing in that deliberation that frightened him. It seemed entirely appropriate for the man he'd become. *The man he'd become.* He'd never killed in cold blood before. And on the long list of his sins, murder had never appeared.

What had happened to the idealistic young man who so ardently wanted to ride to battle to protect his country and its citizens? What had happened to the man that boy had planned to become? He'd disappeared and it seemed suddenly very important that he find him again.

He looked down at the man whose eyes were glazed with fear, then over at the scar-covered dog. He vacillated. Whatever else he knew or wished, he knew that the world did not need this man in it.

In the end, the dog saved the man's life.

She whimpered, drawing Strand's attention. He went over and squatted, letting his hands rove over her scrawny form to feel for broken bones. When he looked up, the man had disappeared.

And Giles was relieved.

Chapter Twenty-Four

Giles made a bandage of his handkerchief and shoved it under his sleeve, trusting the coat's tight fit to keep it in place. The knife wound didn't seem to have affected his movement. He'd deal with it properly later. Right now he had an appointment he needed to keep.

It took him some time to find the address scrawled on the greasy bit of paper the boy, Will, had handed him. There were few people on the streets, none of them by choice. A frigid wind was blowing in off the river, freezing the muck into deep ruts. Overhead the buildings leaned towards one another across narrow passageways, their windows boarded over in an attempt to hold in what little warmth their hidden rooms contained. Those without the wherewithal to rent a cot for the night huddled together in whatever doorway they could find. A few would be dead come morning, victims of the bitter cold that had gripped this city for weeks now.

Strand finally found his destination, alerted by the presence of a big man wearing a thick knit cap and a heavy coat standing outside. He was stomping his feet and blowing into his hands. When he caught sight of Strand, he motioned him over.

He was a bruising great hulk of a man, his forehead stove in above his right brow, causing the eye beneath to cant down and outward. Black stubble covered his cheeks and his lips were tinged purple. "Took ye long enough, din' it?" he groused, swinging around and tromping down a short flight of steps. At the bottom, he banged twice on the door.

It swung open on a scene as improbable as it was homey. A merry fire burned in the little hearth of a small room with a low ceiling. A gimcrack assortment of upholstered chairs formed an arc around the fireplace. A half a dozen men occupied these, most of them balancing plates filled with food on their knees. One was smoking a fragrant pipe. They looked round at Giles's entrance, their expressions guarded.

One of the men seated before the hearth rose. He wore his dark hair long and tied in an old-fashioned queue. In most ways, he appeared ordinary enough, being of middling height, middling weight. But his jaw was malformed and his mouth contorted with scar tissue and when he smiled, which he was doing now, he displayed a perfect set of teeth. They were not his own. Sergeant Alfred Bees had lost his teeth during the war when he'd taken a musket blast in the face.

"Giles, me lad. To what do I owe the pleasure? You've surely not come looking fer a dog fight, 'ave you? Because that poor old thing yer 'olding is more than 'alf spent." He nodded at the bitch cur Giles cradled in his left arm.

"No. This is my pet."

Alfie Bees roared with laugher and clapped his hands. "Oh God, Giles. Ye always knew how to make me laugh. Joff, pour m'lord here a proper drink."

The giant with the dented skull reached across the wooden table for a bottle.

"Thank you, Mr. Bees," Giles said, "but I won't be here long."

"Well, now. That remains to be seen, don't it?" Alfie Bees said.

"Do you know something that would warrant a longer conversation?" Giles tried to keep any eagerness from his voice.

Alfie Bees was a criminal, an extortionist, a thief, and undoubtedly a murderer, but in London's underground hierarchy, he stood as close to royalty as one got. As any king, he kept a close eye on all other claimants to his crown. Anything worth knowing that happened on these docks eventually came to his attention. And all of it was for sale for the right price, because, though a self-acknowledged scoundrel, he styled himself first and foremost a businessman. If he thought that by withholding information it would fetch a better price elsewhere, he would do so.

Giles didn't have the time or patience for such games.

Alfie pointed to an empty chair. With a quick, assessing glance about, Giles took it, setting the dog at his feet and angling around so he could keep an eye on the rest of Alfie's "court."

While he knew that it would gain Alfie nothing, and cost him much, if he were to try to roll him, Giles hadn't lived through innumerable precarious situations by trusting in madmen's good sense. He kept his left hand in his greatcoat pocket, a finger resting on his pistol's hammer.

"Have you heard anything about that matter we discussed?" Giles asked.

"No," Alf said. "If someone done Seward in, he didn't come from 'round here. But," he touched the side of his nose, "there were a pair of Germans at the Haldergate dog fights a month back. Sailors they said, only in port a day or two. Interesting lot.

"Had me lad inquire of the harbormaster and seems there weren't no German ships come in that week. 'Course"—Alf shrugged—"German sailors don't just work on German ships, do they? Then again, maybe they come in for a special purpose, ye kin? Like slitting throats."

"Then where would the bodies be?"

Alfie smiled. "Wash yer sins away in the river, me mum used to say."

An image of lovely Anne Seward being dumped like so much refuse in the Thames darkened Strand's voice. "Find out what ship those two came in on. Find anyone who spent time with them." He withdrew a small purse and let it fall on the table between them. "I'll pay handsomely for that bit of news. You can reach me in the usual manner."

"You'll come down here?"

"Don't I always?" He pushed his chair back, preparing to rise.

Chapter Twenty-Five

It was well past midnight by the time Giles made his way down the short flight of steps to his townhouse's servants' entrance. The only person he expected to find awake was Travers, who would hold vigil despite Strand's repeated orders not to wait up. With a rising time only four hours away, the rest of the staff would be ensconced in their beds.

And, indeed, Travers hovered just inside the doorway, clad in a paisley robe and holding a lantern. Without preamble, Giles stepped inside and thrust the dog into his arms. The little bitch looked up into his startled face, drew her lips back, and snarled.

The display did not faze Travers. He closed the door and sniffed, scowling. "What is this?"

"That is my dog. Its previous owner, a scrawny little urchin, is lurking about in the garden. He's laboring under the misconception that I have not noticed he's followed me. I'm afraid the boy is equally malodorous. Find the boy a bed with Sam in the stables tonight, then in the morning have Mrs. Silcock clean both the boy and the dog up."

"Yes, sir." Travers scowled, moved closer. "M'lord, is that *blood* on your coat? It *is* blood. Are you . . . have you been injured?"

"Nothing that won't heal."

"What happened? An accident of some sort? Is your arm broken? I shall send for a doctor at once—"

"No," Giles said. "You will not. There is nothing broken. I wasn't in an accident. It's a knife wound."

"*What?*"

At the sound of the female voice echoing down from the servants' staircase, both Travers and Giles swung around. Avery materialized from the darkness and flew to his side. Without a second's hesitation, she began pulling off his coat, her brow knotting fiercely.

Though she hadn't bothered to cinch his dressing gown round her waist, leaving it billowing out and concealing the figure beneath, and the lighting was poor, she still managed to look damnably appealing. Her bare feet peeped from beneath the hem and her hair sprang in a tousle of auburn curls around her pink, scrubbed face. She managed to pull off his greatcoat and let it fall in a heap to the ground then set to work on his coat, her head bent to search for his wound. The nape of her neck looked vulnerable and silky and tender.

His fingers itched to touch her there. To touch her anywhere. And kiss her once more—

She let out a cry of dismay as she peeled his coat from his shoulder, exposing the bloody wad of his handkerchief. Her gaze met his accusingly. "You need to have this attended to at once."

Her vehemence took him aback. "I will."

"I'll send for the doctor," Travers said.

"No." Avery stabbed her finger at Travers. "They'll only bleed him and he's bled quite enough as it is. I'll tend to him."

"You? I don't think that's proper," Travers said.

"Proper or not, I don't care." Her chin rose obstinately. "My father sewed up more dogs and horses than most doctors have men and, I'll warrant, with far fewer of their wounds turning septic. And you know it, Mr. Travers. Just as you know that I helped him."

She turned to Strand, eyes narrowing in challenge. "You are going to wait for me in the kitchen. You"—she glared at Travers—"are going to bring a bottle of the strongest liquor the house owns while I sneak into Mrs. Silcock's sitting room and pinch her sewing kit."

The two men regarded each other mutely.

"What shall I do with the dog?" Travers finally asked, holding up the little terrier as if she were somehow preventing them from taking any further action. The cur eyed Avery with open malevolence.

Without a word, Avery strode to the servants' door and yanked it open. A small, raggedly figure tumbled in at her feet.

She reached down and hauled him up by his ear. "*You* take that dog to the stables and you tell the stablemaster—Sam is his name—to find you a bed. You and the dog sleep there.

"First thing in the morning you present yourself at this door. You tell whoever answers that Lord Strand wants you clean. Very clean. You're to bathe not once, but twice. With hot water.

"*Then* you go back to the stables and you do the same to that dog. Then, and only then, you can come back and have a proper, hot meal. Do you understand?"

The boy stared at her, round-eyed and open-mouthed. Giles empathized. He was very much afraid that his mouth was a little slack, too. She had just commandeered not only Travers and his own person, but his dog and his boy, too. He wasn't sure he liked it. But it was damn amusing.

"*Do you understand?*"

"Yes . . . sir. Ma'am. Sir," the boy stuttered.

Avery rolled her eyes. "*Now.*"

With a squeak, the boy nabbed the dog from Travers's arms and bolted back out the door, kicking it shut behind him.

She turned and regarded Travers and Giles with an expression that did not brook any argument. "Well?"

There was nothing for it but to obey.

Five minutes later, Avery returned with the lidded basket she'd stealthily procured from Mrs. Silcock's sitting room and plopped it down on the tabletop. Giles was looking about uncertainly, holding a napkin pressed to his shoulder. It occurred to her that he'd never been in this kitchen before, though as a young man at Killylea he'd been as comfortable in the kitchen as the drawing room.

She did not like the color of his face, or rather the lack thereof. "Sit down before you fall down." She pointed at the chair.

With a mocking tip of his head, he did as told, leaving her to examine the huge, modern, enameled stove that squatted against one wall. It took her a few minutes, but she soon figured out how it worked. She started a fire in its cast iron belly and set a pot to boil on its top; then, satisfied, she wiped the soot from her hands. She turned to find Giles watching her.

She was well aware that few men would allow her to do what she intended to do and she wasn't certain Giles was amongst their number. He would be used to being tended by trained physicians and was bound to be more confident in their abilities than hers. She would have been, had their positions been reversed. She had a great deal of respect for doctors, but—and herein lay the rub—her respect was for their academic acumen.

Her observations suggested that people like her father and Mrs. Bedling and the midwife in Killylea Village, with their years of hands-on experience, had a greater understanding of how to *practice* medicine.

"Do you trust me?"

He smiled wryly. "To do what?"

"To tend that cut."

He grimaced. "For heaven's sake, Avery. It's a simple cut. Travers will bandage it and that will be that."

"That would be most ill-advised. I assume you were cut by a knife. I also assume that it was filthy. My father has long observed that the wounds that hounds or horses receive from dirty or rusted blades or nails often fester. By cleaning them thoroughly before they begin to scab over, he found he could prevent a great many of them from becoming putrid."

"You want to wash the cut."

"Yes. Then, possibly, sew it shut."

He regarded her with a quizzical look then shrugged. "Fine."

"Fine?"

"Yes. Fine. It's obvious neither you nor Travers will be content until something further has been done to my person and as I'd like to retire to my bed, I acquiesce. Have at it."

She'd expected him to put up more of an argument. Now that he hadn't, she felt unaccountably awkward. "Take off your shirt."

"You promise not to faint?"

She rolled her eyes at that, her equanimity fully restored. "As magnificent as your physique is reputed to be, I have every faith that I shall be able to maintain consciousness in its presence," she said dryly. "I have been to museums, you know."

His brows shot up with what she was sure was feigned amazement. "Why, Miss Quinn, I was referring to the sight of my blood, not the sight of my body."

Her equanimity vanished. Her gaze dropped from him and heat boiled up into her cheeks.

"Of course, now I shall be on tenterhooks worrying that my reputation promises more than I actually deliver."

She peeked up. He was grinning at her, his gray eyes sparkling like sunlight on an icy sea. She refused to be chased from the room by his laughter. She lifted her chin.

"I'll let you know."

She didn't expect him to laugh, but he did. She pointed at his ruined shirt. He unbuttoned the top and, with a slight grimace, pulled the ruined shirt over his head.

Thank heavens the pain distracted him from noting her reaction because as far as she was concerned his reputation could not possibly have overstated his beauty. Yes, she had seen statues, idealized versions of masculinity, but they were fashioned of cold marble; Giles was vibrant, living flesh.

His body was a hard, muscled landscape, from the dramatic hills of his shoulders and pectoral muscles, to the smooth valley along his spine, to the chiseled steppes of his ribs, all of it perfect. Deep bronze hair covered his chest, darkening as it narrowed to trace a path down the middle of his belly and disappeared beneath his waistband.

Unwillingly, her imagination conjured up the memory of his kiss, the feel of his mouth covering hers, and his arms surrounding her. *Just a kiss,* he'd said. She'd reminded herself of his trivializing words a hundred times since and still could not begin to match his insouciance.

But at least she could pretend.

"Well? How do I measure up?"

She turned away so he couldn't see her blush. "Frankly, you are average at best."

He chuckled. "Oh, I think we both know that's not true."

"You are the most vain, narcissistic man I have ever met."

"I know," he said cheerfully. "I was cosseted to a criminal degree as a child."

She was about to make some caustic reply but then she remembered that he *hadn't* been cosseted as a child. At least, he had not been cosseted as a sixteen-year-old, which is how old he'd been when she'd first met him. His father had been aloof and distant with his second son, his mother absent, his siblings dead or gone. She might well be one of the few people who knew that but he'd forgotten she did.

She frowned, thinking how odd it was that he would purposefully misrepresent his upbringing. Like her padded corset, an over-indulged childhood seemed to be part of some disguise, just like his vanity and narcissism.

A clean towel hung on dowels above the huge sinks. She took it down and used it as a mitt to carry the pot of simmering water to the table. She looked around until she spied a pot of soft lye soap near the sinks and brought that over, too, just as Travers returned.

He handed an opaque bottle over to Avery. " 'Tis some sort of spirits made from potatoes that the Russian laundress swears will numb any pain, mental or physical. Shall I pour him a glass?"

"It's not to dull his senses, it's to clean his wound."

"You're going to use the liquor to *clean* his wound?" Though Travers sounded doubtful, he didn't outright object.

"Yes. I intend to wash it with soap and water then soak a bandage in this liquor and apply it. Tomorrow, I shall rebind the wound with a poultice of honey and herbs." She glanced at Giles. "With your permission."

"I'm assuming the request is merely a matter of form."

She wasn't sure how to answer.

"Truth to tell, I never saw a beast that Dermot Quinn treated that didn't recover." Travers's unexpected championship made her smile. "Mostly."

"Ah. Mostly." Giles nodded, blew out a little breath, and looked up at her. "I don't suppose you'd consider following the proscribed route of simply letting my poor shoulder be?"

She sniffed. "It's up to you, of course. But if I were you, I would opt for my treatment rather than risk having to have a putrefying limb chopped off."

He stared at her, bemused. "You haven't an ounce of finesse in you, do you?"

"Not an ounce," she agreed, though inside she cringed. He thought her not only unwomanly, but common.

She'd thought . . . Oh! Who knew what sort of inane nonsense she'd thought? That there was some sort of sympathy between them? That he enjoyed her company? That his kiss had, in fact, not been "just a kiss"?

She turned and applied some soap to the towel and dabbed it in the hot water, her brow knotted. The simple truth was that Giles found it easy to speak to her because he didn't feel the necessity to edit what he said. If he was always a gentleman with her, it was only because that was his nature, just as her "lack of finesse" was hers. He would speak to his dog in just such a friendly, open fashion. The dog wasn't going to be affronted.

Well, neither should she. She knew they were not equals, could never be equals. She'd always known it. Or, if there had been a short time when she had thought it could somehow be something else, well, she had been very young and it had been very long ago, and the sound of Giles's voice coming through the heavy library door saying, "*She's your gamekeeper's daughter*, by all that's holy. And now she has no place in *any* society, either that to which she was born or that which her father serves," had set her straight on that accord.

"Avery?"

She ironed the ridiculous anguish from her face and turned around. "Yes?"

He frowned, searching her face. "I said that as having an arm lopped off would be bound to upset my tailor, you'd best get on with it, hadn't you?"

"Yes." She began wiping the blood from his forearm and biceps, working quickly, trying to keep her concentration fixed on the task at hand and avoiding his eye. It proved an impossible task. Because though it only showed her to be as base and common as he supposed, she could not entirely ignore how his muscles played effortlessly beneath his smooth skin, or how warm he felt, or how smooth. And though she worked as gently as possible to avoid hurting him, she feared she failed for more than once she felt him tremble.

When she'd finally cleaned the blood away, she was relieved to see that the knife wound was neither as long nor as deep as she'd feared.

"If you can manage to keep the arm inactive for the next few days, I believe I shan't have to stitch it up." She looked up from frowning at the wound to discover his face only inches from hers. He was regarding her with a frown of his own.

"I'm sorry." She picked up the laundress's bottle and took out its stopper. She gave it a quick whiff. Her eyes began watering. "I'm afraid this is going to sting a bit."

"Ah, well. Good for my soul, I imagine."

She tipped the flagon and spilled the liquor over his cut. He flinched and shot her an aggrieved glare. "That didn't sting a bit. It stung like blue blazes."

"I know," she admitted. "I cut my leg on a rusty scythe when I was fourteen. My father dealt with it in the same manner. I cried."

"I may still yet. Next time I'm injured, I shall make sure you are nowhere in the vicinity."

"Mr. Travers, I will need some strips of linen to bind his lordship's arm. Could you find me some?"

With a bob of his head Travers left the kitchen. Carefully, Avery pressed the wash cloth over the wound. Now that Travers had left, she could ask the questions that had been plaguing her.

"How did you come to be cut like that? Who is that boy and why are you dressed in this fashion? Why did you come in through the servants' entrance so late at night? Where have you been that you smell of gin and smoke and your boots are caked with excrement?"

Though he regarded her with a mild, quizzical expression, Giles's eyes were as sharp as steel spurs. "I would much rather know what you were doing lurking about the servants' staircase in the middle of the night. If you weren't so committed to your masquerade, I would suspect you of meeting a lover."

She had no answer for such a patently ridiculous statement.

"You weren't, were you?"

"Of course not. I was up in the attic."

"The attic."

"Yes. The attic. The only way up is by the servants' staircase."

His deceptively mild expression segued into one of long-suffering equanimity. "And what, pray tell, were you doing in the attic in the middle of the night?"

"Looking out the window."

He nodded encouragingly. "Because . . . ?"

"Because that is the highest point in the house and tonight has been the first evening since my arrival that the miasma called London fog has not befouled the sky. Tonight I could finally see the stars again."

"You were in the attic looking at stars."

She nodded. "Yes. I brought with me a viewing lens such as is used at sea. It's not a parabolic telescope, but one makes do. I was taking down some notes when I chanced to see a figure approaching the house from the mews. Thinking we were about to be robbed, I made my way down the stairs."

He stared at her, appreciation for her courage and resourcefulness nowhere in evidence. "With an aim to what end?"

"With an aim to preventing the robbery."

"Are you a fool?" he exploded. "What if I *had* been a thief and you had surprised me? I might have slit your throat!" He surged to his feet so swiftly that in her haste to back away she bumped into a kitchen chair and nearly fell over.

He caught her by her upper arm, hauling her back to her feet. He did not release her. He stood glaring down at her, his jaw clenched tight and his eyes ablaze.

She glared back.

In her entire life, no one had ever called Avery Quinn a fool and for a very good reason. She wasn't. The one thing she had, the only thing she possessed that no one could deny or take from her, was her intelligence. And now he dared to call her a sapskull!

"Don't *ever* do something so reckless again. *Ever*," he ground out.

"I heard you the first time," she snapped, knowing she sounded petulant. "And you are hurting my arm."

He looked down at where he clasped her tightly around her silk-covered upper arm and released her. "I am sorry."

He stepped away and turned from her, raking his hair back. "But when I think of how you might have been—" He wheeled around. Once more she backed up. "What the bloody hell were you thinking?"

"I was *thinking* very clearly, thank you very much," she shot back. "In spite of your much-vaunted familiarity with my gender, it is apparently a very circumscribed one. You really ought to use something other than the size of a woman's bosom or how easily she simpers at your quips as the sole criteria by which you judge her."

She took great pleasure in the way his jaw bunched up and his eyes narrowed at that.

"Some women, myself included, are actually capable of reasoned, judicious action. I did not come down here unarmed." She reached deep into the pocket of his banyan and produced a small pistol. "I was going to shoot him. Or rather, you. Luckily for you, I am *not* a sapskull and thus waited to see what was what before acting."

"What in blazes are you doing with a pistol? Where did you get it? *Is that loaded?*"

She didn't know what she had expected him to say—something about what sort of woman he found appealing being no concern of hers, maybe an apology for calling her a fool, perhaps even another spate of curses—but it wasn't that. "I brought it from Killylea because I was traveling by public coach, some of which, on occasion, have been known to be robbed, and of course it's loaded. A fat lot of good it would be unloaded."

With an impeccable sense of timing, Travers chose that moment to return carrying an armful of linens. He looked from one of them to the other.

"Did you know she has a pistol?" Strand demanded.

Travers blinked. "I . . . I can't say I knew specifically, but I am not surprised."

"And this does not alarm you?" Strand's tone was icy.

"No, sir. Why would it? After all, her father was your gamekeeper. She's been shooting all manner of firearms her entire life." He hesitated before adding, "And, reluctant though I am to offend your lordship, I'd warrant she's a better shot then you. I *know* she's more cautious," he added with a telling glance at Giles's bloodstained bandage.

With Traver's endorsement ringing in her ears, Avery lifted her chin, gave an audible sniff, and swept from the room.

At least she'd left without getting the answers to her questions.

That, Giles thought grimly, was the trouble with educated women. They thought too much. No, he amended, that was the trouble with Avery Quinn. *She* thought too much. She thought too much, saw too much, and asked too many questions, and she refused to be fobbed off with answers that did not fit her observations.

He didn't worry about what the boy had seen or heard. His focus had been entirely on his dog. Growing up on the fringes of the ratting and fighting rings, Will would have seen plenty of "toffs" out slumming. He would doubtless think Strand was one of them. Avery was entirely another matter.

He had to figure out an explanation for tonight that would satisfy her. She already knew things about him that no one else in the ton did. Too many things. With any luck this masquerade would soon be ending and then he wouldn't have to worry anymore . . . except he would. He would wonder where she was, where she would go, and what she would do when she wasn't here bedeviling him.

Damn it. The only thing he needed to be concerned with was what to tell her, because he had no doubt that he hadn't heard the last of her questions.

For an instant, he considered simply telling her the truth: that he'd been an agent for the crown, working sub rosa during the war. That at its end he'd retired but had been drawn back into service to aid a friend, who'd since disappeared, and that he had been injured in the course of investigating that disappearance.

What prevented him wasn't a matter of trust. He trusted her.

But he held too many other men's secrets. While he would willingly trust her with his life, he had no right to make that decision for anyone else.

Chapter Twenty-Six

"I can see by the way you are moving that your wound is causing you no discomfort this morning. My treatment was apparently effective. Nothing short of miraculous, considering the source. Just think what an imbecile might have accomplished."

Giles looked up from the pile of mail he was sifting through as he ate his breakfast. Avery stood in the doorway, a ridiculous figure with her round torso, her arms set akimbo and her fists planted on her padded hips. He picked up his teacup and took a sip, eying her over the brim.

Such a proud, touchy creature. How could she be so naive in some respects and so canny in others? He motioned her in.

"Please, sit down. It's not even nine o'clock yet. Too early for sarcasm. Even for me. I find sarcasm before noon sours the stomach."

He said this last with deliberate nonchalance; he'd noted how much Avery enjoyed her meals.

The thunderous expression remained in place. If anything her straight, dark brows—blessedly, as yet unaugmented for the day— dipped more sharply, but he noted her gaze stray towards the sideboard.

"Why don't you fill a plate and join me? We can discuss my short-comings, my ingratitude, and your doubtless justified grievances against me while we eat. So much more civilized than you standing in the door-way glowering at me, don't you think? Not to mention much less likely to provoke comment amongst the servants."

Her head whipped around as if to catch a spy lurking behind her. She turned back. "There's no one out there to have overheard."

"Splendid. Pray, come in. No. Leave the door open. There's a silver vase on the table in the hall outside. I can see anyone coming towards the room in its reflection."

She only ventured in a few steps before stopping again.

"The scones are particularly toothsome this morning. Candied or-ange peel, I believe." She had a particular penchant for oranges. "And, by the way, I do thank you. Sincerely."

Apparently, this was not good enough. She dragged her feet to the table, yanked the chair out, and flopped gracelessly down in it.

"Brava. I applaud the detailed depiction of awkward, sullen adoles-cence. But I thought you were supposed to be closer to twenty then twelve."

She glared at him.

He slipped the silver letter opener beneath the wax seal of the envelope he held. "Do you ever worry that after your masquerade has ended you will be so accustomed to striding, flopping, and slouching that you will be unable to return to the relative—and I hope you appreciate my diplomacy here—the relative inhibitions imposed upon a woman's movements?"

The corner of her lip quirked in an unwilling smile and, as he'd hoped, she gave up her belligerent pose. It was one of her better quali-ties, the inability to hold on to a grudge. "No. Truth to tell, it will be a relief. I'm not saying pretending I'm a male doesn't have its gratifying moments, but it's exhausting. I have to preplan even the tiniest gesture."

And often fail, he silently added. How many lads nipped their front teeth into their lower lip when concentrating, or feathered the air with their fingers when illustrating a point? He remained tactfully mute.

"It's not only that. It's difficult to think of what to say to most men."

"I am sure you well know you are every bit as capable of intelligent conversation as any man."

"Indeed, I am," she agreed. "Or would be if there *were* any conversation. That's the problem. There's not." She sighed. "There's a great deal of *talk*, mind you. And it's all about one thing."

He waited.

"Sexual congress."

Bloody. Hell.

"I had no idea men were so single-minded."

Very carefully, Giles set the envelope he'd just opened down beside his empty breakfast plate. He should have foreseen this. The most prevalent topics of conversation amongst men were women, horses, women, politics, and women. "You don't say?"

"I do." She regarded him pityingly.

He supposed he ought to ask her to what specifically she was referring. He didn't want to. Because then he would feel obliged to call out whichever rotter had despoiled her tender ears. And how was he to do that when those same tender ears supposedly belonged to a twenty-year-old male?

"I demand satisfaction for insulting Mr. Quinn's sensibilities by making mention of your mistress's nipples."

Damn it to hell.

Yet every fiber demanded that he shield and shelter her; it was a reflexive response. Like breathing.

"Does the same hold true of you, Strand?"

"What?"

"When I am not around do you compare your lover's breasts to various types of fruit?"

He hadn't . . . It wasn't the same. . . .

"I see you have."

Damn the girl for looking disappointed and doubly damn him for caring. How could he explain that Giles Dalton, Lord Strand, was a character he played without revealing why?

"You were never meant to meet the men you encountered at White's," he said. "Had you stayed here, which you promised me you would, you would not now be in possession of your current knowledge."

"And that would be better." It was a question.

"Don't you think so?"

"No," she answered at once. "Ignorance is never better. I may not like what I learn, but I would rather know the truth than naively give credence to something that does not exist."

She looked him directly in the eye as she spoke and he realized that she'd imagined a standard she'd believed he'd upheld. Not only had he inadvertently destroyed her innocence, but he had also fostered her cynicism. *Well done, Giles.*

"Not all men are like me and my friends, Avery."

"Why would you choose such men to be your friends?"

He shrugged. "They chose me."

"But you didn't have to put yourself in their way. Why did you?" She studied him more intently than anyone had in a long time. Too intently.

She was too discerning by half. He couldn't let her get closer to the truth of who and what he was for the very simple reason that his secrets were not his alone.

"I enjoy their company," he said. "They amuse me. I find there is nothing I want so much in a friend than that he amuse me."

"I don't believe that for a moment. And you are *not* like that."

"My dear girl, as much as I would like to promote your perfectly charming notion that all my sins are based on false rumor or misunderstanding, I cannot. I am not a good man, Avery."

"Oh, I have no doubt about that." This unexpected avowal startled him so much he nearly dropped the letter opener. "But your delinquency is not the same as your companions'—and I refuse to consider them your friends because I do not believe that you do."

He casually scanned the contents of the letter he'd removed from the envelope, barely noting the wording, his thoughts racing. She would persist now until he convincingly illustrated that she'd made a mistake.

"Your discernment is nothing short of amazing," he said without looking up. "Especially since it is based on a renewed acquaintance only a few weeks old and during which time we have spent less than a handful of hours together. But then, as you are quick to point out, you are a genius." He set the letter down and calmly met her gaze. "Tell me, however did you arrive at this fascinating conjecture?"

She flushed, but rather than desist, as could be expected of any well-bred lady—though no well-bred lady would have ever entered into such a conversation in the first place—she continued doggedly on.

"It's not that you look contemptuous or sneer at your companions the way Lord Vedder does when he thinks no one is watching." Begad, the woman really was discerning. "And you aren't ostentatiously offended by them like Lord Douphton. Or even covertly offended." Thank God for that, at least. "You just look . . . tired."

He waited.

"As though their company was a burden. Or," she tipped her head, "a duty."

"What an imagination you have, Avery. Again, I am flattered by your romantic notion of me." She tensed. He'd hit a nerve with that comment and troubled her vanity. "But as the philosopher says, water seeks its own level. Which means that apparently my level is quite low indeed."

For the first time in the course of the conversation, her gaze fell away. Spots of color appeared high on her cheeks. She looked wounded. And that, Giles realized with a sharp intake of breath, wounded him.

Because he loved her.

He was not in love with her, he was not falling in love with her, he *loved* her. Whatever alchemy that worked in the human heart must have occurred in his long ago, for the realization of his feelings occasioned no surprise, only an awakening of his spirit, a ridiculous sense of homecoming, of releasing a breath after a long battle, of yearning and release. Why now? After all these years, why this moment must he finally realize the truth? And what was he supposed to do about it?

"I'm sorry," he heard himself murmur.

She glanced up, her indigo eyes searching his face. He opened his mouth to say more but as he did so caught a reflection in the vase outside the dining room and settled back in his chair.

Burke appeared in the doorway, trailed by a small figure carrying a little dog. "Begging your pardon, sir. But Travers said I was to ask you what is to be done with this boy. And the dog."

Giles forced himself to attend to the problem at hand. Neither the boy or the dog was recognizable from the night before. Both had been scrubbed clean, revealing the boy to have wheat-colored hair and the dog to be brown with white spots. Both were undernourished and bony, and both had a fair number of scars and missing patches of hair.

"The dog is mine. I purchased her last night." He glanced over at Avery. "Her former owner and I disagreed as to her price, ergo . . ."

He trailed off, letting her imagination supply the rest. Perhaps she would accept that as explanation enough for last night's events. It was the truth, after all; the boy could attest to it. It just wasn't all of the truth.

"It's a *sir*, then?" the boy suddenly said, frowning at Avery.

Burke cuffed him smartly on the ear. The boy cupped his ear, looking more offended than injured. "What? I din' know. Who would?"

"Watch your tongue," Burke warned him.

Avery, Giles noted, had to bite back a smile. It was another in a long list of unanticipated charms.

"What's your name, lad?" she asked.

"Will," he said.

"Why did you follow Lord Strand home last night?"

"I was worrit he was going to ditch me dog 'alfway back and she weren't be able to find 'er way 'ome."

As Giles watched, the amusement faded from Avery's face, replaced by dismay. So softhearted, his love. "Well," she said, "he didn't and he won't, Will."

"Yeah? What if she don't like it here? What if she tries—" He paused, blinking away a suspicious shimmering in his eyes. "What if she tries to find her way back to me? You can't let that 'appen. It'll mean the death of her. You got to promise me ye'll keep a weather eye on her until she's settled in good. Promise."

Once again, Burke cuffed the boy, but it was a cursory thing, without much behind it. "Mind your manners."

"Enough, Burke," Giles said. He looked the boy over. "And no, I won't be making any such vow. Surprising as it may be, I have better things to occupy my time than making sure some half-feral dog doesn't run off."

"Strand—" Avery's voice was soft and pleading, far more so than when she'd asked for his aid at Killylea. But that had been for herself. This was for a guttersnipe and his cur.

"There's only one thing for it," Giles continued as if he hadn't heard her hoarse whisper. "She must have a keeper. Would you like the job?"

The boy's narrow, waxy face puckered in confusion. "What's that you say?"

"I'm proposing hiring you to train my dog. You did say she was a ratter?"

The boy's head bobbed in affirmative.

"Then she will have plenty of work in the stables. Of course, there will be other duties that do not involve dog handling. In addition, you will be apprenticed to my coachman, Phineas."

"Ye mean you wants me ta learn ta drive a rig?" The boy looked dumbfounded.

"Yes. You appear to have a knack with animals. Do you?"

"Yea. Yea, I do!"

"Good. You can either sleep in the servants' quarters here in the house or take up residence in the stables. Which would you prefer?"

"Can Belle sleep wid me in the house?"

"And savage anyone who comes within ten feet? I think not."

"Then I'll take the stables with 'er."

Giles nodded. "I trust you were warm enough there last night?"

The boy nodded.

"Now then, Mrs. Silcock—have you met Mrs. Silcock yet?"

"Old biddie with a stinky eye and a grip tighter than a pit dog's locked jaw? She near drowned me."

"Yes. That would be her. You will take your meals with the rest of the staff at her table and listen to her as to the voice of God. Are we clear? Good. In exchange, you and my dog will have a place to sleep, meals, a new set of clothing and"—he glanced at Burke—"what do you say, Burke? Three shillings a week?"

"Seems a mite excessive to me, sir."

"Ah, but he will be performing two jobs. Three shillings it is."

During this recitation, Will's mouth had dropped open and Avery had turned to regard him with an unreadable expression.

"That's the terms of employment I'm offering, Will. Before you answer, will you need to discuss it with your father?"

The boy shook his head vehemently.

"Your mother?"

"Ain't seen her nor me sisters since summer afore last."

"I see. What say you, Will? Have we a deal?"

"Yea. I mean, yes, m'lord."

"Then you may take my dog out and begin acclimating her to her new situation."

"Say what?"

"Show her 'round the stables."

Understanding illuminated the pinched little face. For the first time since Strand had met him, Will smiled, exposing a pair of crooked teeth in a gamin grin. "Straight off, m'lord," he said and, unable to contain his joy over this unexpected rise in his prospects, lifted the terrier's face to his.

"Did you hear that, Belle? You gots a job and so do I." He planted an unabashed kiss atop her scarred head before hurrying off, as if afraid Strand might change his mind. Burke followed at a more discreet pace.

With a slight smile, Strand picked up the letter he'd been reading when he'd been interrupted by Will's arrival.

"You are a good man, Giles Dalton. That was well done."

He stilled. Of all the things a woman had said to him, in all varying degrees of intimacy, he could not recall any that had ever meant more to him. He didn't know how to reply, what to say. Giles Dalton, Lord Strand, ever ready with a quip, as facile with words as he was with a rapier, was afraid that whatever he said would reveal too much. He stared at the letter before him and realized he had a ready change of topic.

"I'm delighted you approve," he said. "And I warrant you'll approve of this even more." He held up the letter for her perusal.

"What is it?" she asked.

"An invitation for us both to attend a party hosted by Sir Samuel Isbill."

Chapter Twenty-Seven

"—and remember to keep your voice low and your glasses on. And be polite to the ladies present," Giles instructed as the brougham slowed to a halt. Avery stared outside. They'd entered a private square off Regent's Street, not far from the river. Elegant broughams and barouches lined the street, depositing their titled owners outside a magnificent house. Her mouth went dry.

"If the situation requires and there are not enough gentlemen present, you may be required to dance," Strand continued as it became their turn to pull before the mansion's front door.

"I don't dance."

"Why not?"

Avery shot him an incredulous look, knowing that nerves more than ire were making her tense. "It was not part of my curriculum. You keep forgetting I was not being groomed to take a place in Society, but as a scientist. Scientists are not required to dance."

The carriage door opened and Will, newly apprenticed to the coach-man, Phineas, unloaded the block stairs. Giles automatically reached out to aid her then, realizing how odd this would look, waited for her to descend, then followed her out.

Giles glanced at Will. "Keep an eye on things, eh?" He tossed the boy a coin. Will caught it one-handed, giving a curt nod in reply.

Wordlessly, Strand followed Avery up the staircase. The mansion door swung open and a tall, liveried footman stepped aside to allow them to enter. "If I may take the gentlemen's coats?"

Avery shed her outer garment and handed it over, then waited for Giles to do likewise, trying to calm herself. With every step she felt more vulnerable and exposed. The rooms in Giles's house were lit by only a few tapers. Here she would be exposed under the light of five hundred candles.

She tugged at the coat Strand's tailor had hastily made up using one Mrs. Bedling had sewn for a template. If possible, it fit even worse. She was horribly aware of the ridiculous figure she cut, toad-bodied, spindly legged, in a coat that stretched across the belly and puckered at the shoulders, with country brogues on her feet. At least her cravat would excite no criticism; Giles had tied it.

He'd taken one look at it as she'd entered the carriage and, *tch*'ing lightly, bid her sit beside him so he could redo it properly. His fingers had worked quickly and impersonally, barely brushing her neck, and yet she had been as exquisitely aware of his touch as if he trailed his lips along her flesh. *Why* couldn't she forget about that kiss?

"Remember," Giles said as he led the way towards the ballroom, "I cannot spend the evening at your side. It would invite interest, and interest is something we want to avoid. Hug the edges of the room. Move about. Eat. But stay in the shadows if at all possible."

And then they were through the doors and in the midst of the most magnificent ball Avery had ever attended. Not surprising, since it was the only such ball she'd ever attended. She couldn't help but be awed. The place was afire with light. It shone from the enormous twin chandeliers on the ceiling to the mirrored back plates of elaborate sconces and the multi-stemmed girandoles lining the walls. Jewels sparkled around slender necks and from the snowy nests of perfectly tied cravats. Heavy silver and gold threads gleamed in fantastic embellishments on hems and waistcoats. Crystal and sequined birds flashed and glinted from elaborate coiffures. Even the ladies' bare shoulders and décolletages seemed to glow.

And it was loud, a cacophony of voices vying to be heard above the faint strains of a musical ensemble seated in the minstrel gallery. Avery, bedazzled, stood at the entrance until Giles secured her elbow and led her to the side of the room where Sir Isbill was dolefully greeting his guests. Beside him stood a tall, pleasant-faced woman with iron gray hair. Sir Isbill looked up and his blunt-featured face lightened.

"Ah. My comet-finding young friend. How good of you to come. You, too, Strand," he said, sparing Giles a cursory glance.

"Sir Isbill, thank you for inviting us," Giles said. "Lady Isbill, a pleasure."

Lady Isbill smiled distractedly, her gaze traveling to the door where the footmen were assisting an antique fellow in a wig. With a quick apology, she hurried off to greet him.

Sir Isbill leaned forward and lowered his voice. "Don't generally go in for this sort of thing, but my wife insists on at least one party for those poor souls obliged to return to town in the middle of winter."

"I'm sure her efforts are appreciated."

He looked anything but convinced. "I suppose. Happily, the Royal Astrological Society is also holding its yearly conference, so at least there're some like-minded men about. Donald Fuller should be here soon. You'll want to talk to him, Mr. Quinn. I've told him about your design for a new parabolic lens. He's intrigued."

She flushed, worried and pleased all at once. "I shall look forward to it."

"Good. I'll point him in your direction as soon as he arrives." He looked over their heads to where his wife was bodily supporting the old gentleman. She stared fixedly at Sir Isbill. "Yes, yes, Martha. I'm coming. I'll speak with *you* later," Sir Isbill said and tapped Avery directly on what would have been her bosom had it not been buried in padding before heading towards his wife.

Avery's eyes went round with shock. Giles cleared his throat, looking almost as uncomfortable as she felt. "Hazard of the game," he said a little gruffly. "Let's find you some place less well illuminated. No lad has ever had such smooth cheeks as yours."

He led her along the side of the room, lifting a hand in greeting to various men, though he did not stop to introduce her. She could not help but notice the admiring glances, both female and male, that covertly followed their progress. She quite understood why. Strand looked splendid. His hair gleamed like polished gold. His gray eyes seemed to catch the light like quicksilver. His freshly shaved jaw was firm and square above the immaculate white of his cravat, and where her coat was crimped and wrinkled, his stretched in a smooth, flawless expanse across shoulders that needed no augmentation.

He managed to convey both dash and self-possession, with a confidence and ease that was as attractive as it was envy producing. Yet, with each passing moment his mood seemed to darken. She had no idea why. Finally he found a place out of earshot of the rest of the company and turned her so they could speak in relative privacy.

"I can't offer to fetch you a drink. I can't stay with you. I have to leave you to your own devices for a while. Do you understand why?"

Is that why he was acting so odd? How peculiar.

"Perfectly." She nodded. "You don't want anyone to think I'm your catamite."

"Dear God. Why in the name of all that's holy do you even know about such things?"

"It's a Latin word derived from a Greek word. I'd been taught both languages by the time I was twelve."

He closed his eyes as if he were trying very hard to keep his temper under control. "That doesn't explain how you know the meaning of that word."

"Every household I have ever boarded in has had an extensive library that included many books written in both Latin and Greek. Indeed, I have long suspected most people collect such books simply because they look impressive on their shelves even though they might not be able to read them."

She lowered her voice confidingly. "I daresay many a lady would faint dead away if she knew the contents of some of the books populating her library. The Greeks in particular were most descriptive in their writings."

He muttered an oath, passing a hand over his face.

"So you see, I quite understand your concerns. And I would share them if I were you. So please, go forth. I shall be fine. Do not worry about me. Besides, Sir Isbill will be looking for me as soon as Mr. Fuller makes his appearance."

His expression filled with a pained sort of concern. "I hate this," he finally said in a low, harsh voice.

"I know. But soon enough, it will all be over one way or the other," she tried to reassure him.

It didn't seem to work. He gave a slight shake of his head and said, "Be unobtrusive," and, without waiting for her answer, left.

She watched him go, feeling well and truly alone then looked around, intent on finding some value in the situation. She decided to consider it a study of her fellow man. And woman. Unfortunately, none were so fascinating to her as Giles Dalton, the Marquess of Strand.

A beautiful, dark-haired woman in a ridiculous state of near undress all but tripped over herself in her haste to put herself in Giles's path. He had to swerve to keep from walking straight into her and his hand shot out to keep her from colliding with him. Her pink mouth formed an "o" of feigned surprise and she flicked open her fan, waving it agitatedly before her face before snapping it shut again and rapping him playfully on the chest.

For the shadow of an instant, Avery thought she detected a sort of tired resignation in Giles's expression. But then it was gone so completely she doubted herself, especially since the look he now bent on the beautiful woman was anything but distracted. Before Avery's eyes Strand turned from a man unsettled by his would-be ward's unsavory knowledge of sexual proclivities to a fashionable fribble and womanizer. His keen gaze grew hooded and lazy, seeming to caress the woman's person. His smile became inviting.

She ignored the fillip of jealousy that goaded her, focusing instead not on how he had changed, but why.

When they'd dined with Sir Isbill, he'd asked insightful questions and made well-reasoned observations. And when they were alone, though his humor could be quick, it was never caustic. In private, she saw the man that the boy she'd known had promised to become: astute, discerning, but with a ready smile and an easy laugh. But his public face was just the opposite: cavalier, supercilious, and careless. Why?

And what had he been doing the other night dressed like a cit and coming into the house where no one would see him? Where had he been and why had he gone to such pains to distract her from asking questions? And why was his home not a home at all, but an impersonal setting for the character he played . . . ?

The character he played.

That was it exactly. Just as surely as she was playing a role, Giles was playing one, too. But for whom was this show intended? And why did he not drop it in the privacy of his own home? But then, she had only to look to the servants to find her answers.

The "servants' network," he'd called it up at Killylea, when he'd asked how she knew about Sophia's presumed pregnancy. For whatever reason he wanted all of London to know him as nothing more than a fop and dilettante.

"I say, Quinn. Is that you?"

At the sound of the booming voice, Avery swung around to find Neville Demsforth descending upon her, beaming with delight.

"I am *so* glad to see you!" He reached out, grabbing Avery's hand in his great paw and pumping it heartily. "What are you doing back here? You should be out in the ballroom, looking over next spring's gaggle of debs. They're all here, you know. Not officially out, course, but that don't matter. Come along, we'll go see if we can spot the next toast."

Avery hung back. "I'd really rather not, Neville."

"Why not?"

"Well, what's the point? It's not as though I'm in the market for a bride."

Neville had the grace to look embarrassed. He'd clearly forgotten that Avery and he did not share the same social position and she could not help but like him all the more for it. He recovered quickly. "Well, I am. Or will be if Mother has her way. So come along and let us see if we can spot a likely Lady Demsforth amongst the flock."

He was so congenial and so good-natured she could not refuse. Besides, the alternative, to stand about holding up the wall, was not appealing.

"You won't insist I ask some chit to dance?"

He looked appalled. "Lord, no. Not unless you do me a similar disservice. Never did discover the knack of keeping me feet under my knees."

She followed him out into the ballroom and together they sauntered along the edges, Neville keeping up a running commentary on the potential bridal material in every girl that passed within ten feet of them.

"Has a squint. Can't abide a girl with a squint."

"Her mother is a friend of my own. I need not say she is therefore out of contention."

"Too thin. Looks like she'd break if she stepped too hard. Dress is awfully pretty, though."

The dress was lovely, ivory-colored gossamer silk edged in tulle ruffles, the bodice spangled with sequins and piped in pale blue grosgrain. Avery had never owned a dress anywhere near as lovely. She had never wanted to before this evening.

She glanced over at where Giles was talking to Lucille Demsforth. Neville's sister was even more beautifully gowned. And she was smiling at Giles tonight, her pretty face alight with interest in something he'd said. He did not appear dismissive of her tonight. Not at all. His expression was filled with admiration.

Would he look at her with similar admiration if she were dressed in the height of fashion? Would he find her appealing? Desirable?

"—as a wet cat in a kennel."

"Excuse me?"

"The Mills-Appel gel. She seems as comfortable as a wet cat in a kennel. She can barely lift her eyes above the floor. Pity. She has nice eyes."

"Oh."

"Her sister's just the opposite. Too cunning by half. While the cousin—that's the cousin standing behind the pair, the one with the yellow hair—the cousin is lovely, but poor as a church mouse."

Already feeling handicapped and frustrated, Neville's last comment rubbed Avery on the raw. "I didn't realize a fortune was a requisite. I thought your family was well-heeled."

"Oh, we are," Neville stated ingenuously. "Positively dripping in gravy. It's just, well, I never thought of marrying a *poor* girl. Mother's always said I must marry a girl who could add to the family's consequence, not deplete it."

"Certainly there are other ways a young lady may augment a family's good name besides monetary ones," she said.

He raised his brows questioningly.

"She might bequeath certain traits to her offspring that would enhance future generations."

"You think people are like dogs and you can breed characteristics into the line?" He appeared intrigued by the idea.

"I do. What would you like your children to be like, Neville? Besides rich." She hoped she had not gone too far, but he did not take offense.

"I should like them to be able to stand up to my—for themselves. To have courage. And intelligence. So they could outwit her—anyone."

Avery nodded approvingly. "Then that should be your criteria for marrying. Not how much money is in the girl's dowry."

"Gads, but you're a smart fella, Quinn. 'Struth, just being with you I feel bright as a new penny. And you're a good sport, too, with more bottom than you look to have, that's for sure. Gads!" He laughed. "When I think about how you were whooping like a Red Indian when me cattle got away from me on St. James! Splendid. Haven't had a bit of sport since." His face fell. "Mother has been most demanding."

His expression brightened on a sudden inspiration. "I have an idea. Heard about a faro game being held down near the docks. Different sort of group, not the usual toffs and dandies, ya understand, but real men. What say we slip out of here and go have a look-see?"

"I don't think I better."

"Come on. It's not all the way down on the docks, just near enough to make it exciting. It's considered prime sport. Slumming, ya know."

She didn't know. She didn't want to know. She shook her head.

Neville sighed gustily. "Well, if you change your mind, let me know. Oh, lord. Here comes me uncle towing some relic along behind him. I'd rather dance than be stuck listening to them blather on about moons and suns and stars." He turned to make good his escape. "Coming?"

She smiled. "No. I'll stay. You forget, I'm here precisely because I like blathering on about moons and suns and stars."

"Eh? Oh. Yes. I had forgotten." He grinned. "It's just that you seem like such a regular bloke. . . ." He trailed off as his gaze surreptitiously swept over her bespectacled face, egg-shaped body, and thin legs. "In many ways," he finished diplomatically and, with a quick nod of his head, vanished into the crowd.

Chapter Twenty-Eight

Giles spotted Sophia across the room. She looked beautiful, her red hair aflame under the candlelight and her lips pouting prettily. Her dress skimmed the contours of her shapely young body, doing more to reveal than conceal with its low bodice and nearly transparent weave.

And he did not feel a scintilla of desire. Without conscious volition, his gaze strayed to the antechamber where he'd left Avery. It was simply unnatural how a woman dressed as an unappealing young man could stir him to such a degree when a girl in a dress designed to excite the imagination brokered no response at all.

But then, it was not Avery in her guise as a young man that made him tighten with desire but the woman beneath. Grimly, he refocused his attention on Sophia.

He'd had no idea she was in town. He'd supposed her father would have taken her to Brighton for the gaming tables. The only people in town in December were politicians preparing for Parliament to convene. And North was no politician.

Sophia spotted him.

Gravely, he bowed his head, wondering how she would handle the situation. For her sake, he hoped she didn't try to cut him directly. Such a contemptuous act could not turn out well for the girl by virtue of the simple fact that she was Sophia North and he, as Avery had so artlessly noted, was Strand. His standing, his consequence, his desirability far outstripped hers, and if she had an ounce of sense, she'd realize it.

Apparently she did, for she inclined her head in return before plucking at the arm of her escort, Lord Vedder. The pair exchanged a few words then came across the room to meet him.

"Miss North," Giles said, executing an elegant bow. "Vedder."

"Strand. Parading your pup about again?"

"Yes," Giles drawled. "Like all pups, he needs an occasional airing."

"Who is this young man, Strand?" Sophia asked as though there were no bad history between them. She'd very astutely decided that nothing could be gained from publicly playing the part of outraged virtue. Besides, few people who were acquainted with Sophia North would give her any credence in such a role.

"No one, really. Has no birth, no name, no fortune. Just a brilliant mind."

"Hm. I'd like to meet him. Where is he?"

Giles glanced about casually. "I don't see him. Despite Lord Vedder's interesting analogy, I don't keep the boy on a leash. But if you'd like, I will contrive an introduction." He smiled. "Though, I'm afraid you'll be disappointed. He has even less looks than money."

She laughed. "Vedder says you found him in the Netherlands. I swear you must have left Killylea and found him within days of my departure."

"Well," he said, "having suffered a grievous disappointment, I felt the immediate need to lose myself in travel."

The explanation clearly delighted her. Her chin notched up a degree and her brows arched. "Yes, well . . ." She turned to Vedder. "M'lord. I am overcome with thirst. Would you kindly endeavor to find me a cup of ratafia?"

Strangely, Vedder did not seem to take exception to being sent on a servant's errand, but bowed and left them.

Sophia looked back at Giles, hesitating. His attention sharpened. Sophia was not given to hesitation. "M'lord," she said, "if we could have a few moments alone. There's a matter of some delicacy I wish to discuss."

Caution made him reluctant. "Then this is hardly the place for that conversation."

At that, she laughed. "Oh, come, Giles. You had me in a cloakroom at the botanical garden. You can hardly refuse me a few moments of conversation."

His recollection was that she'd tricked him into the assignation and had more of him than he'd had of her. He'd never numbered near-public fornication amongst his transgressions until Sophia. But she was right; to suddenly act like a prig was ridiculous.

"Of course."

"There is a small reception room just across the hall from here. It is not being used. I shall meet you there in five minutes."

"This is new. Discretion, Sophia?"

She gave him a hard smile. "I have to watch out for my reputation now that I am back on the marriage mart."

"Very well," he said as Lord Vedder reappeared carrying the requested cup of punch. "Five minutes, then."

"You might at least say you're looking forward to it." She pouted prettily.

"That remains to be seen. Ah, Vedder. Timely as usual." He inclined his head. "Miss North. Vedder."

Five minutes later, with a great deal of misgiving, Giles crossed the hall into the room. He could see no possible way out of the interview. It would be unutterably cruel to leave Sophia waiting for him. At best, he foresaw Sophia making an awkward attempt to blackmail him over his "sister's" madness—at worst, an even more awkward attempt at reconciliation.

He did not, however, anticipate that she would try both.

He was standing at the window, staring up at the dark sky, recalling Avery's remark that "there are no stars in London, only murk and obfuscation" and thinking that "murk and obfuscation" applied to more than the heavens, when he felt the slight puff of air that heralded a door opening. A moment later he heard the swift soft fall of kid-slippered feet but before he could turn a warm body pressed itself against his back and slender arms entwined him.

"I've missed you," Sophia purred, rubbing against him like a cat.

He turned and placed his hands on her shoulders, gently pushing her away. "I'm still the same man you rejected, Sophia. I still have the same family. My brother Louis was still a dwarf."

She shuddered slightly, her mouth twining in a moue of distaste. "So I have since learned, and I must own I think it shoddy of you not to have told me."

"It was never a secret."

"No. But no one told me about it."

"Louis died fifteen years ago. He was never well enough to come to London and so no one here had ever met him. I doubt anyone remembers him at all." Except *he* remembered. As did his mother and sister. And Avery.

"Oh, a few do," she said. "I also learned that he was only your half brother. The taint that affected him may well have come through his mother, not yours." She smiled as if she were offering him the best possible gift.

"Then again, it may have come from my father. Who is to know? And what of Julia?" He wondered if anyone remembered his sister, too, and had told Sophia that the woman she'd seen had been an imposter. He doubted it. After all, Julia hadn't died. She had simply entered a convent before she'd entered Society, very soon after Louis's death. It was a cloistered order and Julia had asked only one thing of her family when she'd joined them, that they respect their privacy and sanctity. And so they had.

"Well?" he prompted.

She was struggling, he could see. "An aberration," she finally said.

So, Society had not remembered Julia, or perhaps they never knew.

"It only makes sense. They are . . . l-l-l-like that, and you are, well, you."

Why had the same words on Avery's lips charmed and amused him but from Sophia they made him feel vaguely embarrassed? Perhaps because Sophia's words reverberated with his father's long ago condemnation, *"A beautiful person like you knows none of the struggles, failures, and setbacks that mold a superior character. Gold is beautiful, yes, but soft and malleable. No man would choose gold over steel in a war."*

"There was nothing wrong with Louis's mental faculties. He was a dwarf."

She was growing irritated. She shrugged elaborately. "What difference? I don't wish to talk about him. Or . . . *her*. I only told you so that you would feel reassured."

He could not bring himself to thank her.

"Is that all?" he asked.

She frowned, her gaze sliding away from his. "Your brother's condition might not be noteworthy, but I daresay your sister's is. I have asked around and no one seems to know anything about her." Her glance grew sly. "I suspect there's a reason for that."

Ah. So he *was* about to be blackmailed. He waited politely.

"Your man of business was most generous to my father."

"I'm gratified to hear it."

"Unhappily, my father has not been anywhere near so generous with me. Indeed, he has been positively stingy. Added to which, he has been losing at the gaming tables again."

"I'm sorry to hear that."

"Yes, well, never mind him." She turned her back to him. "Since I am the person who suffered the greatest from the termination of our engagement, I think it only fair that I should be compensated to a similar degree for my distress."

It was an effort not to blow out a sigh of relief. A few thousand pounds was a small enough price to salve his conscience. Sophia had badly mismanaged just about every facet of her young life but he had aided in it.

"I see. I'm sure something can be arranged."

She wheeled around at that, her eyes flying wide in surprise before narrowing with sudden inspiration. She stepped close to him. "I may have been too hasty in calling off our engagement."

He confessed himself startled. He could not believe she would seriously consider taking the risk that her child would be like Louis or what she imagined Julia to be . . . But then, she wouldn't, would she? If he wed her, he realized, he would never have an heir. He owed her a debt, but not one that great. It was best she understood that clearly. "You did what you needed to do."

She studied him a moment. For all her faults, stupidity was not one of them. She clearly understood the implicit message: There would be no renewal of his offer. She took it with more grace than he'd have assumed.

She gave a small laugh. "No? Ah, well. Baron Nickelbough has been most assiduous in his attentions and he already has his heir."

"He would be fortunate."

She laughed again. "Always the gentleman, Giles. I don't think I quite appreciated that when it mattered. But yes, he would be."

Her fingertips danced up his chest. "We had some fun, did we not?"

"Fun. Yes." That is exactly what they'd had, but fool that he was, now he wanted something else. Something more. Avery.

"We might . . . again."

Her hand curled around the back of his neck and she stretched to her tiptoes, running the tip of her tongue along the edge of his jaw. He froze as her hand scooted down his chest to his waist and below, cupping his member. He was only too human, God knew, and his body reacted where his spirit flagged.

She drew back her head and regarded him triumphantly. "I knew it!" She flung her free arm around his neck, pulled her body up against him, dragging his head down and finding his mouth while her hand worked busily over his erection. She swayed heavily into him, so that he had to clutch her to keep them both from falling.

Angrily, he wrenched his mouth free of hers. All that was needed was a witness for him to be obliged to renew his offer to Sophia. And he did not for an instant put it past her to arrange one.

Chapter Twenty-Nine

Avery stood in stunned silence, not quite believing what had just happened. She had done it! Accomplished the impossible. Everything she had ever dreamt of achieving was soon to be hers.

Sir Isbill had introduced her to his fellow Royal Astrological Society member, Mr. Donald Fuller, a renowned astronomer in his own right. Immediately he'd congratulated her on her impeccable research in anticipating the orbital reoccurrence of the Quinn comet. Her heart had stuttered a few beats on hearing the appellation applied to a comet from lips other than her own and she'd only been able to nod mutely.

Mr. Fuller and Sir Isbill had exchanged what she could only term "twinkling" glances and Sir Isbill had casually announced that not only had he nominated her for admission into the society but, as there had been a quorum present at yesterday's meeting, they had voted on it. She had been accepted as a member. *And*, Sir Isbill had added, leaning forward with a finger alongside his nose, he had a strong, no, make that a *very* strong suspicion that between the comet and her design for a new telescope lens she stood a strong—no, make that a *very* strong—chance of being awarded the Hipparchus medal.

And the two thousand pounds that went with it.

A short conversation about asteroids had followed, but only between Sir Isbill and Mr. Fuller. Avery had been far too excited to participate. She needed to find Giles. She had to tell him.

She hunted around a little frantically, unable to keep from smiling, scanning the guests for his distinctive gold head, but she didn't see him anywhere. She went in search of him, grinning in anticipation of his response. He would be so pleased.

But after a few minutes her smile began to falter. Giles was not in the room set aside for dining, nor was he in the room where some guests were gambling. She could not believe he would have left her without saying something, but she had looked in every room that had an open door.

Which meant he must be in one of the rooms with a closed door.

She did not spend time wondering why those doors might be shut or consider whether their being closed meant they were to remain that way. If she understood opening one's host's closed doors was inappropriate, she chose to ignore it. She had one idea: to find Giles and share her triumph with him.

The first two rooms she opened were empty. From behind the third door, however, she heard voices—a male and female—but the door was heavy enough that she could not recognize them.

She put her hand on the knob, but an unexpected sliver of tact caused her to turn the handle carefully rather than sweep in unannounced. She peered around the cracked door.

There was no mistaking that golden head, the broad shoulders bolstering the slender female form above him. There was no mistaking the passion of that embrace. There was no mistaking what was happening, what the next minutes would bring. Not with the woman's hand pressed so intimately where it was.

Avery's fingers fell from the doorknob. Her breath stoppered in her lungs. She heard a pounding in her ears, but distantly, like drums from some distant plane. And then she was running, her feet carrying her away while her mind remained a frozen witness, jeering at her, *"Fool! Fool! You knew what he was! He told you himself a hundred times!"* and her heart replied, *"I didn't believe him. . . ."*

"Quinn? Quinn, my good fellow!" Large hands caught hold of her, ending her headlong rush down the hallway. Blinking, she peered up into Neville Demsforth's good-natured and concerned face. "Good heavens. Are you feeling all right? You're positively gray! Shall I send for Lord Strand?"

"No! No." She clutched at his arm. "I'm just out of sorts. I don't belong here. I feel out of place, is all."

Neville, bless him, grew grave. "Did someone insult you?"

She shook her head. "No. Actually, quite the opposite, but it's all rather much, you understand. I just want to be able to be myself without worrying about how others see me." The words tumbled out of her, far more truth than she'd meant to tell, but she could not have found a more sympathetic ear than Neville's.

"I understand. Mother has me taking dance and bowing lessons and French lessons and I'm no good at any of it! I am sure everyone thinks I am a laughingstock and pity any girl who has to spend more than five minutes in my company." He glanced over at her. "I'm sure you understand."

She had nothing to say, her mind's eye was still riveted on the scene she'd witnessed. She choked back a sob.

"There, there! I'm sorry. Didn't mean anything by it. Gads, you're even more of a disaster than I am, aren't you?" he asked wonderingly.

"I expect so."

"Come on. We've both had enough of me uncle's party. Let's find that card game I told you about. No one to judge there. No one to nag." He said this last with a telling glance towards his mother who stood craning her neck and critically surveying the crowd.

Avery didn't care where they went, as long as it was away. Panic filled her at the thought of facing Giles. "Yes," she said. "Yes. Can we go at once?"

"Of course. It's not that far away. We'll slip out now, while Mother is towing poor Lucy around trying to hunt down Strand."

He grabbed hold of her elbow and wheeled her around and in a matter of minutes they'd collected their coats and were gone.

Will sat huddled in the interior of Lord Strand's brougham coach, Belle curled in his lap. She made a comfortable armful, warm as a hot water bottle, and if he hadn't been given a task he might have fallen asleep right there and then. It weren't bad inside, what with the wind kept at bay.

But he fought the drowsiness that threatened and kept his gaze hard on the front door of the mansion into which Lord Strand and the he-she lad, Quinn, had vanished. Phineas, having spied a couple of his mates amongst the other drivers, had gone off to a public house located halfway down the street. He'd invited Will to join them but, though Will appreciated the offer, he shook his head.

His lordship had said to Will, "Keep an eye on things," and that was just what Will was aiming to do because, as God was his witness, he never intended to give Lord Strand the slightest excuse to be rid of him. Or Belle. He'd lived in St. Giles's squalor long enough to ken there was no future there for an undersized boy with ambitions above getting deported or havin' his neck stretched.

Besides, he had another job to do.

So, Will straightened right up when he saw the odd little bloke Quinn come out the front door. And he was just preparing to run quick and fetch Phineas when he realized that the little bugger weren't with his lordship at all, but in the company of a big, brawny sort of bloke that to Will's eye would have looked more comfortable behind the back of a plow than in some posh drawing room.

As he watched, the ill-matched pair hurried down the stairs but, rather than get into one of the waiting carriages, they set off up the street heading east towards Covent Garden.

It didn't occur to Will to wonder what two young gentlemen would want in such a place. He knew. He also knew their chances of finding it were significantly less than their chances of finding something they neither wanted nor had bargained for. The chances of *that* happening were very good indeed.

Will squirmed, uncertain of what he ought to do. On the one hand, he weren't no snitch. If a couple of green would-be swells wanted to have a peek-o-day down in the stews, weren't no business of his. On the other hand, 'twas clear as black on a crow that his lordship was strange fond of Mr. Quinn and wouldn't like no harm coming to him—which flummoxed Will who, as one who accounted himself a fine judge of men, reckoned Lord Strand must be amongst the manliest the ton had to offer. At least he were a good enough specimen to best his dad, curse his black soul.

Will considered fetching Phineas, but like as not he'd only get cuffed for his trouble and told to mind his own business. And he should. Still . . .

With a curse that would have had the old biddy Mrs. Silcock boxing his ears 'til they rang, Will set Belle down and exited the carriage. He pulled the scarf the footman Burke had given him up over his head, covering his ears, then he tucked his bare hands up the sleeves of his new coat.

"Stay here, Belle," he sighed and started trotting up the street. "I'm just gonna go see where them two is goin', is all."

Chapter Thirty

L ike an ant's nest kicked open by a cruel boy, the low, mean rooms of
The Crown and Cock churned with life. Dustmen and costermongers, linkboys and porters crowded together in a raucous spectacle,
shoving and pushing and embracing one another. Some slouched against
walls, others crowded the benches, banging their tankards or singing in
boozy chorus. Everyone seemed to be shouting either encouragement or
invective while half-clad girls rained bawdy invitations down from the
overhanging balconies that led to smoky backrooms.

"It's marvelous, isn't it?" Neville shouted above the din. "So . . . natural. None of that Society claptrap! These are real people, Quinn. No one
here will judge or find fault with you. Here you're free."

Yes, Avery thought cynically, free to be plucked clean of any loose
object one carried. Sure enough, as she watched, a girl in a dirty shift
sniggled the handkerchief from a bemused buck's coat pocket while he
ogled a barmaid.

Not that Avery cared. Her mood was dark, her thoughts swinging
between hot jealousy, disgust with herself, and fury that Giles had
wanted that unknown woman . . . and not her.

What a fool she was!

A fat woman in a tight bodice appeared at their sides and thrust heavy tankards into their hands. "On the house, gents!" she said, lifting her head to answer a shouted order from nearby.

Avery set her tankard down, untouched. Not Neville. He took a hearty swig, choked, laughed, and took another. "Terrible stuff. Appalling!" he declared and finished the rest off.

The woman must have been irresistible for Giles to have risked her reputation in so public a place. He hadn't even bothered to lock the door. Why? It made no sense. Unless he'd been carried away by desire.

No man would ever be carried away by any passion she could inspire . . .

She turned to blink away suddenly threatening tears and, as she did so, noted a rough-looking man sitting near the room's only window, covertly studying her and Neville. Realizing he'd been seen, he nodded and lifted his tankard in salute. His smile did not reach his eyes.

She forced her thoughts away from Giles to the matter at hand. Coming here had been a mistake.

"We should go." She tugged on Neville's arm.

He looked down at her in surprise. "Go? My dear fellow, we've just arrived! Why would we want to go? It's most convivial! Look at that fellow over there with the peg leg sawing away on his fiddle! Have you ever seen a jollier man? No, and do you know why? He isn't concerned about his station or consequence, his titles or his inheritance. Or his mother."

"Because he doesn't have any," Avery said, feeling increasingly uneasy. She wasn't sure what sort of place she had imagined Neville had been bringing them to, but it wasn't one as low as this. The fiddler sawing away did so with more grim determination than pleasure, his smile a rictus. Over the entire mob hung an air of manic desperation fueled by huge quantities of gin. A young man, a cit by the look of him, suddenly let out a yell and the girl straddling his lap leapt to her feet. He grabbed her wrist and Avery saw she held an enameled watch fob.

From seemingly nowhere, a pair of men appeared. The girl snatched free and the men hoisted the young cit under his arms and carried him away. It was all done so quickly and with such little fanfare that no one who wasn't watching would have realized what had happened. And no one was.

As she stood there, a boy of no more than nine years shoved a jug in her hand, winked saucily, and shouted, "Have a pull, mister. It's on the 'ouse."

"No, thank you." Avery started to hand the bottle back but Neville grabbed it from her, tipped it over the back of his wrist, and took a long draught.

"Are you elbow shakers?" the boy asked when Neville had returned the jug. "You look like a pair of prime coves. I'm guessing you are."

How many times had the boy said the exact same words to how many other green lads who'd come slumming from the west side of London? Neville looked at her askance.

"I think he's referring to dice." She didn't want to see Giles. Ever again. But she didn't want to be here, either.

"Oh! Of course!" Neville exclaimed, enlightened. "And of course we are."

"Then yer in luck. There's a game starting soon in the back room." The boy jerked his head towards a smoke-clotted doorway.

"Splendid," Neville said. "Come on, Quinn. Let's see whether our fortunes blow hot or cold."

It seemed ridiculously dangerous. And heaven knew, she felt they were already in enough danger. "I don't have a fortune, Neville. I don't have any money at all."

"I'll stand you fifty pounds."

The boy's watchful gaze flew wide and he and the jug abruptly disappeared.

"You don't understand. If I lose it, I have no means to repay you. None."

Neville clapped her on the shoulder, nearly knocking her over. He beamed boozily down at her. "Then I shall make a gift of it."

"I couldn't accept that—"

"Of course you can." Neville draped his massive arm over her shoulders, pulling her towards the back room.

It was darker than the outer room, lit by a half dozen cheap candles, but just as crowded. The players, a motley assortment of merchants, clerks, and hard-eyed habitués, stood three deep around a hazard table, their eyes riveted on the ivory dice tumbling across it. The dice came to a halt and a third of the table erupted into whoops of pleasure. The other players snarled or cursed or fell into grim silence, while a jovial few called out for more bottles of "blue ruin."

"Please, Neville," she said in a voice pitched for his ears alone. "This place is dangerous. Don't you see? Everything around you, all these convivial, natural people you admire . . . it is stage dressing. The only ones here who are not drunk are thieves and captain sharps. It's designed to make young men such as you feel at ease, feel . . . *free.*"

"Young men such as me?" he echoed, looking highly amused. "What of young men such as yourself?" His booming voice drew attention. Avery figured that their best chance of leaving here in the same state in which they arrived lay in not drawing attention to themselves.

"Come along," Neville said, accepting the bottle being passed to him across the table. "Where's the brave lad that shouted such gallant encouragement to me horses? We're here to have fun, Quinn. So let the fun commence!"

He filled an empty glass and tossed back half of it. She regarded him with a sick feeling of dread and helplessness.

"Yer bold friend here has the right of it, young sir," a well-dressed man with an unctuous smile said, sidling up to them. "We're all here for the same thing: a spot of merriment, a song or two, a little gambling, then back to our snug beds by dawn. Where's the harm in that?"

She didn't like him, nor did she trust him. He might *look* like one of Neville's peers, but she knew he wasn't.

Unfortunately, Neville did not share her misgivings.

"That's right!" he said. "Where's the harm that? I'm sick of having to listen to simpering girls and boring old antiques. And Mother. I deserve a night to do whatever I want, with whomever I want!"

"Indeed, you do." The man refilled Neville's glass.

"And unless you wish to find your way back alone, I'm afraid, Quinn, old man, you'll have to stay and enjoy yourself, too." Neville's smile was almost apologetic. Almost.

Where in the bloody hell had the girl got to?

Giles had been hunting for Avery for an hour, ever since informing Sophia that, as flattering as her offer was, he was not interested in renewing any sort of relationship with her.

He had sought Avery at once, like a man seeking fresh water after drinking something polluted. He asked around, but the last anyone had seen of her had been some time earlier when, having delivered the news that she was now officially a member of the Royal Astrological Society, Sir Isbill had left her in a state of what he'd called, "euphoric inarticulacy." Thinking she might have been drawn to the night sky, Giles'd even climbed Isbill's bloody cupola, damn near freezing his hands on the metal ladder in the process. She wasn't there.

He was becoming concerned.

A footman appeared at his side. "Lord Strand?"

"Yes?"

"There's a boy at the front door. He claims to work for you and says it is most urgent that he speak to you."

Boy? Oh, Lord. It must be Will. The damn dog had probably run away. He considered having the footman tell him to go back to the house, but that seemed unduly harsh if he'd lost something he cared about deeply. . . .

He followed the footman to the front hallway where Will stood beside a liveried footman who frowned down at him, a heavy hand holding the boy in place. Will looked openly belligerent and, upon spying Strand, he shrugged neatly out of the footman's grip and darted down the hall to meet him halfway.

"What is this about, Will?"

The boy cast a quick, furtive glance at the footmen behind him.

"It's Mr. Quinn, m'lord."

Strand checked. "What about Mr. Quinn?"

"He and that big cove is gone ter The Crown and Cock in the Garden."

The Crown and Cock was a notorious flash house. "When was this?"

"Hour or so back. I seen 'em leave and I followed after 'cause you said as I was to keep an eye on things and I figured Mr. Quinn counted as a thing."

"Quite right," Strand forced himself to reassure the anxious-looking boy. "You followed them inside?"

"Nah. It'd mean my skin to have one of me dad's mates clamp his peepers on me in that place. I hung about outside, thinking they'd have their bit of fun and be out again right quick. But after a while when they didn't come out, I reckoned I best come inform you before they get rolled proper."

"Get my coat," Strand said to the footman. "Quickly." He looked down at Will. "You did right. Is Phineas with the carriage?"

"No. He's in a public house down the road. Should I go get him?"

"Which would be faster," Strand asked as the footman reappeared at a trot, carrying his greatcoat, "to fetch him and drive or walk?"

"Walk," Will said without hesitation.

Quickly, Strand donned his coat and accepted his hat. The footman, alert that time was of the essence, had already opened the door. Strand grabbed Will's shoulder and wheeled him around, pushing the boy ahead of him.

"You get Phineas and have him drive down there and wait for me."

"But how'll you get there, m'lord?"

"I'll run."

Chapter Thirty-One

Welcome, m'lord!" The flash house's owner, a small middle-aged man with the obsequious manner of an abused schoolteacher and the eyes of a reptile, greeted Giles within a few feet of the front door.

Tension surging through him, Giles schooled his expression into one of foppish disdain. Avery was here. In this vile hole.

"Allow me to introduce myself," the man cooed. "I am Oliver Uttridge, the owner of this tavern and, may I say, I am honored to have entertained the Marquess of Strand."

Strand was too canny to be flattered that the man knew his name. Uttridge would have been watching the entrance from some hidden vantage point, keeping an eye on the clientele. He would know the name of every gambler of the ton, as well as how often they played and, more important, how often they lost, and, most important of all, if they paid their debts promptly. Not that it would matter if they didn't. There could be certain advantages in having a peer in one's debt.

"Hopeful or vain?" Strand drawled.

"Excuse me, m'lord?" Uttridge asked, nonplussed.

"You must be either hopeful or vain, to already claim you'll have entertained me," Strand said playfully, surreptitiously scanning the crowd. He did not see Avery—or Demsforth—anywhere, and with his height and breadth Demsforth would be instantly noticeable. "Which is it?"

"Ah!" Uttridge called up a laugh. "Call it confidence, m'lord. I am certain we'll be able to find something to your liking. Or someone." The man didn't quite wink, though Strand surmised only because at the last minute he thought better of it. "Just tell me your preferred pastime."

Where the *hell* was Avery? Flash houses like this were usually warrens of vice, some rooms used as a brothel, others for drinking and gambling. And other were used for darker reasons still—

He should play the hand, take the time to finesse the matter. He couldn't. The idea of her here, at the mercy of God knew what sort of man or woman, compelled him to act impulsively. Something he never did. But then, Avery had never been in danger before.

"Actually," he said, "I did not come to partake of your entertainments. I am here looking for a young friend of mine."

Uttridge frowned, seeing his chance to lighten the Marquess of Strand's pockets fade along with the opportunity to add to his flash house's cachet. "Oh?"

"Big, blond buffoonish-looking boy. Probably towing a plump little bespectacled mouse in his wake."

A flash of recognition flickered across Uttridge's narrow face. He *had* seen them. Strand bit back his eagerness. The more Uttridge thought he wanted to find them, the longer this would take.

Uttridge held up his hands, the picture of consternation. "My lord. I am so sorry. I hope that you, of all men, will understand."

"Understand what?"

"That even if I knew of such a pair, I would not be able to tell you their whereabouts. The patrons that drift over from the west end of town come here to lose their identities, not to have them discovered. Even *if* the young man is a friend of yours."

He'd given himself away. Now Uttridge would hold his information ransom. Assuming he even had any. Avery and Demsforth could have parted long ago by a different door. Will might simply not have seen them leave.

Or they could be somewhere within, unconscious and hurt, having been set upon for whatever valuables they carried. In which case Uttridge would most definitely not want Strand to find out since he had claimed friendship with the pair.

Damnation. Fear was obscuring his ability to assess the situation. "Friend," Strand repeated, saying the word as though it was badly flavored. "Yes. Well. Truth be told, he's less a friend than a burden."

Uttridge tipped his head inquiringly. Like all men in his position, he was a very good listener.

"You see earlier this evening he won a bauble from . . . a friend of mine in a card game. Nothing of value. A little lock of hair. My friend assures me he would have won the trinket back but, alas, he was called away from the table. When he returned it was to find Demsforth and his little sycophant had decamped."

"Your lordship is fortunate to have so many friends."

Good. Uttridge was feeling he had the upper hand. He would not risk mockery, even so well masked, if he didn't.

"Am I not? At any rate, the owner of that lock of hair is a lady who is, can you warrant this"—Giles opened his eyes wide, inviting Uttridge to share the joke—"*another* friend of mine. She would like it returned before her husband"—he leaned in closer—"decidedly *not* a friend of mine, becomes aware of its existence. And I have offered to fetch it for her."

"How noble of you."

Strand bowed his head in modest acceptance of the accolade. Uttridge believed him. He could read it in the man's face, the contempt that rippled just beneath the surface servility.

But then, why would he question it? This was just the sort of thing Lord Strand, of the roving eye and loose morals and lax conscience, would do: take a lady's lock of hair as a love token, then wager and lose it in a card game where he'd risked not only the lady's reputation but his own blood should her husband discover her indiscretion and challenge him to a duel.

"So, there you have it." Giles shrugged. "I hope now you are more sympathetic to my finding this young man."

Uttridge's face twisted with distress. "Sympathetic, yes. But, m'lord, that does not change the situation."

A cold finger of fear raced down Strand spine. Uttridge's incomprehensible reluctance to barter for information had dire implications. He didn't have time for this. Avery needed him.

"Well," he said with a sigh. "I can at least tell the lady I tried."

"Yes, m'lord."

Strand half turned as though preparing to leave, then hesitated and turned back. "You know, since I am already here and it looks like the remainder of this evening is not likely to be nearly as pleasant as I'd hoped, I may as well see what sorts of entertainment you have, eh?"

Uttridge's eyes glittered with avarice and triumph. "Of course, m'lord. I'm sure we can oblige."

"Don't want a big party. Hate a crowd around a table. Makes me nervous," he confided. "Just a half dozen like-minded fellows with, say, a few hundred quid to spare? Think you can oblige?"

"I am sure I can, m'lord." Uttridge practically rubbed his hands together. "There's a room in the back that's currently unoccupied. If you'd follow me, I'll see you comfortably settled before finding your lordship some amiable companions."

"Splendid."

Uttridge threaded his way through the jostling, noisome crowd, every now and then fixing some drunken lad or laughing, brazen girl reeling into their path with a hard glance that sent the would-be pickpocket veering off to look for other prey.

Soon enough they were in a small corridor pockmarked with a half dozen doors, some hanging halfway open to allow glimpses of the card and dice games within, others closed tightly against intruding eyes. With a bow, Uttridge opened one of these and stepped aside.

Strand wandered inside, eying the room with the air of a connoisseur.

"I'll send a girl in with some refreshment—"

Strand wheeled around and grabbed Uttridge by the collar, jerking him into the room. With a deft move, he kicked the door shut and slammed Uttridge into the wall along side it. His hands at Uttridge's throat, he lifted him bodily from the ground so that his toes barely brushed the scarred floorboards.

Every resemblance to a schoolteacher disappeared from Uttridge's face. His lips curls back over yellowed teeth, his face contorting with rage. He clawed frantically at Strand's hands, kicking out violently, but could find no purchase.

Strand dodged his kicks, pressing his thumbs hard into the man's carotid artery. Uttridge choked, twisting, fear replacing his anger.

"Let me go!" he gasped. "Fer gawd's sake, lemme go! Yer killin' me!"

Giles shook him violently, part of him aghast at the bloodlust singing in his veins, the fury that drove him. *But this man had Avery.* He shook him again. "Where is she?"

"Who?" croaked Uttridge. "Ain't no high class mort here! Not tonight, not never!"

Had he said "she"? Worse and worse. "Not she, you fool. *He!* Where's the taffy-haired young man and his friend?" He eased his hold on Uttridge's neck, allowing him to catch his weight on the tips of his shoes.

At once Uttridge tried to knee him but Giles anticipated the move. He grabbed Uttridge's arm and twisted it behind him and spun him around, locking his forearm around Uttridge's neck and shoving his face into the wall. He yanked Uttridge's hand high between his shoulder blades. Uttridge howled.

"Quiet," Giles ground out.

"Ye'll never get off this street alive," Uttridge panted.

"Right now all you need to worry about is whether you'll get out of this room alive. *Where are they?*"

"Go to hell."

He jerked Uttridge's hand higher. Uttridge squealed in pain. "Last chance. Where?"

"Top of the stairs! Second door in!" Uttridge yelped. "I got nothin' to do wid what 'appens to 'em once they're in that room. Nothin'!"

Strand let him go, shoving him away as he did so that when Uttridge spun around, his arm swinging in a roundhouse punch, he easily ducked it. He blocked another blow and stepped close, feinting left as he pulled short and drove his fist into the man's gut. Uttridge doubled over and Giles felled him with a sharp blow to the back of the head.

Then he headed for the stairs.

Chapter Thirty-Two

Avery huddled in the corner of the room, watching impotently as the bull-necked man she'd noted downstairs stood astride Neville's unconscious form and went through his pockets. Her whole body trembled, her heart thundering in her ribcage and her breath coming in little gasps.

She had never been so afraid in her life.

The woman who'd begged Neville's aid in helping her stumble up to her room—Nan? Nancy?—sprawled amidst a pile of dirty bed linens and discarded clothing on a narrow cot pushed to the side of the room. Every now and then she'd pour herself a drink though she never took her eye off her confederate, no doubt to keep a close tab on exactly what the man was taking off Neville.

"Check under his boots, Bill. I bet his stockings is made of silk."

"Shuddup," the man, Bill, replied, but nonetheless moved to Neville's feet and began tugging off his boot.

Avery closed her eyes, pulling herself into as small a ball as possible, trying to be invisible. Part of her was appalled at her own cowardliness, but a much greater part of her held close to the simple desire to survive.

Poor, gullible, chivalrous Neville had offered resistance and been knocked senseless for his trouble.

Avery slit an eye open, nausea rising at the sight of the cut oozing blood down Neville's face. The boot popped off into Bill's hand and Neville moaned. At once, Bill raised his cudgel to deal him another blow.

"No!" Avery squeaked. "No. *Please.* He's not any threat. He's not even awake. Don't hit him again. Please."

The man eyed her. "Listen to 'im, Nan. '*Please!*' This little squeak makes a prettier plea for his mate than any you'd make for me."

"His mate's a sight prettier lad than you," Nan snapped back.

The man lowered his cudgel. "Just keep yer maw shut," he told Avery, "and ye might make it home with all yer teeth, boy," he muttered and went back to peeling off Neville's sock. He gave a humorless laugh. "'Less, that is, they be really *nice* teeth . . ."

Avery shivered and once more desperately searched the room for any way out. There was none.

As soon as Neville had helped "poor, sick Nan" into the room, Bill had appeared from behind, shoving Avery in after them. The ensuing struggle had been sadly short-lived. Within minutes Neville was unconscious, and she'd been pitched into the far corner of the small, windowless chamber. A short conversation between Bill and Nan followed during which her fate was discussed and summarily dealt with. Surprisingly, it had been the man who'd argued for restraint.

"Look at 'im. He's scairt as a leg-trapped cunny. He ain't goin' make a peep, are ye, boy? No reason to hurt him. Might break 'im permanent-like."

But what would happen when he discovered she was a woman? And what could she do about it? Nothing. Her hands fisted in her lap, terrifyingly aware of her helplessness and vulnerability.

A scant few hours ago she had been jubilant, filled with her own consequence and importance. She'd imagined toasts raised in her honor. She'd imagined basking in Strand's sardonic yet gentle gaze. Instead, she was shivering under Nan's implacable glare. Likely, Avery's antecedents were little different from hers.

Avery, too, might have reached adulthood unschooled, untutored, and illiterate. She might have drifted to London in search of work and ended up in a place like this, as so many girls with no family and no skills did. Only her father's chance encounter with a highwayman's bullet may have separated her fate from Nan's, stood between luring men into your bedroom to rob them and naming a comet.

Her great achievement.

It all seemed so terribly senseless now.

For years she'd focused on making a fantastic astronomical discovery, something that would gain her fame and accolades, because by doing so she could manufacture a sort of faux nobility for herself, one that would allow her to see herself as . . . as Giles's equal. There. In this, her desperate hour, she admitted it.

But now, she didn't care about the comet or prestige or nobility or *anything* except seeing him again.

Because she loved him. Lord, how she loved him. She always had.

She shut her eyes again, conjuring his image as a charm against fear.

She had spent her life with her gaze fixed above her, so that she needn't see what was right before her. Because she'd known that what was before her was as beyond her reach as those stars. Perhaps that was why they meant so much to her. Giles and the stars: perplexing, fascinating, beautiful, and unattainable.

She bit back a sob. It wasn't fair that she should die before she had a chance to experience what passion could mean. She wanted to feel Giles's arms around her, urgent and needful. She wanted Giles to kiss her, Giles to hold her, Giles to . . . to *love* her, a thing infinitely more precious than the discovery of any star could ever be.

"Your turn, squeak."

Bill's voice shattered the cocoon into which Avery had retreated. Terrified, she watched him negligently roll Neville onto his back. He'd stripped him down to his shirt and a pair of underdrawers.

"Come on, now. Sooner begun, sooner done." He held out his hand and twitched his fingers impatiently, motioning her to stand.

Frantically, Avery scurried back, drumming the floor with her boot heels. She clutched her coat tight across her chest and shook her head violently.

The man sighed.

"Gar, Bill. Just grab hold of the little puff-guts and have done. Why're you treatin' him with kid gloves?" Nan called out resentfully.

"Lookit 'im. He ain't gentry. He's just some squinty-eyed bumpkin what found himself in the company of swells. Can't fault him fer wanting to stay there."

"Aye. That's right. No one's t'blame fer nuthin'," Nan said sourly.

"Stubble that," Bill said. "Stand up, mouse. Let's see what yer guardin' under that coat."

"Please," Avery pleaded, shrinking back. "I don't have anything. I swear. Please, let us go."

"I've had enough of this shit," Nan said, propelling herself off the bed and stomping across the room. She grabbed Avery's collar, hauled her to her feet, drew back her arm, and swung hard. Avery tried to dodge it, but the blow still found her.

Her spectacles flew off and lights exploded across her field of vision. Her knees buckled as she fought against unconsciousness. She reached out, grabbing for Nan's arm.

"Ah, Nan . . ." Dimly, she heard Bill protest. She felt herself yanked back to her feet, the coat collar cutting into her throat. Something warm dripped down her cheek. She choked, stumbling, and out of the corner of her eye saw Nan draw her arm back again.

"Let him go."

And that quickly Avery was free, falling down on her knees with bone-jarring impact, catching herself on the flats of her palms. She looked up, blinking through the star-sprinkled room.

Giles stood in the doorway. But a Giles she barely recognized.

Everything about him suggested violence barely held in check. He moved too carefully, with a coiled predatory grace, stepping forward and almost gingerly shutting the door behind him. His gaze glittered with cold, deadly assessment as it swept the room. Tension seemed to hum through him. In his hand he carried a pistol that he pointed directly at Bill. His thumb rested on the hammer.

Bill must have spied what she did in Giles's face for his own went pasty white. "Lookit. You don't want to do somethin' that'll see ye dancin' at the end of rope."

"Don't I?" Giles's voice was a lethal caress.

Nervously, Bill licked his lips. "We'll give back everyt'ing we took. Swear it."

Giles ignored him, speaking instead to her. "Are you badly hurt, Avery? Can you walk?"

She nodded. "Yes."

She managed to stagger to her feet and stumble across the cramped room and to Giles's side. He divided his gaze between Bill and Nan. A muscle bunched and released repeatedly in the corner of his jaw.

"Go into the hall. Wait outside the door. Don't move. If anyone touches you, scream."

"Neville . . ."

Neville had come round and rolled to his hands and knees. He lifted his head. "Wha' ha'pened?" he asked blearily. "Where's me trousers?"

"I've a mind to leave him for bringing you here."

"You can't."

He spared her a brief glance. "As you will. Now, please, wait outside."

Nan's face twisted in fury. Bill looked belligerent but also, she thought, stoic. Like a dog thrown into a baiting box. "She hit me. The man told her not to," Avery said and disappeared out the door.

Giles waited until he heard the door shut, then motioned with the barrel of his gun towards the slattern with the vicious eyes. The one that had hit Avery. Only the deeply ingrained lessons of a lifetime kept him from acting. A gentleman did not hit a woman, no matter how much she deserved it.

"Tear up one of those sheets and tie him up," he ordered her, jerking his head at her companion.

With a sullen glance, the woman ripped a few strips off the bed linen and crossed to her companion, who stood mute and choleric.

"Turn him around so I can see. Now, tie his wrists behind his back."

With a muttered curse, the woman did as he'd instructed. "What are these lads to you? More to the point, what's that *boy* to you?" She sneered. "Is he yer fancy boy? You and this big cove share 'im? Shoulda guessed. Squealed like a little girl when I planted him a facer, he did."

"Shut your mouth." His hand trembled with his effort to keep from shooting. He was a stranger to himself.

She laughed. "Gor, handsome. Ye could do a sight better than that bloated little tick." She finished tying the knots then stood back to admire her handiwork, her hands on her hips. "So. Whatcha gonna do wid me?"

Every fiber of his being urged him to take his revenge and make an example of them, to send out the clear and unambiguous message that anyone who harmed Avery Quinn would meet a similar fate.

It was a barbaric, primitive impulse. Nearly irresistible.

He forced himself to ignore it, reminded himself again that he had been raised to a strict code as a gentleman, one whose nearly every rule he had at one time or another broken. But not that one. Not yet.

"Bring me another strip of linen and turn around," he said as he released the hammer on the pistol and tucked it beneath his waistband at the small of his back.

With a bizarre and repellant sauciness, the woman scooped up a piece of linen and came towards him, hips swinging. She had just about reached him when suddenly she plunged her hand into an unseen pocket and produced a blade. She flew at him, the knife flashing lethally.

Without a second's hesitation, he drove his fist into her jaw. She collapsed in a senseless heap at his feet like a slaughterhouse beef.

Now, he'd broken all of them.

Bill jerked forward, impelled by some vestige of gentlemanliness that Giles apparently no longer retained. His face purpled with impotent rage.

Giles studied Bill narrowly. The man had threatened Avery. Had he discovered she was a woman, God knew what he would have done to her. The thought made Giles's hands curl into fists at his sides.

But Avery had vouched for him.

"Don't. Move."

Bill took his advice, freezing in place and swallowing hard at the expression on Giles's face.

Giles crossed the room and, taking hold of the back of Neville's collar, hauled him to his feet. He swayed drunkenly, his shirt billowing about his knees. He'd never make it out of here under his own power and Giles wasn't about to act as his valet. Neville could count himself fortunate to have only lost the price of his clothing.

Even though the bastard had put Avery in terrible danger and Giles was not feeling generous towards him, Avery wanted him saved so Giles bent down to hoist him over his shoulder. Demsforth took it in mind to protest. "I can walk. Don't need yer help, thank ye very much," he muttered. "Jes . . . lemme get me boots on. . . ."

Damn the boy. He started to shove Giles out of the way. Giles clipped him neatly on the jaw, catching him as he slumped and heaving him over his shoulder.

He smiled as he did so.

Chapter Thirty-Three

Once outside the room, Giles dumped Demsforth unceremoniously on the floor. Avery had grabbed hold of his arm as soon as he'd left the room and still clung to him like she was afraid she might lose him. She wouldn't.

Gently, he clasped her chin, angling her face to see the cut on her scalp better. It was not deep, but still oozed blood. Somewhere, she'd lost the hideous fake brows. He reached inside his coat for his handkerchief and gently wiped the blood from her face and neck.

"How badly are you hurt? The truth now, Avery," he said, working with brisk efficiency. "You're shaking like you have palsy."

"I'm all right," she said. "It's fear that has me quaking like this. Fear and the release from it. Oh, Giles, if you hadn't come—"

"But I did." He refused to entertain for a second the grim images of what might have happened if he'd arrived twenty minutes later. He bunched up his handkerchief and returned it to his pocket. "Can you walk?"

She nodded. Luckily she hadn't taken off her outer coat. It was cold outside. Neville would not fare so well. Giles didn't much care.

215

"You're certain?"

She gave a shaky laugh. "Well, I'd best better be able to walk, hadn't I? I can't see you toting both Neville and me—"

"Neville be damned."

She swallowed at his tone, her eyes frightened. Damn it. He hadn't meant to scare her. He hadn't meant any of this to happen and he didn't have time to apologize. Uttridge or Bill could appear at any second.

He brushed by her and dragged Demsforth more or less upright then went down on one knee and hooked his shoulder under the big lad's arm. With a grunt, he lifted Demsforth back over his shoulder and stumbled upright.

"He weighs as much as a bloody ox." He jerked his head towards the stairs. "Act as if you and Demsforth are jug-bitten. Stagger, stumble, mutter," he said, grunting as he resettled Demsforth more comfortably.

"That won't be a problem."

She tried to smile but her lips trembled and the smile broke, tears welling in her beautiful blue eyes and trickling down her cheeks.

His throat tightened. She should never have known such fear.

He was to blame. He should never have agreed to her charade. He should have realized there would be consequences, but he'd never anticipated how dire they could be. Or that they would include mortal blows to his heart.

"Keep your head down, like you're about to toss up your accounts. Your eyes will give you away."

He gave her an encouraging smile, unbuttoned his waistcoat halfway down, and wrenched his cravat askew. Then he started down the stairs, a foolish, lopsided grin plastered on his face. "Lord love a Titan!" he roared good-humoredly. "'S good thing I come along when I did or young Hal here would be strolling home buck naked!"

They'd reached the bottom of the stairs where the patrons whooped at the sight of the big, half-clad lad draped unceremoniously over Giles's shoulder.

"Now that's a game I wish I'd been in!"

"Get on with you! What would you have done with that giant's coat?"

"I'd a made me two coats!"

Riotous and bawdy comments marked their progress through the room. Giles nodded, shouted, and replied in kind: lewd, earthy, filled with sloppy camaraderie. He even stopped long enough to take a swig out of some barmaid's bottle while fervently hoping he'd struck Uttridge hard enough to keep him insensible long enough for them to make their escape.

And then they were through the door and heading down the street to where his carriage waited. Will's head popped up over the top. As soon as he spied them he leapt to the ground and hurried to the carriage door, pulling it open in time for Giles to dump Demsforth's body onto the floor.

Freed of fear, Avery's limbs went liquid. She swayed where she stood, her eyes beseeching. Without hesitation, he caught her round the waist, not giving a tinker's damn who was watching, and swung her up into his arms then ducked inside. He settled her beside him, snapping out an order to Will: "Have the driver take us to Lord Demsforth's house. Then home. Tell him to hurry."

"Aye, m'lord!"

He shut the door. In the dim interior with only the guttering light to illuminate them, Avery's eyes looked huge and tragic. With a little sob, she leaned against him. His arms went round her, drawing her tightly into his embrace. She was terrified, trembling violently.

He reached for the thick lap rug on the seat across from them and snapped it open, settling it over her shoulders and tucking her close, hoping to share some of his warmth with her. The carriage jerked into motion.

"Shouldn't we get Neville up off the floor?" she whispered against his chest after a moment.

"No." He was still angry, still wishing someone would pay for the blow Avery had sustained. Demsforth was an excellent candidate.

He wanted to demand to know what perversity of reason had led her into following Demsforth to such a place but now was not the time. His temper was barely under control as it was. He did not want to compound her distress by shouting at her.

And he did not want her to draw away from him.

The feel of her small hand curled so confidingly over his heart was a benediction; her warm, light figure pressed so intimately to his side, an unlooked-for favor; and the gentle buffet of her breath against his neck, a sweet gift.

"But he'll freeze." Her voice was small but insistent.

Wordlessly, he reached beneath the seat and produced another blanket. He tossed it over to Demsforth. She leaned down and adjusted it, regarding Neville with concern. "I wonder that he hasn't come around yet, don't you?"

"No." The bloody idiot. What had Demsworth been thinking? What had *she* been thinking?

She straightened, returning to the warm nest she'd made at his side. His breath quickened with gratitude. "You're not worried about his condition?" she asked.

"No."

"But he was coming around back at . . . at that place and now he's lapsed into unconsciousness again. Don't you find that worrisome?"

She wasted entirely too much concern on this worthless boy. "No."

"Why?"

"Because I *caused* his relapse," he said tightly, keeping his gaze fastened outside the window.

"Oh." She didn't speak again.

As the streets were mostly empty, they did not have long to travel before arriving at the Demsforths' magnificent house. Will appeared at the carriage door, peering in curiously. "M'lord?"

"Fetch the footmen to carry his lordship inside and be sharp about it."

"Right."

A minute later a pair of bemused servants arrived and began maneuvering their young master out of the carriage. Demsforth was coming round again, peering owlishly about as he was being manhandled. "What's happenin'? Where'm I?"

"Thank heaven, you're sentient." Avery sounded vastly relieved.

Demsforth squinted at her. "Who're you?"

Too late, she realized her spectacles were missing. She flushed and looked away.

"Get him to bed," Giles ordered and shut the carriage door, rapping on the ceiling. The carriage sprang forward.

"I'm sorry," Avery said worriedly. "Do you think he realized I was a woman?"

"He'd have to be an even greater fool than I credit him not to."

Once again, she fell silent and he cursed himself for the roughness of his tone. He, too, was still coming to grips with the events of the evening. His body was still tight with the last vestiges of fear. Fear? Terror. Pure, unadulterated terror. He had never been so *bloody* afraid in his life.

Apparently, he reacted rather poorly to terror.

The carriage lurched to a stop and Will came round and opened the door, reaching in to pull out the stepping block.

"Forget that." Without preamble, Giles caught Avery up in his arms and swept her from the carriage. He ignored her gasp. If she thought he gave a bloody damn for her bleeding charade any more, she was sorely mistaken. He needed to feel the reassurance of her heart beating against his chest as he carried her up the steps.

The door swung open before he'd reached the top. Burke's astonished visage appeared, framed in the doorway.

"Out of my way." He carried her into the brightly lit interior. Burke was the only one in attendance. He reached to take Giles's greatcoat, but Giles brushed past him and started up the stairs.

"Shall I send for Mr. Travers, sir?"

Just what he did not want: Travers ringing a peal over his head for his negligence. He knew his culpability in Avery's injuries well enough without Travers reciting them.

"No. Don't disturb him." He left the footman staring after him from the bottom of the stairs. At the top, he went directly to Avery's room. Only then did he lower her feet to the ground.

He tried to step back but she clung to him. Surprised and uncertain, he looked down into her face.

"You're safe now," he reassured her. "No one will hurt you."

"They could have followed us."

"No. And even if they did, no one will take you from me." He'd meant to say "from here" but somehow the other word came out. The truer word.

She regarded him somberly with eyes the color of a moonlit sky, a deep, incandescent blue. She was pale. He bracketed her face between his palms, tipping her head to examine the bruise just becoming visible beneath the blood-matted curls.

"Does it hurt much?"

She shook her head. Her eyelids slipped closed.

"If it does, you must tell me. This is no time for false courage, Avery. I will remind you of the words you spoke to me not a week past—"

She pulled his head down and kissed him, stunning him into immobility. Then she let him go, dropping back to the flat of her feet. But she did not retreat. Not even a step. And her eyes never left his.

They stared at one another.

She was flushed and breathing heavily and he could not think of one bloody thing to say, one word, because— He grabbed her more roughly than he'd intended, snatching her into his embrace and covering her mouth with his.

Caught by surprise, for a second she pushed against his shoulders but then, with a small cry of abandonment, she wrapped her arms around his neck. Her mouth opened under his and his tongue swept deep inside, tasting her, stroking the sleek inner lining of her cheek.

He looped one arm around her waist, lashing her small frame to his. With his free hand, he cupped the back of her head. The cool, silky curls slipped between his fingers, the warmth of the skin beneath penetrating his palm. He plundered her mouth, impelled by a desperate yearning. Still holding her, he broke off their kiss and lifted her into his arms and carried her deeper into the room.

"Kiss me," she said, her lips on his neck, her fingers digging into his shoulders. "Want me."

Want? He *ached* for her. "Dear Lord, Avery," he muttered thickly. "Don't tempt me. I'm just a man."

"I don't want to tempt you," she said. "I want you to make love to me."

How often had he lain near sleep, the image of Avery in his bed, appearing at the last instant of consciousness because he refused that specter entrée in the cold, practical light of day? She was his charge, and if not his ward, still a responsibility passed down from his father.

But she was also a woman. *The* woman. The one who complicated his thoughts and disrupted his reason, who hovered in the background of his imagination all day and disturbed his sleep all night.

"What happened tonight has intensified your emotions. This is just a reaction against your previous fear."

"A reaction . . ." she acknowledged, her mouth trailing a path along his jaw. His eyes closed as he focused all his attention on the amazing sensation. ". . . that led to an understanding. I want to know what that other woman knows."

There were no other women. There was only her. His head swirled, dazed by the feeling of her hands moving down his chest in untutored exploration, his waistcoat's buttons coming undone in their wake. "What other woman?"

Darkness clouded her eyes. "The woman at Sir Isbill's."

She'd seen him and Sophia? Bloody hell. "Avery. That wasn't—"

She covered his mouth with her fingertips, shaking her head. "No. I don't want her here. In any way."

She languished a kiss on the corner of his mouth, causing him to catch his breath as she untied his cravat the rest of the way. She tugged it from around his neck and dropped it to the floor. Her fingers danced down his open shirtfront, sniggled beneath and brushed against his bare skin. Every muscle in his chest leapt into rigid response. "Avery—"

She rose up on her tiptoes and caught his lower lip gently between her teeth. "Shh." Her tongue touched his, sending a jolt of searing desire straight to the core of him.

"Avery," he managed, "what are you doing?"

She looked straight into his eyes. "I'm seducing you."

By God, she was. She *had*. Years ago.

Without another word, he swept her high into his arms and headed for the bed.

Chapter Thirty-Four

Inside a hired carriage, Sophia North made her plans.

She had waited for over an hour after Strand had left Isbill's before following him. She didn't worry about offending Lord Vedder. Oddly, it was Vedder who'd suggested she reconcile with Giles in the first place. When she'd agreed, he'd presented her with a nice ivory and silk fan.

Then he'd gone on to explain that he and some of his friends were very concerned that "poor Giles" was acquiring new, low habits and that if she learned that he'd been haunting diverse places or if he mentioned any names with which she was unfamiliar, Vedder and his friends would be interested and *most* grateful.

Sophia gave scant credence to his innuendos. If Giles had developed new, unsavory habits he wouldn't likely give a tinker's damn what Society thought. Most especially not Vedder. Giles was nothing if not autocratic. Still, if carrying tales about Giles—though God only knew why Vedder and his "friends" cared—garnered her some pretty new trinkets, she was not averse to the arrangement.

But tonight she had other plans. Tonight she meant to secure something for herself. She intended to seek Strand out in his own house and continue the conversation they'd begun in Isbill's library.

Strand had been adamant that he would not "endanger her reputation" by indulging in an impromptu assignation. Sophia was no fool. She realized he was not so much worried about her reputation as his marital status should they be discovered. He would have been surprised to realize that, after the initial titillation provided by the possibility of being found out had faded, she'd shared his concern.

Her visit this evening was twofold, the first being by far the most important.

Strand had promised to set her up with funds, but he hadn't said how or when and she was broke. She needed to know exactly when she could expect his gift and how much it would be, and impress upon him the need for secrecy. If her father discovered their arrangement, he would simply take the money from her for himself. She needed it. Only a princely sum would satisfy the gambling debts she'd incurred.

Until now, she hadn't been too concerned over whether she would be banned from the tables. She was pretty and lively, acting as both an ornament and a distraction to the gentlemen players. The question was when would the money she owed exceed the value she had in that role. She feared it would be soon.

The farther into debt she'd slid, the more she had rued her loss of Strand. He was wealthy enough to have provided for her *and* any pastimes she might have pursued, he was ungodly handsome, and he was a considerate lover—something she'd always sneered at before, thinking that a lover ought to be forceful and audacious, but in the last months had come to realize that forcefulness could hurt and that too often audacity went hand-in-hand with callousness.

'Twas true that Strand had often seemed in some fashion *absent* from their couplings. Not physically absent. He performed very prettily and with a rigorous attention to her satisfaction, but she always had the impression that he held part of himself back and that that part was, well, somehow *saddened* by their bed sport. She wouldn't have minded nearly so much had she thought him disgusted or disdainful. She actually found the idea that he was compelled to take her against his higher nature stimulating. But the idea that their coupling saddened him both irritated and offended her.

Not that she'd let such fine feelings bother her now.

No, now that cool reason had returned to prevail, she had no intention of trying to coerce Giles into marrying her. True, she could prevent any unwanted pregnancies but accidents did happen. Bedlam was filled with them. And she had not been overstating the matter when she'd declared that she would rather die than be forced to breed some horrifying monstrosity.

But she didn't need to marry Strand to reap the rewards of such a union without the liabilities. She could become Strand's mistress.

Discreetly, of course, and in such a fashion that it would not interfere with her plan to marry Lord Nickelbough. Such a solution would satisfy all her needs. She would be the wife of a peer—true, not a marquess, but still a wealthy member of the aristocracy; she would not have to worry about some little horror crawling out of her birthing canal; and she would have the cachet and the gifts that came with being the Marquess of Strand's lover. His last mistress had received a new phaeton and a matched pair of bay geldings as parting gifts.

So, it was with a great deal of confidence that Sophia arrived at Strand's townhouse. She had never been inside before, not even during their short engagement, because Strand was not one, as he'd put it, "to waste time entertaining when I prefer to be entertained." It was just as magnificent as she'd imagined and again a fleeting regret that it would never be hers clouded her good mood. She dismissed it. She had no doubt she would visit it many times in the future.

The lights were mostly extinguished in the windows, which suited her purpose. As she could not very well knock on the front door, she would be obliged to go round back to the servants' entrance. Lady Caroline Lamb had often visited Byron by just such a means, though she'd been dressed as a page.

Sophia pulled the hood of her dark cloak up, covering her bright red hair, and exited the carriage, pausing to instruct the driver to wait an hour. She and Strand would either be done with their business by then or, more likely, she'd be staying the night, in which case it would be up to Strand to make arrangements for her discreet departure.

She slipped through the garden door to the back of the house and hesitated. She had no doubt any servant that answered her knock would let her in; she was well-known to them all and did have some consequence. But perhaps, if the door had been left unlatched, often the case where tradesmen arrived to make deliveries well before the household rose, she could simply enter and search for Strand's bedchambers herself? While the former would certainly be easier, the latter provided a deliciously illicit flavor to the encounter. But which chambers would be his?

She backed up and tipped her head to scan the windows on the second floor. Only two of them were lit. One was bound to be his.

Ah, there! She smiled triumphantly. She would know that tall, broadshouldered physique anywhere. . . . The smile faded from Sophia's lips. For Strand was not alone.

His back was mostly to the window, obscuring Sophia's view of his companion. All she could see were his elegant hands clutching a blanket covering the shoulders of a slight figure. He dipped his head and with an urgency and passion he had never shown Sophia covered his companion's mouth with his own. For a moment it appeared as if Strand's attentions were unwanted, for small hands appeared on his broad shoulders, pushing at him.

He ignored them.

Sophia stared, amazed. When had Strand ever forced himself on a woman? When he'd been with her, he had retreated at the slightest hint of reluctance on her part. He was not a man who took, because, she'd always assumed, he'd never needed to. He'd never known what it was to "need." Well, apparently he knew now.

For a few seconds, the small hands on his shoulders remained defiantly clenched but as Sophia watched, the slender fingers unfurled and one hand curved around Strand's neck as the other melted up and over his shoulders, clinging to him.

She could almost see the tension in Strand's body as he held himself in check but then abruptly, hungrily, he lifted the small figure in his arms and, their mouths still locked in a passionate kiss, turned and vanished from view.

Sophia's mouth dropped open. She hadn't seen Strand's lover's face, only the back of a head and a smallish form covered in a blanket, but she knew those short, tousled auburn locks. They could not have belonged to anyone else but Avery Quinn.

What would Vedder pay for *this* information?

And just that quickly, Sophia's plans for the evening changed.

Chapter Thirty-Five

Jaw in a hard line, eyes glittering like shards of broken glass, Giles carried Avery to the bed and lowered her gently in its center. She should be nervous. At least a bit apprehensive. She was a virgin and she'd heard enough ribald tales from the maids and servants to understand that this first encounter did not always go well.

But she wasn't nervous at all.

He worked expertly to divest her of the hated coat and shirt, tug her shoes off, and strip her trousers from her legs. Only the hideous, padded corset gave him pause—and so gave her pause.

She turned her head, afraid of what she might see on his face. He mustn't laugh. Not now.

Her earlier terror had awakened in her a certainty of what she wanted, *who* she wanted. Who she'd always wanted. Giles.

And *he* wanted *her*. She recognized the banked fire in his eyes, felt the hunger in his kiss, and with that had come a sublime new confidence, not in her intellect, but in her desirability. But he could destroy that confidence just as easily as he'd engendered it. He could shatter it with a flippant remark, a caustic grimace.

She glanced around. He did not appear to have noticed the absurdity of the garment but, with obvious frustration, was studying the hooks and eyes, the buttons and strings holding it together. With an unintelligible mutter, he gripped the top edge of the padded atrocity in both hands and, with a jerk, rent it in two. Then he straightened and, with infinite care, turned back the edges of the ripped garment as though he were unfurling a rose, exposing her body.

"My heaven." His voice was soft, reverent, his gaze smoldering. And then, before she had a chance to feel shy at his heated perusal, he was tearing at his own clothes, yanking off his boots before wrenching his coat and trousers from his person, peeling off his shirt until he finally stood naked.

He was big, she realized, but so perfectly proportioned that his size was not always evident. But then, to carry Neville so easily, he would have had to be strong. And he looked very strong indeed. His shoulders were broad, capped by heavy muscle, and his chest was likewise deep and broad, tapering to hard flanks and narrow hips. His limbs were long and sleekly muscled beneath clear, golden skin. Her gaze flickered below a well-defined, ridged belly to where his member jutted from a thicket of dark hair.

Oh, my.

She realized she was staring and blushed. He didn't even realize. His own gaze was riveted on her body, traveling over it with breathtaking deliberation. His chest rose and fell in deep rhythm, his nostrils flaring slightly as though scenting her.

He put a knee on the bed beside her hip and set his hands flat on either side of her head. With an easy, elegant grace he shifted his body over hers and braced himself over her.

The position cast his face in shadows, the hearth light glinting off his burnished curls and limning the powerful slip and play of his shoulders with golden light. Heat seemed to flow off of him like a mist, warming the space between them. His staff bobbed slightly in the air above her belly like a cautioning finger.

"My heaven," he whispered again and this time the words had taken on a different meaning altogether.

She looked down. Freed from their cotton cocoon, her breasts rose round and ample above her meager ribcage. "Now you see why binding would never have worked. They are out of proportion to the rest of me."

He brushed his fingertip along the outer swell of one breast. "Your breasts are glorious."

He bent his head. With exquisite languor, he licked the areola around her nipple. She jerked in response, as though touched by a firebrand, her back arching. His arm slipped beneath her waist and pulled her higher as he took her nipple into his mouth. She gasped at the erotic sensation as he suckled her, slowly, unhurriedly. She clutched at his shoulders, unprepared for a sense of escalating need that uncoiled like a whip inside of her.

"Relax, my love," he whispered. "We've just begun."

My love. Her eyelids fluttered shut.

His free hand slid lower, moving to her buttocks. "You are so soft. So beautiful. My God, but you are exquisite," he murmured as his hand slipped around and between them to cup the mound of curls.

With infinite gentleness, he parted her inner flesh. It was beyond intimate, too raw, a sensory excess. She tried to cross her legs. "Let me. Please." He sounded so pleading, so reverent. She forced herself to relax.

His finger slipped inside and she gasped. "You're wet, beautifully wet." He spoke as if she'd given him some gift. He did not remove his finger, but kept it inside her, unmoving, as he lowered his head and tenderly kissed her mouth, her chin, the side of her neck, her collar bone, her shoulders, her breasts.

It both stimulated and relaxed, incited and turned her body to warm wax. And then he moved his finger, sliding it deeper inside, stretching her. She shifted and the feeling of him inside made her nerves coil in anticipation, heat spread throughout her. She arched into his touch and he moved it deeper, suddenly going quite still.

"Virgin," he said in an odd, desperate sort of voice.

She barely heard him. The nearly painful physical anticipation he'd started was building within her. Her arms wrapped tight around his flanks, a bulwark against the unbearable excitement buffeting her. Her hips pitched instinctively into his touch.

"Please," she heard herself murmur. . . . A whisper? A command? A plea?

Her words seemed to release whatever had held him immobile. He moved his hands to her hips and rolled her on top of him, so that she sat

Connie Brockway

with her thighs spread wide astride his lap. His erection pulsed against her inner thigh. He lightly clasped her shoulders, his gaze hunting her face.

"You're sure?"

She stared down into his eyes. He looked intent, desperate, and . . . anxious.

Good God. Giles Dalton, anxious over the deflowering of a game-keeper's daughter. The servant's daughter. At the unfortunate thought, her brows drew together in a fierce scowl.

"Avery?" He reached up, gently stroking her face. "You can stop. At any time. We don't—"

She regarded him in both consternation and horror. He must not think this was an aberration, that the morning would find her bemoaning the night's events. She had to be clear on that. No matter how much her body ached for a release she somehow knew only he could provide, he must know that this was not the whim of some overwrought girl. She had made this decision as a woman.

But she could not think of the words that could convince him. Her mind was befogged, befuddled by these new sensations, his ravishing touch.

All she could do was answer him in kind. Her hand slipped between them and she wrapped her fingers around his male member. He was hard and heated, a velvety smooth sheath sliding over a thick, solid rod. It was a revelation, a piece of beautiful knowledge: This part of a man's body could be both silken and adamantine. This part of Giles's body.

His teeth flashed in a grimace of agonized pleasure. She might not have experience, but her instincts were sound.

He muttered what could have been a prayer or a curse and she shifted slightly to her knees, bringing the head of his staff to where his fingers had recently played. He was right. She was wet and the rounded head eased effortlessly within.

And stopped.

Her eyes widened. Something was wrong. She knew his entire staff was supposed to penetrate her body, but there was no room.

Abruptly he clasped her hips, keeping her still. His eyes had shut tight and his jaw bulged with tension. "Don't move," he breathed.

He shifted his hips sideways. Whatever he did, it caused that part of him still exposed to drag against the seat of her sexual sensation. Intense pleasure coiled at the place he touched. Another small movement and he had somehow seated himself a little deeper inside. He reached between them and pressed his thumb on a tightening nerve of pure sensation. It was too much. She melted forward.

"*Don't. Move.*"

How could she not when each tiny motion elicited such extravagant reward? Avery spread her hands flat against his chest, digging her fingers deep into his pectoral muscles. A quake ran though him. She wriggled a little, seating him deeper still.

Without warning, he sat up. The sudden movement spread her legs wide and he surged deep within her, up to the very root. She let out a cry, as much in surprise as pain. And there was pain, a sharp pain, hot and deep, but, like a cut, once done, it faded quickly, leaving only an echo behind.

"I'm sorry," he whispered, touching his forehead to hers. He was breathing hard. A thin mist of sweat covered his torso. "There'll be pleasure, too. I swear it."

He pivoted, turning her beneath him while they were still joined. He caught one of her hands in his, holding it close to her face. Watching her intently, he slowly withdrew. She tensed involuntarily, unconvinced that this could be anything as wondrous as what the preliminary fondling and kissing had promised. He felt alien and large. His body overwhelmed hers.

"Trust me," he whispered.

And she did. She did.

She kept her gaze locked with his as he moved, slowly at first, allowing her to get accustomed to him, and then more deliberately. His smoke gray eyes never left her face, watching each reaction as he carefully gauged his rhythm, the depth of his penetration, even as a new sheen of sweat broke over his shoulders and chest and dampened his face.

It built slowly, a feather stroking a nerve end, over and over until the feather was not enough. She stared, amazed, and he smiled, dropping a moist, hungry kiss against her mouth before sliding his hands beneath her buttocks to tilt her up and closer.

Her breathing grew ragged, her body tense in a torment of anticipation. Each thrust grew deeper, harder, and she welcomed it. Unbearable pleasure built inside her, poising her between pain and ecstasy, each stroke driving her nearer to some edge she must know, she must achieve.

"Yes! More! There! Please, God!" she heard herself cry.

He kept moving, strongly, deeply in a primal rhythm, his face set and intent, his gaze never straying from her face. She reveled in his possession, in every powerful movement of his body. She arched her back, stretched on a precipice.

"Oh . . . there. Just . . . just . . . please . . . there. There!"

The climax took her without warning. Pleasure spiked and exploded, racing through her body, filling every quivering nerve ending with repletion. She cried out, caught in ever expanding waves of pure satisfaction, half-sobbing with laughter and crying out with the beauty of it. She wrapped her arms around him, reveling in the power of him, the masculinity, the heat and potency.

"Avery," she heard him say in a rough, low voice as his big body tensed above her. "Avery." His eyes squeezed shut and his lips parted in an agony of sensation. For a long moment, shudders racked his body. Then, slowly, he relaxed. The tension seeped from him and he fell to her side, carrying her with him. His harsh breath pounded in her ears.

An afterglow seeped through her, turning her limbs liquid and warm. She scooted higher and laid her head on his chest. His arms came round her, holding her. His heartbeat deepened and slowed beneath her ear, a counterpoint to the heavy rise and fall of his chest. She turned her face into his chest.

"I wanted it to be pleasurable for you," she heard him say. "I tried to make it last longer, to give you another. But I was . . . you are . . . I could not . . ."

She had never been more aware of her own femininity, felt more keenly her power as a woman. It made her reckless. It made her joyously confident. "What's this?" she teased. "The consummate rake at a loss for words?"

She could feel his breath catch in surprise. She smiled against his chest. Without allowing herself to pause and consider, she flicked the tip of her tongue against his nipple. His arms clenched reflexively around her. He inhaled sharply.

"But perhaps that is the key to your success," she said, dancing her fingertips over his pectoral. Beneath the smooth skin, the thick muscle hardened. "Perhaps feigning inarticulateness serves to disarm unsuspecting ladies of the ton."

Her grabbed her wandering hand and raised it to his lips, pressing a heated kiss in the center of her palm. It was her turn to inhale sharply.

"I might suggest that I do not need to *feign* anything to win a lady's approval, but would not like you to think me conceited." He spoke in a lazily seductive tone, his momentary unease vanished.

"I already do," she said.

"I might also suggest that pretty speeches, or a disarming lack of them, are not foremost amongst those things that recommend a gentleman to a lady's bed."

Pressed against her belly, she felt his member growing hard again.

"Oh?" she asked breathlessly. "And what might those things be?"

With a single easy movement, he flipped her beneath him. "Allow me to demonstrate."

Chapter Thirty-Six

A scant hour before daybreak Avery fell asleep. Giles brushed the short curls from her temple, his fingers lingering on her warm, satiny skin. He pulled the blanket up around her shoulders. The room was cold and he had not stoked the fire all night, having been riveted by the far more devastating fire that burned between them.

What was he to do now? How could he take care of her when he did not know what she wanted? Twice during the long, passion-filled night he'd tried to bring up the future and how the night had changed it. Both times she'd shaken her head. Both times she'd whispered, "This night is mine. I don't care about the others," then wrapped her arms or legs or both around him and pulled his head down to kiss him, banishing every consideration other than the need to make love to her again.

But now the future loomed grim and uncertain. He *did* care about the other nights. *All* the other nights. Profoundly. But he did not know what to do about them.

Part of him wanted to publicly admit to the masquerade, allowing him to just as publicly claim her. But doing so would force her to abdicate her dreams, snatch triumph from her hands, and forfeit everything she had worked so hard to achieve. He could not do that to her. He would do everything in his power to see that she found the acclaim she wanted and deserved.

Add to which, if he did expose the hoax, then what?

He had no illusions. Society *might* forgive a single infraction against its unwritten laws, either the hoax or Avery's lack of antecedents if she agreed to marry him, but he doubted they would forgive compounding them. Was a life with him adequate compensation for being socially ostracized? And even if she were willing to take that risk, would she once she realized the stigma that would attach to their children? Would the sins of the father be visited on them?

His father had been correct in that Society would not easily, or willingly, accept someone without the proper lineage. It didn't matter what side of the blanket one was begot on, as long as at least one of the partners lying on it had blue blood. Avery hadn't a drop of aristocratic blood in her veins. She was as common as a lark. And as rare as a black swan, as flowers made of air, as desert rain.

His lips tightened into a grim line of determination. No, there would be no easy answers, but, by God, between them they *would* find one.

He had always thought he was attracted to women who belonged to other men because the spice of their unavailability piqued his appetite. It was safe to fall in love with someone who would never love you back. There was no danger of failing to meet her expectations.

But now he wondered if there might not have been another reason: He was already in love.

Every woman he'd considered himself capable of loving had in some respect walked outside of Society's conventions. Cat Montrose had not attracted his attention until she had flouted what Society thought a young woman should do. Anne Wilder's initial attraction lay in her outsider status.

But those ladies were simply copies made from a template of which Avery Quinn was the original. Even down to the red hair.

He stared down at her. The revelation did not surprise him. Why should it? At some level he'd known. In one way or the other, he had always loved her. The last few weeks had enriched that emotion with passion and ardor, humor and respect. But what now?

He raked his hair back from his face. Here and now was not the place to try and think rationally. And he owed it to her to consider the future with his intellect as well as his heart. He must do this right; he'd already done so much wrong.

She stirred and he eased himself from the bed, afraid that she needed only to wake and hold out her arms and no matter what best served her, he would not be able to let her go. He mustn't stay any longer. Until he knew what "right" was he could not risk having her masquerade discovered.

He pulled on his trousers and his shirt, collected his coat and boots and, unable to resist, feathered a kiss against her temple before leaving.

It was dark in the hallway outside, still early enough that the staff had yet to begin their daily duties. He made it back to his room, rumpled his bed to make it look slept in, and tossed his clothing on the chair. Then he put on fresh clothing, stirred the embers in the hearth, sat down in front of it, and waited for the day to begin.

He'd left her only moments ago and already he was anxious to see Avery again. He grabbed the poker, stabbed at the fire, then flopped back down. What if she regretted the night? No. Impossible. He was a connoisseur of physical pleasure and on that basis alone he knew she'd been satisfied. But where the heart was concerned . . . ? He might as well admit it: He was as green as any boy.

Had he adequately shown her how much she meant to him? How blessed he felt that she'd shared the ultimate act with him? Had he told her? He couldn't remember. He'd spoken, surely, in murmurs and sighs and whispered endearments. But words had seemed incidental when he could speak so much more eloquently with hands and lips and the rest of his body.

What if she hadn't felt that same way?

He bolted to his feet and paced the room, his thoughts swinging from confidence to despair. He had never been so utterly involved in the act of making love. *Making love,* not fornication. She must have realized this. But how would she? Had he been negligent?

He stared out at the darkness, pressing his fist high on a pane of frosted glass. When would she wake up? When could he begin to make right everything he might have inadvertently done wrong?

He banged his fist against the glass, making it shake. He was acting like a besotted schoolboy. He grinned. He may as well be one. He frowned. She would despise a juvenile display. He moaned and turned from the window, stalking the periphery of the room until he finally flung himself back down into his chair.

The next hour dragged. Finally he estimated it to be a reasonable hour to make an appearance and quit the room, nodding to the little maid carrying a stack of linens outside his door. He was surprised to find Burke waiting outside the dining room. The footman leapt to his feet and opened the door for Giles to pass and then followed him.

Giles took his seat, glanced at the door, and willed Avery to appear. Though he imagined she would not like their first meeting to take place under the servants' watchful eyes. She would probably be exhausted. In all likelihood she would not appear until the afternoon. The thought was unutterably depressing.

"This came for you last night, m'lord," Burke said, placing an envelope on the table.

Giles picked it up and flicked it open. He withdrew a piece of cheap, folded paper, opened it, and read.

Some new bit of information regarding that person wot you have been asking after has come to my attention. I will be wanting more than the usual blunt as it is worth it and will require fifty pounds to tell you what I know. Come straight off to the Fox and Whistle off Maiden Court tomorrow morning and I will be waiting.

It was unsigned.

Thoughtfully, Giles folded the letter and returned it to its envelope. Alfie Bees would not have written demanding a specific sum if he didn't know his information was worth it. He and Bees had far too much respect, if no liking, for one another to do otherwise. If Giles left at once he could be back before Avery appeared for breakfast. Even if it proved fruitless at least it would occupy his time until then.

He had Burke fetch him the battered old greatcoat and soft hat. He didn't bother changing the rest of his clothing. The Fox and Whistle was in a part of town that still had some pretense to respectability. Besides, those who would cut his throat for the price of his boots were nocturnal creatures.

After giving explicit instructions that under no circumstances was Mr. Quinn to be bothered, he was about to head out when he heard a knock on the front door. He frowned. It was not yet seven in the morning. Only tradespeople were abroad so early and they would have come round to the servants' entrance. He waited, curious.

A moment later Burke appeared. "M'lord, Sir Jameson is here." Uneasiness darkened Burke's bright blue eyes. "He says you will want to see him."

Surprised, Giles bid Burke to show Jameson into the library, then shed his outer garment and went to meet his unexpected guest. He had always assumed he would discover Jameson was behind the Sewards' disappearance. Jameson must have found out he was searching for Jack and had come to warn him off.

Sir Jameson would be disappointed.

Giles had no intention of stopping until he knew what had happened to his friends. And should he discover Jameson was behind their deaths he would not rest until the old man had been brought to justice.

He did not care what politicians Jameson held in his pocket or how long it took. If he had done any harm to the pair, eventually Giles would find out and Jameson would pay.

Giles found the old man standing in front of his desk. At once, Giles was struck by the changes in him. Though he still held himself with rigid exactitude, a slight tremor shook his rail-thin frame. Where his head had once reminded Giles of Caesar's profile struck on an ancient coin, gaunt, imperious, and disdainful, now he looked skeletal, the sharp bones pressing from underneath a thin sheath of graying flesh. And his clothing, always so perfect, was slightly disarranged and imprecise.

For all that, Jameson seemed pleased, almost exultant. This itself was noteworthy. Sir Jameson never displayed emotion. Giles had always assumed he had none. He'd once heard Sir Jameson order a man killed in the same monotone that he'd ordered a beef pie from a street vendor.

"Strand," Sir Jameson said. "So good of you to see me. And so early. I'm pleased to find you awake, especially after such an . . . eventful night. Or so I have heard."

Giles was startled. How had Jameson found out about Demsforth and Avery's trip to Covent Garden or his own involvement? He did not ask the question aloud, however. If Jameson thought to unnerve Giles, again, he was doomed to disappointment. Giles had a decade of his own experience to call upon, and he rather thought that in a contest of cold-bloodedness, he might match Jameson.

"What brings you here so early, Sir Jameson?"

Jameson's eyes glittered from behind their heavy, hooded lids. "Let us not play games, Strand. I have come here for information. Information you shall give me in return for my silence."

Giles's thoughts raced as he struggled to mask his confusion. Jameson wanted information he thought he had. About what? And what did Jameson think he knew that would allow him to extort this unknown information? To cover his puzzlement, Giles strolled casually to the opposite side of his desk and sat down.

"Pray. Where are my manners?" He lifted the bell that would call a maid. "Can I offer you something to drink? Coffee? Have you had breakfast?"

"I don't want any damn coffee!" The words exploded from Jameson's lips. Calmly, Giles replaced the bell. Stranger and stranger.

"At least have a seat, Sir Jameson."

As if realizing how oddly he was acting, Jameson collected himself. He grimaced, a parody of his former enigmatic smile, and sat down, shot his cuffs, and draped his hands atop his cane's silver head.

"Now then, what do you want to know?" Giles asked politely.

Jameson laughed, the sound so startling that Giles's brows flew up. "Be damned if you don't remind me of my younger self, Strand."

Once more, Jameson had shocked Giles, but in a far more visceral manner than before. Could it be true? Was he like Jameson, or like Jameson had once been? If so, Lord spare him.

"You're a cool one. Ice wouldn't melt on that brow. Nor would it on mine. But the time for games is past." His smile died. He leaned forward, fixing Giles with a rabid glare. "I want to know where Jack Seward is."

Somehow, Giles kept from gaping. It was the last thing he'd expected to hear. *It meant Jameson was not responsible for the Sewards' disappearance.*

Just as surprising, Jameson apparently thought that Giles knew something about their fate. Giles cast about, trying to decide what to do with this information, how to best leverage it for his own gain. . . . *No.*

Not a second earlier Giles had asked God to spare him the fate of becoming like Jameson and here he was, already trying to figure out the various ways he might use the knowledge he'd just acquired to his advantage. He would not become Jameson. He meant to be the better man. The man Avery assumed him to be.

"I don't know."

Jameson stiffened. His eyes narrowed. "I was afraid you'd say that. Or rather, not afraid so much as resigned."

"I don't know where Jack and Anne are." Giles folded his hands together on top of the desk.

"Anne?" Befuddlement flickered across Jameson's face then cleared. "Oh. The woman. I don't care what happens to her. I only want Jack. We have unfinished business, he and I. Business I will see come to an end, by God." His voice shook slightly.

"Sir Jameson, even if I did know where Jack was, I would not tell you. But the fact is that I do not," Giles repeated.

Jameson stood up and pointed the end of his cane at Giles. "Lord Strand. If you do not tell me where Jack is by evening tomorrow, I will release to the ton a most titillating scandal, that being that the boy the Marquess of Strand has been introducing around as his protégé and lobbying to have made a member of one of London's most august societies is, in fact, his lover. His catamite."

Giles froze. The conversation had suddenly taken a turn that would require immediate action. A hundred threads for a thousand plans streamed through his imagination at breakneck speed while he contrived to keep his countenance from revealing his thoughts.

Jameson took his silence for shock. He sneered.

"And when that happens you may as well be dead. You will never be received anywhere again." He chuckled. "And we all know how very much you love your consequence, Lord Strand."

Giles had heard those words before, from his father. And just as they had been then, they were evidence of how little the speaker knew him. But where those words had hurt before, now they bought him precious time. Time to put into action an idea forming as he watched Jameson gloat.

"So then?" Jameson demanded. "What's it to be?"

Giles kept his gaze fixed on his clenched fists, allowing Jameson to think panic made his knuckles go white, a plan coalescing in his mind. He must speak to Travers at once, before he left to meet Bees.

As much as he wanted to, he could not delay his visit there. To do so might put Jack and Anne in danger. If Bees had information about their whereabouts, he would not hesitate to sell it twice, the second time to Jameson. Giles had to pick up their trail before Jameson knew there were breadcrumbs leading to it.

But the plan he'd just concocted could still be put into play during his absence. Words could begin to be whispered in the right ears. He would have to put Burke's talents and connections to use. It would be risky, but then they already stood on the precipice of disaster.

"Tell me now and save yourself a trip," Jameson said softly.

"You're mistaken in your assumptions about me."

Jameson chuckled.

"For the last time, I don't know where Jack is."

Jameson's eyes went flat and cold. He spun on his heels and yanked open the door. He glared at Giles over his shoulder. "You have until tomorrow night to rethink your position."

Chapter Thirty-Seven

"Here I am, Alf. What do you have for me?"

Alfie Bees continued daintily peeling a hard-boiled egg. A milky shaft of light fell over the table where he sat, revealing the dissipation marring his face.

Alf's ever-present retainers occupied a table a short distance away, their beefy paws wrapped around tankards of small beer. They nodded to Giles and glanced incuriously at Will, who Giles had bid follow him into the tavern.

The boy still didn't have an adequately warm pair of boots and still he'd insisted on "attending to his duties" as apprentice coachman when Giles had sent for the carriage. Walking would have taken too long. Jameson was hunting Seward with murder in his eye. Giles meant to destroy any trail Bees might have unearthed.

Alf looked him over with bleary eyes. "Got the blunt?"

"Of course."

Alf grinned. "Right, you do. Okay then." He wiped his fingertips on his shirt and reached into his coat pocket, withdrawing a filmy piece of cloth. He wafted it gently in the air.

Giles reached for it but Alf shook his head and grinned, setting his forefinger alongside his nose. Wordlessly, Giles withdrew a small purse from inside his coat and tossed it to Alf. He snatched it out of the air and handed the handkerchief to Giles. It was blush pink, made of the finest linen, and edged in Belgian lace. A monogram delicately picked out in white silk spelled the letters AW. Anne Wilder?

"Where did you come by this?"

But Alf was not going to be denied the pleasure of explaining his cleverness.

"I put out the word that it was worth a quid to anyone finds anyt'ing havin' to do wid Colonel Seward or his lady. I had no luck wid that. Then, yesterday I was looking over some bits o' this and that what come into my purview." He looked up at Giles and grinned. He'd undoubtedly been receiving stolen items from his league of pickpockets. "And I sees this bit of pretty and it suddenly comes to me that the captain's lady's name were Anne Wilder afore she married him."

"Who brought it in?"

"Ragman," Alf said and they both knew he was lying.

"And where did he acquire it?"

"Some lad what pinched it off a lady on Hawke's Wharf. She was stepping down into one o' the sloops that carries folks to the passenger ships anchored in deep water. Easy mark."

"Where can I find this boy?" Strand asked. Natty lads tended not to be found when they were sought. The specter of the workhouse or, worse, of deportation, sent them fleeing.

"Don't suppose you can." Alf shrugged. "But I might be able to locate him. Fer another pony."

Strand nodded. "How soon can you arrange a meeting?"

Alf scowled. "I'm not his bleedin' mum. I dunno where any of the lads sleep or where they work. They shows up once a week and we have a bit of business." Apparently Alf had decided to dispense with the imaginary ragman. "Which reminds me," he glanced past Giles towards where Will waited, "yer da's been lookin' fer you, lad."

"How sad that he won't find him," Giles replied, holding Alfie's eye long enough for the slighter man to look away.

"'Course not."

"What day do the boys meet up with you?"

"Tuesdays."

"If you can find him before then I'll pay you fifty pounds."

Alf's brows rose. "Two ponies? I'll see what I can do."

Avery felt Giles's absence before she'd even fully awoken. The large, warm body that had curled around hers all night was gone. She glanced at the clock. It was going on ten o'clock and she was alone.

Her heart kicked into a gallop. What was he thinking this morning? Did he regret making love? *Making love.* Did he think of it that way? Or was this what a Corinthian did? Was she simply one of his lovers? Like that woman she'd seen him with last night. Had he been planning to spend the evening in *her* bed and then, when he'd been obliged to save Avery, and she'd thrown herself at him, had he simply accepted her as substitute?

No. No, no, no.

There had been tenderness as well as passion in their union, a whole-hearted and happy commitment to giving her pleasure. He'd whispered how beautiful she was, how desirable, how she made his body sing and all rational thoughts evaporate. But might not that simply be the way of an unselfish lover? Had he said anything about his heart?

She swung her legs over the side of the bed, snatched up his banyan, and jerked it on. She should have been asking herself these questions before she ripped his clothes off.

But her earlier terror had been so concentrated and prolonged and then when he'd arrived and taken her out of that place her relief had been just as intense, just as visceral. There had been no *thought*. There had been no plan. There had been no past or future. There had only been the present, overwhelming relief and the just-learned lesson that tomorrow might not come so she best pursue what she wanted today. And she'd wanted Giles.

She still wanted him.

But she didn't know what he wanted from her.

In many ways Giles was a cipher, a collection of discordant parts: this cold, gorgeous house without a soul; his reputation as a Pink of the Ton; his drawling sneer, careless mockery, and dandified pretentions. But then there were his strange nocturnal ramblings dressed like a cit and his prowess with his fists. His kindness to an orphan and his old dog. His honorable determination to abide by their deal. It did not make sense.

She needed to know more.

She stood, looking around for the hated corset, and only then noticed that the door between her bedchamber and the smaller room next to it was ajar. Light spilled on the carpet in a thin wedge. It had always been kept locked before. Giles must have opened it. But why?

"Mr. Travers?"

Travers looked up from the book he'd been reading and saw Avery in the doorway. For once, she was not wearing the horrible padded corset. Nor the glasses. Instead, she wore Lord Strand's dressing gown.

"Ah, Avery. You are awake. Good."

"What happened to him, Mr. Travers? To make him like this?"

He sighed. So it was like that, was it? He was supposed to appraise Avery of Lord Strand's plan, but one look at her drawn and anxious face and he realized it would have to wait. He'd known, of course. Only a fool wouldn't see what was between the two of them. And he didn't mean just since coming to London, either.

He'd been sitting beside the fire, a cup of hot chocolate in hand, his feet toasting on the hearth. As per Lord Strand's instructions, he'd told the staff that Mr. Quinn was feeling very poorly, very poorly indeed, and they were to vacate the floor, lest their cleaning disturb him. He was then to go to the room next to Avery's and make it look as if someone had spent the night there, occasionally moving about so that anyone passing in the hall would hear him. Once Avery woke he was to make sure she didn't leave her room until Strand returned.

Avery slipped into the room and took a seat across from him. "What happened to Strand? Why does he act like two different people? Here he's Lord Strand, a dandy and a rake. But at Killylea he's . . . not. Sometimes, when there is no one else around, he is still the man I know from Killylea. Why? Please."

Travers considered. This was not his tale to tell. But one look into her eyes and he realized it was her tale to hear. Still, it was not an easy story. He sighed.

"France had taken over the world, or so it seemed," he began. "Young Lord Giles was eighteen and he begged his father to buy him a commission in some regiment that would see action. He wanted to fight for his country alongside his schoolmates.

"The old marquess refused. He'd already lost Louis and Giles was the last of his line. He would not risk the Dalton name dying on a foreign battlefield and he *was* convinced that if Giles went to war he would die. He had little faith in Giles's judgment or his character. In fact, he thought Giles was mostly enamored of an officer's uniform so he offered to buy him a commission in a regiment that never strayed off English soil, a stylish regiment, whose raison d'être was to protect fashion's sensibilities and populate Society's dance floors with dandified officers." He shook his head lightly.

"Why would he think that?" Avery asked, astonished, and Travers liked her for that, for her surprise that anyone who knew him could think so poorly of Giles.

"It's complicated. I'm not sure how to explain."

"Try."

"Louis's mother died in childbirth and Louis himself was sickly from birth. It was the reason the marquess remarried so quickly. He knew Louis would never live to inherit and he needed an heir. The new marchioness was a convent-raised girl blessed with a fine intellect and strength of character. She was also, if I might say, the most beautiful woman I'd ever seen. And she loved Louis as if he were her own."

"She sounds wonderful," Avery said, blushing lightly. She was comparing herself to this paragon, Travers surmised, and believed she fell short. Good heavens, did she really not understand her own beauty?

"At first, it seemed like the marriage would be a success. The marquess showered his new bride with gifts and in short order she produced two children, just as bonny as herself. But for all that the marquess always loved Louis best.

"He didn't see Louis as bizarrely small, with a twisted back and stunted limbs. He only saw his beloved son. The new marchioness and Giles and Julia loved him, too. Deeply and sincerely."

"They were happy," Avery affirmed softly.

Travers shook his head. "The marriage soon faltered. The marquess either could not or would not give his wife the one thing she craved: companionship. The marquess did not understand her dissatisfaction. After all, he lavished her with wealth, consequence, money, and freedom." He picked up the cup of hot chocolate and stared into it, his thoughts sifting through the tangled memories of the past.

"When Louis was twelve, he became bedridden. The family did whatever they could to comfort him. The marchioness would sit by his bedside for hours reading to him, and Julia—well, Julia had always had a religious bent. She spent hours in the chapel praying. The marquess retreated to his studies. . . ." Travers frowned thoughtfully.

"And what did Giles do?"

"He laughed." He shot her a quick, apologetic look. "Oh, not at Louis. *For* Louis. For his mother. For Julia. Even for the marquess."

Avery looked at him askance.

"Everyone was so grim, you see. The marchioness's smiles faded as soon she quit the sickroom and Julia could be heard weeping at her prayers. Their grief exhausted poor Louis. In spite of the fact that he was dying, he always seemed to be the one comforting those who would survive. Except for Giles.

"Giles was his only respite. *Their* only respite. He was so alive. So hale and beautiful and audacious. He made Louis laugh at the tales of his misadventures and his mother smile over his ridiculously overwrought compliments. Even Julia tittered at his blustering obliviousness and cocksure conceit. He never seemed to take anything seriously and somehow that allowed the others to be a little less serious, too.

"It was all an act, of course." He looked at her sadly. "One he kept up even after Louis died. He'd learned the value of being easy company, you see. Soon after, the marchioness, who had only stayed for Louis's sake, left. She wanted to take both her children with her but the marquess refused and Giles, who by this time was away at boarding school, begged to stay near Killylea. He had always loved the place and took most seriously the knowledge that he would someday be heir to it. In the end, the marchioness acquiesced and left with Julia."

He glanced up and saw the indignation in her face. "The old marquess was not a bad man, Avery, just a very stupid one. He was more comfortable with facts than the subtleties of human nature. He never did see beyond the persona Giles had adopted to the man beneath."

"But how could he not know his own son?" she cried.

"The old marquess never realized that the role Giles had adopted had been one of the few things that provided respite during the long years of Louis's decline. He only saw a gorgeous, cocky boy apparently insensitive to the sadness around him. He considered him a popinjay, nothing else."

"But if he could see past Louis's exterior, why could he not do the same for Giles?" Avery asked, her expression tense with outrage.

Travers regarded her unhappily. "I don't know. Perhaps the effort was too much. Perhaps he didn't have it in him to love another son."

"But Giles was just a boy!"

"You can't give what you don't have, Avery." He looked down at his cup of hot chocolate. It had gone cold. "You knew what the marquess was like."

"Yes. I knew what the marquess was like," she admitted. "But nothing you've said explains"—Avery struggled to find the word, gave up, and swept her hand across the room in an encompassing gesture—"this."

Travers nodded. "Until their argument about the commission, I don't think Giles really understood in how little esteem the marquess held him. The incident left him badly humiliated, and deeply wounded. And angry. Pray remember he was only a lad and do not think too harshly of him."

"Harshly? For what reason?"

He met her eye. "Giles went to London and proceeded to live up to all of his father's worst expectations. He gambled deeply and drank deeper still. He spent extravagantly, on tailors and horses and boot makers, on anything that took his fancy. Or anyone." His gaze skittered away from hers. "He took up with the most raffish set and soon became their leader. He mocked and drawled and dueled. Everything he did, he did to excess. By the time he was twenty-one, he was well on his way to becoming a libertine and a wastrel."

He heard her breath catch.

"But then something happened. I'm not sure why, but even though he remained one of the ton's most celebrated rakes, there was a change in him. He seemed more cynical." He shook his head, trying to find some way to explain. "At the same time more . . . vulnerable. He would come home to Killylea more often after that, looking burnt from within. He tried to make peace with his father."

"That makes no sense," she said, frowning.

He shrugged. "You asked what happened to him. I've told you what I know. You must speak to him to find out anything more."

Someone knocked on the hall door and he called out, "Enter."

"Travers!" Avery whispered. "I am not in my costume!"

"It's all right," he said as the door swung open on a breathless Burke, still in greatcoat and hat, carrying an armload of ladies' gowns. Travers stood aside and the young footman strode briskly to the bed and heaved the dresses atop it. He spied Avery and straightened, his gaze sweeping over the curves revealed by the thin banyan with obvious masculine appreciation.

She colored brightly.

"Ah, Miss Quinn, I presume?" Burke bowed neatly at the waist but when he looked up his eyes twinkled. "And right pleased I am to make your acquaintance, miss. I was beginning to wonder about my, er, masculinity, seeing how your smile always made my—"

"That is enough, Burke," Travers hastily interjected.

"I don't understand," Avery said, her gaze flying between Burke, the dresses on the bed, and Travers. "What is going on here? Where's Strand?"

"Here I am, my dear," a deep voice said. Strand closed the door behind him. "As far as what is going on, it's quite simple really. You are going to die."

Chapter Thirty-Eight

Mr. Avery Quinn was not long for the world.

The sad news came as no surprise to Lord Strand's servants. Burke had witnessed his lordship carrying the young man into the house the night before, blood flowing freely from a wound on his head. A doctor had been called in, of course. Mr. Travers had let him in in the wee hours of the morning and later reported the dismal findings.

Surprisingly it was not the head injury that the doctor anticipated putting an end to Mr. Quinn's short life, but the sudden appearance of a congenital . . . *something*. The details were a bit vague given the quack's use of a long, Latin-sounding phrase. Not that it mattered, it generally being acknowledged that dead is dead no matter what the cause.

The news quickly made the round of London's best drawing rooms, coffee houses, salons, and gentlemen's clubs where it was tacitly agreed that the entire affair must be tedious indeed for poor old Strand, who didn't even know the lad that well. Only in the hushed meeting room of the Royal Astrological Society were heads bowed and prayers offered up for the sake of what everyone who'd read the boy's monograph considered a shining intellect in the world of astronomical research.

Making the situation doubly sad, but nonetheless blessedly serendipitous, earlier the very same night that Mr. Quinn had met with mayhem, his sister, Ava, had arrived to surprise her only sibling with a visit. Burke, who always took evening duty, had received her. Apparently the young lady had instructed him not to bother waking the other servants, so he'd shown her to the room alongside her brother's.

Such a propitious arrangement! But it was all so very sad.

And yet, during Mr. Quinn's swift and woeful deterioration, the young lady managed to maintain her good spirits and contrived to offer more smiles than tears. In fact, no one ever actually saw her shed a tear, the brave lass!

Indeed, in a private exchange with Mr. Travers, Mrs. Silcock had declared she had never seen more dissimilar siblings, not only physically—Miss Quinn being curvy but lithe and Mr. Quinn being round and podgy—but in temperament. Miss Quinn was self-effacing, respectful, and undemanding, and asked Mrs. Silcock's opinion on, well, *everything*!

Clearly, though Miss Quinn was not wealthy—her gowns were not only out-of-mode, but did not particularly fit well, a problem endemic, Mrs. Silcock cannily explained, with country seamstresses—she came from genteel stock, as evinced by her masterful self-containment in the face of such misfortune. True, her manners might be a tad unrefined—when asked to pour tea, she was woefully out of her element—but there again, Mrs. Silcock pointed out, country society is not the same as London Society.

It turned out Lord Strand was acquainted—some vicious tabbies said "well acquainted"—with Miss Quinn. He had met her some years before at the home of mutual friends far north, in a tiny hamlet. No one had ever heard of the hamlet, but then how many unimportant hamlets did one hear of? And if some people speculated that here was finally the answer to why the Marquess of Strand had taken up a protégé, that being that he was seeking to ingratiate himself with a would-be conquest, decent people considered this nothing but nasty speculation.

Besides, what Miss Quinn lacked in social refinement, she made up for in looks. She had a lush, womanly figure and handsome face, with brilliant, thickly lashed blue eyes and fine dark brows. She wore her hair au courant, a tumble of glossy auburn locks of similar hue to her brother's—though Burke opined they were actually quite a bit darker and, after some debate, the other servants had to agree.

She quite riveted the eye, another fact the gentlemen's club members noted with interest. And it was noted that one pair of eyes in particular could not seem to tear themselves away from her.

After all the years, after all the various young ladies who'd cast their nets in his direction, and the line of demi-reps and opera dancers with whom he'd shared his bed if not his heart, Cupid's arrow had finally found the well-hidden vessel lurking in Lord Strand's chest.

The Marquess of Strand was smitten.

And as evidence of how wrong were those who suspected a previous "relationship"—there was one particular, nonsensical rumor that Lord Strand had been seen in a passionate embrace with Miss Quinn just before rescuing her brother—Miss Quinn always acted like a proper lady. She blushed when Lord Strand spoke and her eyes dropped shyly before his ardent gaze. But tellingly, her eyes brightened when he entered a room and her gaze lingered after him long after he'd gone.

Mrs. Silcock was in transports.

Avery hurled the lady's magazine against the bedroom wall. Her *new* bedroom wall. The one she occupied as *Ava* Quinn.

She'd considered throwing a book but feared the noise would only bring the staff running. It had been almost two days since Giles had announced a plan that would protect her reputation, a task he seemed to view with tiresome dedication, guarantee that her name would be forever attached to her comet, ensure that her research was treated with proper respect and given due consideration, and allow her to live freely as a woman.

He then informed her—right in front of Travers, damn him—that in order to do all the aforementioned things, they could not spend any time alone together.

And they hadn't. For the most part he was gone, seeming to avoid her. When he was in the house, there always seemed to be servants about, interested eyes watching.

Early this morning Giles had called a meeting of their fellow conspirators and announced that Mr. Quinn had lingered long enough and would die that evening. The following morning, at *Ava's* supposed behest, Burke and Travers would ready the body in a wooden casket for its final journey to the far-distant Quinn family tomb. It would take a seafaring passage, the length of the coach trip precluding a land one.

They would then convey an empty box to the shipyards where, out of sight, they would dismantle it. The next morning Ava would take a coach north, supposedly headed home. They'd taken into account the fact that it might seem odd that the marquess did not offer the bereaved sister his own barouche, but decided that rather than have his distinctive carriage remarked everywhere it stopped, and since the whole reason for the trip was to obfuscate Miss Quinn's background, she would demur this gracious offer as being too much to ask.

Which was all very fine and good as plans went, but what then? Giles hadn't said. He hadn't projected one day further than that.

It was driving Avery mad.

The only time she'd caught him alone had been in the hallway on their way to dinner last night. He'd moved aside for her to enter but caught her hand first, holding her back just long enough to whisper, "It will all be over soon and we can begin again."

And just what was that supposed to mean?

She'd tried to muster a bit of indignation but when she had looked up into his warm, gray eyes, she had known that if he'd reached for her then, she would have melted straight into his arms. Which did not speak highly for her self-restraint, she supposed. But, oh, she loved him!

Each night, she was haunted by the memory of their lovemaking. She replayed every word he had said, heard again each whisper, each sigh, as she searched for a hint as to his intentions.

Mr. Travers's story about the marquess and Giles had been revelatory. Giles had convinced Society that he was the wastrel his father had considered him. But he paid in private currency for the cost of that public persona. The only wonder was that he hadn't lost himself completely in the role.

But he hadn't.

He was an honorable man. Too honorable. She frowned. Honorable enough? What had he meant by "we can begin again"? Begin to make love again? Begin new lives apart? Together? Argh!

"Miss Quinn? Miss Quinn?"

She looked up. A housemaid hovered anxiously in the doorway.

"I'm sorry, miss," she said. "I knocked but you didn't answer and, well, I was that afraid maybe you'd gone the way of . . ." Her stricken gaze darted to the closed door between her bedroom and the one where her brother was supposedly drawing his last breaths.

"Oh, no, my dear. Please, do not worry about that. Avery has always had a weak constitution. You can tell just by looking at him that something was not right."

The maid nodded her agreement.

"While the women in my family are marked by long, long lives, the men . . ." Avery sighed and shook her head sadly. "Now, what is it you wanted?"

"Oh. Yes. Sorry, miss. Lord Neville Demsforth is in the drawing room. I wouldn't have answered the door but there was no one else to do so, Burke and Travers being gone on some errand."

"What does he want?"

"He wants to see Mr. Quinn."

Avery's eyes grew wide. "What? But . . . that. . . that's not possible."

"That's what I told him, miss. But he refuses to go until he at least speaks with you. Oh, miss, I know it ain't my place to say, but he's terrible miserable, he is. His eyes is all red-rimmed and wretched. I didn't know what to do, Lord Strand being gone, too, but seeing as how Mr. Quinn is your brother, I thought you might see the poor man."

Oh dear. She had feared something like this. It was the reason she had insisted the phantom doctor would blame Mr. Quinn's death on a preexisting condition and not the result of anything that had happened at the flash house. Yet still, poor Neville apparently felt responsible for Quinn's condition. She could not let him him suffer like this. Somehow she had to convince him it was in no way his fault.

"Of course," she said and followed the maid out of her room and down to the drawing room.

Neville sat on the edge of the divan, staring miserably at the floor. Upon hearing her enter, he bolted to his feet and bowed. "Miss Quinn, it is so kind of you to see me." He looked up and stared at her a second, tears starting in his gentle blue eyes.

"You look a bit like him," he said softly. "Well, not really. But the coloring, you know. He has reddish hair, too."

"You must be Lord Neville," she said, coming in and taking his hand. "How do you do? Avery speaks most warmly of you."

"He does?" Neville asked, obviously pleased.

"Oh, yes. Very warmly. Please, won't you sit down?" She lowered herself onto the settee and indicated he might sit beside her.

Blushing, the huge young man complied. She smiled gently. "Avery has told me how you befriended him. He is very grateful for that. As you can imagine, he is not the sort of young man who acquires friends easily."

God bless him, Neville's brow lowered at the implication that there was something not to like about his friend. "I find him quite good company."

"Yes," she said simply. "I know."

The stiffness dissolved from Neville's expression and his blunt features twisted in anguish. "I feel responsible for all this. He didn't want to go, you know. And once we were there, he didn't want to stay. But I insisted." Tears fell from his eyes and he swiped them away, too unhappy to be embarrassed.

"And when that girl asked me to help her up the stairs to her room, I should have refused. Avery said we oughtn't to trust her. But I did. And if I hadn't, he would be sitting here with me and you right now." He hung his head.

She reached over and covered his hands with her own. "No, Lord Neville, he would not. He has known . . . *we* have known for a long time that his was bound to be a short life. He had the Quinn somatotype."

He blinked at her in confusion.

"It's a type of physique," she explained. "None of the males in my family who have such a physique lived to see twenty."

"Really?"

She nodded gravely.

For a moment she thought he would accept this as a sad but immutable fact and be unburdened. But he shook his head, squeezing her hand so tightly she had to keep from wincing. "But I am sure my actions precipitated this crisis. He might have lived another few weeks, at least."

She pulled a hand free and laid it against his cheek. "My dear Lord Neville, don't you see?" He gazed deeply into her eyes and she willed him to believe her. "Avery is already twenty-one. He was already living on borrowed time. He has been for months now. Each moment is an unexpected bonus and that is *exactly* how he sees it."

"Really?" He covered her hand with his great paw and pressed it gently into his cheek.

"Really."

"You are so kind and gentle," he said. "You have eased my conscience greatly."

She sighed happily. She'd done it! "It never had any reason to be troubled to begin with." She pulled her hand from his face.

"I have one last request of you, my dear Miss Quinn," he said.

She tipped her head inquiringly.

"Please, allow me just a few minutes."

"A few minutes?" she repeated.

"With your brother."

"Oh. Oh. I do not think—"

"Please," he implored her, securing her hand again and going down on one massive knee at her feet. "I beg you. Your words have been so kind and I want to believe them more than anything. If I could only hear him absolve me with his own voice, it would mean everything to me, Miss Quinn." He stared earnestly into her eyes. He was so large that even on his knees they were eye level.

Drat. Drat. *Drat.* How could she deny him? She couldn't. She would simply have to don her costume for one final performance as Mr. Avery Quinn. "I will not be able to go in with you," she warned him. "Too much excitement might not be good for him."

Luckily Neville didn't see anything amiss in this rather questionable statement. "Of course," he said eagerly, leaping to his feet.

"I shall go and prepare him. When he's ready I shall send the maid to bring you to his room," she said. "You must promise to stay no more than five minutes."

"I promise! And," he said, "will I, perchance, see you afterward?"

She shook her head. "I must attend to him as soon as you leave."

"Then let me say what a privilege it has been to meet you, Miss Quinn. I would say 'pleasure,' but alas, our situation forbids that happy sentiment, though in different circumstances it would be a pleasure, indeed."

She regarded him in some confusion. "Ah, thank you. I'll send the maid directly after I have seen Avery."

She hurried from the room, motioning the maid to follow. "I have agreed to let Lord Neville see my brother but first I must ready Avery for the visit. As soon as he feels up to it, he shall ring his bell and you fetch Lord Neville and show him into the room. Wait outside until they are done then show his lordship out."

"Yes, miss. But . . . where will you be, miss?"

Avery rolled her eyes. "I'm going to lie down."

The room was murky and unexpectedly cool, surprising Neville. Every sick room he had ever been in had been damned hot. Not that he'd been in many. He was disgustingly robust.

He tiptoed towards the bed where he could see the swell of Avery's stomach under the blankets. Someone, probably his sister, had propped him up on a great pile of pillows. He turned his head at Neville's approach. Shadows obscured his expression, but Neville could make out the thick, single ridge of his brow and a faint smile.

"Ava tells me you blame yourself for my condition," Avery whispered. "Is that what you've come to tell me? Because that's nonsense. Utter rubbish. In your company I have experienced some of the finest moments of my life and your friendship saved me from loneliness in this great, cold city. I do not want you to spend one moment castigating yourself for what has always been a foregone conclusion. I do *not* blame you."

It was a most handsome speech. But it was also not necessary. "I know," Neville said.

"You do?" Avery said.

"Yes. Miss Quinn told me so. That's not why I'm here."

"It's not?"

"No." He stepped to the side of the bed and secured one of Avery's hands. It was a small thing and gave credence to Miss Quinn's assurance that Avery had been born with some sort of weakness.

"I'm here to set your mind at ease, old fellow," he said, smiling down at his friend. "You don't have to worry a mite about your sister."

"I don't?"

"No. Because I'm going to marry her."

Chapter Thirty-Nine

What's going on?" Giles demanded, striding into her room unannounced. "The maid said Demsforth had been to see Mr. Quinn."

"A moment, please." Avery was standing at the ewer with her back to him, scrubbing the last bit of glue from between her eyebrows.

He stalked in, prepared to lecture her on how important it was not to give anyone the slightest reason to doubt their story. He shouldn't be in her room alone with her now, not only because it was improper but because he would not tell her his heart in snatches and hushed whispers. But he had to press upon her the need for discretion. Mr. Quinn must remain completely out of the public eye. No one must make comparisons between the phantom siblings when the memory of one visage was fresh in his mind's eye when he saw the other.

Not that Neville Demsforth was likely to make the connection, the great heedless oaf. Giles had still not forgiven him for putting Avery in danger. He rather doubted he ever would. But Avery seemed fond of the lad, and so for her sake he would aspire to tolerance.

He would do, he realized, a great deal for Avery's sake. Including sending her back to Killylea without him, though every fiber of his being resisted. Hungrily, he filled his gaze with her, his planned lecture forgotten.

The gowns Burke had purchased at a discreet reseller of lady's clothing might not be the height of fashion and might not fit perfectly, being a little too tight across the bodice and a little too long in the hem, but they were excessively feminine. And happily, since Ava Quinn could not have arrived anticipating she would need to go into mourning, they weren't wretched black affairs. This one was iris blue with lacy, ivory sleeves. It was ridiculous and fanciful and utterly unlike anything he'd ever seen her in and he was smitten anew.

"Avery." He wasn't even aware he'd said her name until she responded. "Yes?"

He cleared his throat. "The maid said Demsforth had been in to talk to Mr. Quinn," he repeated.

She glanced over her shoulder at him. "Yes," she said casually. "He wants to marry me."

"*What?*"

"Neville wants to marry me." She looked back into the mirror with a critical eye. Apparently satisfied, she faced him. "It's really quite dear when you think about it."

"No, it's not. It's not *dear*; it's presumptuous! The insufferable pup! How dare he propose marriage with your brother at death's door?"

"Now, that's unfair. He didn't propose, he simply informed my"—she broke off to roll her eyes in exasperation—"he simply informed *me* that he intended to propose."

"Why?"

She went very still. "*Why?*"

"Yes. Why? He's nothing but a boy and he's only just met you. Why would he want to marry you?"

She lifted her chin. Too late, he realized his mistake. "Not that any man wouldn't—"

"Pray, spare me your self-serving temporizations."

He scowled. He wasn't temporizing. He meant it. Any man would be lucky to marry Avery. This, unfortunately, wasn't what he said. What he said was: "I resent that."

"I'll warrant not nearly as much as I resent your words." Her lower lip trembled.

He started towards her. She held up a hand, forestalling him. "No. I realize that I am hardly any Society mama's first choice for a daughter-in-law. Or second. Or any choice at all. And honesty compels me to admit that I suspect some part of Lord Neville's proposal has this very fact at its root. How better to thumb his nose at his mother than to make a nobody his bride?"

"Avery, please," he said desperately, holding out his hand. His heart ached at the hurt in her voice, this recitation of her shortcomings. She had no shortcomings. All the chimerical qualities of breeding and pedigree on which Society placed such importance were simply delusions manufactured to bolster a false sense of consequence.

She shook her head, refusing to take his hand. "No. Please. Allow me my say."

He ground his teeth, unable to refuse.

She took a deep breath. "I do not, however, believe that to be the *only* reason for his planned proposal. Or the most important. Other factors enter in." She glanced at him to see that she had his attention. She did.

"Marrying me will presumably assuage any remnants of guilt he might feel due to his involvement in, er, my death, though I do believe I adequately relieved him on that score. It will also allow him to act honorably and make a heroic sacrifice."

"Marrying you is *not* a sacrifice!" Giles burst out, unable to contain himself. He was rewarded with a tiny smile.

"Why, thank you," she said. "I do not think so either. And I may be doing poor Neville a disservice because I think there is one more reason he wishes to marry me, in fact, the most substantive reason of all."

"And what is that?"

"He is attracted to me."

"The hell you say. The impertinence of that great blond jackanapes! I've a mind to thrash his insolent hide the length and breadth of St. James Road!"

"You can't do that," Avery said, but he thought he detected a tiny bit of gratification in her tone.

"If he offers you any further insult—"

"What insult? He is *offering* marriage."

Damn, she had a point. "I presume that you, I mean you as Mr. Quinn, dismissed the notion out of hand?"

Her beautiful indigo-colored eyes widened. "Why, no. Of course not."

"What do you mean 'of course not'?" he scowled again. Fiercely, again. "Why not?"

"Why not?" She stared at him as if he'd taken leave of his senses, which of course, he had.

She threw up her hands in disgust. "*Because*"—she leveled him with an exasperated glare—"I was supposed to be a dying boy without name or wealth, listening as the titled young heir to a fortune told me he wanted to marry my equally impecunious and inconsequential sister. Of course I didn't say no! Had I done so, it would have immediately awakened his suspicions."

"What did you say?"

Her gaze skittered away from his. "I, ah, thanked him."

He peered at her. "By heavens, Avery, you haven't actually developed a tendre for *Neville Demsforth*?" he asked incredulously and laughed.

He didn't actually feel like laughing. He felt like taking her in his arms and kissing her until she told him she loved him and no one else. But he'd laughed to show her how ridiculous it would be to seriously consider Demsforth's suit. Because she mustn't. She must not consider marrying anyone but him.

Her expression grew shuttered. For a long moment she simply studied him. He shifted uneasily.

"Haven't I?" she finally murmured.

"No."

He was acting badly. He knew that. But he didn't seem able to help himself. What had happened to his much-vaunted self-possession? Why couldn't he act reasonably, with dignified acceptance, feigning deference to whatever she might say? Because where she was concerned he could not pretend. Whenever he tried, his mask quickly cracked, exposing his true feelings and the man beneath.

The realization took his breath away and alarmed him—what if she did not like what she saw? For the first time in his adulthood someone knew who he was behind the construct.

"Why shouldn't I marry him?" she was saying. She started across the room towards him, her brow puckered thoughtfully. "One day Neville will come into a considerable fortune."

"But until then you will have to live with his mother."

She nodded without looking at him. "Point taken. But he also stands third in line to the Higgstinton dukedom."

"Those standing between him and the dukedom are as revoltingly hearty as Demsforth himself."

"Really? How disappointing." She sighed. "Still, I am quite convinced he would be an undemanding husband, one who would never think to interrupt me at my studies. Why wouldn't I marry him?"

He could take it no more. He had waited and planned and tried to keep away until this mess was cleared up and now it was falling about him, leaving him with just one recourse. He strode across the room and swept her into his embrace. "Because you must marry me," he said and, clasping the back of her head in his palm, crushed her mouth beneath his.

With breathtaking eagerness, her arms wrapped around his neck, her soft contours molding to his. Her mouth opened in intoxicating invitation. He speared his fingers through her curls, luxuriating in their clean, silky texture. He kissed her fiercely, deeply, plundering the rich moist vales of her mouth, dizzied by the responsiveness of her lips and tongue. Only after long, luscious moments did he find the wherewithal to lift his head, and even then his lips caught and returned for another heated kiss.

He set his forehead against hers, his breath coming quick. "You must marry me."

She raised her hand and stroked his cheek, her eyes as beautiful and mysterious as a velvety star-spangled sky. He caught her hand in his and pressed a soft kiss on each knuckle and then against her inner wrist where the pulse pattered wildly.

"Why?" she whispered. "I do not belong to the exalted world you inhabit. I never will."

"I do not belong there either," he said, willing her to believe him. Later he would tell her, everything or nothing, whatever she wanted to know. He would keep nothing back. He wanted her to share every aspect of the life he intended them to lead, with full knowledge of what had gone before. But not now. Now, he had to convince her to marry him. "All my life, I've been a tourist, a visitor playing whatever role was required at that moment. Except with you. With you, I am home. With you, I belong."

She looked deeply into his eyes. He had never felt so exposed, so vulnerable. So sure. "And that is why I should marry you?" she whispered.

He thought of all the answers he might give her, considered laying at her feet a list of everything that might possibly recommend him: his wealth and credentials, his titles and his holdings; promises that he would support her studies, follow her around the bloody globe, build a telescope for her if that's what she wanted. But in the end he gave her the only answer that would mean a thing to her.

"No," he said. "Marry me because I love you."

And it was enough.

Chapter Forty

Another peasouper held London in its grip. A sulfurous color tinted a fog so thick one couldn't see across the courtyard of the posting inn where Avery awaited the carriage that would take her away. She perched on a hard wooden bench just inside the door. Several fellow travelers sat at a nearby table, mittened hands wrapped around steaming tin mugs of coffee or thin chocolate.

She shivered, pulling her thick angora cape higher around her neck. Giles stood staring out a front window weeping with condensation, his hands tightly clasped behind his back. More than a few of the inn's female occupants sent fascinated, admiring sidelong glances in his direction. She could hardly blame them. He was incongruous amongst this lot. His dark blue greatcoat set off the breadth of his shoulders and acted as a foil to his golden good looks. Jonquil gloves molded over strong, lean hands and, despite the mud and puddles through which he'd escorted her, his boots gleamed.

He caught her studying him and gave a tight smile before turning back to the window as if the sight of her pained him. They had said their good-byes in the carriage ride over, sitting stiffly across from each other. Though he had not touched her, his expression had been ardent and yearning.

In the end, it had all been so ridiculously easy. All her fears, her concern for his reputation and position, her resolve to continue her astronomical work, her anxiety that someday he might regret marrying someone who had brought so little to the union . . . all of it had vanished in the time it took to whisper, "Because I love you."

She'd been swift to answer that she loved him, too. With all her heart.

"It will only be six months," he suddenly said, his attention still fixed on the swirl of snow that had coalesced out of the frigid fog.

"I know." She hesitated. "Heaven knows I am hardly a font of information on protocol, but I thought that propriety demanded a year's mourning after the death of a relative before one could wed."

"Propriety be damned," he said. "Six months. Unless . . ." He glanced at her waist.

She smiled. "I'm not."

He returned her smile, though his was chagrined. "It would have been a good excuse. This will be the bloody longest six months of my life." He frowned. "You'll write?"

"Probably more than you'll like to read."

"Never."

And then the carriage had been loaded, and the porter was calling out that they were to embark. Around her, the other passengers were rising to their feet, collecting satchels and boxes and bidding farewell to the smattering of friends and relatives that had come to bid them adieu.

Giles did not move. He folded his hands behind his back and tipped his head. "I hate this, you know," he said conversationally.

"I know. But you are the one that insisted we submit to societal expectations. I would elope with you now, if you'd like," she offered. She meant it most fervently. "Right now."

His lips parted and he jerked towards her a step before suddenly halting. Firmly, he pressed his lips together.

"No," he said, so quietly she had to strain to hear him. "No. In this I will not be precipitous. This is not for my sake, Avery. It's not even for your own. It's for our children's sake. The dozens of children we shall have. By chance one or two of them might actually be concerned about

Society's good opinion. They might even require its approval. Though God knows why, but stranger things have happened, I suppose."

She loved him for that. "Dozens of children?"

He grinned. "Give or take."

She grinned back and held out her hands and he clasped them close, helping her to her feet. "I must go. They'll leave without me."

"They wouldn't dare." She had to smile at such arrogance, though she recognized it was true.

"Then I do not want to keep anyone on the coach from their heart's journey's end," she said. "For I swear, if I knew someone was keeping me five minutes from your arms, I would shoot them."

"I had no idea you were such a bloodthirsty little thing."

"I am where you are concerned. Now, see me outside and bid me good-bye."

He nodded, as if not trusting himself to speak, and held the door open for her. Then he followed her to the coach where the porter waited. Giles had secured her a seat facing forward and extra cushions. He handed her up and closed the door behind.

"Every day," she called out the window, feeling anxious now that the final moments were here.

He did not reply and the last she saw of him he was standing beneath the saffron glow of the yard's lantern, the snow collecting on his broad shoulders and catching in his golden hair. He stood gazing after her until the coach turned the corner and he was lost to her sight.

She sank back, sighing. The carriage was making slow progress, lumbering and creaking its way through the twisted alleys towards the wider thoroughfares near St. James. From there they would take the turnpike road north towards Chester and the pace would pick up. She was to get off at the first posting house and change directions, going home to Killylea to wait for Giles.

Home. How wonderful that sounded. How much she missed the sounds of the ocean crashing on the base of the cliffs, the gleaning cries of the gulls surfing in winds above, the salt-sweet air and brilliant, crystalline skies. In six months Giles would join her, and they would never need be apart again.

They had been driving fifteen minutes when the carriage came to a sudden halt, drawing a muttered oath from the man sitting across from her. "What now?"

Outside, voices rose in a brief exchange; the door swung open. A thin, aristocratic-looking old gentleman in a black topcoat, a scarf wound around his neck, peered inside. He spotted her and his noble old countenance collapsed in sympathy.

"Miss Quinn?" he said.

"Yes?" Her heart began to beat faster.

"I have been sent by a Lord Strand to fetch you."

"Fetch me? Why?"

He looked at her sadly, his face filled with compassion. "I was on my way to my office. There was an accident. The gentleman was not looking and he stepped into the street and—"

She bolted forward. "What gentleman?"

"Lord Strand. He's been injured. He begged me to find your coach. I'm afraid . . ." He shook his head. "If you could—"

She was already scrambling past him and out of the coach. "Take me to him," she commanded.

He already missed her. But, he told himself, at least he could use the months to conclude old business, discover what had happened to Jack, then officially—and permanently—resign his services to the crown. The barouche pulled to a stop in front of his townhouse and he got out.

Giles spotted the boy at once, scurrying across the street from beneath the holly bushes where he'd been sheltering.

"Lord Strand?" he called out.

Will jumped down from where he'd been sitting next to the driver. "What are you lot doin' speakin' to his lordship?" he snapped. "There ain't no cadging here. Get on wid ye!"

"Ain't cadgin'," the boy protested.

"What do you want, boy?" Giles asked.

"Gentleman said I was to give you this." He handed Giles an expensive vellum envelope and snickered at Will.

A cold finger touched Giles's spine. He dug in his pocket and pressed a shilling in the boy's hand. The lad tapped two fingers to his cap and darted away.

Silently, Giles opened the envelope and unfolded the single sheet inside.

St. Anne's Churchyard. Miss Quinn is with me.

He jerked the carriage door open and swung inside, banging on the roof and shouting, "St. Anne's Church. Fast!"

Chapter Forty-One

St. Anne's Church existed in a nether region halfway between the mansions of St. James and the squalor of Covent Garden. As though afraid of insulting either contingent, it abstained from the ornamentation that marked the richer area but refused to decline into the shabbiness of the poorer. Not a single light burned from within its small, tidy edifice.

Giles had left the carriage around the corner a block away, hoping to survey the situation before making his presence known. He knew the chances of this were slim; Jameson had not acted as codirector of the Secret Committee for twenty years because he was sloppy.

True to his suspicion, a quick inspection of the church proved futile. No one was there. Instead, he found them in a mausoleum, the centerpiece of the lichyard at the side of the church. It was a huge marble edifice some thirty feet long and half that across. The bronze door stood open, light spilling out over nearby headstones sprouting drunkenly from the frozen ground.

There would be no furtive approach and he had no weapon on him. Fear and desperation had propelled his actions; he'd raced here without thinking to arm himself. He took a deep breath and entered the chamber.

A single lantern sat on the floor, the only source of light inside. Avery stood at the far end of the mausoleum, separated from him by an ornate granite sarcophagus. Sir Jameson gripped her from behind, his pistol to her temple.

She held herself very straight. More than fear shimmered in her direct gaze, there was anger, too. And courage, God love her.

The flame guttered in the lantern, licking Jameson's gaunt face with its insubstantial light. The hand holding the pistol quaked. His finger, Giles noted, was on the trigger. He had to get him to lower the gun before he fired, intentionally or otherwise.

"A mausoleum, Sir Jameson?" Giles drawled, glancing around like a visitor at an art exhibition. "I wouldn't have taken you for a man given to melodramatics. I can't help but think the owner would take exception to making such a use of his ancestors' final resting place."

"Not at all. That is my maternal grandfather, you see," Jameson said conversationally, nodding to the sarcophagus. "However, I do apologize for the gothic setting. Over the years I have found it to be an exemplary situation for this sort of thing."

"And what sort of thing is that?"

"Interrogations. Trades. Occasionally executions."

Avery's face paled in the lantern light.

"And which is this?"

"That remains to be seen."

"Let Miss Quinn go."

"Miss Quinn, is it?" A creaky sound emerged from Jameson's throat. Giles realized it was a laugh. "She's your whore, Strand. Nothing more or less. Oh, please," he sneered, "do not bother with indignation. I know she was in your bed the very night her brother was wounded. You were seen. I thought at first you were buggering the boy. It would have been so much more convenient had that been the case."

"You mean so much easier to extort information from me."

Jameson nodded. "Just so. Now I have been forced to more extreme measures." His smile disappeared as quickly as if someone had snubbed out a flame. "Where is Seward? Where is my beloved adopted son?"

He was mad, Giles realized. Quite mad.

"The Netherlands," Giles answered at once. "In Overflakkee."

The pistol swung towards him. The gunpowder flashed in its pan at the same time pain exploded in his side. Avery cried out, jerking forward. Jameson snatched her back. Giles looked down at the hole ripped through the side of his greatcoat.

"Damn," he said. "This is my favorite coat."

"Next time it will be Miss Quinn's turn. And I shan't miss." Jameson jammed the barrel of the pistol up under Avery's chin. "Do you take me for a fool?"

Giles did not think the bullet had hit anything vital but blood loss was making his head swim. His legs were starting to fail him. "No!" He held up his hand in a placating manner. "No."

Giles did not know how Jameson had known he was lying. It didn't matter. The only thing that mattered was that he had nothing to trade for Avery's life. God help him, he would have given Seward up if it meant saving her. There was nothing he would not have sacrificed to protect Avery.

"Then tell me!" Jameson raged, spittle flying from his mouth. "Tell me so I can put the bastard in the ground!" Every vestige of refinement had fallen from him like skin from a molting snake. He quivered with rage, his face contorted. "Tell me!"

He swung the pistol towards Giles again and suddenly Avery grabbed his wrist, yanked it back, and sank her teeth into his flesh. Jameson screamed and Giles lurched forward, unable to do more than pitch against the sarcophagus.

The gun dropped from Jameson's hand and Avery fell to her knees, scrambling for it. She had youth and agility on her side. Jameson didn't stand a chance. He didn't even try. She sprang to her feet, the second barrel of the pistol already cocked and pointed at Jameson's chest.

Giles gasped, pulling himself upright against the stone coffin.

"Well, now what are you going to do, my dear?" Jameson asked, cradling his injured arm against his chest. "Are you going to shoot an old man in cold blood? I don't think so."

The anger was fading from her expression, panic and uncertainty replacing it.

"Giles?"

"I'm fine. Don't take the gun off him." He was not fine. He could feel the blood flowing from the wound, unconsciousness licking at the edges of his vision.

"I daresay time is ticking away for your lover, Miss Quinn. You best tend to him before he succumbs. I assure you, I have no other weapons. I will just be on my way."

"Stay where you are," she commanded. Her voice shook, but the gun didn't. Her father had taught her well.

She glanced at Giles, anxiety bright in her face. "What should I do?"

She should shoot Jameson, Giles thought. He should tell her to shoot him. If she didn't, Jameson would go to ground and with his resources they would never find him until the day he chose to reappear. They would never be able to relax their guard. They would be condemned to lives spent looking over their shoulders.

But he couldn't say it. He knew too well the sorts of nightmares that killing a man engendered, no matter how necessary. He would not allow Avery to suffer that.

"Let him go, Avery."

"Yes," Jameson said. "You don't want to be a murderer." He started past her.

"No!" she shouted. She had come to the same conclusion as he, Giles realized.

Jameson halted. Licked his lips.

"It's all right," a calm voice said from behind Giles. "You may put down your weapon, Miss Quinn. The matter is well in hand."

Giles turned his head. Sir Robert Knowlton stepped into the room.

"You?" Avery's brow pleated with confusion. But she still didn't lower her weapon. She had learned caution quickly, but thoroughly.

"Yes, Miss Quinn. Me." Knowlton's voice was calm but he did not take his eyes off the gun. "I am sorry for the little deception I perpetuated on you at the coffee shop near Strand's townhouse. I was trying to ascertain exactly who you were. And what. I'd been following you and when you went into the bookstore, I popped into the coffee shop. So obliging that you entered so soon afterward.

"You see, Lord Strand and I have a long-standing professional relationship. When I heard that he had acquired a protégé, I was, of course, curious. One cannot be too careful when one's agent suddenly takes up with someone no one has ever heard of. But during our delightful conversation, and after I realized you were a young lady, my fears were assuaged."

"Agent?" she echoed.

"I see Strand has been discreet. Most gratifying. But, I believe, no longer necessary. Yes, my dear, Lord Strand has worked in his government's employ for some time now. Under my auspices." He glanced at Jameson, who was not paying them any heed, his gaze darting about the room, assessing and discarding plans, looking for a way out that did not exist. "Amongst others."

Knowlton smiled at Avery. "So, you see, you can put the gun down. Sir Jameson is no longer in a position to threaten you. Nor will he ever be. He has shot a peer of the realm, you see, though I doubt he will ever stand trial."

Which meant Knowlton was now the sole head of the committee. A dark suspicion filled Strand. "How did you find us so quickly?"

Alerted by the tension in Giles's voice, Avery turned the pistol back up towards Knowlton. Jameson edged sideways. The pistol barrel swung back to follow him. "Stay where you are!"

For the first time a touch of uneasiness betrayed itself on Knowlton's grandfatherly face. He cleared his throat and motioned behind him. A small figure slipped in beside him. Will.

Knowlton's expression was apologetic. "Young Will here has been working for me for some time, keeping me apprised of Mr. Bees's endeavors."

Giles stared at the boy, surprised by the sting he felt at the boy's duplicity. "You mean, the dog . . . the whole thing was stage—"

"No!" Will said. "That part were true. It were only after I come with Belle to yer house and Sir Knowlton gets wind of it that he asks me to . . ." He trailed off, his face filled with misery.

"Asked you to report on me."

The boy's gaze fell, abashed.

Giles did not blame him. He blamed Knowlton. "You contrived the whole thing, didn't you? You knew Jameson was going mad. You knew he thought I could tell him where Seward was. You probably even encouraged him in that belief. How? Vedder?" He could see he was right.

"Then you sat back and waited, knowing it was only a matter of time before he did something that would take him out of the game, leaving you the sole director of the whole organization."

Knowlton did not deny it. He simply said, without the least bit of gloating, "It's for the best. Now, before you lose too much blood, I suggest you tell your very brave young lady here to let me take Jameson into custody."

He did not wait for Giles to comply but moved to Jameson's side and took his arm. The fight seemed to have gone out of the old man. His chin sank to his chest and he shuffled forward. Giles did not trust this for a second.

"Be careful," he said.

"Do not worry. Mr. Burke is without. Young Will here insisted that he come. And my men are waiting at the lichyard gate." Whatever he saw in Avery's eyes apparently reassured him, for with a slight bow of his head, he pulled Jameson to him and propelled him outside.

"Oh," he said, pausing at the door. "And please, Giles, stop looking for Jack. I promise you he and his bride are safe and well. Had you known where they were, you would have surely given them up to protect Miss Quinn. Which is exactly why you do not know. Nor ever shall."

And with that, they disappeared.

Giles met Avery's eyes. "Put down that gun, you bloodthirsty wench. It's done," he said as he felt the ground swelling beneath him and his knees begin to buckle.

The last thing he remembered seeing was her feet flying across the mausoleum floor.

God, the woman could run.

Epilogue

One year later

After much deliberation, the Royal Astrological Society conferred the 1819 Hipparchus posthumously on Avery Quinn and decided to present the medal to his sister in his honor. But as she was in mourning, they waited the requisite year before inviting her to the ceremony in order to make the presentation. It was a grand occasion, made more so by the fact that the ceremony was being held at Buckingham Palace.

But there was added excitement in the air, for certain members of the society had prevailed upon the palace to make a special presentation of which the new Marchioness of Strand was deliciously unaware.

She had arrived in London with her husband just the night before. A few of the more pompous members of the society were wont to tip their noses up at the unseemly haste with which the marquess had secured his bride's hand, it being no more than six months after Mr. Quinn's untimely death, but they were in the vast minority, the greater portion of their members being secret romantics. As are all stargazers, claimed Sir Isbill, the society's acknowledged leader if no longer president.

Besides, Lady Strand had been revealed to be an astronomer in her own right. Lord Strand had sent much of her brother's research to the society for their edification. In his unexpunged papers, Avery Quinn had quite openly credited his sister with much of the work—though privately Sir Isbill considered it closer to "most." Which is why the rigorously fair-minded gentleman had lobbied so fiercely and relentlessly for the great honor that was about to be conferred upon that unsuspecting lady.

Privately he also considered that the Quinns' parents must have been as odd as their children were brilliant. For instance, they had named both their children, male and female, "Avery"—as well as the family dog. Or so said Lord Strand. Ava was apparently simply a fond contraction.

Sir Isbill looked out on the assembly from where he sat beside His Majesty's representative, a comfortably unassuming old gentleman named Knowlton. He spotted his nephew Neville some ways back. He finally had hope for the lad.

Earlier this year the boy had stood up to his mother and talked his father into purchasing a commission in a very reputable, if unfashionable, regiment for him. At the very back of the room, hovering outside in the hall beyond the open doors, he saw a boy holding a dog. The lad looked extremely self-satisfied. As did the dog. Sir Isbill sighed. Royal protocol was not what it used to be. But then he remembered the royal in attendance and owned it was not surprising.

Behind him, on a raised dais, the Prince Regent rested his bulk, looking quite congenial. And before them all sat Lady Strand beside her husband, listening politely to their new president drone on about the history of the society. Lord Strand didn't even make a pretense of listening. His attention kept wandering towards his wife and small wonder, she was lovely.

Really, thought Sir Isbill, why was it that the most undeserving popinjays always managed to secure the most glorious women? Not that Strand was a dullard. No, indeed. Quite bright actually, but he had never lived up to his potential, apparently being content to waste his life as a fashion plate. Well, perhaps Lady Strand would change all that.

The Prince Regent began addressing the crowd. Sir Isbill eagerly fastened his gaze on Lady Strand. He wanted to see her reaction.

She turned to her husband and a beauteous smile curved her lips. Her hand rested briefly on her stomach before returning to his arm. Beauty *and* intelligence. Sir Isbill admitted himself a little beguiled.

He glanced over just as the Prince Regent stood up and approached Lady Strand. The entire assembly sprang to their feet. Obviously caught by surprise, the marchioness did likewise and then swept into a deep curtsey and held it. Lord Strand beamed. The prince smiled. He was well known to like pretty women, no matter how unfortunately intelligent.

"Do you not love a surprise?" Sir Isbill heard him whisper over Lady Strand's bowed head and then, producing the royal insignia fastened at the end of a satin ribbon, he put it over her head. "It is with great pleasure that We hereby appoint Lady Avery Dalton, Marchioness of Strand, Dame of the Order of the British Empire."

He held out his hand. "Dame Avery, arise."

Author's Note

Where to begin? I loved finally putting paid to Giles's long and varied history. He has been tapping me on the shoulder demanding his "happily-ever-after" for years and I am confident he found the wait worth it.

Both the pain and the pleasure of writing historical fiction, especially historical romance, is deciding where to deviate from facts. It's even harder when the facts are as fascinating as the fiction. German-born astronomer William Herschel was one of the founding members of the Royal Astronomical Society, an entity created a few years after my fictional Royal Astrological Society. But it is his sister, Caroline, who demanded my attention.

Stunted by a bout with typhus, the lady never reached much above four feet in height and though it was assumed that she would never wed, it was also assumed she would be a house servant. Instead, she became her brother's collaborator, making discoveries in her own right, cataloguing stars, fashioning telescopes, and becoming the first woman to receive a salary for her scientific endeavors. In 1828, the Royal Astronomical Society presented her with their gold medal for her work. No woman was to be awarded it again until 1996.

As for the Secret Committee, try as I did and in spite of my ardent belief some such organization did exist, I could find no mention of one. What I did discover was that after the war with France, England had a plethora of agent provocateurs and spies returning to their native soil. While I found this fascinating, this book is a love story and I did not want to distract from that journey with a side trip into politics. To learn more about these spies' activities, I suggest reading about the Cato Street Conspiracy and the Peter Loo massacre.

And that frigid weather? Fact: 1819 was one of the six coldest winters in London's history. Snow fell regularly and fairly deeply. The fact that I am writing this now, in the midst of a fairly cold and fairly snowy and horrifically long Minnesota winter, is pure happenstance.

And finally, while I make every attempt at veracity in my use of language, some words simply have no reasonable synonyms and where I have used the anachronistic term for clarity, I beg your indulgence.

Minnesota, 2013
Connie Brockway

Acknowledgments

I love my job and for that I have many people to thank: my friends at Montlake Publishing, for supporting my vision and renewing my joy in writing, with a special shout-out to Kelli Martin, Nikki Sprinkle, and Jessica Poore; my husband, David, for uncomplainingly (mostly) and once again surviving on take-out pizza for weeks; my friends Lisa, Terri, Christina, Mary—long shall we run!

And most of all, to Susan Kay Law, they simply couldn't make a better friend or editor. And a better sister I couldn't ask for. Love you, Sus!

About the Author

N*ew York Times* and *USA Today* best-selling author Connie Brockway has received starred reviews from both *Publishers Weekly* and the *Library Journal,* which named *My Seduction* as one of 2004's top ten romances. An eight-time finalist for Romance Writers of America's prestigious RITA award, Brockway has twice been its recipient, for *My Dearest Enemy* and *The Bridal Season.*

In 2006 Connie wrote her first women's contemporary, *Hot Dish,* which won critical raves. Connie's historical romance *The Other Guy's Bride* was the launch book for Montlake Romance. Today Brockway lives in Minnesota with her husband, who is a family physician, and two spoiled mutts.

Sign up for more from Connie Brockway!

http://www.conniebrockway.com/mailing_list.php
https://twitter.com/ConnieBrockway
https://www.facebook.com/ConnieBrockwayFans